THE DARKNESS

BY

JOHN MICHAEL OSBORNE

ISBN: 978-1-962905-02-2

TABLE OF CONTENTS

Part One

Dusk

CHAPTER ONE

Jimmy Durham's life changed forever when the cops stepped into the bar.

Before then, he was having a good day. He and his best friend and roommate, Seth Williams, had just moved to a new basement apartment in Morganburg, Virginia.

Seth brought them a couple of beers and sat down at a table near the railing that overlooked the pool tables to the floor below. The place was warm, and the aroma of greasy burgers and fries filled the air. Two women, the only people down there, played a game of pool. The fall semester wasn't going to start for two more weeks, and most of the students hadn't returned yet. TVs around the Hawk's Nest showed early football from the CFL and NFL preseason games. Classic rock played over the crack of pool balls.

The guys toasted their glass mugs.

"To our senior year," Jimmy said. "So it goes fast and painless."

Seth chuckled. "Here, here." He threw out his arms. "Now, we'll be living in luxury for our final two semesters."

They toasted again.

"Amen," Jimmy muttered.

Jimmy's phone buzzed on the table. "Finally. It's Laura."

"Tell her to get her ass here before we get drunk without her."

Jimmy picked up. "Honey, where the hell are you? We're already here."

"Sorry. I was just doing some research for my next article, and I lost track of time. Jimmy, you won't believe what I've found. It's about the campus and the town. It's going to hit Morganburg like a bomb!"

Laura, a writer for the campus paper, was working on a story for the early edition that came out a week before the semester began. Jimmy was so busy with his move he never asked her what it was about.

"Seriously? You gotta tell me about it then."

"I will when I get there. I just got home. I'll see you in about fifteen minutes."

Jimmy hung up. He was eager to see her again. He hadn't seen her in days.

Seth chugged the last of his beer. "What's up?"

Jimmy shrugged. "Who knows? She's working on a story about the town. She thinks it's really big."

Seth ordered another beer from the waitress. "In this little redneck town? Like what? The Possum Day Parade has been canceled?"

Jimmy forced a smile. "Yeah, it's probably something like that." He hoped that's all it was. Lately she'd been acting so nervous, jumping at loud sounds, looking over her shoulder. It was like she thought someone was after her.

He couldn't wait for her to get there so he could see her and hug her again. And then they could finally order something to eat, too. The food in there smelled so good, and he never got a chance to eat since they finished moving and returned the moving van that afternoon.

He ordered another beer and watched some of the preseason games. He checked his watch. The fifteen minutes came and went.

"Damn," Jimmy muttered. "What's taking her so long? She should've been here by now."

"Relax," Seth said. "She'll get here. Girls are always late."

He called her. No answer.

They watched more of the games and checked his watch again. Half an hour went by. They each ordered another beer. He started to really worry and called her again. Still no answer.

Seth set his beer down and checked his own watch. "Maybe she got a call or someone stopped by. Maybe—"

Then two guys, one tall and thin with balding hair and the other short and fat, came to the table and flashed their police IDs.

"Are you Jimmy Durham?" the tall one asked.

"Yeah."

"Will you come with us?" the short one said.

"No," Jimmy said. *What the fuck do you mean, will I come with you? What the fuck for?* "What's this about?"

The tall one asked, "You have a girlfriend by the name of Laura Jenkins?"

"Yeah. Why? What's happened?"

"We'll tell you when we get down to the station," the short one said.

Seth stood up. "Is he under arrest?"

"Easy there, big guy," the tall detective said. "No. We just need to ask him some questions."

Seth shrugged and reached for his wallet. "I'll settle up and follow you down there."

Jimmy went with them to the detectives' car.

My God, I hope Laura wasn't in a car accident driving over here, Jimmy thought. *That's probably it. Damn, I hope she's okay.*

On the way there, he asked, "Won't you tell me what this is about?"

"We'll tell you at the station," the fat one said.

"Why? Because your brains are down there?"

Jimmy hoped that would piss them off enough to start talking, but they remained quiet.

He asked, "How did you even know how to find me?"

"A friend of hers told us we'd find you there," the tall, bald one said.

"Friend? What friend?"

"Traci Frederickson," the fat detective said. "She called a friend of hers. Think it was the girlfriend of Seth's."

Flanked by the detectives Jimmy pushed open the bar door and stepped into the humid night air. Cars shot down the road. A couple pulled into the parking lot.

"I need to know what this is about," Jimmy said. "Has there been an accident or something?"

"We'll tell you at the station," the fat one again replied.

Natalie knew they were at the bar. But how would they know to talk to Traci? Was she with Laura in the car accident?

The police took him down to the station, and he sat in a small interrogation room. The walls were white, and there was one long table and three chairs.

Not exactly a room that made him feel welcome..

Then they left him in there so long, he thought they decided to go eat dinner.

Jimmy met Laura at a bar with some friends. She was a journalism major, and she was intrigued that he majored in creative writing. They shared a love of reading and writing. He had never met a girl like her. They really hit it off right away.

Finally, Laurl and Hardy returned to the room. Jimmy didn't like either one of them. They weren't exactly the most forthcoming duo, and they possessed this funny gray look in their eyes.

Fat Boy sat down next to him. "I'm sorry, Jimmy. There's no easy way to tell you this, but we found Laura murdered in her apartment. We're sorry for your loss."

"Murdered?" Jimmy exclaimed. "When? Why? Who the hell murdered her?"

The tall one leaned his back against the wall and crossed his arms. "We're trying to find that out now."

Tears pooled in Jimmy's eyes. "How can she be murdered? I just spoke to her over the phone!"

"The phone?" the fat one asked. "When was that?"

"Seth and I were at the bar for nearly an hour before she called."

The fat one grimaced like he suffered from constipation. Then the door popped open, and someone called the tall one outside.

Burger Boy remained. He asked, "Do you know of anyone who would want to kill her?"

"No," he muttered.

"Did she have any bad blood with anyone recently?"

Jimmy didn't want to talk anymore. He just wanted to crawl into a hole and die. "No."

"Did she complain about anyone recently?"

"No, no, no. She never—" He was still trying to comprehend how she could be dead when he remembered what she had told him over the phone.

"She never what?"

"Wait. She mentioned something about a story she was working on for the campus paper. She said something about the story hitting this place like a bomb."

The detective wrote that down. "Did she mention what the story was about?"

"No. She was going to when she got to the bar. But—"

"But?"

He muttered, "She never made it."

"We'll look into that. We're trying to find her roommate. Do you know where she is?"

Jimmy shook his head. "Courtney? No. They got along, but they weren't that close. Courtney spent a lot of time at her boyfriend's."

"What's his name?"

"I don't know."

The detective talked some more, but Jimmy couldn't remember about what, and he didn't care. The only thing he knew was Laura was dead, and some stinking god-forsaken son of a bitch murdered her.

Stick Boy came back into the room. "We had someone check the security footage in the bar. It proves what he said. He was in the bar and at the time of her killing."

Jimmy never thought he'd see the day he'd be grateful for Big Brother.

"Okay, Jimmy," the fat detective said. "You can go. If we hear anything or have anything else to ask you about, we'll be in touch."

"How was she murdered?" Jimmy asked.

The detectives glanced at each other.

"We'd rather not say," the tall detective said.

Jimmy stood, picked up his chair, and slammed it down so hard he bent the legs.

"I've had enough of this horseshit from the both of you! You dragged me down here and tell me nothing until you bring me into this pigeon cell. Then you grill me like I had something to do with the killing a girl I really loved when the whole time I was at a bar. I've listened to you. Now you listen to me! I spent two years in a biker gang in between high school and college, and I never took any shit from anyone then, and I'm damn sure not taking any from the likes of you two out-of-shape old fucks!"

Finally, Jimmy felt like he had an understanding with them. They looked like they might crap their pants.

"Now, either you tell me what I want to know, or we may have more than one murder here tonight, maybe more than one in this room, do you read me?"

They glanced at each other before they nodded.

"How was she murdered?"

"She was stabbed," the fat one said. "Nine times."

"We shouldn't tell you that," the tall one said. "But do you know of anyone who had that kind of rage inside them that would do that to her?"

Jesus, Jimmy thought. *Who the hell would want to do that to someone as beautiful and sweet as her?*

"No," he muttered. "Not even when I was on the streets of Virginia Beach did I know anyone as mentally fucked up as that."

CHAPTER TWO

After the funeral, when Jimmy returned to Morganburg, Virginia, a small town two hours south of Virginia Beach, he wanted to talk to the police right away.

Seth drove him to the police station, and Jimmy asked to see the lead detective in Laura's case.

"What's this about?" the receptionist asked.

What do you think this is about, you moron? Jimmy thought. *How many murders do you have in this backwater town?* "Laura Jenkins. I'm here to talk to someone about her case."

"Take a seat, please. I'll call a detective."

They made him wait half an hour in the reception area before Fat Boy came out. Jimmy figured he had to get that triple-decker-deluxe burger down before he came out to talk.

The detective sat him down at his desk. Jimmy wondered why he couldn't have sat there for the first visit and get treated like an actual human being. Not too surprisingly, there was an empty yellow wrapper and an empty container of fries at his desk. The detective crumpled them up and threw them away.

Jimmy was glad he got that out of the way before he got to work. He hated to see the cop hard at work on an empty stomach.

Then he said, "We're sorry. So far, we're still working the case. I have nothing new to tell you. When we find out something, we'll let you know."

Why did I even bother? "What about that story she was working on for the paper? She kept notes in a blue notebook. It should be in her apartment."

"Yeah, that's right. We never found that notebook. And we spoke to the editor of the paper. He said she never told him what she was working on."

That guy still had that funny blank look in his eye, like he was in a trance. Jimmy left the police station feeling worse than when he arrived. Seth drove him back to their new home. Jimmy was grateful they had moved. His old apartment would only bring back memories of Laura there. He swore he could still smell her flowery perfume in that cramped, two-bedroom apartment in Morganburg, Virginia, a small town about an hour and a half south of Virginia Beach.

Morganburg University, a small college of ten thousand students, started as a liberal arts school but gradually added more majors like political science, law school, business, and nursing.

Jimmy wasn't concerned about the outside of the house; that's not what won him over. Now they had a large living room, two larger bedrooms, and a dining area big enough to invite friends over for dinner. Jimmy liked all the added space. When they got inside, Jimmy realized he had never bothered to move a lot of his belongings into his room. Boxes were still stacked up in the living room.

"Dude, I definitely like this place," Seth said, looking around. "I've got more room for my paintings now."

Jimmy nodded. He knew Seth was trying to get his mind off the murder, but it was going to take far more than just talking about the apartment. "Yeah, it works well for the artiste, especially one who pumps out paintings like you do."

Seth grabbed some boxes from the living room. "Do you want these boxes in your room?"

Jimmy didn't care where he put the damn boxes. Throw them outside for all he cared. "Sure, go ahead."

Seth, his best friend since junior high school, said, "Hang in there, my friend. Only two semesters left, and we're outta here."

Now Jimmy thought he couldn't wait to get the fuck out.

Jimmy exhaled like a prisoner stepping outside after serving time. He hated that town so much, the place that had killed his girlfriend. At first, he didn't just want to move out of the apartment but leave Morganburg, although that meant quitting college, and he only had one year left, so he decided to push through his senior year. "Yeah, that's what I keep telling myself." He still didn't like the idea of staying in a town with a killer on the loose.

Seth got a call on his cell phone from his girlfriend, Natalie.

He kept the volume loud, and Jimmy could hear part of the conversation.

"So you're back in town?" Seth asked. "Yeah…He's as fine as can be expected, I guess. "Yeah, sure. Come on over. I'm done unpacking. Jimmy's getting there."

"Traci wants to see it, too," Natalie said.

"Okay. She can come, too."

Oh, great, Jimmy thought. *Like my life isn't miserable enough. Now I have to have her over here, too?*

Natalie Dupree and Traci Frederickson drove over to see the guys' new home. They parked in the driveway at the side of the house and next to Jimmy's car. He breathed in the warm, humid air and gazed up at his new home for his senior year. The egg-white, one-story house stood on the edge of the woods.

Seth, a tall weightlifter, bent over to give Natalie a peck on the lips. "Hi, sweetie."

Natalie reached beneath his long, dark curly locks and flicked the silver earring cross that dangled down his neck.

She hugged Jimmy. He always Seth picked a sweet, pretty girl with her long straight brunette locks and small rabbit nose. "I'm so sorry," she said softly. "And I'm sorry I missed the funeral."

"That's okay."

"Are you hanging in there?"

He nodded.

"Have they found the person yet?" Natalie asked.

"No. Not yet."

"I'm sorry, Jimmy," Traci said. "I really am."

He nodded again. Traci, a blonde with light crystal-cold blue eyes and soft swirling curls flowing down the middle of her back, wore an electric shirt and cutoff jeans. She was pretty, but Jimmy never cared for her.

While he unpacked more boxes, Seth gave the girls the grand tour. Their apartment door opened to the living room, full of Seth's larger paintings. Piles of boxes stood around the table. The bathroom was to the right, and Jimmy's bedroom was to the left, filled with boxes, and two homemade bookcases lined the wall at the foot of his bed. His desk and computer sat by the window, ready to do homework. The dining room stood next to the living room, and the kitchen was in the back.

Jimmy opened a large box. He found his leather jacket with the skull emblem of the Black Knights on the back, and hung it up with a special Harley hanger and plastic bag.

Traci frowned. He knew she hated that he and Seth had been in a biker gang in between high school and college. The Black Knights weren't like the Hell's Angels or the Pagans, just a bunch of guys who liked to ride, hit the bars and music clubs, and hang out together. Of course, knuckles could get bloody on occasion.

Natalie asked, "How did you guys find this house?"

Jimmy placed a couple of boxes full of books right beside his bookshelf. "Last July, I found an advertisement in the campus newspaper. I guess the guy who had lived here went AWOL, and the company wanted to find someone to replace him right, so they offered it dirt cheap."

Natalie glanced into Seth's room. "I think the place is great for you. You were running out of room. Now you have more space for your books, Jimmy. And Seth has more room for his paintings."

Jimmy looked over her shoulder. Seth already had some of his paintings neatly stacked against the wall. He thought Seth was the most organized artist he'd ever seen. "Yeah, I think we're going to like this place a lot better."

Natalie pointed to the back of the kitchen. A large padlock hung above the doorknob to a door beside the oven. "Where does that door lead to?"

"That's like a boiler room area. The water heaters and heating system are back there." Jimmy stuck his pen into his back pocket. Always having a pen in hand was a habit he got into when he registered at college. He always needed to fill out an endless supply of forms. Traci always bitched how he always kept a pen in his hand. She liked to ask him if he showered while holding one.

"Who lives upstairs?" Traci asked.

No one of importance, Jimmy thought.

"Three girls," Seth said. "They're seniors, too."

"Well, I like it," Natalie said. "Maybe out here, it will be quiet so you guys can study and sleep."

"Did you see outside?" Seth asked.

Jimmy grabbed a soda and followed them out.

When Jimmy first saw the house in the bright sunshine, it looked like a cozy home that could be turned into a Bed and Breakfast. Now that the sun crept behind the tree line, the house looked scary, sitting alone like its presence somehow kept the forest at a firm distance.

A rare warm breeze blew through Jimmy's shoulder-length brown hair. It was really a beautiful day. He just wished he could enjoy it. He wore shorts and a black shirt that absorbed all of the sun's heat. Strong storms rumbled through in the early morning, but that did nothing to cool off the late summer day. They only felt like they added more humidity to the air, but the fresh, wet grass smelled clean and fresh.

Natalie jogged up the cement steps that led to the front porch. She looked great in her fiery red tank top and tight shorts. She jogged back down the steps to stand beneath a small maple tree in the front yard. "I like it."

Jimmy and Traci followed her.

"I don't know, guys," Traci said. "Doesn't it look a little creepy out in the middle of nowhere?"

"Creepy?" Natalie laughed. "How can you say that? I think it looks beautiful."

Several skinny pines looked like they reached to the sky, and a few towering evergreens stood around the property. Eight columns, four in the front and two on the sides supported the flat, square porch roof. A black metal design resembling a small fence wrapped around the top of the porch. Beside it stood the rust-colored chimney. Two living room windows flanked the chimney. To the left of the porch was a single bedroom window with a faded striped red and gray awning. Two bushes sat beneath each window, and a black mailbox, for all the residents hung to the right of the door.

Jimmy stepped up to the chimney next to the porch. He hated to admit that maybe the house was a little creepy. "You want to see spooky? Look here. I didn't even see this until we started to move in. Check out these faces on the chimney. Don't they give you the creeps?"

Three stylized faces carved into a rectangle in the middle of the chimney looked like garish theatrical masks of rage. They were almost funny.

"Oh, gosh, yes," Natalie said. "Who the heck would sculpt faces into a chimney?"

Jimmy frowned. "Yeah, I've wondered that myself."

Traci asked, "Don't you think it's quite a ways away from the university?"

Jimmy darted up the porch to check the mail and glanced through the window of the first front door. He saw a couch and part of a coffee table as he closed the mailbox. "Not really," he said. "We just drove around the outer rim of the campus, down Baxter Road to here on Rutledge Avenue. If you walk through these woods, on the other side are the art and political science buildings. It's only like a fifteen-minute walk."

The girls stepped closer to the front steps. The trees gazed down over the roof of the house.

The sun cowered behind them as the damp woods absorbed the last of the light.

Traci pointed to the top of the porch to the center of the metal design. The base of the center piece was thicker than the rest of the spires that decorated the top of the porch. "Check that out up there. It looks like a chunk was broken from the top of that metal design. What do you suppose that was?"

Jimmy shrugged. "Who knows?"

They headed back down the concrete steps to the north side of the house, where Jimmy parked his car. Flapping wings from above startled him. A flock of purple grackles flew to the edge of the woods and landed in the trees. He always hated those birds and the obnoxious noise they made. Their metallic cawing sounded like a predator pounced on them. They immediately shot out of the woods and flew away. Jimmy wondered what was wrong with them.

A few feet from where Natalie parked her car stood at the side entrance. He led the girls through an inner hallway to the front door of the basement apartment. He liked the basement entry and hallway to the front door. It reminded him of his favorite bars back in Virginia Beach.

Seth grinned when he looked at Natalie. That's the first time he'd seen Seth smile in weeks.

The loud partying, late-night noise and fighting from their neighbors at their last apartment building turned Seth into a constant grouch. Seth really didn't seem to care about which house he lived in, but Jimmy hoped moving would bring back the old easy-going Seth.

Seth and Jimmy led the girls out the front door and around to the backyard. The sun had now slipped all the way behind the trees. Seeing Seth do many still life paintings, Jimmy had learned all about the flowers in the area. Seth didn't necessarily care about what he painted, but Jimmy liked researching things. Now he could appreciate that the yard out back was filled with blue flag irises, purple cornflowers, cardinal flowers, and black-eyed Susans blooming along the semi-circular wall shaped like a frown made of large brown and black rocks. The air was breezy and floral.

Natalie breathed deep. "I love this fresh air. And I love the aroma that's out here. I smell pine and wild flowers." She let go of Seth's hand.

Jimmy joined her. He stepped over the rock wall built into the earth and walked up a slope to the edge of the forest. He glanced back at the house gouged right into the hill. An eight-foot white concrete wall emerged from the ground to the home. Concrete stairs between the wall and the house led up to a driveway and parking area for the upstairs neighbors. The parking lot was big enough for four cars. A side street wound through the woods and around the backside of the university. A small screened porch was on the left side of the house.

"I'm planning on painting some pictures of this place," Seth said. "I want to do paintings of the house, the woods, and all of this out here."

Traci lingered by the door.

Jimmy approached the woods. A chilling wind blew from the direction of the trees. No sunlight penetrated the leaves and branches of the tall pines that stretched to the clouds. It looked like a dark hideaway for a murderer. Jimmy shuddered. He said, "It sure did get cold all of a sudden, didn't it?"

Natalie agreed. She crossed her arms across her chest.

"Cold?" Seth asked, chuckling. "Are you kidding? It's in the eighties out here. I'm hot."

The wind cut into Jimmy, and he shivered again.

Natalie turned around and looked at Traci, still standing back by the house. "You feel it getting cold out here, too, don't you?"

"God, yes," Traci gasped. "I want to go back inside."

Jimmy's head snapped back to the forest when he heard twigs snap. Just for an instant, he again caught a glimpse of a shadow figure ducking behind a tree.

"Now what?" Seth asked.

"I thought I saw movement in there," Jimmy said. "Like a shadow."

"You saw an animal?" Seth asked.

Jimmy took a few steps to the woods, crossing the manicured grass until he came to the tree line. It was hard to see, it was pretty dark in there, but he could make out something in the pines several feet deep. He caught a glimpse of a pink blouse; then the figure darted again. He saw blue shorts, bloody like the night she…

"*Laura*", he gasped.

"Jimmy!" she cried. "It's right beneath your feet. It's in the ground! Get out now while you still can!" She shrieked before she disappeared.

Did he see what he thought he did? Or did he want to see Laura so badly his brain was giving him what he wanted? But then again, why would he see her bloody?

"Jimmy." A hand grabbed his arm from behind. Jimmy spun around. "Christ, Jimmy, what's wrong?" Traci said. "You look gray. Are you all right?"

"Will you quit sneaking up behind me like that?" Jimmy snapped.

"Sorry," she muttered angrily. "But you weren't answering me. You were just standing there like you were in a trance."

Jimmy glanced back. His Laura was gone. Was she really there at all?

"What is it?" Natalie asked. "Did you see something?"

Jimmy stepped over the rock wall to the house. "No, it's nothing. For a moment, I thought I saw someone walking in there. I guess it was just my imagination."

"I didn't see anyone," Traci said.

Seth said, "I'm hungry. Am I the only one who hasn't eaten dinner yet?"

"I don't feel like eating," Jimmy muttered.

Natalie grabbed him by the arm. "Come on. You should eat. Try to eat something. You looked like you've lost some weight."

Jimmy gave in. He didn't want to be mean to her. "Okay." He knew the early edition of the campus paper would be out now. He thought news about her murder should be in there. Hopefully, someone who sees it will know something.

Natalie patted him on the arm, and Jimmy glanced at her. "Come on. It will be all right.

You've got us to lean on."

Jimmy glanced back at the woods. "Yeah. Let's get the hell out of here."

CHAPTER THREE

They got into Jimmy's old beater Honda. The old relic groaned a couple of times before the engine turned over, and they and drove to The Little Five Points Deli, the hub of Morganburg, where five major streets joined just off-campus. It was his favorite deli, and new ownership had converted it into a full-service restaurant but kept the name. Before they went inside, Jimmy grabbed a campus paper from a blue newspaper stand just outside the restaurant. The campus newspaper always came out with an edition the week before each semester began. "Want one?"

"No, thanks," Seth said. "I learned to give those up."

Despite the humidity that enveloped Jimmy, his vision of Laura left him cold. It made no sense for his mind to imagine her bloody, as that's not how he remembered her or wanted to see her. But it had to have been his imagination. The aroma of freshly baked bread in the busy restaurant warmed him. A black-and-white checkered pattern stretched across the floor, complementing the dark blue uniforms hurried from one table to another while classic rock filled the restaurant.

Once seated at a small round table, they ordered drinks from a short blonde with a fading bruise beneath her right eye. Jimmy wondered if a boyfriend had given her that. The violence on campus really disgusted him.

Seth ordered a beer.

Jimmy was stunned. He thought Seth had quit drinking for the most part. Seth always had Coke. "You? You're drinking a beer? You haven't had a drink for lunch since last summer. What's up?"

Seth smiled. "What the hell. It's Friday. I feel like a beer."

Jimmy rubbed his face. He thought he could drink a case of the stuff right now.

They didn't have to look at the menus. They knew what they wanted to eat and ordered.

Jimmy opened *The Black and Blue*, the campus newspaper, and the headline screamed, "Student Found Murdered." Jimmy knew more about what happened in Laura's murder than what was reported there, but something caught his eye.

"Laura Jenkins, a writer for the *Black and Blue*, was planning to do a story about the town. 'I think she said it had something to do with graveyards,' Valerie Conway said, a friend of Laura's."

Jimmy wondered what the hell would writing about graveyards get somebody killed. He caught Traci's name under an article. He had forgotten she also was a writer for the paper.

The waitress brought them their beers.

"Who's Valerie Conway?" Jimmy asked Traci.

"Valerie Conway?" Seth said. "I know a girl by that name. She's an art major who's been in a couple of my art classes."

"She was a good friend of Laura's," Traci said. "I'm surprised you don't know her."

"Sorry, I didn't know all of her friends."

Jimmy couldn't explain it. Traci always irritated him. He picked up the paper again and pulled out a pen from his back pocket and slapped it against the paper. He then saw a small article about a student who was raped. "What's up with all of the violence on this campus? Last semester I remember we had three reported rapes."

Someone in the kitchen dropped a tray full of plates. The crash nearly made Jimmy jump out of his chair.

Seth sipped his beer. "When Jimmy and I were freshmen at a small community college in Virginia Beach, there were no murders. And there were no rapes reported."

Traci sampled her beer before she set it down. "Yeah, there's way too much violence here."

The smell of frying burgers and fries made Jimmy's stomach grumble loudly, "You're with the *Black and Blue*. Could you do a story on Laura's case? She was working for the campus paper before she was murdered. I know she was working on some story about Morganburg. What if she found out something, and that's why she was killed?"

"You really believe that, Jimmy?" Natalie asked.

"Yes, I do."

"I'm already working on a story about violence on women here at Morganburg, Jimmy," Traci said. "Laura was *your* girlfriend. I think you would know more about what story she was working on than I would. Why don't *you* do her story?"

Fat chance, Jimmy thought. He felt intimidated by the idea of writing a newspaper story. They'd probably laugh him out of the office. He didn't know how to begin, and all he had was a gut feeling that she had learned something she shouldn't have. Besides, his head felt like it was in a fog. He could barely concentrate on anything. He didn't know how he was even going to get through his final classes now.

"No way, honey. After all, I've been through, I don't have it in me to do a story about her. I don't know how to write a newspaper article. I don't know who I should talk to. I'm not a reporter or a cop. I'm a student. I've got enough work on my hands."

Traci snarled, "All of us on the paper are college students, remember? If you join, you can learn reporting skills."

Seth sketched on a napkin. "I think she's got you there, Jimbo."

Jimmy again folded the paper and set it aside. "I don't think so."

"Why not?" Natalie asked.

Traci sipped her drink. "We need new people. Last spring, we lost a couple of people because of graduation. We're always looking for new writers. Why don't you join us?"

"Listen," Jimmy said. "I'm a creative writing major. You're the one majoring in journalism. You would know what to do. I wouldn't."

"The senior editor could help you with that," Traci said.

Jimmy drank his beer and groaned. "I don't know. Now that its the fall semester…people graduated and have moved on…I wouldn't know where to start."

"She was your girlfriend," Traci said. "Would anyone else have more motivation than you?"

Seth sipped his beer while he wasted napkins by sketching people in the restaurant. "You ought to do it," Seth said. "The experience could only help you."

"Yeah," Natalie said as they were served their sandwiches. "Why don't you try it? You might actually make you feel better. Help find Laura's killer."

Jimmy dug into his roast beef sub. It was just what his stomach needed.

He wondered if the cops couldn't find her killer, who was he to do better? "Look," he said, his voice turning sharp, "I can't. I don't want to have to go through her murder all over again."

Traci nibbled on a turkey sandwich. "Okay, I understand."

But the idea intrigued him. He and Laura dated for nearly a year. When he found out she'd been stabbed to death, he wanted to crawl into a hole and die. It's been a struggle just to get out of bed in the morning. He'd do anything to find the piece of scum who killed her, but he was afraid of making a fool of himself if he ran around playing detective. He didn't think he could pull it off, but he wanted to try anyway. He thought about how he would start such a story.

He never said another word during lunch. He couldn't stop being mad about how she died.

Her killer stabbed her *nine times*. He couldn't stop imagining her, bleeding to death, maybe even calling out his name, and he wasn't there.

CHAPTER FOUR

After lunch, Natalie and Traci left Jimmy and Seth alone so they could finish unpacking and straightening out their new home. Before Jimmy stepped inside, he checked the mailbox again. He shuffled the mail before he peeked through the window in the door to take a longer look at his new housemates' living room. Stockings and shirts hung over the tan couch. Dirty dishes and glasses littered the wooden coffee table.

Jimmy couldn't believe it. He had never seen women live like slobs. He hoped the house didn't have roaches.

He returned to their basement apartment.

"Any mail?" Seth asked.

"Nope."

Seth and Jimmy had bought a case of beer before they returned home. Seth tossed Jimmy a bottle right as Jimmy stepped through the front door. Exactly what Jimmy wanted.

Seth dug into a box and found his paints. "So tell me what's up between you and Traci."

Jimmy popped the top, and suds rushed to the mouth of the bottle. He quickly sucked some down. "What do you mean?"

"I mean, you two are always at each other's throats. For obvious reasons, you two weren't so bad today, but usually, it's like you enjoy arguing."

Jimmy sipped a little more. "Look, I don't ask to be around her. She's Natalie's friend.

Every time I see that girl, she bitches me out about something. Who the hell does she think she is? My mother?"

Seth chuckled. "Honestly, Jimmy, I always thought she was jealous of Laura. I really believe she's got a thing for you."

Jimmy couldn't believe he had just said that. He set his bottle down so hard on the living room table it sounded like a skeletal fist had punched glass. "Seth, don't even go there. She's not my type. Besides, I'm in no mood after what happened to Laura."

Seth's straightened out their two recliners in front of the TV in the living room. "Suit yourself. But I think you've got a lot in common with her. You're both writers. I think if you asked her out, she'd go."

Jimmy sneered as he glanced at his beer bottle. "You're lucky I still got beer in here, or I'd throw this at you. Are you nuts? I can't stand that girl. And I don't feel like it. My mind is on Laura."

"Okay."

Seth went into his room and started unpacking some clothes. He opened his closet and hung up some of his jeans next to his leather jacket.

Jimmy followed him into the bedroom. He smiled slightly, eyeing the jacket. They had come a long way from when they rode with the Knights. "Why the hell would I want to date her?"

"Because I think you've got a crush on her. Honestly, the way you two act, I wish you'd just call a truce and get all warm and cozy with each other because it's obvious to me she wants to."

Jimmy gulped the last of his bottle.

Seth glanced up. "Yikes," he muttered. "Incoming!"

Seth ducked behind his closet door before Jimmy's beer bottle hit him. The bottle clunked against the door. Seth didn't bother to pick it up. Jimmy stepped back to the living room, and Seth chased him. "I think it would be okay if the two of you just hung out together. I know you loved Laura. I think you blame yourself for her death. But that wasn't your fault."

"I'm not the one who killed her," Jimmy muttered.

Jimmy hated how he was out having a good time while she was being murdered.

The sound of heels hammering against the floor told them the neighbors were home. They walked through the home. Jimmy gazed above him. "Jesus Christ! Did you say three women live above us or a herd of water buffalo?"

Seth chuckled and shook his head. "I think they have nothing but hardwood floors up there. They sound like they're big girls." He finished unpacking his painting supplies and crushed the cardboard boxes. "But actually, I got a glimpse of those girls when I was outside. They're thin. One's a blonde. The other two are brunettes."

Jimmy placed a box full of his books in his room. He couldn't understand what was so important that had them moving around so much in the afternoon. They acted like restless dogs. "Can't they take their heels off? Most people are glad to kick off their shoes once they get home."

Seth put one of his heaviest CDs, "Master of Reality" by Black Sabbath, into the stereo and turned the volume way up. "Here's something to drown that crap out."

Once "Sweet Leaf" was done, one of the women angrily pounded her high heel into the floor. It was unmistakably an attempt at communication.

Seth turned off the stereo, grabbed a dumbbell from Seth's room, and smashed it against the ceiling. "Take your goddamn heels off!"

It was quiet for a few moments until the women filed out of the house. "Uh-oh," Jimmy said.

He grabbed a couple more beers and tossed one to Seth. "Now we've done it. I think we're about to get three little visitors who are going to critique our taste in music." He wondered briefly if he could've simply asked them to keep the noise down. They might not realize the sound carried so much in that old house.

"I don't give a fat rat's ass if they don't like our music," Seth grumbled.

A few moments later, someone knocked at the door. Jimmy said, "I guess it's time to meet our new neighbors."

Seth opened the door. Jimmy thought they were really pretty. The girls shook their hands.

Their perfume smelled like jasmine and gardenia. They smiled at Seth.

"We're just wondering," Anne Marie said, "if you could kinda not play your music so loud? It's, uh, the bass, I mean, is vibrating things off our tables and shelves."

Jimmy found a box of his clothes. "We were trying to drown out all of the noise we heard when you came home. Those high heels of yours sound loud down here." The girls ignored him. They stared at Seth.

Michelle pushed some of her hair behind her ear. "Oh, we're sorry. We didn't mean to disturb you. We didn't realize we were so loud." Michelle, the curly-haired brunette, wore a baby blue top and tan shorts. Her voice sounded deep and alluring.

"It's okay," Seth said. "It sounds as if you have no carpeting upstairs."

"We don't," Elizabeth said. "All of our floors are hardwood."

Jimmy wondered if he was invisible.

"Do you girls want a beer?" Seth asked.

"Sure," they said.

Jimmy nodded. "I'll get them."

Seth offered the girls a seat at the table in the living room. Michelle saw some of Seth's impressionist landscape paintings lying around the room. "Are you guys art majors? Those are really good."

Seth spun a chair around and sat down. "I am. Jimmy's a creative writing major. Are you girls undergraduates, too?"

"Yeah, I'm a business major," Michelle said. "Nothing matters to me more than making a lot of money right away. My parents had to take some lousy jobs to make ends meet, and I don't want to have to go through that."

"You want to have a lot of money?" Seth asked.

"*Yes*. Once I get my degree and I get offered a job where the starting pay isn't even fifty thousand a year, I won't even take it. And I want to make a lot more money than that."

Seth cringed. "That doesn't sound like fun."

The girls chuckled.

Jimmy came back with the beers and handed them out.

Michelle opened her bottle. "I like it. I like taking charge of things. I want to run a company, take control of it, and turn it around."

"Do you two feel the same way?" Jimmy asked.

Anne Marie was the smallest. After she sipped some of her beer, she sat with her arms and legs crossed. "I'm studying nursing. My mother is a doctor. I want to help people just like her, but yeah, I want to make some decent money. I'm hoping to save money and maybe become a doctor like her."

Elizabeth held her bottle while she got a closer look at Seth's paintings. "I'm a poli sci major, and I want to be a lawyer."

Jimmy smiled slightly. "Following in your daddy's footsteps?"

"No." She stopped to take a longer look at one of Seth's still-life paintings. "My parents went through a horrible divorce. My father is an attorney, and he really screwed over my mom. You won't find me sleeping while some lawyer gets the upper hand on me."

"You don't have to tell me about a messy split with the folks," Seth said. "Been there, done that."

"Why? What happened?" Anne Marie asked.

Seth took a swig of his beer. "Let's just say it was at least as bad as Elizabeth's parents."

Elizabeth continued to look through Seth's paintings.

"Like what you see?" Jimmy asked.

She nodded. "Yeah, you're really good, Seth."

Seth tipped back his bottle. "Thank you."

"The guy who used to live down here before you was an art major," Anne Marie said. "He took off a couple of weeks ago. He quit school and moved."

Jimmy froze for a moment. The real estate agent who rented the basement to him had just said the prior tenant had moved out without any notice. He'd figured the guy had been failing or ran out of money or something. But after his vision in the woods, he wondered if more was going on. "Do you know why?"

Michelle shrugged her shoulders. "We don't know. But I can assure you, we'd like to have left with him. And as soon as we graduate next spring, we're just as gone as he is."

Seth lifted a box from the floor and set it on the table. "Why? Is there a problem with this house?" He found some glasses.

Anne Marie opened her bottle. With her long blonde hair, high cheekbones, and pale blue eyes, she looked like the girl next door. "No. It's not the house."

Elizabeth long, straight hair gently cascaded over her shoulders. She wore an orange sundress with no bra. Her erect nipples projected awkwardly like she desperately wanted someone to hold her breasts. "It's the woods out back."

Jimmy glanced out the window. "You don't like the woods?"

Anne Marie nodded to the rear of the home. "It's not a forest we've got a problem with. It's those woods."

Seth picked up another box and found more glasses. "What's wrong with them?"

"Sometimes we can hear a woman scream from far away," Elizabeth said.

Jimmy felt a chill run down his back. The vision he'd had of Laura came back to him, and he had a new thought. Could those woods be the cover for a student killer?

"At night, sometimes we swear we can also hear voices coming from there," Michelle said.

Elizabeth anxiously looked outside. "Yeah. But the voices are strange. We can hear several people talking. It sounds like they're complaining or arguing."

Jimmy set his box of clothes into his room and returned to the living room. "What are they saying?" He wondered if these girls were just pulling their legs, but they didn't seem to be joking.

Michelle sipped her beer. "You can't quite make out what they're saying. And that's weird because if people are complaining or arguing, you can always hear them. But these voices mumble or whisper. It's as if they don't want us to hear them. Or maybe it's another language. We think that forest is haunted."

"Exactly," Anne Marie agreed. "It's like something is in there that doesn't want us to hear them because they're plotting something, something *awful*."

Michelle folded her hands around the bottle. "Or maybe the voices are trying to entice us into the woods?"

Seth shot a look at Jimmy before he said, "Jimmy said he thought he saw maybe an animal moving around in there."

"Yeah, maybe," Jimmy muttered. "Just for a moment."

"Really?" Anne Marie shivered. "I knew there was something in those woods!"

Jimmy now feared his vision of Laura wasn't his imagination. But that would mean that someone could read his mind and make his worst fears visible. "Some *thing*?"

Elizabeth forced a nervous giggle. "You haven't seen the fog out here yet. The fog that comes out of those woods isn't gray or white. It's *black*."

Black fog? Jimmy had never heard of such a thing and didn't believe them.

Seth chuckled. "Did you say black fog?"

Anne Marie set her bottle aside. "Yeah."

Jimmy picked up one last box from the floor, put it into his room, and returned to the living room. "Tell us about that fog."

Michelle said, "It creeps out of the woods at night. When we see that, we take off."

Seth asked, "Has anyone besides you seen the fog or heard the voices or screams?"

Anne Marie shivered. "We've had enough talk about that. It's really creeping me out." She glanced out the window. "No way I ever want to find out what's in there or what it wants. I just want to leave here."

Bells chimed, and Michelle answered her cell phone. "Hi! Yes, absolutely. We're just about ready to go. We'll see you soon." She hung up. "We gotta go."

"Just the girls out on the town?" Jimmy asked.

Michelle chugged the last of her beer. "Yes. One of our sisters, Cassie, split up with her boyfriend, and we're taking her out to cheer her up and give her a good time."

"You girls are sorority sisters?" Seth asked.

"Yeah," Anne Marie said.

They stepped back to the living room.

"Where are you girls going?" Seth asked.

"We don't know yet," Elizabeth said. "We just plan on bar hopping tonight."

Anne Marie set her empty bottle on the table. "Anything to get away from here for a while."

"Next weekend, we plan to go to go up to Norfolk to see Cassie's parents," Michelle said. "A weekend away from this creepy town would be a welcome change."

Jimmy gulped some more of his beer.

They didn't like the house. They were even afraid of the town. And they weren't joking around.

Anne Marie finished her bottle. "Thanks for the beers, guys."

"Okay, girls," Seth said. "If you see that fog or see anything else or hear anything that scares you, we're down here now. Jimmy and I aren't afraid of anything."

"We'll keep that in mind," Anne Marie said. "Bye, Seth."

"Bye, Seth," Elizabeth and Michelle said.

Jimmy waited for Seth to close the door, and he asked, "How do you do it?"

Seth grinned as he peeked into a box. "Do what?"

Jimmy finished his beer. "You know. Get women to just instantly fall for you. Do you have a love potion you mix into your shampoo? Or have you learned hypnosis?"

"Maybe the girls just dig my hair."

Sure, that's it, Jimmy thought. "Oh, like hell. I've got just as many long locks as you do."

Seth slammed the last of his beer and threw the bottle away in the garbage can sitting by the front door.

"I think they love those high cheekbones and those velvety-brown eyes," Jimmy said.

Seth picked up another box and took it to his room. "Velvety-brown what?"

"Eyes," Jimmy said. "Eyes, dumb ass"

"I don't think there's any such thing, Jimmy. Brown velvet?"

"I don't think it's so much the color; it's just like the way your eyes look. Like velvet, you want to reach out and touch it. You're drawn to it. And women are drawn to your big brown eyes." He suspected it was more than Seth's looks, but he liked poking fun at Seth.

Jimmy grabbed a box of his CDs and took them into his room. "So what did you make of those girls?"

Seth placed the landscape paintings in his room. "I really don't know. Seem nice enough, I guess."

"You don't think they're crazy? Pulling our legs, you know, joking around?"

"Crazy?" Seth said as he put some shirts away in his dresser. "No, but I think they're a little spacey. Their imaginations get the best of them, and then they all think they see the same thing."

Jimmy grabbed a box of CDs from the living room. "So you don't believe that stuff?"

"I believe they believe. I don't think they were lying to us just because they thought it would be a big joke to feed us full of BS. But I don't believe they saw black fog. There's no such thing. Maybe they were high."

"Yeah," Jimmy mumbled as he peered out the living room window and stared at the trees.

For a moment, he again thought he saw movement in the woods. He suddenly regretted the move. He stared at the trees in hopes to make sure it wasn't his eyes playing tricks, but he didn't see anything again. He wondered if someone lived out there. And he wished he hadn't turned down Traci to join the paper to try to find out who killed Laura.

CHAPTER FIVE

Jimmy awoke to the sound of people arguing, but he couldn't make out the words. The voices came from the woods. Jimmy sat up and looked out his bedroom window.

Laura stood in front of the trees as black fog oozed out of the forest and surrounded her.

She ran to his window. "I have more time if I come to you in dreams, Jimmy. I'm hiding in the campus church where they can't get me. You're walking over the dead. It's in the administration. They have control of everything. You—!" She screamed before she disappeared as the dark fog started to envelope her.

He was pretty sure this time that he wasn't hallucinating or imagining anything, and his instinct was to go to her, to help her. Perhaps she had never died at all, and some other girl had been stabbed.

The house rumbled as if demons below were pounding their fists against the earth. Items rattled off his dresser, a lamp tipped over, and books fell off his shelves. Then the bookcase topped over.

Jimmy thought it was an earthquake.

Jimmy's bedroom floor quaked and cracked open. Concrete snapped and splintered like wood. Small trees erupted through the floor and grew skyward, quickly growing as large as the ones outside, and one tree smashed through the floor beneath Jimmy's bed. Branches caught the bed and pushed Jimmy toward the ceiling. He raised his arms over his head to keep from being crushed and screamed.

Jimmy woke up.

He blinked. His heart beat madly. The sheets stuck to him like a bloody shroud. He felt disgusted as he pulled them off and wiped the sweat from his arms and chest. He looked at the ceiling and then around the room. It was morning. He breathed deeply and mumbled, "It was just a dream." He smiled as he shook his head.

Jimmy drove to campus before his first class and called Laura's roommate, Courtney, but she didn't pick up. He left her a message. He wanted to see if Laura's notebook was still in her bedroom.

Before Jimmy made it into his first class, he got a call from Laura's mom, Brenda. He saw her at the funeral, but they only spoke briefly. They were both too distraught to talk.

"Jimmy, have you heard if they made any progress with finding Laura's killer? Have they arrested anyone? Have they even said if they have any suspects?"

"So far, No to all the above. I've spoken to them, and they're so unprofessional. It's like Laurel and Hardy have control of the case. I'm so disgusted. I won't even talk to them anymore."

She cried, "I don't know what to do. When I've called, they give me the run around, put me on hold, and hang up on me. I drove all the way to Morganburg and went down there. They just left me to sit in the lobby. Then some fat old man came out to me and said they're still working on the case, but they have no new leads."

"They've done the same thing to me."

"And that man had these funny gray eyes. It's like he's hypnotized."

Now he knew she'd see that, too.

"I know who you're talking about, and I've seen that look." He checked his watch. Class was about to begin. "Brenda, I have to go to class. But can you tell me if Laura mentioned anything about what story she was working on?"

"She wouldn't talk about it other than to say it involved the campus administration and the local government. It was like she was afraid to tell me for fear my life would be threatened."

Jimmy shivered. *My God, what did she find out?*

"Jimmy, is there anything you can do? You live right there. Can you pressure them to just do their job?"

Jimmy's heart broke for her. He felt exactly the same way, completely powerless. "Brenda, I vow to you I'm going to find the son of a bitch who did this to Laura."

He hung up. If only he knew how.

Jimmy finished writing a short story for class just as Seth finished with his classes. Jimmy made himself a roast beef and cheese sandwich while Seth put on an old black Morganburg football T-shirt and faded blue jeans and grabbed a canvas, his black tackle box full of oil paints.

Seth grabbed a couple of beers from the fridge. "I want to get all the different colors out back."

Jimmy waved lazily. "Have fun." But he wondered why he brought the beer with him.

Seth set his painting on an easel and began to paint a picture of the house and the trees in the background. Jimmy went outside to check the mail. Seth looked like he had lost himself in his painting.

Jimmy got the mail and thought he heard someone in a deep voice call Seth's name.

"Jimmy?" Seth said. "That you? I'm out back."

Jimmy wondered what he meant. He never called Seth.

Jimmy went down the steps.

"What the fuck?" Seth exclaimed.

Jimmy jogged around to the side of the house, and for an instant, out of the corner of his eye, he thought he saw a dark figure in the backyard, but then it was gone.

Seth walked backward like he backed away from a vicious dog. He stumbled over and screamed. Jimmy glanced at the back. Nothing was there.

Jimmy wondered what had gotten into him. "Seth, dude, what's wrong?"

"Look!" Seth turned back to the woods. Nothing was there. An icy wind blew from the woods. Seth turned back to Jimmy and gasped, "Shit."

Jimmy was unsettled and confused. "Look at what? What the hell's wrong?"

Seth glanced back twice before heading back to the front yard. "Am I losing my marbles?" he muttered. "Jesus Christ, I'm done painting for today." He grabbed his things and headed back inside.

Jimmy joined him. He wondered what the hell Seth was talking about.

Seth went into his room and dumped his painting supplies on the floor. He joined Jimmy in the kitchen, and they each got a Coke.

Jimmy thought the beer wasn't so good on a warm day and empty stomach for him.

Jimmy cracked open his can. "Here. Time to drink this instead. Now tell me what just happened."

Seth chugged his soda. "You'd never believe me if I told you."

"Give me a shot."

"I heard this voice calling me. I thought it was you. But then I realized it wasn't. When I came around the side of the house, I saw this guy with long hair wearing a black robe. He pointed at me and laughed."

Jimmy shuddered even though he wasn't cold. Somehow he knew what his friend was talking about. "You saw someone come out of the woods?"

Seth chugged his soda like he hadn't had anything to drink all day. "No. He bubbled up out of the ground like he came out of his grave. Then I saw trees smashing through the ground. They ripped through the house, and it burst into flames."

Jimmy felt lightheaded, and his hands trembled. That was just like his dream. "I just had this nightmare last night about trees smashing up through the ground and house." They stared at each other for several moments.

Seth never mentioned having premonitions or visions before, but that coincidence between Jimmy's nightmare and Seth's hallucination was too chilling to ignore. Jimmy picked up his cell phone. Hearing that knocked the foggy feeling out of his brain. "Do you know what Traci's number is?"

"What, you want to call her now? You do like her." He smirked.

"Just tell me her damn number."

Seth gave it to him. Jimmy got her on the phone. He believed something bad was going on there. He couldn't sit on it anymore and keep his eyes closed. If he didn't act, who would?"You remember how you wanted me to join the paper to do that story about Laura's murder?"

"Yes, of course," Traci said.

"I changed my mind. I want to work to try to help find Laura's killer and maybe work on something else. I feel like it's all got to be connected. There's something about this town that's beginning to scare me."

And those chilling words from that vision or hallucination or whatever it was still ringing in Jimmy's head.

"It's in the administration. They have control of everything. It's beneath your feet. It's in the ground."

The next day, after classes, Jimmy met Traci. She looked pretty in a green top and blue jean cut-offs, and he admired her from a distance before reminding himself of how irritating she could be. She stood in front of the towering Main Library that looked like a federal courthouse. The center of campus, the courtyard in front of the library, where the law library, the campus chapel, the administration building, and a dorm stood, was a popular leisure spot to study and read for students with its shady trees, grassy areas, and a huge fountain at its core. They made their way out of the courtyard and down the sidewalk under the hot, cloudless day. Students passed by on their way to class. The drab, gray art department and burgundy poli-sci buildings, with a small graveyard in between, stood across the street. In the art building, Seth usually painted nearly every afternoon. Jimmy planned on meeting him there later.

Once inside the Department of Art, Traci asked, "So what changed your mind?"

Jimmy wondered if something bizarre was going on in Morganburg. "Believe it or not, Seth had this weird vision or premonition. And it sounded like a nightmare I had the night before. And we met the girls upstairs. They actually think something is in the woods." He couldn't explain it, but he had the sense that this was connected to Laura's murder.

"In the woods? Like what?"

"I don't know. They weren't sure."

Traci frowned. "Are you serious about Seth having a premonition?"

"Yeah." He felt embarrassed for trusting her. He should've come up with more evidence. Maybe he wasn't going to be any good at this investigation stuff.

"Did he ever have those before?"

Jimmy shrugged. "Not that I know of."

"What was similar about his vision and your dream?"

"We both saw trees erupting from the ground. I'm wondering if that wasn't symbolizing force, like violence and rape. Maybe his subconscious and mine picked up on something."

"Like what?"

"That's what I aim to find out."

Jimmy wondered if maybe there was something in the ground or water there that was poisoning people.

Fried food odors floated through the air. Jimmy and Traci crossed the street to a row of local restaurants and to the old downtown red-brick edifice that once was an apartment building. Now it housed the campus newspaper. A taped yellow outline of a body on the floor surprised Jimmy.

"What the hell is up with that?" he asked.

Traci frowned. "That was meant as a joke. It's a mock-chalk outline of a dead reporter. Ever since Laura's murder, it seems all too real, although Laura wasn't the first student murdered here."

Chills ran down Jimmy's spine. "What do you mean there are others?"

"There's one more before her that I know about."

She led him to a small conference room upstairs. The heat grew worse with each stair they climbed. The office smelled dank, like the grimy brown carpeting sucked in all the humidity of the building and trapped it in that hallway. It reeked as if the place hadn't been cleaned since it was built. The floors creaked and moaned like they walked past an old woman's deathbed. Jimmy felt sorry for the editorial staff that worked there every day. Several yellowed big story-front pages of the paper covered a bulletin board. The edition of the day after Laura's murder hung in the center. Beneath it was a story about Rudy, a student, killed on campus. Jimmy read part of the article.

"The body of the murdered student has now been identified. Rudy Sanchez's body was found behind the art building by Dr. Tom Johnson in the early evening." The article went on with interviews of his friends. Jimmy was disappointed. It didn't give any details as to why or who murdered him.

Jimmy did his best to hide how he felt as the staff trickled in and Traci introduced him. They all sat at a small rectangular table sat in the middle of the room. The stifling heat poured through the windows. No A/C existed in the building.

Traci asked, "Didn't Laura have a roommate?"

"Yeah. I tried calling her, too. I left her a message, but I haven't heard back yet. I'm getting worried."

Edward Frank came into the room. The dark-haired, clean-cut, thin senior editor, dressed in a yellow polo shirt and tan slacks, welcomed Jimmy aboard. Then there was Amanda Madigan, a curly blonde with heavy make-up around her big brown eyes, who wore a short pink dress, and Deanna Matthews, a tall, slender brunette, dressed in a ratty black top covered in paint and cut-off jeans. Jimmy figured her for another art major.

Ed nibbled on a tuna fish sandwich while he told Deanna and Amanda he wanted them to follow up on the student elections. Jimmy hated tuna. The overpowering smell turned his stomach.

Ed bit into his sandwich again before he relaxed in his chair. "Jimmy, Traci tells me you've got a story you want to work on."

"I do. I want to see if I can find any information on Laura's murder."

Ed set his sandwich aside. "That's a pretty tall order for a college student. Where do you plan to begin?"

Jimmy said, "First, I want to find out what story she was working on before she was killed.

Do any of you know what story she was doing?"

Ed ate more of his sandwich. "No."

None of the writers knew what story Laura had been working on.

Ed asked, "Have you spoken to the police, Jimmy?"

Jimmy chuckled. "Yeah, for all the fat lot of good that did me. It's like talking to a corpse."

Amanda snarled, "I've always hated the police. They're useless. They won't tell you anything, and they act like nothing's wrong."

"The university isn't any better," Deanna said. "When there was that Greek dance at the student center last spring, and those frats got into that fight, and two went to the hospital, the university said nothing. They didn't warn the frats about fighting or threaten to kick anyone out who fights. They didn't say anything, not even a 'no comment!' It's like the place is run by the walking dead."

Jimmy thought that was comforting. No wonder the violence there raged on and on.

Ed finished his sandwich. "Jimmy, I remember Laura mentioned to me she was researching something about Morganburg. She said she believed it could be something big."

Jimmy never cared about journalism, and he never took an interest in what she had worked on.

Now he regretted not asking her about it. "She told me the same thing. I wondered how big a story could be in this little town. Now I wished I had paid more attention to her."

Traci said, "Another female student murdered. More violence against women. That hooks into the story about campus date rape that I'm working on right now." She gritted her teeth and let out a heavy sigh.

"Depending on how your stories go, maybe you and Jimmy could work together," Ed said.

Jimmy wasn't fond of the thought of working with Traci. He'd rather do his story on his own. "Yeah, okay, maybe. But first, let me talk to some of Laura's friends and see what I can find out."

"If you need any help with your story, let me know," Deanna said. "Laura was a friend."

Amanda smiled. "I'd be willing to help, too."

Jimmy was glad to hear that. "Okay."

Ed wiped his hands on a paper towel. "I'll have you work closely with me, Jimmy. You see me again once you've got something to let me know what you find out." He stood up. "All right, that's it for now. Get in on it, guys."

The students filtered out, but Ed stopped Jimmy and Traci in the hallway in front of a Coke machine. "You know anything about Rudy Sanchez?"

Jimmy thumbed back to the conference room. "Not until about ten minutes ago."

Ed nodded. "I love this Coke machine. The longer you hold the button, the more Cokes it gives you." He put in a buck. It spat out three Cokes and gave him seventy-five cents back. The cans hit the bottom of the machine like pool balls at the bottom of a corner pocket. "I don't want to give you the wrong idea, but listen to me. Be careful about getting too curious about this town."

"Why?" Jimmy asked. "What do you mean?"

Ed offered his extra Cokes to Traci and Jimmy. "Rudy was on the paper five years ago. He was an art major. He became curious about Morganburg. Didn't Traci tell me you have a roommate who's an art major?"

"Yes."

"Rudy was found strangled to death in back of the art building," Ed said.

Jimmy couldn't believe it. "Jesus," he breathed. "What was he investigating?"

Ed sipped his soda. "I wish I knew! The editor before me was terrible with record keeping."

Traci gulped her Coke. "I heard about Rudy. I mean, I looked into it. But I can't find anyone who knows anything about his death. I can't even find a record of how he died. What do you know?"

Ed said, "When I first started working here, everyone believed it had something to do with his story. Back then, there were students on this paper who knew him. And I guess none of them wanted to take on whatever he was working on."

"Do you know of anyone who knows what story Rudy was covering?" Jimmy asked.

"No, I don't. But if you want to know more about Rudy, you go talk to Tom Johnson, the head of drawing and painting over there in the visual arts building. Have you ever heard of him?"

Jimmy finished his Coke. The hot August weather made him thirsty. "Yeah. My roommate knows him. Seth plans on having Johnson for his senior exit."

"Rudy was one of Johnson's students. He can tell you about Rudy's murder."

"Okay." Jimmy crushed his can and threw it away. "I'll do that."

After Jimmy and Traci left the newspaper offices, she asked, "Where are you headed?"

"Right down to the art building. I told Seth I'd meet him after classes. Seth always likes to rework a lot of his paintings. And after what I just heard from Ed, I want to talk to Seth to see if I can meet with Johnson. Want to come with me?"

"Yes," Traci said. "If you're able to get a meeting with him, I want to hear what he knows."

They rushed across the street, and cars leaned on their horns. People drove impatiently in between classes around the lunch hour. One van ran a red and nearly hit them. Jimmy marveled at how some people in that town acted. They're so rude and obnoxious. It wasn't like this anywhere else he'd lived; even most of the bikers he'd known were really decent guys.

Once they returned to the art building, Traci pointed to the small graveyard next to the Department of Art. "*There's* something I'd like to know about. Why is there an old cemetery stuck in the middle of the campus?"

Jimmy sometimes wondered that himself. "Seth told me he thought that the university was trying to send the students a message by putting a graveyard between the art and poli sci buildings."

"And what message would that be?"

"Artists whose art is political end up in the grave."

Inside the Department of Art, also known as the visual arts building, a small gray fountain in the middle of the entrance welcomed them. A water nymph spewed water from a horn, and behind the fountain, a glass wall faced a stairwell that led to the ceramics and photography studios. They hung a right by the stairs and down the hall. Colorful abstract paintings hung on the hallway walls. The Department of Art put on shows in that hallway year-round. The inside of the Art Department was the only part of the campus Jimmy liked because it was so beautiful. The rest looked more industrial, only concrete, glass, and steel with no yards with foliage.

Seth always worked in a studio down the hall, sometimes all night. The white studio had one wall made of glass covered with tan paper so the lighting inside could always be controlled.

Ten gray metal easels surrounded a portable carpeted stage on wheels for models. Seth worked near the far corner. He was painting a scene of snow-capped mountains.

Jimmy said, "Another landscape painting? You are the only guy I know who can do landscapes in blue."

"I'm in a blue mood, dude," Seth said.

Jimmy waved a hand in front of his face and grimaced. They'd had high hopes for this art building when it was built, but it really didn't work out. There was no ventilation, and his eyes watered a bit from the smell there. He could never stand the turpentine fumes that permeated those studios. Jimmy wished Seth would learn to paint in acrylic.

Jimmy asked Seth about Professor Johnson. Seth told him Johnson was probably in his office. "I want to go see him," Jimmy said to Traci. "Want to come with me?"

"You know I do," Traci said.

Seth grabbed a rag and wiped his hands. "What are you talking about?"

Jimmy said, "We heard about a student named Rudy Sanchez who was murdered here. We think it might be connected with what happened to Laura."

"Rudy Sanchez?" Seth said. "Never heard of him. Before my time, I guess."

"He was murdered five years ago," Jimmy said.

Jimmy and Traci headed to Johnson's office.

Seth threw his rag down. "Hold up, guys. I want to hear this, too. If murders are happening on the campus, I want to know."

CHAPTER SIX

Seth led the way. The art professor's office was just a few steps away from the studio where Seth worked. A short hallway contained two offices, and beyond the second office was an interior design studio. Bright sunshine poured through the studio windows.

Professor Johnson's door was open. He read a book at his desk. Seth knocked on the door.

Dr. Johnson, an overweight man with dark hair and a beard, smiled. "Seth, come in."

Seth introduced Jimmy and Traci to Dr. Johnson.

Jimmy told Dr. Johnson about Ed Frank. "I'm working on a story for the campus paper. I'm looking for some information."

Dr. Johnson smiled. "Sure. What do you want to know?"

Jimmy hoped he wouldn't blow him off. "I want to know about Rudy Sanchez."

The smile and the color faded from Johnson's face, like the color of rotting flesh of a body left out in the summer sun. "Rudy Sanchez?"

Jimmy saw by the look on his face that the name terrified Dr. Johnson. "I'm sorry if this subject digs up bad memories. But Ed told me to ask you about Rudy and this town. I'll understand if you don't want to talk about it—"

Dr. Johnson cut him off. "No, it's all right. That whole episode with Rudy happened four years ago. He was one of the best art students I've ever had. He was working with the paper, too, as I recall. Really bright guy, he did large brightly colored surrealistic paintings." He got up.

"Hey, come with me."

Dr. Johnson led them out of his office, through the hallway, and into the interior design studio. "I want you to see something. One afternoon I was working late. I walked through this studio to the balcony outside." They followed Dr. Johnson through the classroom with large architectural tables. A glass wall, just like the drawing and painting studio next door, faced them. Dr. Johnson opened the glass door to the back balcony, which squealed like a cat. Johnson grabbed the railing and pointed to the ground below. "See that yellow spot in the grass? That grass there never grows no matter how many times they dig the ground up and reseed."

Jimmy felt queasy. "My God," he groaned. "That stain is the exact shape of a body." His knees suddenly turned weak.

"That's what that is," Seth said. "I've seen that since I was a sophomore. I thought it was a prank."

"No," Dr. Johnson said. "I wish it was. That's where I found Rudy. At first, I, too, thought I was looking at some sort of prank. You never know with some art students. So I ran down those stairs and to the body. You'll never believe what I saw."

Jimmy licked his dry lips. *"What?"*

Dr. Johnson's hand tightened as he gripped the railing of the balcony. His knuckles looked like white marble. "I found Rudy lying on his stomach, but his face was looking up at me.

Someone or something strangled him so badly his neck was broken." He grimaced. *"His head was twisted all the way around."*

The students backed away from the railing.

"Rudy had this ghastly look on his face," Johnson said. "It was as if he had seen the most terrifying thing he could imagine. And I'm positive whoever or whatever had strangled him had come from those woods right there."

Jimmy was horrified. He stared at the woods behind the visual arts building. On the other side was the house he and Seth had just moved into. "Did you call the police?" Jimmy asked.

"Yes," Johnson said. "But before I did, I turned Rudy's body over. I didn't want to touch the body or destroy any evidence for the investigation, but I couldn't stand looking at that terrifying face. I ran back upstairs to my office and called the police. After that, I came back out to the balcony here."

"And?" Traci asked.

"What I saw scared me more than anything I have ever seen in my life. I was only inside for a minute or two to call the police. When I came back out here, Rudy's body was turned back over! There was no one around. There was no way anyone could have run out there and turned that body back over again. That might sound strange, but it happened."

Jimmy felt his heart beating like he had run a forty-yard dash. Two girls talked as they came out of the back of the building. They seemed oblivious to the yellow scar in the grass. The imprint looked like the legs were left straight and spread apart, and the arms were wide out. Probably Rudy had tried to fend off his attacker before he died. The head of the stain pointed to the building, and the feet pointed towards the woods like his killer came from there.

"God damn, man," Jimmy muttered. "What did the police say?"

Johnson's voice turned hoarse. "The same thing you just did. They thought it was the grisliest thing they'd ever seen. The uniforms turned the body over. Then they covered it with a sheet."

"Then what did they say?" Seth asked.

"The cops questioned me. We were just a few feet from the body. A couple of detectives came out to look at the body. I saw an officer lift the sheet. You're not going to believe this, but I have to tell you." He paused. *That body was turned back over again.*

"Christ," Traci gasped as she backed further away from the balcony.

"What did the police find out?" Seth asked.

"To my knowledge," Johnson said, "nothing. I think they swept the whole thing under the mat. The murder was reported on the front page, but no details were given. And the university said nothing. I think they're afraid to talk about it because it would make them look bad, and it would be a deterrent to kids coming here. They probably thought with a few spring graduations, no one would know about it anymore."

Jimmy shuddered. "What do you think happened to the killer?"

Johnson leaned against the balcony and glared at the woods. "I don't know. But I do know one thing. Something's not right here in Morganburg."

Jimmy wiped his sweaty brow. He thought the art professor was talking about the police department, but he might have meant something else. "What do you mean?"

"I've seen kids who looked like they've aged ten or fifteen years getting an undergrad degree. I've seen them with these painful lines carved into their faces."

"I've seen that, too," Seth said.

Johnson nodded. "I walk across the street to the courtyard over there in front of the Main Library, and I see these ghastly zombie kids walking in a dazed motion, almost floating.

There's something weird here on campus, and I believe it's coming from that forest."

Jimmy glanced at Seth. He remembered what his upstairs neighbors said about the woods.

"What can be done about that?" Jimmy asked.

Dr. Johnson nodded again. "The university has been petitioning for a variance request for months to expand the university property to accommodate a larger political science department and law library."

"What does that mean?" Traci asked.

"That means me and a few other citizens within City Hall want those woods flattened for that space. We just missed getting that request to pass last spring. This autumn I think we'll get it. I'd ask all of you to show up at the City Hall meetings and speak up during the public comment section."

Jimmy had seen various sections of property around the outer edge of the campus with posted legal signs for variance requests to expand the area of the university. "You'll think they'll do it?"

"We only need two more council votes. And this time I know we've got those votes. These damn woods have got to go."

"Dr. Johnson, Traci and I are working on some investigations for the campus paper about the town and have some of the violence that's happened here," Jimmy said. "What you've told us sounds very scary. Got any advice?"

His brow furrowed. "Yes. I don't care if you do a story about the campus, but forget any story about this town. Just don't do it. And never stay here on campus after the sun goes down. Once your classes are done, get out of here."

Jimmy wondered what he was talking about. "Why?"

"People die on campus after dark."

After being in a biker gang Jimmy was used to dealing with danger and death on the city streets at night. He'd seen his share of road rashes and motorcycle accidents. It took a lot to scare him. And being out at night on campus in a small town didn't seem like such a scary thing until he heard this story. He shrugged and said, "Okay."

Tree branches choked the light of the already setting autumn sun. A cold wind cut through Jimmy's clothes to his skin. The others also shivered as a rotting odor saturated the breeze.

"Come inside, kids," Dr. Johnson said. He closed the door and locked it. "Time to go."

Jimmy, Seth, and Traci said goodbye to Dr. Johnson.

The professor rushed into his office to grab his things, roared back out again, slammed the door, and fumbled with his keys to find the right one. He swore as he picked them up.

Jimmy believed he wasn't exaggerating. He was really frightened of that place after sunset.

Seth walked to the law library to pick up Natalie and go out for dinner. Jimmy and Traci stopped inside the building near the fountain.

"Think we should quit?" Jimmy asked. He was spooked now that he knew two reporters had been murdered. "Not do the story? Hold our peace? Just forget the whole idea?"

Traci glanced at Jimmy and Seth. *"No,"* she said. "I think we should do this story."

Jimmy frowned. "So do I. I want to get to the bottom of Laura's death, and I think the same person killed Laura and Rudy over whatever they found."

They were walking when Jimmy heard what sounded like someone talking to the professor at the end of the hall, but he wasn't paying much attention. It sounded like a student was calling him from somewhere further down the hall.

"Dr. Johnson?" a man said. The accent was Hispanic. "Oh, Dr. Johnson? Won't you come? Dr. Johnson!"

Dr. Johnson never noticed them as he sprinted down the hall, down the back stairs to the parking lot.

Jimmy glanced at Traci.

She shrugged. "What got into him? You think he knows more than he said?"

"I don't know," he muttered. But he sure liked to find out. *What was Rudy's last name? Sanchez?* "Did you hear someone calling Dr. Johnson just now?"

Traci shook her head. "I thought I had heard a couple of people talking, but I couldn't make anything out."

He shivered as he walked back down the hallway. Traci followed him. They stopped in front of the small corridor and Dr. Johnson's office.

Jimmy grimaced. "My, God, can you smell that?" The normal art building smells had been replaced by something foul, like rotten eggs.

She held her nose and nodded. "Yeah, what the heck is that?"

"Smells like something died." He wandered down into the interior design studio thinking he should investigate the smell. The back door slammed shut.

They jumped.

He had seen Dr. Johnson lock that door behind him.

Traci was ghastly white. "Jimmy, maybe we should get out of here."

He wondered if Dr. Johnson let someone in and that's who he was talking to. But why did he just run out of there? He shuddered as he locked the door. "Yeah, I think you're right."

CHAPTER SEVEN

At the end of the week there was still no more word about Laura's murder. Right after Laura's death he thought the police were simply incompetent, but then he believed they were covering up. Jimmy called some of Laura's friends he knew, but none of them remembered her saying anything about the story she researched before her murder.

Saturday, as Jimmy reheated some lasagna, Seth came home from school and dug a bunch of food from the fridge.

"Did you see Dr. Johnson in your class today?" Jimmy asked.

"Yeah, why?"

Jimmy shrugged, but he felt relieved. "I saw him running out of the art building yesterday. I was hoping nothing was wrong."

Seth cut a couple of sandwiches in half. "Nothing that I know of."

Jimmy hoped that was nothing then. Maybe Johnson was just in a hurry.

"What gives? Looks like you're going on a picnic." Seth nodded. "I plan on popping the question to Natalie today at lunch."

Jimmy shook his hand and said, "Congratulations, man."

Seth grabbed a Coke from the fridge. "I'm celebrating tonight. Rafe and Pete are throwing a party at their house.

They work on the paper, and maybe they remember what Laura was working on. You should talk to them."

Jimmy felt better. Maybe he scored a new lead. Besides he'd heard many stories about that house Rafe and Pete rented way out on the south side of Morganburg. It was supposed to be unforgettable. "Okay, "I'll be there."

On his way out the door, Jimmy got a phone call from Courtney, Laura's roommate.

He said, "God, I'm so glad to hear from you. I was getting afraid you had been murdered, too."

"No way. I've been off campus ever since Laura was killed. Are you okay?"

"I'm as okay as can be expected, I guess. Hey, I called because I wanted to ask you. Do you know what story Laura was working on?"

"No, because when I was there, she wasn't. We didn't get a chance to talk much."

"Damn it. Laura always kept a notebook with her for her stories. The cops said they couldn't find it. I want to know what she was working on."

"Why?"

"The night she was murdered, she told me she was working on a story that would hit this place like an anvil. A couple of hours later I find out she's dead. Can you let me into our apartment so I see if it's there? Plus I can check her computer to see if she started typing the article."

"That's a crime scene, Jimmy."

"Hell, I know that, and I don't give a damn. The cops are as useful as a warm bucket of spit."

"I'm not going back there, Jimmy. I don't want to see, you know, where Laura was killed."

Jimmy felt the same way. "Can you give me the key then? I just want to check on those two things."

"I can't right now. I'm at work."

"I'll be at Rafe and Pete's tonight. They're having a party. You could give it to me then."

"Yeah, okay. They live right near where my boyfriend does."

That night Jimmy headed to the edge of town where Rafe and Pete rented a one-story blue house just beyond a strip mall. The place crawled with people, goths in black clothes, Freak People, and even a few sorority and fraternity-looking folks. Jimmy loved the hard-driving rock that thundered out of the stereo system in the living room. Pete was in there showing a video camera to a girl.

Jimmy didn't even want to know what Pete was trying to talk her into.

Jimmy spotted Courtney talking to a friend in the living room. She hugged him.

"Are you sure you're okay?"

Jimmy shrugged. "Not really. But I'm dealing with life day by day."

She handed him the key. "Honestly, Jimmy. I don't know how you can go back there. Just get this back to me as soon as you can, all right?"

He nodded, and she left.

Jimmy found Seth and Natalie sitting at the kitchen table. Seth had brought a sketchbook with him. While Natalie and Traci drank beer, Seth sketched Natalie. Pot smoke quickly overwhelmed cigarette smoke as Jimmy wormed his way through the crowd to the kitchen table. He heard people talk about Seth.

"Hey, he's good," one girl said, pointing at Seth's half-finished sketch.

"Yeah, but I can't imagine why anyone would want to do make scribbles," a guy replied.

"What's the purpose in it?" another guy asked. "What kind of profit would anyone hope to make from such foolishness? What kind of job will that get you?"

A second girl said, "Do you believe people actually spend four years to get a degree to do *that?*"

Seth looked up apparently impervious to their chatter. "Jimbo! Where the hell have you been, man?"

Natalie hugged him.

"Everything go as planned?" Jimmy asked. He grinned at Natalie.

"Sure did." Seth put his sketchbook down and the men shook hands.

Congrats," Jimmy told Natalie. To Seth, he said, "You're a lucky guy."

Seth grinned. "Have you been here in Rafe and Pete's house before?"

Jimmy sipped some beer. It tasted great on such a warm evening and took away the slight sting of seeing his friends happy when had no one for himself. He appreciated Seth changing the subject so fast. "No way. Show me around?"

The legendary house lived up to its reputation. Huge, sloppy-painted murals covered the walls. Some looked abstract, others he recognized as large renditions of CD covers. People had drawn several cartoons on the dining room walls. Several paintings were well done, but most looked like drunken abominations. Someone had written, "Jimi Hendrix is God" at the top of the living room wall. All of it was detailed in dark paints making it unlikely the then tenants would ever get their security deposit back. He had to respect their commitment to art even if most of it was drunken abominations.

Rafe and Pete inched their way to Seth and Jimmy. Rafe's hair was bleached, but his dark roots began to show through. Pete's brown dreadlocks always looked like Medusa's hair.

Rafe gulped a mixed drink while he held a beer in his other hand. He claimed his spare bottle of beer was his chaser, but then he shoved the beer into Jimmy's hand. "Are you guys digging the party?"

Jimmy said, "I mean, the party's great, but I didn't come here to party, Rafe. I came to ask you about Laura."

"Laura?" He sounded stunned. "What about her?"

"Do you know what story she was working on before she was murdered?"

Rafe slammed some of his drink. "Yeah, I remember she said she was working on some kind of story about Morganburg."

"Can you remember what?" Jimmy asked.

"She told me she needed to talk to one of the sororities." He downed the last of his drink.

Jimmy couldn't imagine what sororities would have to do with the history of the town or graveyards. He asked, "Did she mention which one?"

Rafe shook his head. "No. Maybe Pete knows." He shouted back at the kitchen, "Hey, Pete, get your ass over here!"

Pete slid through the crowd and also came equipped with a drink in each hand. "What is it?"

Rafe asked, "Did Laura ever tell you what sorority she was going to visit? You remember she was working on some story for the paper?"

Pete groaned. "Oh, man...no. Wait. Yeah, she said it was the Tri Delts."

The girls who lived above them were from that sorority.

"Did Laura say what her angle was?" Jimmy asked. "Like what story she was working on?" Pete downed one of his drinks. "She looked up the history of Morganburg. She said she found out something bad about the university."

Jimmy set his can down. "Bad? Like what?"

Pete shrugged. "She didn't say. She said she needed to look up something in the library. Like two days later, she was dead."

Jimmy felt queasy. He assumed Laura and Rudy were investigating the same thing if they were both killed for it. But why would the killer stab one victim and turn the other's head backward? Nothing made sense yet. "Did she say which campus library? Or was it even the Morganburg public library?"

Pete shook his head. "Sorry, man. She didn't say."

Rafe got another couple of beers. He twisted the top off his spare bottle and handed it to Seth.

Seth waved his drawing hand. "It's not safe to drink and draw."

Rafe finished his own bottle. "Yeah, whatever. Here. It's our house. It's our party. Now *drink*."

Seth grinned. "Okay."

"Rafe, what's up with these walls, man?" Jimmy asked, sensing it was time to change the subject.

Rafe grabbed a chair and sat down. "When my girlfriend, Candy, moved in here with me, people would call her and she wouldn't have any paper to write on, so she would scribble their phone numbers on the wall."

Jimmy said, "Okay, I can understand that, I guess."

"Then Pete and I started doing the same thing. Then as we talked on the phone, we wrote messages on the wall. From there, Candy began to doodle and write poetry as she talked to her friends."

Jimmy stepped up to the kitchen wall above the counter. A small blue phone sat on the kitchen counter. "All right, I see some poetry here. But what about all this other crap?"

Pete slammed one of his drinks. "After that friends would see all of this shit on the walls at parties, so they started to write their own poetry and do their own little doodles. From there, people started to paint their own stuff on the walls. We never said no."

Rafe said, "Dude, we think it rocks. Now we insist everyone who comes here for parties to paint something. We hope to eventually have an entire mural all over the house. Neat, huh?"

"Neat?" Jimmy said. He believed that was one way to put it. "I guess I'd call it interesting.

Does your landlord know you're doing this to the walls?"

Rafe pounded down his drink and stole Pete's spare.

Pete had a look on his face like *Dude, what the fuck?* He left to get another drink.

Rafe said, "No, he never comes around. We can never get him to fix anything. If something needs repairing, like the toilet or whatever, we have to get it done ourselves. We just deduct the bill from the rent. We write him and tell him if he's got a problem with that, he can talk to our parents' attorneys. Funny, we never hear any complaints."

Jimmy still thought they wouldn't get their deposit back. He nodded to be polite, then checked the time. It was early enough; the campus main library was probably still open on a Friday night. He started to make his way to the door, trying to signal to Seth he was going now when three girls said, "Hi, Jimmy," but their faces really brightened when they said, "Hi, Seth."

Michelle, Anne Marie, and Elizabeth stood in his way with beers in their hands. They wore short dresses and a lot of make-up. They said hello to Jimmy, too. *Speak of the devil.* Jimmy whispered to Rafe, "What'd you do to get their attention?"

"Hey, they know *you* by name," Rafe said.

"That's because those three live above us in our house. How do you know them?"

Pete came back and sipped his drink. "I swear I don't know those girls. They sure are *phat!* I wonder—"

Rafe set his drink aside. "Oh, wait a minute. Those are Tri Delta girls. I have a friend in one of my English lit classes who's a Tri Delt."

Jimmy didn't know any Tri Delts aside from his new neighbors. But he figured he should talk to them if Laura thought they knew something. "What's her name?"

"Cassie Davis," Rafe said.

"What brings you here to this party, girls?" Seth asked. "Do you know Rafe and Pete?"

"Not yet," Anne Marie said. "Cassie does. She has a class with Rafe."

The girls shouted for Cassie, and a girl with dark, waist-length hair squeezed her way to the kitchen table. As she breezed by Jimmy, he mumbled, "Judas Priest."

Cassie's large brown eyes looked equally proportionate to her big bosom. She smelled really clean, like she had just stepped out of the shower, although her curly hair was dry. She wore a tight red sweater and a short black skirt. By the expression on Seth's face, Jimmy could tell that her beauty even impressed Mr. Commitment. Natalie didn't look as impressed.

The girls introduced Cassie, and they all found space to sit down.

"It's nice to meet you, Cassie," Seth said. "Have you met my roommate, Jimmy?"

They shook hands, but Cassie's attention never turned away from Seth. "This is my fiance, Natalie," Seth said.

"Fiance?" Anne Marie said. "I didn't know you had plans to get married, Seth."

"Oh, yes," Seth said as he held Natalie's hand. "I just asked her today. Natalie and I plan on spending the rest of our lives together."

"Gosh, Seth," Anne Marie said. "Congratulations! I didn't realize you were that serious with your girlfriend."

Natalie glared at them, but she didn't say anything. Anne Marie was looking at Cassie apologetically as if she'd planned to hook her up with Seth.

She placed her hair behind her ear, seeming nervous. "I'm sorry. I had no idea."

"Hey, it's okay," Cassie said before she sat down next to Natalie. "I just came here to get drunk and have some fun." She sat down next to Natalie.

Natalie looked pissed off now, with Cassie beside her on the couch. Jimmy thought he better get out of there before a catfight broke out. But Cassie ignored Natalie and watched Seth draw.

Jimmy said to Seth, "I'm taking off, man."

Seth said, "Already? Did Rafe and Pete answer your questions about Laura's story?"

"Sort of," Jimmy said. "I think they pointed me in the right direction."

He started to leave, but Rafe's girlfriend, Candy, stopped him. Her long, dyed black hair hung to her waist. She always wore black and never wore a bra. She smelled of whiskey. She hugged him. He felt her breasts against his chest. He never minded feeling breasts, but it was a little weird knowing Rafe was in the same room. She grabbed his arms hard. "Jimmy, how are you doing?"

He sighed heavily. He still thought about Laura every day, and he supposed he always would. What sort of person would he be if he just forgot about her? "As well as can be expected, I guess."

"I don't think I've seen you since last spring. It's good to see you out tonight." She hugged him again. "Why don't you have a drink?"

"I just came by for a minute to talk to Rafe and Pete."

She turned him back around to the table. "Don't leave now. Stay and have at least one beer."

My God, it's Friday night. Don't you ever stop working?"

"Not really," Jimmy groaned. He was always writing papers and stories for class. That's what he ought to be doing, as he had something due on Monday that he had barely started.

"Please stay and have one beer?" she said.

Jimmy picked up the beer he abandoned on the table and popped it open. "Okay. One beer."

Amanda emerged from the living room and sat down next to Jimmy. She looked really hot in her white blouse and black miniskirt. She moved her chair right next to his. "I didn't know you knew Rafe and Pete."

"I met them through my roommate over there, Seth." He pointed to his roommate.

Natalie saw him talking to a girl and said, "Jimmy, do you have a new friend?"

Jimmy said, "I guess so. I met Amanda this week. She works on the campus paper." He turned to Amanda. "Anything new with you?"

Amanda shook her head. "Nope. I tried to talk to the police to see if I could find anything else about Laura's investigation, but they were so rude about it. I was just asking, you know?

They told me that I could either get out or get arrested. What a bunch of assholes."

Jimmy couldn't believe it. He wondered what was up with that bunch.

Candy asked, grinning like she thought it was all a joke, "What's this garbage I hear about you getting married, Seth?"

A couple of girls moved, and a painting on the wall behind Natalie grabbed Jimmy's attention. He stepped up behind Natalie, abandoning the conversation. The picture depicted a dark figure with long, dark hair in a black robe standing among the headstones of a graveyard. The figure's eyes were solid black. One hand beckoned. Goose pimples sent icy prickles down Jimmy's back. It looked like the figure Seth described in his premonition.

"It's not garbage, honey," Seth said. "I really am getting married to Natalie."

"You?" Candy asked. "From what Jimmy has told me, you were the biggest Freak People in high school. And I also heard about how you two had a couple of wild years between high school and college in a biker gang. I was told you ran around with a lot of girls then."

Seth sipped some beer. "Yeah, yeah, I know, but that was back in the day." He held Natalie's hand. "I've found my one and only girl."

Amanda exclaimed, "You guys were in a biker gang?"

Seth sipped his beer. "You bet."

"Which one?" Amanda asked.

"The Black Knights," Seth said.

Jimmy asked, "Hey, Rafe, who did this painting?"

"That was Valerie," Rafe said. "She's an art major. I haven't heard from her in quite a while. Have you seen her around, Pete?"

"Valerie?" Jimmy asked. "Valerie Conway?"

"Yeah, you know her?" Rafe asked.

"No," Jimmy said. "But I read her name in the paper. She was interviewed about Laura's murder. She was supposed to be a friend. I'd really like to talk to her."

Rafe slammed some of his cocktails. "Hey, Pete, have you seen Valerie?"

Pete savored his drink. "She dropped out at the beginning of the semester and moved. I don't know what happened to her."

That figures, Jimmy thought.

Anyone he wanted to talk to had a way of taking off. He wondered if there wasn't something to that. Jimmy got a closer look at the painting and shivered. Valerie definitely knew something.

Candy chugged more of her drink. "How did you manage to tie Seth down, Natalie? Did you get him drunk and pregnant?"

"Actually, getting him pregnant probably would be easier," Natalie said. "This is the first night since the summer I've been able to drag him away from the studio and get him out. He hardly ever drinks anymore."

Seth eyed his beer bottle like admiring an old weapon. "I don't like drinking that much anymore. When I was a teen, I liked to use alcohol to bury my demons. Now I prefer to paint to purge them. Plus, no hangovers, and it's cheaper."

Don't like drinking that much anymore? Jimmy wanted to say. *Before we moved, you hadn't had a drink more than one beer in over a year.* He didn't much like the thought that Seth would backslide into drinking all the time.

Natalie said, poking him playfully, "There are still demons in you, isn't there, my sweet?"

Before Seth got up to head to the fridge, he said, "College helped me find my true calling, and now instead of wasting my time with all of the drinking and other drug taking, I occupy my time with drawing and painting. But I have to admit; I still like the occasional beer." He found the fridge packed full of alcohol.

Rafe pulled a beer out for a girl.

Seth asked, "Rafe, you got any food in this place?"

"Oh, yeah. Right there on top of the fridge, man."

Seth looked. "There's nothing but a couple of bags of potato chips up here."

"Yeah, man," Rafe said. "That's it. *Food.*"

Seth grinned. He grabbed a bag, then set it back down and returned to the kitchen table.

"Don't want it?" Jimmy asked.

Seth grimaced. "Nah, screw it."

Jimmy didn't like seeing that. Seth liked to skip meals when they were on the streets because he said he didn't want anything slowing down the alcohol in his brain. He wasn't sure what to say now. Potato chips weren't going to slow the beer down all that much, anyway.

"Come on, Seth," Rafe said. "I want you to paint something on one of my walls. You're an awesome painter."

"All right."

Rafe gave him some watercolors to work with. Seth began to paint a landscape scene on the living room wall.

Jimmy finished his beer as fast as he could and snuck away from Candy while she talked to Natalie. He said to Seth, "Hey, man, I'm cutting out of here."

Before Jimmy left, he saw Cassie go up to Seth. She appeared to be interested in his painting. Natalie watched them from the edge of the kitchen. She still looked really pissed. Jimmy thought Natalie surely knew Seth would never cheat on her. Maybe it was the disrespect in the situation that Cassie would flirt in front of Natalie. Whatever was going on, Jimmy was relieved to be taking off.

On his way out the door, Jimmy ran into Traci.

"You're coming to the party?" he asked. "I didn't think those drunk fests were your thing."

"Jimmy, I'm so glad I found you. Natalie told me you and Seth might be here. I've been trying to call you."

Jimmy checked his phone. "Sorry. It's a little loud in there. I didn't hear the phone. What's up?"

"I just wanted to know if you found out anything from Rafe and Pete?"

Jimmy groaned. "They told me Laura was working on a story about the university. They said she found something bad about it, but she didn't tell them what it was."

She frowned. "I'm sorry. Are you leaving already?"

"I saw Courtney. She gave me the key to her place. She wouldn't come with me because she doesn't want to see in there. I want to see if Laura's notebook is still on her desk."

She grimaced. "Are you sure you want to go into…the place she was killed?"

"Hell, yes. If I can find what her story was about, I might have an idea of who killed her."

"Mind if I tag along?"

Jimmy nearly dropped the key. "You want to come with me?"

"Yeah."

Jimmy believed that may not be such a bad idea. After all, the killer was still on the loose, and he might be looking to kill Courtney or anyone else, nosing around in there, looking for clues.

"Sure."

They drove to Laura's place, a ground-floor apartment, and walked right up to the front door.

Jimmy never liked apartments without a security door where you step inside the building to get to your home. And Laura getting murdered was precisely why he didn't like those kinds of apartments.

They crept inside, and an awful odd odor hit them. A horrid stench, like when there's a lot of blood, made them wince. The large red stain was at their feet when they opened the door.

"Someone attacked her right after she opened the door," Traci gasped.

Jimmy felt like crying. "Was she stabbed, or was she gutted?"

Jimmy wondered what sort of maniac is on the loose here in Morganburg. Jimmy wondered.

They walked straight back and turned left to Laura's room, and he felt a surge of rage shoot through him.

A clear square surrounded by dust stood on the top of her desk.

"*Look,*" He stood in front of Laura's desk. "Someone took her computer."

He pointed to the corner of her desk. "This is where she usually kept her notebook." He jerked her book bag from the chair and set it on the bed. He looked through it and found another notebook. He flipped through it.

"Wait a minute," he whispered.

Traci held one of her arms and glanced around. "Find something?"

"She's got Rudy's name here with the number 4 beneath it and circled it. Then she wrote, 'They used Christine to wage war.' Christine? Who's Christine? And who's they? And what war?"

Traci shrugged. "Can we go now?"

Jimmy wanted to throw the notebook against the wall. "What the hell does that mean?"

A shadow passed by the window, and Traci screamed. Jimmy looked outside and saw nothing. He reached for a baseball bat Laura always kept beneath her bed.

He ran to the front door and threw it open. He saw a shadowy figure standing across the street. He looked like the dark figure in the painting on the kitchen wall in Rafe's and Pete's home. His eyes looked deep and black, maybe even gouged out. It also looked like the same figure Seth said he saw.

Traci ran into the living room. "Jimmy, what is it?"

He glanced back at her, and when he looked back, the figure was gone.

Was he just seeing things, or was that dark figure real?

"I honestly don't know."

CHAPTER EIGHT

The following Tuesday morning, Jimmy went to the library and stepped through the glass doors, past a security guard in a white shirt, black tie, and pants. The guard read a book and hardly paid any attention to Jimmy. Jimmy passed the check-out to find the information desk. He never spent much time in this library since the town library was better for fiction, which was what he liked to read when he could.

A young woman, likely a student, with short dark hair asked, "Can I help you?"

Jimmy felt the hairs on his neck rise when he asked, "I'm looking for a history book on the University of Morganburg. Do you have any books like that?"

She said, "Yes, I know we do. Go to the third floor. That's where all our history books are. We have two history books about Morganburg." She gave him the classification numbers.

Jimmy found the books and sat down at a nearby table, and read through the books. He found some information he already knew. The university was first chartered in 1805. It started out as the Freedman College of the Arts.

He discovered the Civil War was fought right through the area that was now the campus. He thought about the graveyard on campus, which he'd never spent any time in. He wondered when the graveyard had been created.

The books quickly skipped ahead to what happened during the '50's and '60's and the Civil Rights movement, and the Vietnam War. Although the university struggled through some turbulent times, he didn't find anything particularly notable about the university. Nothing Laura would write about anyway. He didn't stop reading until the late afternoon when he gave up and jogged over to the Department of Art. He found Seth in the studio re-working another large expressionist landscape painting.

Jimmy couldn't get used to that smell of turpentine in there. "Have you eaten dinner yet?"

Seth laughed. "Dinner? I haven't eaten anything all day."

"Christ, Seth, what's wrong with you? You've got to eat."

Seth let a sly smile creep across his lips. He took his eyes off his painting to look at Jimmy. "Yeah, yeah, *Dad*. I've been so busy I haven't had a chance to eat yet."

Jimmy grinned. If Seth could joke around, he was probably fine. His earlier concern that Seth was backsliding now seemed a bit silly. "Let's go, dude."

"Actually, I'm good to go. I'm just waiting on Nat. She's over in the law library working on some homework. As soon as she gets her cute little ass over here, we can take off."

Seth painted snow-covered mountains. His sky was as blue as sapphires. The painting looked as sharp and vivid as if Jimmy stood on the shore and gazed at the ocean. He could almost smell the salty sea air.

A cool breeze caught Jimmy's attention. He looked behind him. The back door of the studio stood open. Jimmy stepped out onto the balcony and glanced at the mark left by Rudy's body. It was as yellow as a dog's favorite spot. Jimmy looked down to his right. At the edge of the cemetery, he saw a person planting a small tree. The guy didn't seem like he belonged here.

Jimmy stepped back inside and whispered, "Hey, Seth, come here."

Seth put his paint brush down and wiped his hands. He stepped outside with Jimmy and asked, "What?"

"Check that out," Jimmy whispered.

Jimmy and Seth saw a man wearing a skirt and no shirt. He wore a Mohawk, but with his hair long on the sides. That long hair he tied up close to his head. He patted the ground gently and touched the branches like a father running his fingers through the hands of a small child. He turned and looked up at Jimmy and Seth. His face was black, contorted, and small horns protruded from its skull. He smiled. The wind grew much colder. Goose flesh covered Jimmy's body.

"Hey, guys," Natalie said as she and Traci stepped outside. Jimmy and Seth jumped. "Whoa. Peace, guys, okay? What's wrong? You out here telling ghost stories?"

Jimmy thought his heart might drill a hole through his chest. He looked back, and the man was gone. He looked to Seth, convinced that they'd both seen the stranger digging. "What the hell?" he muttered.

Seth turned around and said, "Hey, where did that guy go? You saw him, right? That's what you were trying to show me, the guy in the costume?"

"What guy?" Traci asked.

"There was a guy down there," Seth said. "He was planting a tree."

Traci saw the tree. "So?"

"So, the guy was wearing nothing but a skirt," Jimmy said.

"A skirt?" Natalie chuckled. "Are you sure you saw a guy?"

Seth smirked. "Trust me. I've studied figure anatomy. That was a guy."

"He's not there now," Natalie said, uninterested. "I'm hungry. Want to go eat?" She held out her hand to Seth.

"Absolutely," Seth said, taking her hand.

Jimmy stared at the edge of the cemetery, wondering why he'd found the man so frightening. He closed the door and locked it before he caught up with his friends, and they drove to a fast-food burger joint, The Promised Land, a popular place carved out of an old apartment building just off campus. It smelled of greasy food. They sat at a red booth and ordered cheeseburgers and fries.

"Were you able to get to the library this morning?" Traci asked.

"Yeah," Jimmy said. "I found a couple of books about Morganburg. But I couldn't find anything in there that was bad about this town. Nothing that would get anyone murdered. Back to square one, I guess. Maybe we should try to work out who had something to gain by keeping a story quiet, and then we can work out what the story was?"

Seth raised his eyebrows at Natalie before he sipped his beer. Natalie smiled slightly and shrugged as she drank her soda.

"So, what did you find out about Morganburg?" Traci asked.

Jimmy grimaced. "Nothing useful. I was up on the third floor, where they have the history books. There are all kinds of books about Virginia but almost nothing on Morganburg, and believe me, I checked thoroughly."

"So now, what will you do?" Natalie asked.

"I'm not sure." He asked Traci, "Is the campus news office still open?"

"No," Traci said. "It closes at noon. Why?"

"I wanted to go there to check on the past issue when Rudy was killed."

"You don't need to do that," Traci said. "You just have to go to www.bbnews.com, and you only have to plug in the date of the issue you want, and it will come up. Look, I'll show you. After lunch, why don't you come to my place? We can look it up there. I live not far from here."

Jimmy was relieved he still had some sort of trail to follow. "Okay."

Seth and Natalie looked at each other, and she winked at him. Seth nodded.

After lunch, Jimmy followed Traci to her apartment. She lived way off campus in a large complex with four buildings, in a small one-bedroom apartment. She opened the door to her living room. A computer sat on a desk in the living room, and a TV stood to the left.

Traci sat at her computer and hit the website.

"Do you know the date Rudy was found murdered?" Jimmy asked.

"Oh, yeah. I've seen that front page for the past three years. You remember it's hung up at the office."

"So what was it?"

"October ninth. Here, you do it." She got up so he could sit at the computer.

Jimmy plugged in the tenth on the website. They waited a few moments, and the paper appeared before them. "Student Murdered Behind Art Building," the headline blared. Jimmy read the full article. It never mentioned the condition of Rudy's body, and the police had no suspects. Jimmy plugged in several dates after October tenth, scanning the newspaper. He only saw the murder mentioned again to identify Rudy as the student who was killed. He never saw the death mentioned again. Somehow he wasn't surprised. "It doesn't look like Rudy's murder was solved."

"It wasn't," Traci said. "I heard from Amanda; the police said it's a cold case."

Jimmy shivered. He wondered how such a small college town couldn't find the people who committed such brutal murders. He clicked out of the website. "Well, I've hit a dead end here. How are you doing on your research?"

"I emailed the frats and had them fill out a survey. I asked them if they had gotten into a fight with their girlfriends did they ever hit them? I asked them if they argue or fight more when are together on campus. I also asked them if they thought they could get away with rape, would they do it?'"

Jimmy wondered what she was fishing for with those questions. "Wow. I wonder if they'll even do that survey."

Traci shrugged. "It's due this week. I'll find out then."

After his second class, Jimmy hurried back to the newspaper building and hooked up with Traci. They drove to a deli off campus and ordered subs. He was surprised at how pleasant the meal was. Again they didn't fight. She was actually nice to him.

In the middle of the day, Jimmy returned to the Department of Art to meet with Seth before they went to lunch.

"I'm going to pick up Natalie," Seth said. "She's studying in the law library again."

Seth began to pack up. Jimmy stepped out of the studio to get a breath of fresh air. He couldn't understand how those turpentine fumes never bothered Seth. At the end of the hallway, Jimmy saw a person dressed in the blue of a Civil War soldier, but his eyes were red, his face black with large horns and fangs. He held a rifle with a bayonet over his shoulder.

Jimmy thought it was funny at first. He wondered if there was supposed to be a Civil War battle re-enactment around somewhere. Or was that a frat involved in hazing? And what was up with the creepy mask?

"Jimmy," the soldier called in an inhuman voice as he slowly raised his arm and motioned for Jimmy to come to him. "Jimmy," he said louder.

Jimmy wondered how that guy knew his name. It wasn't funny anymore. He didn't know this guy.

"Okay, dude," Seth said. "Let's rock."

Jimmy whirled around.

"What is it?" Seth asked.

Jimmy looked back at the end of the hallway. The soldier was gone, and he turned back to Seth. "Honestly, I don't know."

Just as they stepped out of the art building, Jimmy got a call. Traci said. "Get your ass over here to the news office," she demanded. "You're not going to believe these results."

"What's wrong?" Jimmy asked.

"Just get over here."

He couldn't understand why she wouldn't tell him on the phone. Maybe there was news about Laura's death. Then he realized she was probably talking about her frat survey. "Traci thinks she found something important."

Seth nodded and smiled. "I bet she did."

Jimmy didn't have time to ask him what he meant by that.

Once Jimmy was done with the class, he arrived at the news office and found Traci in front of a computer, taking notes. "What's up?"

She frowned at him. "Are you okay? You look really pale."

Jimmy groaned. "Just got a lot on my mind, I guess."

"Okay…*Grouchy.*" Traci showed him a sampling of a couple of the frats' survey answers.

"You're not going to believe this. Damn near sixty percent of the frats say they've hit their girlfriends during fights. Almost eighty percent say they felt they argue or fight more when they're in frat or sorority houses. And the screwiest stat, nearly fifty percent say they would want to rape if they thought they could get away with it."

"Jesus," Jimmy breathed. The results felt like a cinder block hit him over the head. "Can these really be honest answers? How do we know they didn't answer those questions that way just to get a reaction?"

"Because they answered as individuals. Unless all of the frat houses called each other and agreed to answer the questions dishonestly as a joke, and I doubt that happened, then I think we must believe these results are accurate."

He still wasn't sure this wasn't a joke. She didn't know humor the way he did. "What do you make of it?"

"It scares the hell out of me. What sort of mentalities do these college educated people have once they graduate? Is this something the school wants? Does it even care? No wonder we have problems with violence here." She collected her notes into a pile and clicked back to Word. "I think we need to get these results published and see what the student reaction is. Hopefully, it'll inspire someone to come forward about Laura's death."

"You think maybe a frat murdered Laura?" He didn't quite follow her logic, but maybe it made more sense to think a frat stabbed his girlfriend because she wouldn't have sex with him. The idea that she was murdered for her reporting seemed a bit thin.

"I think that's a definite possibility."

Jimmy's hands shook. He didn't know why, but he figured he was afraid of something. "I'm not so sure it's that simple."

"How do you mean?"

"Maybe that's why I'm so pale. I think there's something wrong on campus. And I think it's not only affecting the frats; I fear it's affecting all of us."

She seemed dubious. "Affecting us? Affecting us how?"

"Come with me to my place, and I'll show you." A feeling had been building inside him since they'd moved, and he wasn't sure how to explain it, but something wasn't right.

They drove to his place, and once they stepped inside Jimmy's apartment, he looked for Seth to make sure he wasn't there. Jimmy went into Seth's room and grabbed a landscape painting.

He asked Traci to come outside with him. He showed her Seth's painting of the house, then told her to look at the woods.

"Tell me what's wrong with this painting."

Traci chuckled. "Jim, there's nothing wrong with this painting. Seth has a wonderful sense of color. His reds and browns lead you into the background, and shades of green and yellow keep bringing you back to the foreground. Once again, Seth has made another awesome painting."

"Forget all that. I don't mean the painting was painted poorly. I mean, Seth has an inaccuracy in his painting. Look closer at his trees. He's painted the tree line here in his painting, but if you look at the woods, the trees are closer to that rock wall."

Traci chuckled again. "Well, obviously, Seth made a mistake. I mean, after all, those large trees haven't grown forward in just a couple of weeks."

"Yeah, I know. But Seth doesn't usually make mistakes like this. He's a very realistic painter when he paints people or homes." He stopped short of saying what he'd really been thinking, which was Seth has been hallucinating.

Traci shrugged. "It's just a painting, Jim. Artists don't have to be photo-perfect."

"I realize that. But this isn't an impressionist painting. Let me show you something." Jimmy led Traci around to the front of the house. "I want you to take a look at one more thing. Remember the day when I drove you and Natalie out here for the first time, and I showed you girls the faces on the chimney?"

"Yeah."

Jimmy hoped she wouldn't run away screaming when she saw what he was getting at.

"Remember what Natalie said when she saw them? She saw their angry, mean faces, right?"

"Yes, Jim," Traci said impatiently. "What's your point?"

He felt like he was losing her attention, but he wanted her to understand. "Look at the faces on the chimney."

"What? Seth has those mean, angry faces on the chimney in his painting."

Jimmy's back was to the house when he said, "And what do the faces look like up there now?"

Traci's eyes opened wide. "Oh, my God!" She backed away like the gruesome faces had spoken to her. "They're smiling!"

Jimmy glanced back at them. The painting shook in his hands. He felt his eyes grow misty, and his legs felt like wet clay. Jimmy feared he could lose it and cry right there in front of Traci.

This was supposed to be a good house, and he didn't have the money or time to move again so soon. "That's right. They're smiling."

"Christ, Jimmy! What the hell is going on? How can that be? Brick doesn't change like snow melting in the spring."

"No, it can't." Jimmy looked down, hoping he could trust Traci. He had to tell someone what he'd seen, and he was starting to wonder if he was losing his mind. "I fear there's something in those woods."

"You mean you saw something? Or heard something?"

"I thought I saw Laura in the woods that first day you and Natalie came out here. I thought it was just my imagination, but now I'm beginning to wonder."

An icy wind blew from the woods. The tree branches banged against each other.

Jimmy didn't mention the Civil War soldier. He wasn't sure if that was a hallucination or just a frat playing a prank. Besides, he'd gotten Traci freaked out enough as it is.

He added, "Yeah, and don't forget Seth had a vision."

"You said he thought that was a premonition?"

"I'm hoping that's what it was. But after these things I'm seeing lately, I'm not so sure."

Jimmy waited for her to say something.

She bit her lip.

He felt a deep sense of panic that she'd start laughing at him. He asked, "Have you suffered any visions like that?"

She shook her head. "No…except maybe for that chimney."

"I think there's something in this town that is forcing us to suffer from hallucinations. The question is," Jimmy said as he raised Seth's painting, "were we suffering from a hallucination in the past?" Jimmy glanced back at the chimney again. "Or are we suffering from one now?"

Tears pooled in Traci's eyes. "Christ, I don't know! What do you think we should do?"

"Right now, I have to go to class. Then I'm going to hop on the internet to do some research.

Hopefully, I can find some answers."

"But what do you think we should do about us? Are we okay? Do we need to see a doctor?"

Jimmy glanced back at the chimney. "Traci, I honestly don't know what to tell you. I don't know what we could tell a doctor until I get some more answers. I'm afraid if we went to a doctor with this, he'll only tell us we were mistaken when we first looked at the chimney. And I hope that's what has happened. I hope all three of us made a mistake because right now, I can freely admit to you, I'm scared. I'm *really* scared."

CHAPTER NINE

After classes the next afternoon, to save himself time of having to drive back home, Jimmy ran to the library and had no trouble signing up for a computer at that time of day. Only two girls sat at the computers beside the information desk. Their fingers clicked over the keys like marching skeletons. He hopped on one and looked up companies in town that sold products with chemicals, thinking maybe there was something in the water here. That might explain a lot. The internet bounced him to parent companies, and he learned where those companies were based and how many employees worked there. But he looked for chemicals that existed in certain products and their possible side effects if those products were misused, abused or improperly stored, or dumped. Aside from maybe the strange yellow mark in the grass on campus, there were no indications that someone had dumped anything. He felt like he wasn't getting anywhere there, so he abandoned that direction of research.

Jimmy clicked back to a local lawn care company. He read more of the same. He found out where the parent company was based, how many employees worked there, and how many smaller companies it owned. Finally, he found a site that explained health concerns. He discovered the names of chemicals they used, but protection agencies and watchdog groups kept their eyes on lawn care companies. He found studies done on pesticides and fertilizers that lawn care companies used. Some of those groups still raised concerns about those chemicals, but thus far, all evidence supported that those chemicals were practically non-toxic, and even if evidence existed to the contrary, people were concerned with cancer. No one worried about chemicals causing hallucinations, making people violent, or driving people mad. He did feel like these things were connected, that whatever would make him and Traci see the faces differently might also be responsible for the rapes and beatings on campus and in the community.

And those haunting words he heard Laura say still replayed over and over in his mind. *It's in the ground. It's beneath your feet.*

Jimmy thought he'd hit a dead end unless he could find out whether the university is using different chemicals. He asked the librarian, a blonde with straight long hair and dark circles beneath her eyes. "Do you know who I could call to find out which university department is responsible for taking care of the grounds?"

"I can tell you that," she said. "That's the physical plant."

Jimmy returned to his computer and looked up the number, and grabbed his cell phone from his backpack. He got in touch with a secretary. "I'm with the campus paper. I need some information about what types of chemicals you use on the grounds." He continued to jump around the physical plant's website as he spoke. He was getting way more comfortable with internet research now that he had done more of it.

"I can assure you, we use the very same chemicals as all lawn care companies." Then she said, "I can also tell you this if you want more information about lawn care chemicals—"

"Holy shit," Jimmy whispered and hung up on her. He discovered the EPA had its own website. He clicked to that. "Bingo," he said aloud. Everyone looked up at him. "Whoops," he mumbled. "Sorry." He found a plethora of chemical names. He pulled out a notebook from his black book bag and took notes. He read about bioaccumulative toxic pollutants, Benzene, dioxins, and many other poisons. Within an hour, he got pretty familiar with biological and man-made chemicals, but none of what he found was what he looked for. With each toxin, he thought he may have had something, but then he hit another dead end. Maybe scientists just didn't study the mental health effects of chemicals.

Jimmy couldn't understand that if chemicals weren't messing with people's minds here, when what was causing their hallucinations? It wasn't just Jimmy seeing things.

Jimmy believed he needed to turn his attention to the town of Morganburg. But the only thing the internet would reveal about Morganburg was that it was a small college town in Virginia. He read more about the town's history, but that also told him nothing. It was just the standard story of the South, plantations, peanuts, and things like that.

He sighed heavily as he shut off the computer. He still thought maybe there was some chemical to blame, but he'd be damned if he knew which one, or how it got into the water, or why it wouldn't have affected them at their old apartment. His last chance was to find something in the books. He returned to the third floor, determined to find something. He stared at the bookshelves, but he didn't know where to begin or even what to look for. All these books surrounded him to quench his thirst for knowledge and yet he didn't know if any of them could help him. He felt as if he were lost at sea.

Pete said Laura found something bad about the university, and maybe that was in the ground, but Jimmy couldn't figure out what that could be.

Jimmy figured the answer had to be in front of him somewhere. He grabbed more history books on Virginia and started to read.

As long as his schedule allowed, Jimmy camped out at the library to read about Virginia's history, but he never found anything particularly interesting about the university. By Friday of that week, he was exhausted. He read so much his eyes ached. He rubbed them and checked the time. The library was about to close.

He ran across the street to the art building looking for Seth. Before Jimmy entered the studio, he glanced over his shoulder, half expecting to see the Civil War soldier there. He breathed a sigh of relief when he saw nothing at the end of the hallway, then wondered immediately if he was spooking himself. He entered the studio and found Seth working on a new landscape painting. It looked like he was trying to paint a wooded area with a stream.

"You got plans for tonight?" Jimmy asked wearily.

Seth stopped painting. "I'm going out. Natalie is studying all night."

"I've been doing what must be the longest bout of research for a college student. I'm so tired I think I'm too exhausted for sleep."

"Want to come blow off some steam with me? Rafe's new band is playing at the Oddyssey. He plays guitar."

"I don't know," Jimmy muttered. He really didn't feel like going out, especially if there was another excuse for Seth to drink. He didn't mind a few beers, but he didn't want Seth getting hammered. He checked for messages on his cell phone and saw Amanda still hadn't returned any of his calls. Since Amanda was at Pete's and Rafe's party, he hoped she would come to the show. "On second thought, maybe that's not such a bad idea. I could use a break."

"Great. I'm feeling a little burned out myself. This painting is pissing me off. For some reason, I just can't seem to get what I want. Maybe I just need to get away from it for a while."

Jimmy never asked Seth why his forest painting hadn't matched the forest, even though he'd shown it to Traci. He didn't feel like it was a good idea to confront Seth about it.

"I know three is a crowd," they heard behind them, "but do you mind if a friend joins you?"

Jimmy was startled to see the beautiful brunette. He wondered why she was there in the art studio. "Cassie, right? We saw you at Rafe's and Pete's party."

She grinned. "That's right."

She and Seth stared at each other. He thought it was a little odd that Seth would get engaged and then flirt with another woman if that's what Seth was doing. "I get the distinct impression that after I left the party the other night, you two got a little chummy."

Seth and Cassie chuckled.

"Yeah, I guess you could say that," Seth said. "We talked a little."

"I like your painting," Cassie said.

Seth cleaned his brushes. "I wish I could say the same thing."

Cassie looked really hot in her tight blue shorts and a sheer white blouse. "Hmmm," Jimmy muttered. "You know, when a friend looks like that, I don't think three is a crowd." He didn't feel like it was his role to protect Natalie, but he wondered if it was appropriate for her to be here.

Seth grinned. "You want to come with us, sweetie?"

"You bet," Cassie said.

Seth ran over to the law library to tell Natalie where he was going that night so she wouldn't come looking for him in the art building. Then he rejoined Jimmy and Cassie. They drove to the Oddyssey, a downtown bar just up the street from the newspaper office. Jimmy opened the door. It creaked so loudly it sounded like bones snapping. The overwhelming stench of cigarettes hit Jimmy in the face. They looked up to see a flight of stairs leading to a platform. Black webbing wrapped around the railing and on the wall. On the platform, a disjointed Grim Reaper sat behind a table. A black cobweb hung from its cheek down to the table. Jimmy tried to touch him, but the Reaper's scythe fell onto an open deck of Tarot cards.

They jumped back.

The tip of the blade fell on top of the Death card.

The others laughed uneasily. Jimmy thought that was unsettling, but he believed the figure was rigged to do that. He wanted to try to touch the Reaper again, but he thought he saw eyes in the skull mask. "Jesus!" he exclaimed as he yanked his hand away.

"What?" Seth asked.

Jimmy looked again, and the eye sockets looked dark, eyeless, and soulless. The whole setup might've looked hokey and cute to someone else, but he felt reminded of the shadow figure he kept seeing. "I can't tell if that's a prop or if there's someone in that costume. I think I no longer want to find out."

They climbed another flight of stairs. A white spotlight from the stage, like a full moon out in the country, made the two robed bouncers look like mere silhouettes. They never spoke as they extended their hands. The three seniors gave them their IDs. The hooded figures handed them back and gestured for the three to go ahead.

"That's some welcoming committee this place has tonight," Cassie said. "I didn't know we were going to a haunted house."

"Wow," Seth said as he got a good look at the stage. The walls looked like old stone. Hanging from them were whips, chains, and shackles. A couple of emaciated and tattered dummies hung from chains on the wall. Two girls dressed in bikinis, with long curly hair, locked inside cages, writhed and danced to the music being pumped through the speakers.

Seth started talking like an art history student. "It looks more like a Gothic cathedral than a bar with those vaulted ceilings. And those look like clerestory windows."

It looked too creepy for it to remind Jimmy of a church. "You see a cathedral? This place looks more like the inside of a castle to me. And the dancing girls don't quite seem period appropriate."

The whole bar contained candelabras and sconces. The stage had a second story for band members to sing and play their guitars. The stage reminded Jimmy of a dungeon or at least the descriptions of dungeons he'd read. On the second tier of the stage, crouched on pedestals, were two statues of gargoyles. Their wings were spread open, and appeared like they were prepared to pounce.

"I've never been in this place before," Seth said. "Does it always look like this?"

Jimmy remembered that Seth hardly ever did anything besides paint. "Never? Jesus, Seth, this is the hottest bar in town, and you've never been in here before? You need to get your ass out of the studio, man. Are you going to paint your life away?"

Seth grinned. "Actually, that was sort of the idea, Jimbo. Keeps me out of trouble."

They sat at a brown table and ordered drinks. Cassie excused herself to go powder her nose.

Jimmy was glad to get a chance to talk to Seth alone, just as the band tuned up and did sound checks. "So tell me, what did you find out about our little Venus love kitten?"

"We talked about art mostly. She was interested in the painting I put on Rafe's wall."

Come on, Seth, Jimmy thought. *You know that's not what I'm asking. Give me the goods.* "Yeah, I don't care about that. What did you find out about her?"

"She's kind of pissy about guys. She split up with some frat named Ernie."

Jimmy chuckled. "Ernie? Like Sesame Street Ernie?"

Seth smirked before he rubbed his face and yawned. "Yeah. She's from Virginia. She's a business major. I don't know. We talked, but I was drinking pretty heavily for the first time in months. The booze really went to my head. I'm afraid a lot of that party faded into a fog."

Damn, Seth, Jimmy thought. *You're drinking like when we were riding in the Black Knights.* He didn't want to say anything and sound like a nag, though. Jimmy almost opened his mouth, but he backed down.

Cassie returned to the table. Jimmy wanted to ask her some questions about the frats, but just as he opened his mouth, Amanda snuck up behind him, hugged his arm tightly and sat down. She wore a short black dress that showed lots of cleavage, and she looked great. "Jimmy!" she said. "I figured I'd find you here."

Jimmy exclaimed, "Where have you been? I tried to call you all week." He was relieved to know she hadn't been blowing him off on purpose.

"You did? I never got any of your calls."

"Is your phone working?"

"My phone is working fine. Maybe yours isn't working." She ordered a grasshopper from the dark-haired woman with Egyptian brown eyes. "What did you want to tell me?"

His phone worked. He didn't want to argue. "Information about Laura's murder. The article in the campus paper never mentioned the names of her friends. I only knew a couple, and I called them. They didn't talk to the police. Do you have the names the cops talked to? Can you put me in touch?"

"Yes. Actually, Deanna Matthews was one of her friends the police spoke to."

"That doesn't help me much. She already said she doesn't know anything."

Amanda dug into her purse. "Yeah, but I think Deanna knows the others. I've got their names and phone numbers. Call her. She might be able to help. She wrote down three names and their numbers. Here. The police don't consider any of them suspects."

Jimmy glanced at the names and frowned. Besides Deanna, he knew none of them. He stuffed the paper in his pocket. He was glad he came tonight. He not only got what he wanted, he believed for at least a little while, he could relax, see Rafe's band, and enjoy the night. "Have you ever seen Rafe's band before?"

"No," Seth said.

"Jesus, do you ever get out of the painting studio?"

Seth grinned. "Only when I have a good reason."

The band finally finished tuning up, and Rafe, with a beer in hand, strolled by their table.

Jimmy said, "Dude, that shirt is awesome," pointing to Rafe's red and black tie-dyed shirt.

"Thanks. I thought it would go great with these black pants and boots." He sipped some beer. "I'm glad to see all of you could make it."

"We're glad to be here," Seth said. "When the hell are you going on? And now that I think about it, what is the name of your band?"

"We're called the Chosen. And we'll be on in a few minutes. So what do you think of the place?"

"It sort of reminds me of the strip dives in Virginia Beach Jimmy and me and the Knights used to hang out in," Seth said. "But this place is truly spooky. You've done a great job with the decorations."

Rafe chuckled. "Oh, yeah. Jimmy told me about those bars you had as your old stomping grounds. Nothing spooky ever happened there."

Jimmy nodded. He wished like hell he was back on his old favorite hangouts. He missed Virginia Beach. "That's what I like about this place. It reminds me of those old bars. I miss the city. I can't wait to graduate and move back home."

Rafe peered over his shoulder. "It looks like the guys are going on, so I guess I gotta go. I hope y'all like the show."

After Rafe hit the stage, Amanda asked, "When were you two in a gang?"

Seth ordered a Jack and Coke. "Jimmy and I didn't go right into college from high school. We spent a couple of years in the Black Knights."

"How did you get into a gang?" Cassie asked.

"We had a friend who was a year ahead of us in high school," Jimmy said. "After Seth and I graduated, he asked us to join."

"What did you guys do in the gang?" Amanda asked.

Seth laughed. "A lot of booze, other drugs, and girls."

Amanda frowned. "No, I mean, how did you make a living?"

Seth gulped his drink. "We did construction. Some of the guys were licensed contractors, and we got some pretty good stuff."

"So, how did you end up in college?" Cassie asked.

Jimmy sipped his beer, and it tasted really good. The air was thick from the heat and humidity. "We just got sick of the lifestyle. The booze and drugs stopped being fun. Construction is hard work; we were always bruised and sore. We didn't see a future. So we abandoned it for college."

They kept talking while the Chosen did one final partial practice. Pete asked a guy at the control board to turn up his guitar.

When the four-piece kicked in its first set, the loud music forced Cassie to shout into Seth's ear. Seth moved his chair closer to Cassie's so they could keep talking. Jimmy also scooted his chair closer to Amanda's. Amanda rubbed his back and played with his hair as they talked. It felt really nice to have a girl touching him. Then he saw Traci squeezing through the crowd with a look on her face every guy would recognize as bad. She pulled him aside.

"I want to talk to you!" she shouted.

Jimmy couldn't believe this. He was finally beginning to enjoy himself, and now she showed up. What right did she have to treat him like that? "Now? I want to see Rafe's band. They're just starting."

"I don't care. We need to talk."

"How did you even find me here?"

"I've been calling you at home and your cell phone. I looked for you in the English library and in the art building thinking you may be with Seth. Then I went over to the law library and found Natalie. She told me you and Seth were here."

He couldn't help but be impressed with her investigative skills, but it still felt really weird that she would focus on him like this.

"Can't this wait?"

"No! I want to speak to you right now."

Jimmy was in no mood to deal with Traci. And he was willing to tell her that, too. She'd definitely grown on him recently, but he was back to finding her irritating. "What's wrong with you? You know, sometimes I feel like you think I'm married to you."

"Don't say that! And there's nothing wrong with me." She grabbed his wrist and shouted, "Come on!"

Jimmy groaned. He turned to Amanda. "I've got to go. I'll be right back."

Be he left, he glanced back at the stage. A woman screamed. Jimmy looked up at the band, and the Grim Reaper rushed out of a tunnel on stage. He opened a cage door and seized one of the dancing cage girls. The Reaper looked exactly like the one on the stairway. The woman squealed as she struggled to fight off Death.

The crowd raised their arms and cheered.

Jimmy couldn't stay to watch more. He chased after Traci.

The Reaper's scythe was raised upward again and away from the Tarot deck. The Grim Reaper at the table sat with his feet propped up on the table. A lit cigarette burned between its teethy-grin. Jimmy shuddered. He no longer thought that was a prop. He believed that was someone in a costume.

Jimmy stopped her outside. The music could still be heard outside, even with the front door closed. The night was still muggy.

Jimmy yelled, "What the god damn hell is your problem?"

"I need to speak to you!" Traci shouted. "I want to know what you found out in your research. Are we in any kind of danger?"

Jimmy closed his eyes, gritted his teeth, and moaned. "I don't know. I couldn't find anything. I looked all week. I was so exhausted tonight that I went out with Seth to see Rafe's band. Why don't you join us?"

She crossed her arms testily. "What's Amanda doing there?"

The Chosen started their show, and they heard their music rumble from inside. "She's friends with Rafe and Pete, too. I hoped she'd be here. I got some names of Laura's friends. Now I can talk to them. Why are you so mad?"

"Did you see my article published on the front page of Thursday's paper?"

"Yeah. You did a good job," he said begrudgingly because she did do a good of the article, and he hoped saying so would calm her down some. "Get any reaction?"

"Yeah, I got a couple of death threats."

Jimmy couldn't believe it. It was just a story about what was on the minds of the frats. No one was likely to take it seriously. Why would anyone get that upset? "Death threats? Is that why you're asking *me* about danger? Seems like you know more than I do."

She stormed off. "Go back in there with Seth and your bimbo. I'll somehow try to survive without your help, you know?"

Jimmy couldn't understand why she was so mad at him. Did she think they were going out because they'd started working together on the paper? He did appreciate her work, and he didn't want to fight with her. Maybe he should be more understanding; if she was getting death threats, she must be scared. "Wait a minute, Traci—"

"Oh, screw you! You're obviously too busy getting drunk with your sluts all weekend long; I guess that's my own tough luck! I'm glad by Monday you'll be willing to do further research, but I'm not sure I'll be alive then!"

Jimmy was getting irritated despite his effort to be sympathetic. "Hey, wait a minute. Traci, come back!"

"Fuck you, Jimmy!" she screamed before running away. Jimmy started to run after her, but he was slammed to the ground, rolled over, confused, and found himself looking at Seth.

Seth flew out of the bar and collided with him.

"Jesus Christ!" Jimmy exclaimed. He staggered back to the sidewalk. *What the hell are you doing, Seth?*

Seth crouched at the front of the building, and he spat on the sidewalk a few times. Seth, a weightlifter since junior high school, weighed nearly two hundred pounds, and when he collided with Jimmy, it nearly knocked him unconscious.

Jimmy gasped for air. "Seth, what the God damn fuck?"

Seth spat on the sidewalk one last time. He wiped the sweat from his face. "I got so damn sick, I bailed! I thought for sure I was going to heave right onto someone's back."

Jimmy put his hand on Seth's shoulder. "Are you okay? What happened?"

"Yeah, man, I am now. I feel a lot better now that I'm out in the cooler air. It was so hot and stuffy in there. I could hardly breathe."

"Damn, Seth," Jimmy muttered. "How much did you drink?"

Seth sat up on the step in front of the bar. "I don't know. Couple of shots, couple of drinks. Then I saw this guy in a Reaper costume rape this girl on stage. The crowd just stood there and egged him on."

Jimmy shook his head. "Dude, it's a show. Didn't you see all the decorations?"

Amanda ran out of the bar. Even as she stood still, she swayed back and forth. Her speech was slurred. "Jimmy, what the hell you doing out here?"

Jimmy feared this was going to be another fight.

"I'm talking to Seth. He felt sick, so he came out here to get some air."

"You didn't come out here to talk to Seth!" she shouted. "You came out here to talk to Traci. What's up with you two? Is she your girlfriend?"

Jimmy's jaw dropped. "Girlfriend? God, no! Are you nuts? She'd never be my girlfriend. My girlfriend was just murdered. I'm not looking to date right now."

"What's it with you and her then? You're always around her. When we're together, she always wants to get you alone.

You're always doing stuff with her. Would you rather be with her than me?"

"No!"

Amanda chuckled incredulously. "You know, Jimmy, your actions speak louder than your words. You want me on a real date, let me know. I'm tired of playing second fiddle to Traci."

She stormed off. Her high heels sounded like a horse clopping off.

Date? Jimmy wasn't looking for a date. He wondered if she was completely clueless.

Seth chuckled like a little boy. "Dude, you are so smooth with the girls. You just had two women blow you off on you in one night in less than ten minutes."

This just isn't my night, Jimmy thought. "Hey, fuck you, Seth, you know?"

Seth laughed even harder.

"Just for once tonight, could all of the female assholes in this world go to hell?" Jimmy said.

He started laughing, too.

"What happened out here, Jimbo?"

"Hell, if I know."

"Maybe if you weren't so cold to them. Somehow you got them both thinking you were great, but you just didn't manage to seal the deal with either one. "

"Hey, screw you, Seth," Jimmy said as he continued to laugh.

Cassie stepped outside. "What are you guys laughing at?"

Jimmy asked, "Are you going to start yelling at me, too?

She smiled slightly. "No. What are you talking about?"

"Then nothing is really happening out here," Jimmy thought. "We're just kidding around."

"What are you guys doing here on the front stoop?" she asked.

"Seth is recovering from nearly throwing up while the entire female population of the town is out here telling me to kiss off. As long as you're here, do you want to tear into me as well?"

Cassie smiled. "No, Jimmy. I'm not mad at you." She looked at Seth. "Are you all right?"

"Yeah." He rubbed his face. "Did you see the Reaper on stage?"

"No, I was in the bathroom."

Jimmy suggested, "If you like, we can go back inside and see if that girl is okay."

Seth waved his hand. "No. I'm sure what I saw was all a part of the show. That girl's okay. I just drank too much too fast, and it was so hot in there. I don't know how those guys could play in that heat."

Jimmy rubbed the sweat from his own forehead. "It is a hot, sticky night, isn't it?"

Seth breathed deeply. "I wasn't doing anything but standing there, and I was ready to faint. Those guys were performing as if they were possessed! There's no way I want to go back inside. It's too hot. I'm afraid I'll get sick again. Let's just go."

"Okay," Jimmy said. "I'll take everyone home."

Jimmy wanted to call it a night. He just wanted to lay his weary head on a pillow and get some decent sleep.

CHAPTER TEN

Jimmy woke up to the sound of one of the upstairs neighbors shouting. He rolled over and looked at the clock. It was eight in the morning. He felt like he needed about three more hours of sleep. His eyes burned. He thought it might take a forklift to pry him out of bed. But those damn women above got up early and sounded like horses being led to the stable.

Jimmy thought about Traci. He tried to call her last night, but she still wouldn't pick up. He was worried about her. She hadn't been acting like herself last night.

Jimmy wondered why those God damn women had to get up at the ass-crack of dawn. As if clomping around wasn't enough, they started shouting next.

"Elizabeth!"

"What?"

"Phone!"

"Who is it?"

"Cassie!"

A woman clumped across the house. Jimmy believed those women must sleep in their high heels. He jumped into the shower. The water was warm, and it felt good. He wanted to beat Seth to the bathroom, but after he got out of the shower, he realized Seth was in no condition to race. Seth was at the kitchen table drinking a can of root beer and looking like death itself. Obviously, Seth didn't stop drinking after he left the bar.

"It's alive!" Jimmy said.

Seth glared at him. "Yeah, but just barely, Jack. I've got one foot in the muddy gutter and the other in the bloody graveyard, but I'm still breathing." He rubbed his face. "I think."

"Why don't you just stay in bed? It's Saturday." He was getting up anyway to do more research, but all Seth was going to do was play with his paintings.

"How the hell am I supposed to get any sleep when we got a herd of blasted cattle wandering the plains upstairs?"

Jimmy toweled off his hair. "They woke me up, too."

"What's it with those girls? Did they have their shoes surgically attached to their feet?"

Jimmy smirked and shook his head. "I was wondering the same thing myself."

Seth scratched his curls and held his head in his hand. "I had nightmares all night. I kept dreaming about women being raped and butchered."

Jimmy combed his wet hair back. A wave of chills crawled down the length of his body. It was all that drinking he did last night. And Jimmy hoped that's all it was. Just because Seth said, he saw a show didn't mean the girl on stage had been raped. "Why don't you go back to bed? Even with all of that noise upstairs, I'm sure you'll fall back to sleep. If you looked any more tired, you'd be dead."

"No dice. I promised to take Natalie out for lunch." Seth set the can down hard. He watched it tip over and roll off the table. He never picked it up. "What are you doing today?"

Jimmy moaned. "I guess I'm going over to Traci's to see if I can smooth things over." He didn't know why she thought they were together.

"Good luck. I hope your day goes better than mine has thus far."

Jimmy fixed himself a roast beef sandwich before he took off. He turned on the microwave beside the kitchen door, aside from the room full of water heaters and the heating unit. It sounded like one of the girls stood near the basement door as she washed some dishes and put them away.

"Why don't you fix me some breakfast?" a guy asked.

"Why don't you get off your dead damn ass and fix your own damn breakfast?" the girl snapped.

"Because you're the god damn woman, and you should make me breakfast!"

Jimmy felt bad hearing them argue. Neither of them seemed like they were much of a treat to wake up to. He wondered which of his neighbors had a jerk for a boyfriend. A pot hit a wall, and someone thundered out of the house. Those girls dated frats. Lately, he had heard them fighting more and more with their boyfriends. And the fights turned increasingly more violent. Jimmy thought about how he and Traci always fought. Before recently, he just thought she was annoying, but since he'd spent some time with her, he'd found her to have a nice personality, so it didn't make sense that she was back to fighting with him. He realized fighting always happened at the house or on campus. Never in town. He suddenly lost his appetite and left without saying goodbye to Seth.

Jimmy drove off campus, made a stop downtown, and then headed to Traci's apartment building and buzzed her door. On his way to the apartment, he spotted a flower bed in the middle of the courtyard.

Shit, I could've just saved myself the money and yanked one out of the ground from there.

He knocked on her door and leaned against the doorjamb, and waited. When she opened the door, he handed her a single long-stemmed red rose. "Truce, okay? I just want to talk. Please, let's not fight."

Traci smiled when she saw the rose. She took the flower and smelled it. "Thank you.

It's beautiful." She invited him inside. "Where did you find a single rose?"

"Well, don't let your apartment manager see you with it, okay?"

"You stole this from the flower bed outside?" she exclaimed.

Jimmy chuckled. "No, I'm *kidding*. I was just kidding. Calm down. I got it from the little flower shop downtown."

She smiled and smelled it again. "Oh. You know, it's hard to get a fix on you, Jimmy. Sometimes you're really sweet."

"Are you okay?"

She shrugged. "Yeah, I'm fine."

"I don't know why you were so mad last night."

Traci sat down on her couch. "I'm sorry. I was worried about the death threats. I guess I thought you would protect me or something."

"I didn't mean to seem like I didn't care about you. It's just that I really wanted to be out, and I wanted to see Rafe's band. Did you get the threats over the phone?"

Traci sighed after she put the rose in a vase and placed it on the coffee table. "No. They stuffed the threats in the mailbox at the front door of the news office."

Jimmy sat down next to her. "Did you call the police?"

"The paper did. The police are doing an investigation."

He nodded. She already knew how he felt about the police.

"Do you have any idea who is doing this?"

Traci shrugged her shoulders. "It's obviously one of the frats who fears the survey makes their frat house or all of the frats look bad."

Jimmy wasn't sure he wanted to mention this. Some people reacted badly to it when he brought it up. They hear a biker gang, and immediately they think the Hell's Angels.

"Listen, you know Seth and I were in a biker gang before we got into college."

She frowned. "Yeah, Natalie told me."

She didn't look happy about that, but she also didn't look horrified.

"Our primary responsibilities in the Knights were to watch all of the guys' girls and our bikes when we were out at bars and other hangouts so no one would give the girls any trouble. I make a good bodyguard. If there's anything I can do to make you feel safe, I'll do it. Just tell me what you want me to do."

Traci smiled slyly as she looked down.

Jimmy recognized that look in her eye. He had seen it in Laura's when she wanted something. "There is something, isn't there?"

"I'll think about it," Traci said. "I've never had a bodyguard before."

Jimmy smiled. "Okay, so we're friends again?"

Traci's smile widened. "Were we friends before?"

"Weren't we?"

"I'm not so sure about that. I don't think we got along so well in the past."

Jimmy knew that much was true. They usually bickered. He wondered if maybe he was wrong about her.

"I'd like to change that. Can't you tell from that flower I got you?" It had been a spur-of-the-moment decision, but he felt bad for not taking the death threats seriously. And maybe he did like her some.

Traci scooted forward on the couch. "If you keep being as sweet as you have been with me today, I don't see why we can't be friends. Just don't go back to the way you were last night."

Jimmy didn't think of himself as Jekyll/Hyde. He thought he was a consistent person all the time. But he didn't want to argue. He thought they'd been making a lot of progress with their relationship since he joined the paper. Their relationship was now good for the first time ever."

"Did you try calling any of the names Amanda gave you?" she asked.

"No. She said Deanna knows them. I'm going to call her first to see what she knows about those girls. But first, I still have to see Amanda today."

"Amanda?"

"Yeah, I also need to go over to Amanda's to see if I can patch things up with her as well. I kinda screwed up with her, too. I need to talk to her. She was really pissed at me last night."

"You two had a fight?"

Jimmy smiled weakly. He hoped this wasn't going to lead to yet another fight. "Yeah."

But Traci only looked sympathetic. "I hope it goes okay." She admired the rose again. "After you're done with her, are you free this afternoon?"

He nodded. "Yeah, maybe. I still have to hit Blackboard to review a student's short story. I'll call you, okay?"

"Okay. You be careful."

Jimmy nearly laughed. He never heard anyone say that to him before. It actually felt kinda good. "Careful? You're telling an old biker to be careful?"

"Yeah."

He looked into those exotic crystal-cold blue eyes. For a moment, he forgot about how much he missed Laura and just appreciated how pretty Traci was. "All right. I will." He closed the door and stood there for a moment. Jimmy couldn't understand it. They get along so well at her apartment. And they did fine at a restaurant way off campus. But every time they were on or near campus, they always argued.

Jimmy got into his car and tried to call Amanda on his cell phone, but there was no answer. He stopped by her apartment, but she wasn't there. Jimmy figured if she wanted to talk, it was up to her.

That next day Jimmy tried to call Deanna, but she didn't pick up, and her answering machine was full. Maybe he could find her at school.

Once on campus, the day was beautiful. The middle September sun hung in a cloudless sky. The trees hadn't started to turn color yet, and the spring-like day inspired Jimmy to want to get up right away. Between classes, Jimmy saw a couple of students cut across the graveyard to get to class. He thought it was about time he finally went in there.

He realized in all the years he went to school in Morganburg; he never wandered into that little cemetery between the art and political science buildings. He stepped over a short white wall looking for the tree he thought that Mohawk man had planted. Only a handful of old weather-worn gray graves protruded from the ground, some so decayed the names were no longer legible. For those gravesites that could be readable at the time of preservation, some fresh, duplicate headstones stood by the originals. Mere rocks marked a couple of graves. Jimmy headed across the street to the Main Library.

The dates on the headstones read from the Civil War, some older. Jimmy glanced back at the graveyard. Out of the corner of his eye, he thought he saw a dark figure shrouded in black standing at the edge of the woods, but when he turned to look, the figure vanished. Jimmy shuddered, telling himself it was just his imagination, although he didn't believe that.

He quickly turned to go to the library, but Traci stopped him.

He was glad to see her again. He wished he had never left her that afternoon. He had been thinking about her ever since.

"What happened?" she asked angrily. "You never called me like you said you were going to."

They walked down the sidewalk. Jimmy moaned. "Oh, damn. I forgot. Listen, yesterday turned into a disaster. I was studying when Seth and Natalie had a huge fight. They really screamed at one another. You wouldn't believe it. It was awful."

"My God, those two have been going together for over two years. Didn't they just get engaged? I've never known them to act like that before."

"I don't know. But I've never seen them fight before, and that fight was truly ugly."

"I'm sorry to hear that. When you didn't call, I was upset."

Jimmy had so much on his mind; lately he didn't feel like explaining. "I didn't mean to. Forget about it."

"I don't suppose you made it over here to the library, did you?"

He shook his head. He trusted there was something to learn at the library, but all of his efforts had only led him to lose faith in the idea that had made sense, that Laura had found something and someone wanted to kill her rather than let her expose it. This felt hopeless-like he was dying of thirst in the middle of the ocean. "I did, but I didn't find out anything. I've got to hit the internet again."

"How did it go with Amanda?"

"It didn't. I couldn't get in touch with her. I think she's still pretty pissed. If she wants to talk, she knows where to find me."

"You busy now?"

He felt a little bad that he had to say he was. "I need to talk to Deanna to see what I can find out."

He wished he had asked her out to get a bite to eat the last time he was at her home. Now he's not going to let that chance pass him up.

She asked, "Have you got enough time to spare for lunch first?"

Jimmy smiled wearily. "Lunch?" Actually, a little fuel sounded like a good idea. "Yeah, sure. We sure are doing that a lot lately."

"If we're to be partners, the more we're around each other, the better we'll get along. Besides, you said something about being willing to be my bodyguard, didn't you? I feel safer the more you're around."

Jimmy liked hearing that. He thought briefly about putting his hand on her shoulder but decided not to.

That warm, humid day, they made their way by the cemetery between the art and poli sci buildings to the parking lot behind the Department of Art. Traci wanted to eat at The Varsity, a fast-food joint that boasted to be the greasiest place in town. It was popular with all the students. To get there, Jimmy drove down fraternity and sorority row, the street with all of the antebellum homes that housed the Greek organizations.

When Jimmy reached the end of the street, he pointed across the road to a black steel fence with a small brick wall at the corner. "What's that?"

"What?" Traci asked.

Traffic whizzed by in front of them. "That right over there."

"You mean the old cemetery?"

"Another one?" Jimmy said. "Just how many little cemeteries are there around this campus?"

"I know of a couple more."

This was a new angle to the problem of violence and shadowy figures on campus. Maybe there was some sort of angry ghost problem, even though he found that very hard to believe. "Where? Show me."

Traci told Jimmy to hang a right. They drove around the edge of the campus beyond the student center. Traci showed him the first one. Then she gave him directions to the second one, which was near where Jimmy and Seth lived. As Jimmy drove around the east end of campus, they found another one.

"God damn," Jimmy said. "All four of these cemeteries surround the campus."

"Oh, and I just remembered. There's another old, larger Civil War cemetery on Wilson Street. I always think they're kind of neat, you know? Especially the older cemeteries just aren't that scary."

Jimmy went down the road past the football stadium and beyond the science building. After Jimmy saw that one, Traci asked, "What's up with you and these cemeteries?"

"Hang on," Jimmy said. "This may be nothing, but I want to check something out. I need to get a map."

"A map?"

"Yeah."

Jimmy drove to a gas station for the map and then to The Varsity. The smell of grease in that restaurant was so overpowering Jimmy thought he'd need to wash off a layer of the stuff after he got home. Students packed the eatery in between classes. Large flat screens hung up high on the walls all over the restaurant. Each TV aired a different sports channel. After Jimmy and Traci ordered their burgers and fries, he spread the map across the table.

"Damn it," he mumbled after his cheeseburger dribbled some grease onto the map. He loved their burgers, but they really weren't exaggerating about how greasy they were. He wiped the grease off with a napkin and grabbed a pen from his back pocket.

"What are you doing?" Traci asked.

"Look here," Jimmy said as he made a dot with his pen as he marked where the first cemetery was located. "The cemetery down the road over there is here. The two you showed me are here and here. Okay, we found the fourth one here." Jimmy marked where they found the final cemetery. "And here's where that Civil War cemetery is."

"So?"

"Hold on. The cemetery between the art and political science buildings is right here in the middle of campus." Jimmy turned the map. "Holy shit."

"What?" Traci gulped her soda and washed down some fries. "What is it?"

Jimmy turned the map around again. "Don't you see it?"

"No."

Jimmy used his pen to connect the dots. He drew five straight lines.

"Jesus," Traci gasped. "It's a pentacle, like a pentagram. Isn't that a symbol Satanists use?"

"Yeah. And this top line runs right down fraternity and sorority row."

And Laura's story involved something about the sororities.

"You're on to something, aren't you?"

He wished he knew. Seemed like every time he had figured something out, he ended up back at a dead end. "Maybe. I need to get back on the internet to check something."

"Can I help?"

"I don't know. I wish I could find someone who could get a soil sample analyzed—"

Traci perked up. "Is that what you need? I think I can help you there. I've got to finish writing a paper, but I'll go dig up some ground in the woods, and I'll have a lab analyze it. I'll bet you they find nothing. Chemicals don't cause the kinds of problems we have here."

"You know of a lab that will do that?"

"Yes. I have a friend who studied soil science here. Now she's a scientist. Want me to?"

"You bet! Then you tell me if they find anything." This was a win for him, especially if she found something. He really wanted there to be an explanation for why the town was so violent, and nobody seemed willing to do anything about it.

"Damn, that would be great! Let me get you back to campus, and your car and I'll let you get on with it."

Traci grinned. "You bet."

After classes, Jimmy returned to the library. More students checked out computers at that time. He jumped on the last one, still thinking that chemicals might be a part of the problem on campus, as surely so many people weren't violent without reason. He did a little digging and found out the university took care of its own grounds. His parents paid a lawn care company to take care of the yard at the house he grew up in. That lawn care company treated most of the lawns in his neighborhood. Problems with violence and hallucinations didn't exist there. Jimmy searched for any company capable of dumping chemicals. None existed now or in the past.

He hit the University's website and discovered that Morganburg started as a small settlement back in the late 1600s. It was one of the original towns that the English settled in the new America. The college was first chartered in 1795. The university was built before chemical companies existed. At best, there may have been an old apothecary in that town at one time.

Jimmy figured the damage that sort of business could have caused, even if it maliciously discarded the product, would've been minimal. Jimmy still suspected that dumped chemicals may be causing side effects on the students. And the side effects caused violence and hallucinations. But Jimmy found no such evidence either now or at any time in the past.

Jimmy decided he needed to read more about Morganburg and the university. Maybe the school had contracts with chemical manufacturers or something. But that would have to wait. Time had flown by, and he hadn't even called Deanna. He couldn't believe the time. He was exhausted. He not only researched the afternoon away, he sat at the computer for most of the night. He wanted to see if Seth worked on a painting in the studio. He stepped outside. He remembered how Dr. Johnson warned him not to hang around the campus at night, but he didn't say why. He spotted a Civil War soldier walking toward the Academic Building. He looked again.

"What the hell?" Jimmy mumbled. His eyes opened wide. Was he walking? He looked like he floated above the ground.

Jimmy jogged across the street. Did he see that figure floating, or was the figure a hallucination? Before Jimmy crossed the street, he heard a woman scream. From her cries, it sounded as if she was being stabbed.

"No! Stop! No, no, no!" the woman wailed.

Jimmy knew that was no hallucination. He took off at a run towards the sound. After what happened to Laura, he'd be damned if he let another woman get hurt.

The screaming came from behind the law building. He sprinted back across the courtyard to behind the law building. He found no one. No one stood from behind the law building to the Academic Building. The woman screamed again. This time it sounded like it came from behind the art building.

"What the *hell?*" Jimmy whispered. He'd heard of auditory hallucinations. *Was this screaming real?*

The disembodied voice floated around the campus. Nobody else seemed to hear it. Jimmy quickly walked away from the law building and back through the courtyard. He looked behind him several times. He walked faster. He ran across the street and looked behind him again before he entered the art building. He never felt fear like this before, not even walking the streets of Virginia Beach late at night. But back then, he always had Seth, Billy, Hat Trick, and his gang friends with him. Right now, he felt very isolated and alone. He ran down the hallway and burst into the studio. Seth wasn't there. His easel was there, but even the smell of turpentine had diminished as if nobody had come in today.

Jimmy heard the front door of the art building close shut. It sounded like the door of a tomb. Footsteps, heavy like someone wore boots, echoed down the hallway toward the studio. He looked around for a weapon. Outside of a stray paintbrush, there was nothing he could use. He had no interest in finding out who was in the building late at night. He cut out of there through a side studio door.

A figure with long dark hair, drenched in black, stood in the cemetery. His eyes looked sunken, hollow, and soulless. This looked like the same person Seth described seeing at home. He'd assumed it was a hallucination, but the figure looked so real. This was the same figure he saw outside Rafe's and Pete's home and painted on their kitchen wall.

The person watched Jimmy walk across the street. Jimmy sprinted to his car and sped away.

Jimmy believed Dr. Johnson was right. This campus is no place to be at night. In fact, it was no place to be at any time.

CHAPTER ELEVEN

The next afternoon Jimmy got home after classes; he found some beefy-smelling substance with cheese melted over it in the fridge. Looked like Seth attempted some dinner and abandoned it. Before As it warmed his make-shift meal in the microwave, Jimmy heard someone knock on that side door of the upstairs residence.

"Cassie!" a woman shouted. "It's Ernie!"

CLUMP, CLUMP, CLUMP, CLUMP, CLUMP.

Jimmy wondered if those women weren't part Minotaur.

"Get the god damn hell out of here, Ernie!" Cassie screamed. "We're through! Get that through your head!"

"I just want to talk," a guy said. "I just want to see you."

"I don't want to talk to you! It's over! Now get out!"

Jimmy cringed, listening to them. He liked Cassie well enough. He didn't want to hear her fighting.

"Are you seeing someone else?"

"I'm seeing no one! Now get lost! I have nothing to say to you anymore!"

A shouting match ensued. No one listened. They only yelled louder than the other. Jimmy heard more female voices join the fray. A struggle broke out. It sounded like the women forcibly removed Ernie from the house. Glasses fell and broke. Plates hit the floor. Cassie screamed incoherently.

Jimmy's muscles tensed as he gripped the edge of the kitchen sink. He wanted to go up there and straighten out that punk, but then he relaxed when a door slammed, and a car engine roared. Metal and glass objects hit the car until it sped off. The girls sounded like they emptied the entire kitchen into the upstairs driveway. He was just glad that it seemed to be over, and he wouldn't have to go upstairs and remove the unwanted guest. He grabbed his meal from the microwave and retreated to his room.

He called Deanna, one of the girls he met at the campus news office. Amanda gave her the names of some women, and she said Deanna knew them. "It's Jimmy Durham. Can we talk? I've been trying to call you, but I haven't been able to reach you and your answering machine is full."

"Oh, sorry. I didn't realize. I'll check that right away. What's on your mind?"

"Did Laura ever mention to you anything about something bad about the town government or anything about corruption?"

"Oh, shit. Hang on now. I remember last spring Laura mentioned something about a vote to take down some of the woods to expand the university. But then she said the vote wasn't likely going to happen until the fall. And Laura was interested in it. She was going to make some phone calls to the city council members.

Shivers ran down Jimmy's body. "Do you know why?"

She didn't answer right away. He heard her fighting to keep herself from crying. "Jimmy, I don't know. I never got the chance to ask. If only I had known—"

"I got some names from Amanda. Do you know any of them? Barbara Sands, Tiffany Spencer, or Hillary Byron?"

Deanna composed herself. "Barbara and Tiffany are sorority girls. Hillary was a good friend."

Suddenly Jimmy felt like he had scored a lead. Good friends tell each other everything, especially girls. That's exactly someone he needed to talk to. "If I called those girls, you know, do you think they'll talk to me?"

"I think Hillary dropped out or transferred."

Jimmy hung his head. *Naturally. Seems to be a lot of that going around lately.*

"The other two I don't know. They're Tri Delts and I'm not a sorority girl. And I didn't know them that well."

"Okay." He should probably talk to some Tri Delts, but he wasn't sure what to ask them.

Before Deanna hung up, she said, "I'd love to help you, Jimmy. Is there anything I can do?"

"Probably not. But Pete told me Laura found something at the library. I've tried to look there, but I couldn't find anything, not anything about the town that would cause her to be murdered."

"I've got some free time, Jimmy. Between classes, I'll take a look, okay?"

"Sure thing. Thanks for the help. It means a lot to me."

Once he was off the phone with her, he tried to call Hillary, but she didn't answer. He feared she saw some of the things he had or she knew what Laura did and she got the hell out of Dodge. He needed more help and he might know somehow who could. He looked at the ceiling where the Tri Delt girls lived. One of the girls stormed out. The rest griped to each other but couldn't make out the words.

Jimmy thought things were getting worse in the house. The girls didn't use to fight with their boyfriends that intensely. He remembered how Seth and Natalie fought the time last he was with them here in the house, just like the girls upstairs fight with their boyfriends. And here was where he and Traci had their worst spats. The cemeteries, the pentagram, sorority row, the hallucinations, the figures, people here fighting…There was something bizarre going on in this town. That was certain. And it felt like it was getting worse.

The next week Jimmy finally found Seth in the art studio where the stench of turpentine still ruled. To his delight, Cassie was there. He didn't know what she was doing there, but he needed to talk to her.

Seth looked pale and tired, and he swore and muttered to himself as he worked on a painting.

He struggled with his landscape scene. Jimmy wondered what was up there. Seth usually knocked out a painting a week, sometimes two. Now it was pushing late in September, and he still couldn't finish one. Seth's still life was set against the wall. It looked like he experimented with cubism. He wasn't having a lot of luck with the experiment.

"You going to be at this all night?" Jimmy asked.

"Yeah," Seth grumbled. "I'm trying to get this right."

Jimmy looked at the painting. "I'm no art major. But it looks fine to me."

Seth smirked. "You're right. You're no art major."

Cassie looked hot again. She wore a revealing pink sweater she kept unbuttoned low and pants she didn't fasten to the top. "You're just the girl I'm looking for," Jimmy said. "Got a minute?"

"I am? Why?"

"Aren't you a Tri Delt?"

"I am, but I don't live in the sorority anymore."

"Would you help me set up an interview with at least one of them? I'm working on a story for the campus paper, and I'm not sure they will speak to me. "

"After Traci's story about the frats, I wouldn't be surprised," Seth muttered.

"Yeah, I can do that," Cassie said.

"I'm hoping to speak to Barbara Sands or Tiffany Spencer. My girlfriend was planning to talk to them before she was killed, and I want to try to find out why."

"Laura was your girlfriend? I'm so sorry."

Jimmy nodded and smiled a little. "When can we do this?"

She shrugged. "Let me call Barbara. Maybe we can do this tomorrow night."

As long as Seth was busy, Jimmy was going to let him work on his painting. He returned home to work on a story for his creative writing class until it was nearly time for him to go to bed. Just as he shut off his computer, he got a call from Traci.

She said, "I just talked to my friend, and she said she could do the lab work on the soil sample, but she wants it right away. I'll get you a sample from the woods behind the art building."

Jimmy felt a wave of shivers run down his body. "*Hold on.* Where are you?"

"I was at the library. I've driven over to the art building."

"You're on campus now? At night?" He thought she knew better than to wander around on campus then. "Traci, don't do it now. Wait until tomorrow morning."

She groaned. "I can't. I have to work all day tomorrow. You don't understand; there are rules about who gets access to the lab equipment. I wouldn't be able to get the sample until tomorrow night. And my friend wants it right away. She wanted it tonight, but if we wait, it might be a while."

Jimmy grabbed his keys. No way did he want her to do anything on campus late at night, especially if she was going to try to find answers about the campus grounds. "At least wait until I get there. Don't go out there yet."

Traci chuckled. "Natalie said you and Seth were bodyguards to girls when you were in a biker gang before you got into college. I guess that sorta thing doesn't leave you, does it?"

"*I mean it*, Traci." Jimmy ran to his car and got inside. "Wait until I get there."

She chuckled again. "I'm not afraid. I've studied at the library at night for years. Nothing bad has ever happened. Dr. Johnson spooks easily."

"I don't care." Jimmy hit the gas and headed to the university. "There are a lot of funky things happening at night there. People have been murdered."

"Oh, my gosh, Jimmy. *Okay* already." He heard her open her car door and pop the trunk of her car. "I'm just getting a plastic bag and a small garden hoe from the back of my car. It sure is a warm night, nice though it's really quiet. I can't even hear any insects. But this whole campus at night does seem like a graveyard."

"Just hang on. I should be there in less than five minutes."

"All right. I don't see anyone or anything out here. Is it okay with you if I wait here by my car? It's parked right by the building."

Jimmy exhaled. "Okay. Just don't go near the woods until I get there. And stay on the line." He turned onto Jackson Street and passed the art department.

"I just saw a red car by the building," she said. "That you?"

"Yeah."

He turned around the block and headed down the road to the street to turn into the back parking lot. "I'm almost there." He nearly dropped the phone as he went to make the left turn. Darkness spilled out of the woods and bled across the street to the parking lot. *"What the hell?"* he gasped.

Over the phone, Jimmy heard something pop like a branch snapped. "What was that?"

Jimmy exploded into the parking lot and the brakes squealing, stopped thirty feet from Traci's car.

"Traci!" he shouted.

"Oh, my God!" she screamed.

Dear Lord, he thought. *What is that?* "Traci, look out!"

She spun around to run but turned her ankle and hit the blacktop. The dark fog rushed to her, missed her, bashed into her car, and knocked it a few feet forward. Black and green claws reached out from the blackness and grabbed her ankles. Traci shrieked several times before she freed herself. Jimmy started to get out of the car to help her. The stench of sulfur around him was overwhelming.

He heard several voices whispering, *"Come to us, Traci. Be with us, Traci."*

"We want you, Traci."

"Come with us, Traci."

"Come, Traci, Traci, Traci…"

"Traci, Traci, Traciiiiiiiiiiiiiii……"

But once she broke free, he lurched the car forward some more, and she shot to her feet. Jimmy leaned over and opened the passenger door, she hobbled to the car, and jumped inside.

"Go, go, go!" Traci screamed.

Jimmy slammed the car in reverse, tires squealing and smoking as he turned. Then yanked the stick back into drive….and he saw the fog turning to them.

Jimmy thought, *What. The. Fuck.*

Jimmy stomped on the gas, but the fog accelerated too, slamming into the side of the car, nearly tipping it on its side.

Traci wailed like a banshee as the black and green slimy claws, dripping with sores, pus, and black ooze, emerged from the black, and scraped across the window.

Jimmy floored it, tires squealing louder than the claws' metallic grating and carving ridges into the passenger side window, and turned left, the fog in the rearview mirror.

My God, what sort of evil possesses this campus?

PART TWO
DARKNESS

CHAPTER TWELVE

Once they got to Traci's apartment, she slammed the door, locked it, jerked her curtains shut, and peeked out her window.

She gasped, "Whatever that black stuff was, I don't think it followed us home."

He collapsed on the couch. "You really saw that then, right?"

"No way could I miss that! If you're hallucinating or going nuts, then so am I."

Jimmy breathed so hard he nearly hyperventilated. "What was that? What did we see?"

Traci kept looking. "I don't know what that was. It was like fog, but it had substance. It hit the car like a wave of water. And what were those claws? Did you see those? They were in the fog!"

Jimmy's heart rammed in his chest. "Yeah, I saw them. I don't know what those were. I don't know what the hell is going on at this campus."

He still had trouble processing what he had seen. Black fog? What could cause that? His neighbors were actually right. And he thought they were nuts. A part of him could believe he suffered a hallucination by seeing black fog, but not with the car getting nearly rocked off the road. It really did seem like the campus was possessed by a supernatural force.

"And to think I've been busting my ass trying to find what could be causing hallucinations in this town. What's going on here has nothing to do with chemicals."

Jimmy thought nothing made sense. If he could believe he'd seen Laura's spirit and everything else he'd seen, he believed it now. It's beneath our feet. She said it was in the ground and it was in the government, and she told her mom it was also in the campus administration. What the hell is 'it'?

Traci stopped looking out the window. "I don't think that black soup, whatever it was, followed us here."

"No, I lost it when I left campus. In fact, I think it only exists on campus. Once we get away from the university, it seems to lose its power, whatever 'it' is."

"Do you think we should call the police?"

Jimmy laughed. "Oh, yeah? And tell them what? The campus is possessed by black fog that nearly tried to kill us? They'll take that seriously."

Traci sat down next to him. "So now what?"

"Whatever that is, I think it's what killed Laura."

"Wasn't she stabbed to death?"

"Yeah, but what's in that blackness? That just isn't fog. We saw black figures with claws. It was coming straight for you, but when you ran to my car, it turned to follow you. That means it's intelligent. It has intent. And its intent was malevolent."

"But what's in there that wanted Laura dead?"

He shrugged. He wished he knew...or did he? "She was going to write about it, or write about something, warn people. She figured out something about it. And that's what got her killed."

He felt his heart finally begin to slow down a little. He clasped his hands as he placed his elbows on his knees. "Being from a biker gang, I can tell you I can take on a killer, but I don't know how to fight what we just saw."

"So what do you want to do?"

Jimmy thought there was only one thing he could do. "I don't know about you, but I'm ready to give up. There's something dangerous in this town, and it's killing students. I'm also ready to pack it in and leave."

The next afternoon, after classes, Jimmy found Seth in the studio. Jimmy hadn't seen him in days. He wanted to hang out with Seth again and see if he would like to get something to eat and talk about. The landscape painting Seth had been working on lay in the corner like Seth had tossed it over there. And Seth grumbled to himself with the still life he now worked on.

"Hey, man," Jimmy said.

Seth angrily peeked around his painting. "Hey."

"How about we get some lunch? It's been a while since we did that."

"I'm not hungry. This painting is driving me up the wall, and I'm trying to rework it."

That was odd. He had never seen Seth struggle with his paintings like this. "Then why don't you give a rest. You could probably use some food."

His tone turned sharp. "I'll get something to eat later."

Seth rarely passed up a meal. Jimmy wondered what was up with him all of a sudden. "Okay, well look, I just wanted to tell you the girls upstairs were right. I saw that black fog. It nearly attacked Traci right here outside in the parking lot. We got off campus just in time. You won't believe it. The stuff actually rammed my car."

Seth laughed heartily. "Yeah, sure it did, Jimbo."

"I'm not kidding, Seth! That really happened."

Seth scoffed. "Oh, come on, Jimmy. There's no such thing as black fog."

That pissed him off that Seth would believe him. He believed Seth's story about his vision at home. "I *saw it!* Look, we've got to get out of here. We—"

"Fuck it!" Seth kicked over his painting. "I don't know what the fuck is wrong with my painting lately, but it's like I couldn't even paint a smiley face."

Jimmy nearly jumped back. He never saw Seth kick his canvases. He felt scared and confused. Seth never had problems with his art. If he felt frustrated with anything in life, he'd turn to painting. The more stressed out he was, the more he'd paint.

"Maybe you need to take a break," Jimmy said.

"Yeah, I could use a breather." Seth grabbed a sketch pad and some pencils and blew right past him.

Hello? Jimmy thought. *Jesus, Seth. I'm trying to talk to you here.* Jimmy followed him. "Listen to me, Seth. I'm not kidding. We need to get the hell out of here. Forget the damn deposit. We can transfer to a different school. We'll lose some credits from this semester, but we can figure it out. "

They walked down the back steps of the building and down to a Coke machine.

Seth got some coins out of his pocket. "Jimmy, I don't know what you saw or what you think you saw, but it doesn't matter. We can't leave. We've signed a lease. We're here for two more semesters."

"We'll break the lease. People break leases." And Jimmy remembered the last person who lived at their place went AWOL on the rent. Jimmy thought they should've smelled the manure downwind and never signed the lease.

Seth punched the button on the Coke machine. "*No, we won't.* I can't afford it and neither can you. Look, we just got until the summer and then we graduate. After that, we can do whatever we want. I want to finish my Master's, but I thought we'd all eventually end up back together in Virginia Beach."

The machine plopped down a paper cup, dumped in some ice, and filled it with soda. Seth grabbed a Coke and headed out the back door. He wouldn't even wait for Jimmy. Jimmy grabbed a Coke for himself and chased after him. He couldn't believe Seth wouldn't believe him. They had been like brothers since junior high. Never once before did Jimmy tell something to him and Seth didn't believe him. At least when Seth was sober. Now he wondered about what Seth saw at the bar when he ran out.

As Jimmy ran after Seth, he caught a glimpse of a flyer on a campus bulletin board that announced a haunted campus tour. That sort of thing had never interested him before, but after what he had seen last night, he wondered if maybe he should start paying attention to things like that.

Jimmy caught up to him. "I can't believe what I saw happened last night doesn't scare you. I believed you about your vision of the dark figure. I can't believe you don't want to leave."

They walked past the cemetery, and Seth said, "Come on, Jimmy. There's *no way* you saw that. Were you drinking?"

"No!"

"We can't leave. We have to finish school."

They walked down the sidewalk and crossed the street. He knew Seth was right. They couldn't leave, but he didn't want to die. He didn't know what to do.

"Where are you going?" Jimmy asked.

Seth chugged his Coke. Some of it ran down the corner of his mouth. He wiped his face. "I don't know. I'm just looking for something to draw."

Before they got to the student center, they heard Brother Leroy shouting at students. They found Rafe and Pete sitting at a stone table in front of the place, a stone-white building no bigger than Jimmy's basement apartment. The bookstore, a blue building with a black roof the same size as the student center, stood side by side. Rafe and Pete sketched the raving redneck and the gathered students before them. Seth opened his sketchbook and joined them in their fun.

Jimmy finished his soda and crumpled the can. A preacher, Brother Leroy, stood on the wooden stage outside the bookstore. Rock bands used the stage to play on Thursday and Friday afternoons for free promotion. Preachers also liked to use it as their own personal pulpit to warn students about the evils of education, being a college student, and the college student lifestyle. A crowd of students gathered around the stage to heckle the preacher. Jimmy approached Brother Leroy from behind. He threw his crushed cup in the direction of the minister. He hit the brown-haired, obese preacher right in the head. Jimmy kept walking around the crowd. By the time the preacher turned around, Jimmy was already facing the stage. The crowd laughed and cheered with Jimmy. He wasn't even aiming. He didn't actually think he'd hit Leroy.

"Whoever threw that will burn in Hell!" Brother Leroy yelled.

Rafe, Pete, and Seth laughed and gave Jimmy the thumbs-up sign.

Jimmy sat down with them. "What the hell you two are doing here?"

Pete stopped drawing for a moment. "We're out here for a class. Our professor wanted us to draw something outside."

"We decided to come out here to draw," Rafe said.

Pete resumed drawing. "We had no idea Brother Leroy was out here again."

Jimmy turned around and looked at Leroy. "Yeah, he's a frequent visitor. Too bad he doesn't come equipped with an off button. Why students want to come out here to argue with that twit is beyond my comprehension. I know why he does it. He wants the attention."

"People like to come out here and argue with him," Rafe said.

"Exactly," Jimmy agreed. "But they're actually feeding his desire. No matter how loudly people shout at him, they will never change his mind. He's got his one book that gives him all of his opinions, including why he should come out here and scream at college kids. I'm sure that's in the Gospel according to Leroy."

Jimmy looked at all of their drawings. Rafe's sketch looked great. He drew the student center and the bookstore next to it. Pete drew Brother Leroy carrying on like a lunatic. But Seth was working his eraser as though he might burn a hole through the paper.

Leroy shouted, "Now I know some of you women are lusting after my body right now!"

"Don't flatter yourself, you fat slob!" a woman shouted.

Brother Leroy opened his Bible. "And some of you guys are, too!" He flipped to a page.

"People, turn to your Bibles!" He paused even though he knew no one had brought a Bible with them. "Now I'm going to read this for *double emphasis!*"

The crowd knew his routine. They heckled him and said, "double emphasis" with him and laughed. A guy way in the back yelled, "Read it for triple emphasis, Leroy!"

Leroy announced, "Turn to the Book of Ephesians, chapter five, verse three. 'But fornication and impurity of any kind—!'"

Jimmy tuned him out, watching Seth and feeling worried for him. If Seth couldn't do art, he lost his emotional outlet. He had already started partying more.

Seth mangled his drawing. He swore and threw his pencil away.

"What's going on over there, Seth?" Rafe asked. "It sounds like good things aren't happening."

Seth sharpened another pencil like he tried to turn a screw into cement. "I don't know what's wrong with me lately. But I can't seem to get any of my paintings or drawings right, including this sketch."

"Don't you people realize that you are damning your souls by coming here and lusting after each other and fornicating?" Leroy screamed. "This whole town is a den of sin! I am warning all of you what will happen when you become college students! Fornicators! Masturbators! Liars! Perverts! Intellectuals!" Leroy scowled and listened to the students ridicule him. "But I'll tell you the most blasphemous abomination in the eyes of the Lord!" Leroy swung around and pointed his finger at the guys. "Artists!"

Seth's pencil tip broke. "And I'll tell you something else," he growled. "Between this sketch and that backward ass-country fuck, I'm beginning to like the idea of shoving this pencil right up his ass! I'm sick of that hillbilly and his whining."

Seth's eyes turned black. A large dark cloud covered the sun, and a cold wind cut right through Jimmy like a large, broken, jagged branch. Brother Leroy stopped in mid-sentence, clutched his chest, and staggered forward. He toppled off the stage. People in the crowd rushed to him.

"Somebody call an ambulance!" a girl shouted. "He's not breathing!"

A guy whipped out his cell phone and dialed nine-one-one.

Jimmy looked back at Seth. Seth rubbed his face like he was exhausted. "The hell with this drawing," he spat. "I've had enough! This isn't working. I need new pencils anyways."

Seth ignored what happened to Leroy and stormed off to the bookstore. Jimmy wasn't sure what to believe when it came to things he had seen lately. Did Seth's eyes really turn black? It looked like Seth caused Leroy's collapse. *But that's impossible, isn't it?*

Jimmy got a call from Cassie. She said, "Can you meet with some of the Tri Delta girls tonight? I've some girls who said they'd be willing to talk to you."

Jimmy wanted to quit the story, just in case he was right that someone was murdering students, but she went to the trouble to set up the meeting, and he still wanted to find out who killed Laura. The more he thought about it, the angrier he got. Laura was dead and he swore to her mother that he'd find out....or even what had killed her. He wanted to find out about Laura. He wanted to that for her. He'd just have to be careful. *Very careful.*

"Okay," he said. He glanced at his watch. "I'll be at home by seven."

"Good. I'll come pick you up."

Before he hooked up with Cassie, he wanted to stop at the library. He didn't care about what happened to Brother Leroy and left.

Jimmy went to the library to try to find more books about Morganburg. Maybe he should speak to a librarian again. Or maybe he needed to go to the Morganburg Library. Pete said Laura had found something at the library. He had assumed Pete meant the one on campus.

He started to go up the front steps of the main library when Amanda came out. She wore a red top with black buttons and a super short red mini skirt, and black nylons. She didn't just look hot. She looked like solid lava.

"Jimmy," she said quietly. "Where the hell have you been? I've been trying to call you."

"Well—" Jimmy started to say.

She grabbed his arm, and her breast nudged up against him. "I'm so sorry we got into that fight. I don't know what got into me. I guess I was really drunk."

This was a whole new side of her. He liked it. "It's okay, Amanda."

"Would you like to go have some dinner? We can talk."

Traci suddenly came out of the library. She shouted, "Jimmy, what the hell are you doing?"

She startled him. "I'm just talking to Amanda." Jimmy felt anger surge through him. "What the hell are you doing, Traci?"

"I've been trying to find you. I thought you needed my help with your story. I thought this story was important to you. But every time I turn around, you're with this bimbo!"

"Hey, screw you, bitch!" Amanda snarled. "What business is it of yours what Jimmy does?

"Are you jealous that he doesn't spend his nights in your bed?"

Traci's jaw dropped. "Jealous? How dare you say that to me, you little whore! I have no more interest in bedding down with him than I would with you, which I hear isn't a problem for you because you like to row both sides of the boat if you know what I mean."

"Why, you fucking cunt!" Amanda raised her hand to slap Traci.

Jimmy stopped her.

"Both of you knock it off!" he shouted. He shoved Amanda back. "What the God damn hell is wrong with you?" Jimmy yelled at Traci. "It's none of your damn business what I do, God fucking damn it!"

"That's right!" Amanda screeched.

"And you shut up," Jimmy snapped. "You're only making this worse!"

People stopped to gawk at them.

Amanda stared at him for a moment. "Well, fucking excuse me! I don't get you at all, Jimmy. *Are* you sleeping with her?"

"Sleeping with her? I'd no more do that than I would screw an ape!"

"What did you just say?" Traci fumed. "You obnoxious pig! You know, Jimmy, you can take your precious article and any help you expected from me, and you can shove it right up your ass!" She stormed off.

"After what you just said to me, as far as I'm concerned, I never want to see you again!"

Amanda said. "Obviously, you two have some sort of thing going on, so go to her! I can tell you care more about her feelings than you do mine, so you can go to hell! I hate you!" She stormed off in the opposite direction.

Jimmy regretted his comment about the ape. He wasn't sure why he'd said that. He couldn't understand what was going on. He warred with two good friends, and he couldn't understand why. He spoke better to guys he got into fights with on the streets of Virginia Beach. Amanda walked by the law library. Traci headed in the direction of the art building. He wanted to stop them both, but he could only stop one, but which one?

"Damn," Jimmy mumbled. He ran after Traci. "Traci, wait up!"

"Go to hell, Jimmy!" Traci said without stopping or turning around.

"Damn it, Traci, stop!" Jimmy ran up to her and grabbed her by the back of the arm. She jerked away.

"Don't you touch me!"

Jimmy couldn't understand why she was acting that way. He let go of her and pleaded, "Will you calm down? Look, can you please tell me what the hell just went on between the two of us?"

"We hate each other and we had another fight. So what else is new?"

Traci began to storm off again, but Jimmy said, "I thought we both agreed that we liked each other. Remember?"

Traci spun around and opened her mouth as if she was going to start tearing into him again, but she said nothing. She looked confused. Traci even appeared to not know where she was.

"How'd I get here?" Jimmy expected her to say, but she remained silent.

"Traci, what just happened back there? I was there talking to Amanda. I had gotten sidetracked by her, but I realized after I stepped outside I still had work to do. I planned on going on back inside to do more research."

Traci held her head as if she had a headache. She shrugged her shoulders and shook her head. "Hell, I don't know what came over me. I thought you were going to patch things up with her."

"Yeah, I had until today. Now I think all of that is right back into the crap hole." Jimmy held Traci's hand. "Listen, I'm sorry about how I spoke to you. I also don't know what got into me. You know what I think we need to do? Let's get off campus and talk."

Jimmy and Traci drove to the Hawk's Nest way on the outskirts of Morganburg, the same bar he was at before the police told him Laura was murdered. A large stage stood at the front of the bar upstairs. A lower floor was for pool tables, darts, and other games. A dark-haired woman in a pink and black jumpsuit shot a game of pool. The aroma of fish hung in the air. A large screen on the wall had CNN reporting the normal daily grind. Only here in Morganburg seemed like the world turned upside down.

They sat down at the bar. A pretty brunette named Brittany, with long legs and a tight green top, served them a couple of beers. Jimmy and Traci sat in a booth. Two old barflies sat at the other end, burying suds and griping about politics. After Jimmy ordered a couple of beers, Traci sipped hers. Jimmy slammed half of his bottle.

"How do you feel now?" Jimmy asked.

Traci smiled. "I feel fine." She held the smile, but her eyes seemed a little confused and scared.

"Are you sure?"

"Yes."

"We were at each other's throats only a few minutes ago. Do you remember?"

Traci sipped some more of her beer. She smirked and shook her head again. "Honestly, I really don't know what got into me. I just saw you there and thought that something was going on. You have me that rose, so I thought maybe you wanted to be with me. I guess I overreacted to everything. I should call Amanda and apologize. I'm sorry we fought. Really. I didn't mean any of those mean things I said."

Jimmy knew a woman would probably blame herself, but he felt like the campus was to blame somehow. They couldn't seem to keep control of their emotions when they were on campus. "Do you have some sort of problem with me being with Amanda?"

"Of course not. Why should I care? I mean, really, why should I? It's your life."

"Let me ask you this, then. Don't you think we fight more when we're on campus or just off campus, like at my place?"

Traci thought for a few moments. "I don't know. We just seem to argue a lot."

That didn't make any sense to him. "But why is that? We've already told each other we like each other. So why do we keep fighting? And I mean, when we fight, we don't just ever have a little argument; we go at each other like a couple of junior high school kids behind the school."

Traci smiled slightly. "I don't know, Jimmy. I guess that's just the way we are."

"Well, honey, that's not how I normally am. I don't speak to anyone the way I speak to you. And I don't talk to you that way except when I'm on campus or around the campus. I just don't understand, but I'm sorry. I'll try to do better."

"Maybe this university has bad vibes."

"You know there's more to it than that after what I saw. Sometimes when I'm with you, I feel like a drunk."

She looked at him quizzically.

He said, "I mean it in the sense that it's like I just embrace the rage and anger, so I'm almost high on it or something. I stay mad, so I keep getting drunker. That way, I won't pass out. I feel this rage shoot right through me. I need to vent so I don't explode into pieces."

Traci shrugged helplessly.

"Maybe there's something about me that brings that out of you."

She grinned.

Talking about this wasn't getting him anywhere. He gave up. "So why did you want to see me?"

Traci's smile turned to a frown. "I've been trying to call you. I tried to talk to the police. They wouldn't help. In fact, they were downright rude. They say they're not releasing any more information to the public about Laura. Supposedly they're still investigating."

"That's what Amanda told me. Same thing with Laura's mom—" Jimmy glanced at his watch. "Oh, crap. I nearly forgot. I gotta go. I have to go to the Tri Delta sorority house to see if they know anything about Laura. Come on. I'll drive you home."

Traci looked down and said weakly, "Okay. Good luck." As he got up, she said, "Hey, when are you leaving Morganburg? Didn't you say you were going?"

Jimmy frowned. "I guess I can't because of the lease. I talked to Seth. He reminded me we only have two semesters left. I guess he's right, but I'm only going on campus when I absolutely must."

"All right. Be careful, Jimmy."

He breathed deeply as they left the restaurant. "You bet your sweet ass I'm going to be."

CHAPTER THIRTEEN

Jimmy arrived home and found Cassie there waiting for him. "Sorry, I'm late. I had a bit of a mini-emergency and lost track of time."

When they arrived at Delta Delta Delta, she said, "I'm glad we could do this now. "This weekend is the big Morganburg-North Carolina A&M game. All of Phi Beta Kappa plan on going down to North Carolina to see the game. They're studying for exams this week. Then they leave Friday afternoon. Otherwise, you'd have to wait until Monday."

Jimmy definitely didn't want to wait. "Okay. Let's get this over with."

A blonde let them in and said, "Cassie! I heard you were coming over. I'll get the girls. Come in and sit."

A large crystal chandelier hung over their heads. A den full of glasses, books, and leather chairs was at Jimmy's right.

Jimmy wondered if the place was a house or a palace. The place reeked of privilege.

He peeked into the den to get a closer look. The antebellum frat house, built sometime in the seventeen hundreds, had its interior remodeled. Large hand-crafted cream ceramic lamps softly lit the room. Full bookshelves lined the walls. Blue sectionals and recliners stood in front of a rectangular coffee table with a glass top and wooden legs. Brandy and shot glasses sat on an end table in the corner of the room. All of the glasses had Greek letters of Tri Delta on them. A Giorgione replica of *Tempestuous Landscape with the Soldier and the Gypsy* hung above the fireplace. Its dark and murky setting, along with the ominous storm in the background, fit in well with the atmosphere of the town. The fireplace set looked like it was made of gold. A large oak desk stood near the fireplace. A tall grandfather clock ticked away in the corner of the room.

"Books," Jimmy muttered.

"What's that?" Cassie asked.

"Oh, nothing. I was just thinking out loud. It's been so hard it is for me to find the research that I need for what I'm working on. Do you realize how many books there are on this campus? Do you even know how many libraries this university has?"

"I know about the Main Library."

"There's also the English library, the art library, and there's even a math and science library. I feel as if I'm drowning in an ocean of books, yet I'm not able to find one to help what I'm looking for."

Two girls came down the stairs. Cassie introduced him to Barbara Sands and Tiffany Spencer. The girl who answered the door asked if they wanted anything to drink. Jimmy declined, but Cassie said she did. She wanted to get caught up with Cassie, so they went together into the kitchen. Jimmy and the other girls went into the living room.

Perfume permeated the sorority house. It seemed all homes had their own unique scent, as if the house was a living entity. Cassie led Jimmy into the living room. Prussian blue lamps sat on the end tables, and eggshell white curtains covered the windows. Above the upholstered beige couches, two paintings of scenic countrysides hung on the walls. A glass table sat in front of the couch. Recliner chairs occupied the corners of the room. An alizarin crimson vase set upon a credenza. The dark blue lamps and the soft white walls and curtains made Jimmy feel very calm.

Barbara Sands, a long-haired honey blonde, wore a bright purple and white dress, and Tiffany Spencer, a brunette whose straight long hair hung nearly to her waist, wore a white blouse with tan slacks. Both wore high heels. Jimmy thought it looked as though they were heading to a college career seminar rather than staying at home to hang out.

Tiffany asked, "So, want do you want to ask us about?"

"I'm working on a story about my girlfriend's murder, Laura Jenkins. She wanted to meet with you about something. Do you know anything about that?"

The girls glanced at each other and shook their heads.

"No, not really," Barbara said. "I remember her calling to ask about that, but it got delayed, and then, you know, unfortunately, she died. I thought she wanted to ask about the haunted dorm."

"Haunted dorm?" Jimmy asked. He had never heard anything about that, but he'd never lived on campus.

Tiffany said, "Yeah, you ever heard the story about the curse?"

"Curse?" Jimmy sat on the edge of the sofa. "What curse?"

"This girl had a fight with one of the frats," Barbara said.

"What was the fight about?" Jimmy asked.

"I think they split up," Barbara said.

Tiffany got up. "I'm going to get us some beers."

Jimmy asked, "What's that got to do with a curse?"

Tiffany came back with the beers. She handed Jimmy one. He set him aside. He didn't care about drinking. He only wanted to hear about the girl.

Barbara opened her can of beer. "She was a Satanist. And it's believed she placed a curse on him and all the frats."

"All the frats?" Jimmy asked. Jimmy thought that was interesting. Very interesting. He wondered if that could be where that dark fog is from. It seemed demonic or at least evil But Traci wasn't a frat. Why did it try to abduct her? Because she planned to take its soil? Or because she wanted to have it analyzed?

Tiffany sipped her beer. "Yeah. I also heard she could've placed a curse on the university or the town. They give haunted tours of the dorm around Halloween every year."

Jimmy wrote that down. Halloween was coming up. "Maybe I'll—"

They knelt on the sofa and faced each other. The lights dimmed.

"Jimmy," Tiffany whispered. "We can give you anything."

Barbara ran her hand up and down Tiffany's body. "Anything you want."

Tiffany licked her ear. "You just have to let us have what we want."

What the hell is going on? Jimmy couldn't move. He couldn't speak.

The girls kissed. "We can give you all sorts of pleasure."

Barbara said, "We can show you things you've never seen before."

The girls kissed each other again.

Tiffany squeezed Barbara's breast and licked Barbara's face. Barbara moaned. "We can give you Heaven on Earth, Jimmy," Tiffany cooed.

"Join us, Jimmy," Barbara pleaded. "And you will know pleasure like no man."

He wondered who he was supposed to join. Satan? Was that the curse spreading all over the campus and town? Was that what was causing the hallucinations? Was that why he kept fighting with Traci? Tiffany unbuttoned Barbara's dress and exposed her white bra. "All of us Tri Delts will be your servants, Jimmy."

Barbara unbuttoned Tiffany's blouse and ran her hand all over Tiffany's aqua-green bra.

She yanked Tiffany's bra aside and sucked on her small brown nipple. "We promise, Jimmy," Barbara said.

Tiffany jammed her hand up Barbara's dress. Barbara moaned loudly. "We promise," Tiffany whispered.

The girls kissed again.

"Don't try to stop us," Barbara gasped.

"We're always watching, Jimmy," Tiffany said. Then she snarled, "We're always watching."

Barbara hissed. "And our wrath is great."

Jimmy saw a dark figure with long black hair and hollow, dark eyes scowling from the window. *My God, is that a demon?*

Something growled louder and louder, drowning out the moans of the girls, drilling into Jimmy's brain as it took over everything, and the figure just watched…its eyes…its eyes…

"Did you find out everything you needed to know?" Cassie asked.

Jimmy blinked. The girls were suddenly back on the couch. They were fully dressed. The lights suddenly shone bright again.

"Are you okay, Jimmy?" Tiffany asked.

"Yeah, you look a little funny," Barbara said.

Jimmy cleared his throat. "Yeah. Just a little tired."

Barbara drank her beer. Tiffany took a can from Cassie.

Barbara smiled politely. "I'm still fine."

Another hallucination? Jimmy could move again. He cleared his throat. He hoped his erection wasn't obvious. "Actually, I think I've got all I need. I'm ready to go."

Tiffany pouted. "Already?"

"Yeah," Jimmy said and hoped it didn't sound like a gasp.

"Come back anytime," Barbara said seductively.

"Yeah, *anytime*, Tiffany said.

Jimmy darted out the front door, but he froze when he saw the dark figure again out on the front lawn. This time he was with a woman. She also had long dark hair and wore a black robe.

Jimmy trembled.

"Cassie!"

She was still saying goodbye to the girls. Finally, she closed the door. "What?"

"Did you see—?" The figures were gone.

"Did I see what?"

Naturally, he thought. "Never mind. Let's get the hell out of here."

CHAPTER FOURTEEN

For the rest of the week, Jimmy slept on Traci's couch and avoided the house and campus except for classes and when Jimmy needed to use the computer. He believed he may have discovered *what* had killed Laura but not why. And so long as he wasn't trying to find that out, he saw no strange things and was starting to feel a little safer. He still wanted to know why, but not at the expense of getting swallowed by that dark fog. He hoped things would remain quiet until the end of the semester.

That Saturday, Jimmy returned to the house to see if he got a check in the mail from his folks. When he drove up, Seth was outside painting a portrait of the house.

Jimmy got out of the car and looked at Seth's painting. "Another outdoor picture of this house?"

"I'm getting sick of figure anatomy. Seeing the same model in the same position all week long is becoming sheer drudgery. I decided I wanted to paint something I already had some success with, so I thought I should paint the house again."

"Are you still having problems with your art?"

Seth stabbed the brush into the canvas. His paint was so thick it looked like he worked his second or third layer. "Yeah. I hoped this would keep me from going out of my skull. I want to get one decent painting in before Natalie, and I go out for lunch."

Jimmy was glad he was at least painting. He seemed like he was having problems lately with his art for whatever reason. Jimmy darted up the porch.

"You want me to put you in the painting?" Seth asked.

"No, smart ass. I want to check the mail. I'm looking for my little care package from home."

"Oh, yeah." Seth dropped his paintbrush onto the edge of his easel. "That reminds me. My mother is supposed to send me my check, too."

They jogged up the front porch and Jimmy grabbed the mail out of the box. He shuffled for his check. "Hey, what do you know, you got yours, too. But it wasn't sent with loving affection like mine was."

Seth smirked. "Yeah, ask me if I give a crap, pal." Seth grabbed the letter and gave Jimmy's shoulder a light shove. Jimmy lost his balance and fell against the girls' front door. It popped open.

"Whoops," Jimmy said. He expected someone to come running to him to find out why he just burst into their home, but no one came. "I guess no one's home."

"Don't they believe in locking their doors?"

"It sure doesn't look like it." Jimmy started to close the door, but Seth stopped him.

"Wait a minute," Seth said. "I want to see what the inside of the place looks like."

"Seth, you can't just walk in there. Someone could come back at any minute."

"I doubt it. This is the big football weekend. You know, practically this entire town is down in North Carolina because the Pirates are there playing A&M. Most of the frat fucks and sorry-ass sisters go. And I'm positive those girls are down there."

Jimmy supposed Seth was right. And he was curious about them, too. Just how many pairs of heels do they have?

Seth and Jimmy stepped inside. The living room looked like a disaster. They found clothes lying on the floor and draped over the tan couch. Dirty dishes with rancid food were left on the coffee table in front of the couch. The smell of rotten food filled the house. A black phone sat on an end table next to the couch. Flies buzzed around their heads. Jimmy couldn't believe women lived like this. Maybe some guys, but not women.

"You'd think these women knew how to clean up after themselves," Jimmy said. It was disturbing to think such cute girls were so gross.

"They fight like animals. They live like animals."

One bedroom stood to Jimmy's right. A side door inside that room led to the back porch. A clock ticked away in there. To Jimmy's left was the bathroom. The bathroom stood in between two bedrooms. They looked like girly rooms, frilly white and pink bedspreads, a red dress hung from a closet door in the room to his left, and a stand-up white oval mirror sat in a corner in the room to his right. The bathroom smelled strongly of soap and perfume.

Seth looked around the house. "You know, I swear there are some days I could come up here and slaughter these bitches when I hear them fighting, screaming, and making all of the noise they make late at night. Sometimes I wonder if they even sleep."

Jimmy frowned, thinking Seth must have just been making a crude joke about murder. "You've seen their place. Satisfied?"

"No way. I'm sick of being kept awake night after night because of them."

Jimmy knew that wouldn't help Seth with his painting. He had a sinking feeling about what Seth planned to do, and he wasn't sure how to stop him. "What do you have in mind?"

"I don't know," Seth muttered. He stepped into the kitchen. A long white counter space and a white and black dishwasher stood across from the tan refrigerator. He opened the cabinets and drawers. He found the door that led downstairs to the boiler room. He unlocked the door and peered downstairs. The steps faded into the dark. "One night, I was in our kitchen. I heard a woman open that door, and she asked what was down there, and a guy said it was Hell." He shut the door and locked it.

"I'm beginning to think this whole town is Hell."

He turned to the living room again and stepped on a piece of paper. He picked it up, flipped it over, and read a message aloud. "Elizabeth and Anne Marie, I called all our sisters and I've got eleven who said they go with us on a road trip after midterm. We just got to get Cassie to agree to come."

Seth came up to Jimmy and looked at the note. He ripped it out of Jimmy's hand and crumpled it. "Like hell they will."

Jimmy was startled. "Damn, Seth. What do you care?"

"Because Cassie and I are doing something that weekend."

Jimmy wondered why he was doing something with Cassie for the weekend when he was engaged to Natalie.

"What would you be doing with her?" Jimmy asked.

"It's not important." Seth opened a drawer and found a hammer and nails. "I know exactly how I'm going to get even with these clods."

"How?" Jimmy thought it wasn't cool that Seth was just making decisions in a home that wasn't theirs. The girls were rude, maybe, but that didn't make what they were doing now okay.

And he couldn't think of what he could or even should be doing with Cassie.

Seth grabbed the hammer and nails. He walked into one of the girl's bedrooms and opened the closet.

Jimmy didn't like the looks of this. "What are you doing to do?"

Seth nailed a couple of high-heeled shoes to the floor. "Fuckers. I'm so sick of hearing those women walk around up here with their damn shoes on twenty-four-seven."

Jimmy laughed. "Seth, this ain't funny, man. You can't do that. You're going to get us into so much trouble! You know they're going to know that this is us. There's no one else around for them to pin the blame on."

Seth stopped hammering for a moment. "Yeah, there is. We can make it look like a frat prank."

"And how do we do that?"

"Go into all of their drawers and find their panties. Run them underwater and stuff them into the freezer."

Jimmy chuckled uncontrollably. He couldn't believe Seth had said that. He never acted like this before. "You're a very sick boy, Seth. That will make it look a dumb frat prank, but they will still pin the blame on us."

"No, they won't. I've got another idea. You just start looking in their dressers while I finish nailing their shoes to the floor."

Jimmy found the girls' panties. He ran them under the kitchen faucet and threw them into the freezer. Jimmy liked getting even, but he knew this would mean war. After they walked out of the girls' home, he said, "Man, we are so dead."

"No, we're not," Seth said. "I need to go up to the bookstore tomorrow. While I'm there, I'll buy a greeting card. You'll see. If they still think it's us after they find their underwear in the freezer, I'll mail them the card. I'll have them suspecting their best friends."

Jimmy left Seth to head to Traci's apartment to pick her up. The partly cloudy, early October afternoon finally began to cool off a little. Underneath a Titian sky, the leaves in town began to burn a fiery Cezanne still life.

Down the street from campus, not far from Jimmy's home, two pizzerias stood right next to each other, Geribaldi's and Italy's Finest. Large wooden decks stood out in front that the students packed nearly every day. Seth and Jimmy kept a ritual of hitting each one every other time. But today skipped their normal routine. They usually came with Laura and Natalie, and since Laura was no longer there, Jimmy changed it up and hit Geribaldi's twice in a row.

They sat out on the outside deck. Because of the big game, almost no one was there; only a group of five guys sat on the other side of the deck. A waitress came out to them, and they ordered a pitcher. When Traci looked up at the waitress, Jimmy noticed something caught her attention. Once the waitress went inside to get the beer, Traci stepped up to an orange flyer taped to a post.

"Oh, this is freaking tacky," she grumbled.

"What?"

"They're doing a haunted ghost tour here on campus, and they go to this haunted dorm where a girl committed suicide."

Committed suicide? Jimmy thought. *That must be what those sorority girls were talking about.*

Traci sat back down as the waitress brought out their pitcher. They still hadn't decided on what they wanted on their pizza, so the waitress said she'd come back.

Jimmy grabbed the pitcher and poured a glass for Traci. "What's the name of the dorm?"

"Meyer Hall."

"*Meyer Hall?* I just heard about that dorm—"

"Yeah, and they named the girl who had killed herself Christine Walters. "That's—"

Jimmy nearly choked on his beer. "Wait. *What?*"

"Christine Walters," she muttered. "Why?"

Jimmy went over to the flyer and then came back. "*Christine.* Don't you remember? That was the name Laura had written in her notebook."

"Oh, my God," she gasped.

Jimmy sat back down. "I want to sign up for that tour."

Traci reached for her cell phone. "There's an opening later this Monday. There. Got it. We've got a reservation for later this month."

"You want to go, too?"

"Sure. Can't leave you alone at night on campus, can I?"

"Are you sure you want to go back there at night again?"

"No. But we have to figure this out together, don't we? I mean, after everything we've been through to try to find out what happened to Laura—"

"That's what I wanted to talk to you about today. I talked to those sorority girls."

"Yeah, you mentioned that. What did you find out?"

"I—"

"Looky who we found," Jimmy heard to his left.

It was Seth, and Natalie was with him.

What the hell? Jimmy thought. He was just going to tell Traci they should investigate Christine's death. Why was it that once he made plans to do something, he suddenly gets stopped?

Seth said, "Okay, what gives? We're breaking the rule. This is our second stint at Geribaldi's. We're not supposed to break the chain, remember? We're going to make the pizza gods mad. It's supposed to be bad luck. We've been bouncing back and forth like a ping-pong game since we came here."

Jimmy said, "Yeah, well, we always did that with Laura. I wanted a change."

"I see," Seth muttered. "Sorry. Maybe that's a good idea."

Seth and Natalie sat down with them.

Jimmy was so relieved to see Seth, and he seemed like he was in a good mood, too.

"What brings you two here?" Natalie asked.

"We wanted to talk about the story," Jimmy said.

"How's that going?" Seth asked.

Traci flashed a concerned glance at Jimmy. He shook his head.

"Hard to say yet," Traci said. "We're still checking out leads."

Jimmy gave her a wink. *Good girl*, Jimmy thought.

The waitress brought out more glasses and Seth poured two more beers. The four of them decided to order a large pizza with damn near everything on it.

"So, what brings you two here?" Jimmy asked.

"We're celebrating," Natalie said. "I got accepted to the University of Virginia, where I'm going to law school."

They cheered and toasted. Jimmy and Traci congratulated her.

"Are you going to be a big corporate lawyer?" Traci asked.

Natalie drank some of her beer. "No way. I want to help people. Maybe I'll become a lawyer for some legal aid group."

"You're going there too, aren't you, Seth?" Traci asked.

"Yes. I'll be working on my Master's in drawing and painting."

Jimmy was relieved to be reminded of that. All of them needed to leave. The sooner, the better.

"Are you going on to school, Jimmy?" Natalie asked.

"I'm thinking about it. I think I might need a master's in creative writing if I'm going to get a novel published."

"Where?" Traci asked.

"A school in Virginia Beach. I miss the big city. I want to go back."

Traci grinned. "Hey now, really? That's where I'm from. I'm thinking about going there to do an internship."

"Hey, we got to toast this, people," Jimmy said. The four of them raised their glasses.

"You're the second one of us that is going to grad school. May the rest of us continue to have the foresight to see all of our dreams come true."

"Here, here!" the rest of them said.

Jimmy carefully watched Seth's drinking. He hadn't seen Seth down so much so fast since their days in the Knights. "So let's see. We've got us an artist, a writer, a journalist, and now a lawyer. Which one of us is going to become successful first?"

Seth laughed before he gulped some beer. "We'll probably all be dead before that happens."

Traci set her glass down. "Seth, don't say that."

"That's not true, Seth," Natalie said.

Seth chuckled again.

Traci sipped some of her beer. "You look tired, Seth."

Seth downed more beer and finished his glass.

Jimmy was amazed. *Damn, Seth. Did you drink all that, or is there a hole in the glass? What's your rush?*

Seth filled his glass again. "I am tired. And it's all because of those God damn women who live above us."

Jimmy heard them fighting with their boyfriends again this morning as he worked on his computer. "They're getting worse."

Seth said, "I know. I don't really want to call the police, but I'm beginning to believe I'm going to have to."

"Why don't you stay at Natalie's place?" Traci asked.

Seth groaned as Natalie smiled slightly. "I have been some nights. But she lives so far off campus. I prefer to sleep here. I can sleep longer that way when I'm allowed to. I keep thinking those girls will eventually stop fighting."

The waitress brought their pizza out to them and everyone dug in.

Natalie set her beer down. "Okay, now that I've got you drinking beer, eating pizza, you should be feeling pretty good right now, Seth."

Seth groaned. "Here it comes. I knew this had something more than just celebrating."

Jimmy ate some of his pizza and wondered what Natalie was up to now.

"I spoke to my folks yesterday." Natalie hesitated as if she was expecting Seth to blow up.

"Yeah, so?" Seth said. "What's up? There's nothing wrong, is there?"

Natalie wiped her hands. "No, Seth, nothing like that. I just spoke to them, and they said they wanted to visit next weekend. I told them they should be here in town, and they could come here for lunch."

Seth cleared his throat.

Natalie said, "Uh, I mean, sorry, guys. They can come to Italy's Finest across the parking lot, and we can all have pizza and beer together. And the invitation goes to both of you guys."

Jimmy stopped eating his pizza. He wasn't too sure if he liked this idea. He glanced at Traci.

Traci nibbled on a slice. "Oh, I'd love to meet your folks, Natalie."

"I've told my folks all about you, and they've always wanted to meet you. I told them you might be really busy with some of your paintings for a class, so you won't have to stay very long. Does that make you feel better, Seth?"

A stray warm breeze blew by. Birds sang from the trees out in the back of the pizzeria.

Seth gulped his beer. "Yeah, I guess so."

Really, Natalie? Jimmy wanted to say. He was already busy enough with school and trying to find out who or what killed Laura...without getting himself killed. "Gee, I don't know, Natalie," Jimmy said, hoping he sounded a little sarcastic even though he wasn't. He glanced at Traci again. "Do we really want to meet Natalie's parents?"

"Sure we do," Traci said. "We'd love to meet them. Are they from Virginia?"

"No, they live in New York State. They went to school here. My father is a lawyer, and my mother is a judge. Once I got get my law degree, I want to stay here in Virginia. I like it here a lot, but I don't think my folks will be so happy about that, especially my father."

"They don't like the South?" Seth asked.

"No, that's not it. My parents are from there, but they moved here as kids. They went to Morganburg, but they moved back after graduating, and they think a better opportunity is up there. That's why I'm hoping you'll help me, Seth convince them that staying here with you will be best for me."

Seth waved his hand like Zorro holding a sword. "Have no fear. I'll cut through all the Yankee negativity he's used to up there and turn on the charm. He'll feel all the warmth and hospitality of the South coming off me in waves."

Yeah, if he isn't bludgeoned by the drunken vibes shooting out of your pores, Jimmy thought.

He knew they'd have to make sure Seth didn't do any drinking that day. Maybe it was a good idea for Jimmy to tag along. His investigation could wait one day.

Jimmy flashed a look of concern to Traci. "I guess I can come. But I've still got important things I want to get done. I can't make a whole day of it."

Seth drank some beer. "Yep, we both can't."

Natalie finished another piece of pizza. "Don't you guys start. It'll be okay. You'll both be here on your own turf. You'll be involved in your favorite pastime, swilling beer and eating pizza. And you won't be alone, Seth. You'll have a couple of friends, plus me, with you."

"Yeah, I suppose that's true," Seth said.

"You like those odds, don't you?" Natalie asked. "It will be the four of us against the two of them. You won't feel so nervous meeting my folks then, will you? This way you'll have three friends your own age here. You don't think my parents will give you a hard time, do you? They're nice people."

Seth polished off another glass of beer and looked at Natalie for a moment. He snatched his second slice. "No, I suppose they wouldn't. I guess I wouldn't be so nervous then. Okay, let's do it. We might as well get this over with. Your parents are going to really love me."

Jimmy was glad he finally agreed. For a moment, it looked like an argument would break out there that afternoon.

Natalie grinned. "I know they will. Nothing will go wrong, trust me."

Traci asked, "You get along fine with your parents, Nat?"

She sipped her beer. "You bet. They were strict but fair. I never had problems with them. 'Make me proud,' my dad always said to me. I think I have. I sure hope I have."

"That's not what my old man said to me before my mother booted his ass out of our lives," Seth grumbled.

"How come you guys don't want to meet Natalie's parents?" Traci asked.

Seth and Jimmy chuckled bitterly.

"If you had parents like ours, you wouldn't have to ask," Jimmy said. "When we were in high school, it seemed like all adults were out to get us. We hated our parents, our teachers, other parents, the cops, and just adults in general. Why do you think we ended up in a gang after high school?"

"Your parents mistreated you?" Traci asked.

Seth ate like he hadn't all week. "My old man was rough on my mother and me before the split when I was twelve. Let's just say it wasn't fun growing up."

Traci asked, "Have you seen him since?"

"Nope." Seth chugged hard. "Don't miss him. When he'd go into his rages, I'd lock myself in my room, turn up the music and draw."

Natalie frowned. "Gosh, Seth. I didn't realize it was that bad."

Seth shrugged a little. "That's how I found art. And I found there's nothing I couldn't paint. I couldn't control people, but I could create anything I wanted to see. Only beauty. No negativity, no ugliness, no war, and no hate. Through my paintings, I was in my own little peaceful world."

Jimmy noticed four guys sitting in the corner of the deck, right next to the front door. The stacked empty plastic cups like building a plastic tower of Babel. The drunker they got, the louder they became. Jimmy feared if they kept up that kind of drinking and before long, they were going to be in trouble.

"I promise you I haven't seen her ever since," one grumbled. "I got half their fucking kitchen cookware thrown at me the last time I went there."

"Just make sure you stay away," someone else said.

"I keep telling you; I won't damn it. I didn't even go to the game to avoid her."

"Okay, Ernie," one of the guys said. "Take it easy. I got an earful from Michelle because you showed up there."

"She's made it clear to me she doesn't want me around anymore."

The mention of Cassie and Ernie and the fight involving them made it pretty clear what they were talking about. Jimmy decided not to look directly at Seth for a while for fear they'd both break out in uncontrollable laughter.

"Let's just go," someone else grumbled.

They mumbled before shoving their chairs away. They walked behind Jimmy and Seth. They bumped into the backs of their chairs as they left. Seth scooted his seat forward a little.

"Jesus," Seth muttered. "Isn't the aisle big enough? Maybe it's time that bunch lay off the beer and pizza for a while."

"They weren't overweight," Jimmy said. "Dude, I think that was Ernie and the boyfriends of the girls upstairs."

"What's their problem?" Natalie asked.

Seth said, "Those girls upstairs are always fighting with their boyfriends at all hours of the night, I couldn't take it anymore. I called the cops on them. That's not really working, so Jimmy and I found their front door open this morning."

"Oh, my God," Traci gasped. "What did you do?"

"Seth nailed all their shoes to the floor," Jimmy said.

Natalie dropped her pizza back onto her plate. "Have you guys completely lost your minds? That was breaking and entering."

"We knew that," Seth said after he finished his second beer. "We didn't care."

Jimmy raised his hand. "I cared. I tried to warn him."

"And that card you mailed could be construed as harassment, and if that's true, you used the postal service to harass those girls, which could be a federal offense, and you wouldn't want federal charges on your ass, Seth. You could have kissed everything goodbye, including college, a decent living, money, a job, and probably everything else."

"Hell, you don't think I know that?" Seth snapped.

"Then why did you do it?" Natalie demanded.

Seth emptied the pitcher. "You try living beneath that bunch of assholes! Most nights, they're up until three or four in the morning screeching at their boyfriends. I think they got off easy. If I had to put up with clods like that when I was with the Knights, I would have gone up there with a garden hoe and really given those broads something to scream about."

"Seth, you would not and you know it," Natalie said. "The next time they keep you awake, give me a call. You can sleep at my place, just like before. Please don't do into their house again. Honestly, Seth! I don't know what's gotten into you lately. You're not acting like yourself."

Once the frats stormed off, Jimmy noticed a woman sitting at a table with her back to them. Something about her looked familiar. Then she turned around, eyes black, blood gushing from her chest. She grinned and Jimmy's blood ran cold. Prickles formed across his scalp and danced down his body.

Jimmy thought, *My God, it's Laura, and yet—*

"You're not doing that again, right, Jimmy?" Traci said.

Then Jimmy's attention snapped back to the conversation. "Uh, yeah, right." When he looked back, Laura was gone.

Jimmy glanced at Traci. She stared at him. Her smile faded. He knew Traci recognized a look of concern on his face. Seth gunned down beer like some folks drink shots.

"I think we may convince those girls that it was one of their own who was in the house," Jimmy. "But I don't think we're going to convince their boyfriends."

"Yeah, well, we can handle anything that bunch of rednecks can dish out," Seth growled.

Jimmy feared this was going to get a lot worse. He would always be loyal to Seth, and he didn't know how to stop him.

CHAPTER FIFTEEN

Late Sunday morning, Jimmy returned to his apartment to work on reviewing a story submitted to class by one of his classmates. He no longer felt safe in that house so close to the woods, but nothing bizarre happened, so he believed he could work on his computer at home during the day. He believed the best thing for him to do was stay focused on his classes and make the time pass as quickly as humanly possible.

Seth still struggled with a painting, so he said he wanted to take a break by drinking and watching the NFL games.

Jimmy finished his review and was going to start looking up Christine Walters' death when the neighbors came home, and it sounded like they cemented their feet in steel pails. Jimmy came into the living room and Seth grinned.

They heard voices, but they couldn't immediately make anything out. One of the girls walked right over to Seth and Jimmy. "I just want to change before we go out to eat!" she shouted.

Jimmy joined Seth in the living room and held his breath for a few moments. *They're going to be so god damn mad.* It was until they heard a body crash to the floor and hit the back of the closet. Jimmy and Seth laughed hysterically.

"What the fucking hell?" the girl screeched.

Jimmy and Seth laughed even harder but tried to keep their laughter as quiet as possible.

"Oh, my fucking God!" she wailed.

Jimmy laughed so hard he sat down on their threadbare recliner.

"You sure this isn't funny?" Seth asked.

Jimmy couldn't answer him. Both guys now held their hands over their mouths so the girls couldn't hear their laughter.

The girls and their boyfriends rushed to her. "What is it?" one girl asked.

"Some fucking God damn fucking asshole nailed all of my fucking God damn shoes to the God damn fucking floor!"

Seth laughed so hard; he also fell out of his chair. People scrambled to other parts of the house. Seth and Jimmy heard the other two girls scream to the others that they found their shoes nailed to the floor.

"Man, who the fuck did this?" a boyfriend shouted.

Jimmy and Seth still laughed uncontrollably. "Oh, man," Jimmy said. "This was worth it!"

People ran around the house looking for things that were missing or in disorder. Jimmy and Seth finally collected themselves and sat back in their chairs until they heard a girl shout, "What the hell?" Seth and Jimmy struggled to keep from falling out of their chairs again. "God damn it!" she screamed. "You guys, come look at this!"

The crowd rushed into the kitchen. It sounded like a many-legged monster scrambling through the house. "I think they just found their underwear," Seth said. They laughed more.

"Oh, dear Lord," Jimmy gasped. "They're pissed. And you think we're not in trouble with them?"

"Relax. I've got our asses covered."

"You better be right because if we got a problem with the frats, we don't have enough art and English types to help scrape our backsides out of this mess."

"We won't need them. We'll be fine."

Jimmy wasn't so sure about that. He feared Seth was getting ready for war. Moving here hasn't made him better. In fact, Seth was getting even worse.

CHAPTER SIXTEEN

Early in October, things stayed calm and quiet for a couple of weeks. Jimmy started to relax a little. He hoped things were settling down and backing off for a while. Or maybe it's remaining dormant for now to rebuild its power.

Jimmy shuddered at that thought.

As long as nothing bad was happening, he didn't care much. He avoided his apartment as often as possible. He didn't go there or on campus at night. He concentrated on his studies to help make the time go as quickly as possible. If things remained quiet until the end of the semester, he'd be grateful.

The day before Traci reserved their spot to go to Meyer Hall for the haunted Halloween tour, she called him and asked, "Are you sure you still want to see where Christine Walters killed herself? We're going to be on campus at night."

"Yeah. I'm hoping the tour guide can tell us about the evil on campus and what had happened to Christine."

Traci insisted on going with him. He really didn't want to argue. He didn't want to go alone. When she arrived, she wore jeans and an electric blue top that zipped up in front.

Jimmy and Traci drove to the student center to meet their tour guide, Jeff Duncan, a short, pudgy clean-cut kid, exactly the opposite of what Jimmy expected to see on a tour such as this.

"I'm expecting another couple still," Jeff said.

Traci glanced outside. "Back when I first made our reservations," she whispered to Jimmy, "I was excited to see this dorm. Now that it's night and we're on campus, I'm petrified."

Jimmy nodded. He tried to keep himself calm, but his heart wouldn't stop racing. "I hope all the witnesses we're going to have around us were going to keep us safe. Whatever's loose on this campus may have a lot of power, but it attacks like a coward. It waits for people to be alone."

They only waited a few minutes before Amanda and her new boyfriend, Stan, a tall, thin journalism major, joined them. Jimmy said hello to her.

After they drove to Meyer Hall, Amanda whispered to Jimmy, "I always knew you really liked Traci. I think you two will make a great couple."

"A couple?" Jimmy muttered, but Amanda grabbed Stan's arm and walked away before Jimmy could ask what she meant by that, even though he knew.

The university abandoned Meyer Hall, but it kept the lights on inside for security reasons. "I hate going into this building," Roger confessed. "Usually, something weird happens during these tours."

"How long have you been doing this?" Jimmy asked.

Roger unlocked the front door. "This is my third year. I'm a senior, and believe me, after I graduate, I'm out of here."

"You don't like it here?" Traci asked.

"Let's just say there's something about this town that makes me nervous."

Jimmy and Traci glanced at each other.

Jimmy realized it wasn't just them. There were others, Roger, the women upstairs, and maybe many others experiencing unexplainable events.

Roger led the four up to the second floor. "This is where Christine lived back in the middle eighties." They followed Roger down the hall. He unlocked a door to a residency room. "There's not much known about her. She was a goth girl and a loner. Police couldn't find anyone who called Christine a close friend. No one on this floor liked her."

Jimmy said, "I had heard she was into black magic, and she placed a curse on all the frats."

Roger nodded. "She was into black magic. And rumor has it she briefly dated a frat. She thought the guy really cared for her, but the story goes that he was lured into one of the frat houses; he and a couple of his friends made fun of her for being a goth, humiliated her, and raped her. After that, she placed a curse on all the frats."

"But is that true?" Traci asked.

Roger led them to a set of stairs. "I think the whole thing about the frats is mostly Morganburg legend. Let me take you up to her old room, and I'll show you something."

Jimmy shuddered. That story is at least partially true, then. No wonder this place is the way it is.

After Roger led everyone into her room, he said, "I want you to take a look at this wall."

They saw a bunch of brown symbols and words that looked as if they had been painted over.

"Before Christine hanged herself, she slashed her wrists and used her own blood to draw these symbols and this Baphomet here."

"That's awful," Traci said. "Why doesn't someone wash that off?"

"Believe me, the university has tried," Roger said. "They've had maintenance people scrub those off and paint over those symbols numerous times. But those symbols keep reappearing."

Everyone on the tour shuddered and groaned. Jimmy felt a waterfall of shivers cascade down him.

Roger explained, "It's getting so the maintenance people don't even like coming into this building anymore. They complain that they hear and see strange things when they're in here, things like objects floating in the room and banging on the walls and footsteps in the halls. The university right now is considering the idea of just tearing this wall down. In fact, the school is considering a number of ideas. One is to gut this building, and use it for storage. Another is to just level the place."

Jimmy eyed the wall closely. "Do you have any idea if these symbols mean anything?"

"I had a friend who owned books on the occult, and he said they were pagan symbols."

Stan stepped closer to the wall. "What are these words?"

Roger stepped. "Please don't touch this wall. The message is, 'The One with the Devil-Black Eyes Shall Return,' whatever the hell that means."

Devil-Black Eyes. Jimmy felt queasy. He had seen Seth's eyes turn black.

Amanda stepped up to the wall and reached out to touch the symbols.

"Don't do that!" Roger shouted. "Everyone who has touched that wall has committed suicide."

Amanda chuckled. "Oh, come on. You don't really expect us to believe that, do you?"

Roger nodded. "Yes, I do. I've done several tours here. There have been two people who have touched that wall, and both have killed themselves just days after. Please don't touch those symbols."

"Oh, that's just silly," Amanda said before she placed her hands on the symbols.

"Superstitious silliness."

Traci pointed to a closed door. "Is that where Christine killed herself?"

Roger cringed. "I wish you hadn't done that. But yes, that's the bathroom where she hanged herself. We keep that door closed all the time now because maintenance people have said that they've seen a girl hanging in there."

They jumped back when they heard three loud bangs against the bathroom door.

Amanda looked back at Roger and said, "Oh, that's cute! Is this part of the tour? You're trying to scare us? Who's in the bathroom? A frat pledge?"

Roger scrambled back to the front door. "No! Don't open that door, okay? Let's just get out of here."

"Oh, right," Amanda said. "This gag isn't scaring me. It isn't even funny. This is a typical prank you pull every Halloween, isn't it? Once I open that door—" She shrieked, ran out of the room and down the stairs.

Jimmy couldn't get a look at Amanda's face, but her scream seemed real enough.

Stan ran after her. "Honey, what is it? Are you okay?"

Jimmy stood right behind Amanda. Before the door swung slowly closed, he saw a girl hanging from the showerhead. That horrifying specter looked nothing like the woman in black he'd seen on campus. The hanged girl's tangled jet-black hair hung over one side of her sickly cottage cheese-colored face. Black make-up heavily tattooed her eyes and lips. Blood dripped from her wrists. The door slowly opened again, and she pointed at Jimmy and spoke in a choking, deep voice.

"Leave well enough alone, Jimmy. Let it go, or we will destroy you!"

Jimmy felt his stomach lurch. "What the hell?" he mumbled.

"Jimmy, what is it?" Traci tried to push her way by Jimmy. "What did you see? I heard someone in there say your name. Who's in there?"

Jimmy's heart smashed against his rib cage. "No, wait."

"I want to see!" Traci said.

"No, you don't!" Jimmy shoved Traci away from the bathroom. "Come on! We're getting out of here."

The girl's body swung. Then she floated and ripped the noose apart.

"Jimmy—!" Traci said as she tried to push Jimmy out of the way, but Jimmy forced Traci out of the room.

Roger screamed, "Oh, my God!" and slammed the door. "Fuck! I don't believe it! Fuck! Fuck! Fuck!" Roger pushed his way past Jimmy and Traci on the stairs and kept running.

They rushed down the stairs and joined Roger, Amanda, and Stan.

"What was that about?" Traci asked. "Why wouldn't you let me look?"

"My God," Amanda gasped. "I saw a girl hanging from the ceiling!"

"Where's the nearest exit?" Jimmy asked.

"It's at the end of the hall and down the stairs here in the back," Roger said.

They sprinted down the hallway to the staircase.

Jimmy heard a door open upstairs, and footsteps descend the stairs. A long shadow of a figure reached the bottom of the steps.

The girl sang in a high but scratchy voice, "Someone's going to die tonight."

Roger tried to open the door, but it wouldn't budge. "Oh, my God! I don't know how to get out of here! We're trapped!" He crumpled to the floor.

Oh, crap, Jimmy thought. He's having a panic attack. I'm going to have to find a way out of here.

Jeff and Amanda helped Roger to his feet.

"Jimmy," a girl called at the end of that hall behind them. It was Laura. Oh, thank God. Right when I need you. "This way!"

Jimmy ran down the hall.

Traci screamed, "Jimmy, what are you doing? Don't go to her!"

Laura reached out to him and grabbed his hand. He shrieked. It felt like she jammed a hot pin beneath his fingernail, and fissures of searing pain shot up his arm. Her nails dug into his flesh, and blood rolled down his arm. Darkness wrapped around the corner, and she pulled him back to it. Laura's eyes blackened. A choking, gurgling sound emanated from her mouth as her face darkened and contorted. Her lips formed a sickly grin.

It's Christine!

"Come on, Jimmy," she said with a gravelly voice. "Join us." She jerked him back as the encroaching Darkness nearly reached the tips of his feet. He struggled to break free of her burning grasp as the Darkness blacked out the end of the hallway and billowed up behind her.

He kicked her in the chest, and she doubled over. He ran back to the others.

This evil here can force us to see what it wants us to see.

"Oh, God, I don't know what to do!" Roger cried.

Jimmy said, "We're getting away from that vision! That's what we're going to do."

Christine's maniacal laughter echoed behind them as they ran down a long hallway and turned the corner to find a door.

Stan tried to open it. "I don't know why these doors won't open! They're only supposed to unlock from the outside. They shouldn't lock them from the inside. I don't know how we're going to get out of here!"

Jimmy yanked a fire extinguisher down from the wall. "I do."

He slammed it against a window. It took three times before the glass cracked open. A security alarm blared so loudly Jimmy feared it would damage his hearing. But he knew the alarm would bring the cops. Jimmy cleared away the broken shards of glass clinging to the edge of the window frame.

"Everyone out now!" Jimmy shouted.

"But—" Stan started to say.

"Go!" Jimmy ordered. "Just go!" he walked a couple of steps towards the end of the hall. He saw a shadow creeping around the corner.

"Oh, Jimmy?" a girl sang mockingly. "Come here. I want you to come play with me!"

Jimmy fired the extinguisher at the end of the hall. He didn't think that would do any harm to whatever or whoever crept around the corner, but he wouldn't be able to see that grisly vision again. Stan was the last person to crawl out of the window. Jimmy launched the fire extinguisher down the hall and jumped out the window. After he got outside, he motioned for everyone to get back.

"Keep going!" Jimmy shouted. "Get as far away from the building as you can!"

"That's the last time I do a tour here," Roger gasped. "The hell with it. No pay is worth that!"

Jimmy bent to a knee and caught his breath.

"Look!" Roger said.

Jimmy gazed up. A girl looked out a second-floor window. He spotted the dark figure standing by a tree across the street. He glanced back up at the window, and the girl ran away. The dark figure vanished.

"Is everyone all right?" Jimmy asked. Roger, Stan, and Traci said they were. He didn't hear from Amanda. He couldn't see her. "Wait a minute. Where's Amanda?"

They looked around.

Roger sat down on the ground. "She's over there beneath that tree." He wiped tears from his face. "I knew this was going to happen one day. Someone was going to touch those symbols, and we'd see Christine hanging there."

Amanda sat back against the tree, her her arms wrapped around her knees. Jimmy knelt beside her. "Amanda, are you all right?"

"I'm okay. I'm okay. I'm okay," she said. Her eyes stared straight ahead, and she didn't look at him.

They waited for the police. Jeff explained to the officers what had happened. The cops had that funny, gray look in their eyes. Their look really creeped out Jimmy, and he couldn't wait to get away from them. The police searched for the girl but found no one. After the cops were done with their search, one of them pulled Doug aside to speak to him.

Another one got Jimmy alone and said, "You've had plenty of warning, Jimmy Durham. Now take Traci and leave Morganburg before something happens to you and all your friends."

Jimmy shivered. *This force has control of the police, too.*

He got Traci and left for her apartment.

Once inside her home, Jimmy sat down on her couch and hung his head. "This place is one giant nut house."

She got him an extra blanket. "You might as well just stay here from now on. It's too dangerous to be on or near campus."

He nodded. "What did we just see back there?"

He shook his head. "I don't know what we saw. Pure evil possesses this town. And I don't know how to describe what I saw. I never believed in any of this kind of crap before."

She sat down next to him. "You know you can stay here for as long as you like." She parted the curtains to glance outside. "Do you think we're safe here?"

"I think so. We're far from campus."

"What did that cop say to you?"

"To take you and get the hell out of here."

"Really?" she exclaimed.

"Yeah."

"Whatever's here, it's got the campus police, maybe the school administration, and who knows who else."

"Yeah," he muttered. He wondered if Dr. Johnson wasn't trying to insinuate that when he told them about Rudy and the campus.

She held his hand and squeezed it. "What's going to happen to us?"

"I'll tell you what's going to happen. We're getting the hell out of here as soon as our classes are done. We're not going to graduation. I'm not even sure we should stay here for the final semester. I'm leaving. You're leaving. And Seth and Natalie are coming with us."

They stared at each other for several moments.

Jimmy believed if there was no Laura, he could really love her. He really could.

She asked, "If we leave, what about our final classes?"

"That's what I'm going to have to check. I think we can go to another college and have our remaining classes transferred. If not, I'm willing to move back to Virginia Beach and just commute every day. The hell with it. Nothing we're going through here is worth it."

"Okay," she held his hand. "I'm going to bed. I'm not sure if I can sleep, but I have to get up tomorrow." She kissed him on the cheek. "Good night," she whispered.

He watched her walk to her bedroom, and she glanced back at him before she went into her room.

CHAPTER SEVENTEEN

For a week, Jimmy tried to find Seth with no luck. He left Seth messages, but he never called back. He wanted to talk to Seth about what he saw at Meyer Hall.

But was that such a good idea? Seth wouldn't believe him about the black fog. Jimmy feared Seth would really ridicule him for telling Seth what Traci and he saw at the dorm.

Reluctantly, he returned to the apartment to work on his computer. Finally, he found Seth at home. He was working on a painting in his room. And judging by his swearing, it didn't sound like it was going well.

Seth came into the living room. "Well, well," Seth muttered. "Loverboy is back. Looks like things are going well with you and Traci."

The comment infuriated Jimmy. He was going to tell him he wasn't cheating on Laura even though Laura was dead.

Before he could let Seth have it, the upstairs neighbors came home. One woman ran to the center of the house, slammed her heel down onto the floor three times, and ran back out. Cars started up and drove off.

Jimmy thought this was going to get ugly. "No, Seth," he said sarcastically. "They definitely don't think what they found upstairs was because of us. We actually have them believing that it was us, not a frat prank. Now we're never going to get any sleep at night ever again."

"I told you to be cool." Seth removed a greeting card from a dresser drawer in his room and brought it out into the living room. He sat at the table.

"What are you writing?" Jimmy knew he should be working on his homework, but he was procrastinating.

"Dig this," Seth said after he put his pen down.

The cover read, "What's new with you?" Jimmy read what Seth wrote. "Dear Michelle, Elizabeth and Mary Anne, the three of us came by your place last Saturday, but you weren't home—" Jimmy glanced at him. "The three of us? Who's that?"

"I'm just trying to throw them off a little more. If we want them to believe it was a frat prank, then I think we should have them believing it was more than two people."

"The door was unlocked, so we let ourselves in. We knew you wouldn't mind. You didn't come back, and we got bored, so we decided to amuse ourselves. We know you girls are mad.

"Girls, don't be mad! It was just a joke! We realized you didn't suspect a thing when we saw you on campus. You girls are so sweet to us. We love you. We're sorry we made you upset. We don't want anyone who wears bras and panties as sexy as yours to be mad at us."

Jimmy thought this was the nastiest thing he ever read. He threw the card at Seth. "Jesus, Seth. You're one sick puppy. After all these years, I never knew there was a perverted side to you."

Seth chuckled like an evil troll. "I'm only trying to sound like a dumb ass frat who would do something stupid like that. I'm going to sign it, 'Guess who?'" Seth sealed the envelope. "I'll mail this. They should get it in a couple of days."

Jimmy shook his head. "I hope you're right about this."

"I am, believe me. They'll think it's some of their friends, or they will believe their friends will know who it is. You'll have them questioning some of their friendships."

Jimmy frowned. "I think you're turning back into the Seth I knew on the streets."

Seth chuckled before he grabbed a beer. "They don't know who they're messing with."

Cars sped back to the house. Several people burst into the residence upstairs and walked all around the house.

Seth smirked and gulped some beer. "That was just too obvious, girls."

Seth wasn't just acting like his old self. He was also drinking like in the old days. And his drinking picked back up right after they moved to this house. Jimmy wanted to talk to him about leaving Morganburg, but not while he was drinking like that and when he was in such a mean mood.

Is it just because the neighbors kept him up the past several nights, or is something else influencing his behavior?

A couple of days later, Jimmy returned to the house to work on a story for a creative writing class. When he checked the mail, he recognized a certain envelope addressed to the upstairs residence. Jimmy went into his apartment. He hadn't eaten all day, and as long as he was there, he wanted lunch before he returned to school. When Jimmy was in the kitchen, he heard one of the girls go to the center of the house and come back to the kitchen upstairs.

"Oh, my God!" she said. "You won't believe this! Whoever was in this house wrote us a letter! Listen to this…" Jimmy chuckled as she read the letter aloud. "Can you believe that?" she said. Jimmy heard their phone ring, and that girl picked it up. "Whoever was in your house just sent us a letter," she said again. "Listen to this…" She read the entire card over the phone. "Can you believe that?" As Jimmy made his turkey and cheese sandwich, he heard the phone ring three times. The girl read the card over the phone to everyone. "Can you believe that?" she asked over and over again. "Do you swear you don't know who this is?" the girl asked all of her friends. Jimmy ate his sandwich, drank a Coke, and listened to the girls talk to each other. He couldn't make out everything they said, but in that old house, you could hear a lot.

"Maybe this is some sort of secret fraternity sect pulling a prank," one of the girls said, "like the Skulls and Swords."

"Or maybe it's just a few jerks who want us to think it's a fraternity sect," another one said.

"But who could it be?" another girl asked.

The three girls kicked around several names. Jimmy laughed as he realized Seth pulled it off. He got the heat off them. And now they suspect their own friends.

After the girls said several names aloud, they were quiet for a while. Then they said together,

"Ernie!"

"That's who it must be!" one girl said. "Ernie and a couple of his friends. Ernie can't get over the fact that he and Cassie are over, and he's always hated us because we've been protecting her and trying to find a new boyfriend for her."

Jimmy's lunch filled him. He laughed as he threw his dishes into the sink. He was relieved that Seth got the heat off them. That should solve that problem permanently. His laughter died after he walked into his room. Seth sat in his bedroom talking to Natalie. They started to argue, and Jimmy didn't want to hear it. He finished his story, submitted it to Blackboard, and went to Traci's.

Jimmy shared a late afternoon lit class with Rafe and Pete. As they walked out of class together, Rafe said, "We need to make a short film for class."

As they stepped out of the building, Pete said, "But we're having trouble with ideas for our scripts."

Rafe said, "You're a creative writing major, and you get A's in your classes. Would you be willing to look at what we've got written so far?"

"Sure. Let me see them when you get a chance."

They walked by the law building and in front of the Main Library.

"We were hoping to have you look at them now, like maybe in the library."

Jimmy checked his watch and chuckled. "Guys, it's getting late in the afternoon and I never hang out here once the sun goes down."

"Why?" Rafe asked.

"You guys wouldn't believe me if I told you."

"Try us," Pete said.

They stopped at the library.

Jimmy shoved his hands into his coat pockets. "Okay, I saw this black fog come out of the woods behind the art building."

The guys laughed.

"Black fog?" Rafe snickered.

"See," Jimmy said. "You don't believe me." He started to walk away.

Pete grabbed his arm. "Now wait. Tell us more."

"If you don't believe me, you can ask Traci. She saw it, too. And it nearly grabbed her. I got to her just in time. When she got into my car and we sped off, the stuff rammed my car."

The guys glanced at each other.

"Seriously?" Rafe asked.

"Yeah. And I've seen this Civil War soldier on campus at night. But his face doesn't look human. That's why I won't stay here after dark. This place gets weird and dangerous once the sun goes down."

They headed to the library parking lot, where the guys parked their cars.

Rafe said, "The Civil War soldier is likely just a frat pulling a prank."

"Yeah, but the black fog I want to see," Pete said.

"So do I." Rafe opened his trunk and pulled out a film camera. "If that shit's real, I want to get it on film."

"Yeah, and that could help me with my class project," Pete said. "I like horror. And I'm writing a horror script."

What was going on campus still gnawed at Jimmy. If he had the Black Knights with him, he wouldn't be afraid to go anywhere or find out anything that was going on around campus, including who killed Laura. But the Knights were so far away, and he hadn't doubted they could come without much notice, but they're not right there all the time. If Jimmy wasn't going it alone, he wouldn't be so afraid. Rafe and Pete feared nothing. If they captured the black fog or any other paranormal events on film, that would not only give him something documented proof to the police that something dangerous was here at night, but then maybe Seth would realize they needed to leave Morganburg.

"Are you guys afraid to be on or around campus late at night?" Jimmy asked. He thought it if he could just make it sound fun, they might be into it.

Rafe chuckled. "We're not afraid of anything here at night. We've been out late at bars and around campus all the time."

"If we see those Greek fucks dancing around in their costumes, we'll punch them in the face!"

Jimmy forced a grin. *Maybe now I can finally get some answers.* "Sounds good."

CHAPTER EIGHTEEN

Jimmy grabbed a copy of The Black and Blue from a nearby newsstand, and he waited with Rafe and Pete on the front steps of the Main Library for dusk to turn to night. A cool breeze blew by in the fresh, crisp air. A few scattered yellow and red leaves scooted down the sidewalk. The passing leaves were the only things out there.

Jimmy sat down and opened the paper. "Jesus," he breathed.

"What's wrong?" Rafe asked.

"Deanna has been reported as missing," Jimmy said.

Pete turned on his camera and checked to see if it was recording. "Really? I haven't seen her in a few days."

"Neither have I," Rafe said. "I wondered what happened to her."

Jimmy feared what could've happened to her.

Just as he was reading about some sort of fall festival brunch the Tri Delts were hosting in their backyard in two weeks, a woman's scream echoed across the campus. Waves of goose flesh traveled down the length of Jimmy's body.

Are we actually witnessing a student being attacked? "You guys hear that?" Jimmy exclaimed.

"I did," Pete said. "You'd have to be deaf not to. It sounded like it was over by the student center and the bookstore."

"Let's check it out," Rafe said.

They sprinted around between the Main Library and the law library. They ran through the journalism-psychology complex and to the student center.

"See her?" Jimmy asked.

Pete and Rafe said no.

They heard the woman scream again, but it came from the direction of the library. Jimmy gasped. "Look!"

Rafe and Pete whirled around. They saw someone dressed as a Civil War soldier making his way up the steps of the journalism-psychology complex.

Jimmy felt his knees turn weak. My God, he's actually floating. I've never seen anything like that before.

"Holy crud," Rafe said. "Are you guys seeing what I'm seeing?"

"Yes!" Jimmy and Pete said.

"Is that the soldier you were talking about?" Rafe asked.

"Yeah," Jimmy breathed.

"You getting this?" Rafe asked.

Pete aimed his camera at them. "You better believe it."

They ran after the figure. They got to the complex and then heard something growl loudly.

"What the hell was that?" Rafe exclaimed.

"I don't know, but it sounded like it came from the political science building," Pete said.

They sprinted down the steps and toward the art building, but they found nothing. They heard another scream that sounded like it came from the courtyard. So they ran in that direction.

This time they saw a row of four Civil War soldiers march around the campus chapel, but when they ran around there, they found nothing. They heard another scream again, this time back near the football field. But this sounded like it was neither human nor animal, like huge, jagged machinery grinding against another metal surface. Once again, they chased after it but found nothing.

They saw a shadow figure running by the bookstore heading in the direction of the courtyard. The figure moved at an inhuman speed. Again the guys chased after him but couldn't find anything.

"Damn it!" Rafe shouted. "Where'd he go?"

Jimmy leaned against on the short brick wall that surrounded part of the Main Library and caught his breath. Jimmy thought his heart was trying to pound a hole through his chest.

The guys heard another scream. This time it sounded as though she was past the football stadium and student center and near the science building.

"Let's go," Rafe said.

"No way," Jimmy said.

"What?" Rafe asked.

Jimmy waved him off. "I mean it. I'm sick of this. I'm not running all over campus chasing a disembodied scream that floats all around this university like those Civil War soldiers and that shadow figure. You guys saw what I did. I'm satisfied. Now I know I'm not going nuts. If you guys want to keep running around campus, fine. But I'm done."

Rafe turned to Pete. "Want to keep going?"

"Hell, yeah. This is cool!"

"Good luck, guys," Jimmy said. "I hope you get that black fog caught on camera. I really do. Just stay the hell away from it. And if you do, I want to see it. I'm showing it to the police and to Seth."

"Okay," the guys said.

They said goodbye to Jimmy and ran off after the invisible screaming woman and left Jimmy standing by the wall outside the library parking lot. He quickly headed to his car, and he looked down to see bloody footprints on the sidewalk.

"What the hell?" he mumbled.

The sidewalk turned bloodier the closer he walked to the library. The prints turned into puddles. So much blood ran down the sidewalk it looked like a hog had been slaughtered in the library parking lot. He suddenly remembered he was alone again on campus at night. He hopped over the wall and ran across the parking lot to his car. Jimmy heard a man scream again.

He turned to look, casting his vision across the vaguely illuminated outline of the Main Library parking lot. From the darkness below the buildings imposing rim, the figure of a soldier shambled toward him, slow and stumbling. Jimmy gulped involuntarily, his body crying out for moisture inside his rapidly drying throat.

As he turned back to face the car, another scream ran out, and a blast of hatred and agony punched right into his ear. It was way too close. Startled, Jimmy simultaneously spun and jumped back. His legs danced an uncoordinated St. Vitus Dance; he tripped, falling to the ground. He looked up from his sprawled position, and before he floated the source of the scream, another soldier, his figure outlined by the parking lot's lights like some kind of demented angel. The soldier floated forward, head hanging loose on his neck as if the corpse were suspended from wires, and this was some kind of grotesque stage trick. This one looked like someone had chopped and gutted him with a machete. Profuse amounts of blood dripped from his mutilated face. Bloody pieces of flesh hung from his head, and blood-soaked bits of muscle fell to the ground in front of Jimmy's feet.

Jimmy scrambled backward and stood as quickly as the onset of panic would allow. Glancing to the right, he saw the first soldier moving closer. And more were coming from the courtyard.

"Jimmy," they called like a groaning chorus of the dead.

The mutilated one moaned, "Get out of Morganburg, or I'm going to do to you what I did to Laura."

Then their mocking laughter echoed in his ears.

Jimmy was horrified. As he opened the door, he heard two people scream. They sounded like Rafe and Pete. He jumped into his car and jammed the keys into the ignition. The soldier floated up to the car. The figure reached out and wiped a bloody smear across Jimmy's window. Her bony hand scraped like a jagged piece of rock. Jimmy sped around the campus. He thought he had eluded them, but then the soldiers appeared in front of him, and they floated to his car again. Jimmy sped around them and fled the university to Traci's apartment, giving up on Rafe and Pete.

Jimmy hoped she'd be home. He buzzed her door until she answered.

"Yes?"

"Get your ass down here!" Jimmy screamed.

"Jimmy, is that you?"

"Yes, God damn it! Get down here now!"

Traci ran out to Jimmy. She wore a robe and tennis shoes like she was just getting ready for bed. "My God, Jimmy! What's wrong? You're so pale and sweaty; you look as if you've been swimming."

"Come here. I want you to see something." Jimmy grabbed Traci's wrist and jerked her to his car. He needed her to see the blood so she'd take him seriously. Her wrist felt cold. She smelled good, like she used a nice body wash.

"Jimmy, what are you doing? You're hurting me!"

He loosened his grip. "I'm sorry, all right? But I need you to see this." Jimmy led her to his car and pointed at the window. "There! Do you see that? Do you?"

"Good God, what happened?"

"So you see that?"

"Yes, I see that! It looks like a bloody smear. What's going on? What did you do?"

Jimmy ran his finger through the blood and drew a bloody line above the smear. He felt the blood between his fingers. He couldn't believe it. That blood should've dried on the drive to Traci's place. He looked at her. "Did you see that smear I just made?"

"Yes, Jimmy! Where did it come from?"

"That right there is definitely not a hallucination! If you're real, then so is that blood on my car."

"I agree. Now will you tell me where it came from?"

"I need a drink, like, right now. Have you got any booze in your apartment? Make me a drink, and I'll tell you all about it." He didn't want to be that guy who needed a drink in order to think, but he figured he deserved a drink tonight. Hopefully, it would at least get him to calm down a little.

"Did you hit someone?"

Jimmy's whole body trembled. He felt awful that she had to ask him that, that she thought he'd be the kind of person who hit someone and ran. "No, and I wish it was only that bad. I can't just have a beer. I need hard liquor. Have you got that?"

"Yes, come on." Traci grabbed Jimmy's hand and pressed his arm to her breast.

He collapsed on her couch. He couldn't control the shaking in his hands. Traci poured him a Jack and Coke. He slammed the whole glass.

"Honey, you got to make this stuff stronger."

She made him another one, looking concerned. She filled the glass half full of whiskey.

Jimmy recoiled after he got a sip. It burned his throat. "I'm sorry," she said. "You said you wanted it stronger."

"No, don't be sorry. Really, this is exactly what the doctor ordered." Jimmy gulped. He ran his hand through his hair and breathed like he had run from campus to her apartment.

"Now, will you tell me what happened?"

He feared he'd freak her out as much as he was. "I saw this Civil War soldier on campus. He was bloody, hacked to pieces. He ran his bloody hand across my window." Jimmy gulped more of his drink. "I swear, the more I try to find answers, the worse things I see. And I don't understand why I'm seeing these things. None of it makes any sense."

"I don't know what to tell you, Jimmy. How did this start?"

"Rafe and Pete wanted to see this weird crap for themselves. And they did. They can tell you they did."

"Okay, but those boys have a weird sense of humor. Are you sure it wasn't a prank?"

Jimmy still breathed heavily. He glared at her. "Pranks don't float! Blood doesn't stay wet on a car window when you drive across town! The research I've been doing for the article is over! I really mean it." He thought of the dark figure with the hollow eyes. It seemed like the figure knew he was chasing it, the demon or curse or whatever it was. Because he wanted to find Laura's murderer, and he thought maybe he had. And he didn't want to chase it anymore.

Traci sat down and squeezed his hand. "But Jimmy—"

"No buts!"

"Jimmy, there are a lot of people who want to see you follow up on what you've been—"

Jimmy gulped the last of his drink. "Forget it! I'm a college student who wants to be a writer. I want to graduate and get the hell out of here while I still have a choice in the matter."

Traci cradled her knees up against her chest and stared at him. "Okay," she whispered.

CHAPTER NINETEEN

That whole week, Jimmy tried to call Rafe and Pete, but he couldn't reach them. He wasn't sure if those guys were playing a joke on him or if something really happened to them. He was pretty sure he'd heard screaming and that they weren't joking by pretending they'd heard it, too.

Jimmy tried to find Seth, but he wasn't at home. He called Natalie. Natalie said she only saw him Saturday night. She was very busy studying for a big poli sci exam. Jimmy didn't like that; not even she knew Seth's whereabouts. It wasn't like Seth to disappear. Where was Seth for the entire weekend? He hoped to see Seth that day in their martial arts class. Jimmy returned to the campus paper offices and told Ed Frank he quit.

Ed smiled coldly. "You sure that's what you want to do?"

Jimmy noticed a funny gray look in Frank's eyes. "Yeah."

"Okay, I understand."

Jimmy shuddered and left without saying another word. He walked back to the courtyard. It was a gorgeous day, sunny and in the upper sixties. A couple of disjointed, fluffy clouds floated across the sky. They reminded Jimmy of the couple he had seen the night before. He walked across the campus to his class.

Jimmy thought about everything he'd seen lately. Was there really a point to it all?

He saw a guy with long, dark hair who looked draped in his own funeral shroud and then a woman who looked the same. He saw some weird-looking dude wearing only a skirt. He saw a floating soldier that looked hacked to pieces, but Rafe and Pete saw it too or said they did. He saw faces change on a chimney, and Traci said she did as well. Was all of that due to the curse those sorority girls told him about? Was everything he had seen the cause of demons? It just didn't add up.

He felt fine until he began his newspaper story. Now he had nightmares every night when he could sleep. The violence above was growing even worse.

There's a big wide world out here to run around in. Look at it out here. It's beautiful. Jimmy believed he should be outside eating lunch and reading a good book. He should enjoy his time in college. He should work hard and learn but also enjoy his freedom. Instead, he was getting himself scared out of his wits, chasing after bloody phantoms and insane visions. Was this really worth it?

Was his mind really in danger if he stayed here, or was his life in jeopardy if he continued to try to figure out what was going on here in Morganburg? Had he been suffering hallucinations or seeing these strange visions because there was a force in the town that didn't want him to find something evil spreading here?

Jimmy glanced at the cemetery between the art and political science buildings. He stopped and looked back at the Department of Art. Rudy apparently died from trying to find answers here. What was he could he have been looking for?

Did he want to write that this town was possessed, and that was why he was murdered?

"Jimmy," someone said behind him. He was so lost in thought; he wasn't even paying attention. "Jimmy! Hello? Earth to Jimbo."

Jimmy spun around. He had raised his fist up close to his face, ready to fire a punch toward someone's throat or face. He expected to see that bloody couple standing behind him. Instead, it was Seth holding his hands up to show he was unarmed and looking startled.

"Jesus, Jimbo," Seth said. "Take it easy, man. I didn't mean to scare you. What are you doing? You're standing out here as if you're in a fog."

"Christ, Seth, what are you doing sneaking up behind me?"

"I wasn't sneaking up behind you. I kept saying your name, but you weren't hearing me."

Jimmy frowned. "I guess my head is somewhere else today." He didn't think Seth would pull his leg about something like that. "I'm sorry. Let's go to class."

As they passed by the student center, Seth asked, "What were you thinking about?"

"Rudy."

"Rudy? Why that guy?"

Jimmy told him about the floating couple he wanted to get on tape and why. "I finally gave up. I got sick of the wild goose chase. But they chased after that creepy couple. I heard two people scream. It sounded like Rafe and Pete. I've been trying to call. Have you seen them?"

"No. They weren't in class today. Do you really think something happened to them?"

Jimmy felt his stomach turn. "I hope not. After what I've learned about Rudy and—" He didn't want to tell Seth about Christine or the soldiers. Seth wouldn't believe him about the black fog. "Well, getting really nowhere on research, and now that Pete and Rafe might be missing, I've decided to give up. Maybe it's a coincidence that I started seeing all this crap after I decided to investigate, but I'm done."

"I don't know everything you've seen, but Rafe and Pete missing class isn't exactly unheard of with them. But if you think you should give up, then do it. If it doesn't feel right and you don't like it, or think it's too dangerous, then maybe it is time for you to set that aside and move on."

Jimmy and Seth walked past the student center to the gymnasium. They needed phy. ed. classes to graduate. They didn't care for a lot of sports, so they both grabbed PE credits in the two things they were involved in since they were in the Black Knights, weightlifting, and martial arts. After they put on their white uniforms and yellow belts, they stretched out before their taekwondo class began.

"You look like hell again, by the way," Jimmy said. "Were you out drinking last night?"

"No, all night long I was tossing and turning with nightmares."

"Nightmares? Do you remember what were they about?"

"I was out in the woods," Seth said. "And there were these decaying bodies littered everywhere like there had been a war. And this guy with really long dark hair came out of the darkness and pointed his finger at me as if I was to blame for all of that, or he wanted me to do something about it. Somehow in the dream, I was the murderer."

Jimmy shivered. This guy with dark hair was everywhere, even in dreams. "Sounds like that guy you saw in behind the house."

"Yeah, that's exactly who it looked like. I don't know why I keep dreaming about him. I wish I would stop. That dream gives me the creeps."

Jimmy finished stretching. "Do you believe in ghosts?" He wasn't sure how to tell Seth that the dark figure was real, not just a dream. Maybe if he could convince Seth the figure was real, they could both move out and get away from the malevolent spirit, whatever it was.

Seth smirked. "Ghosts? I believe in the human spirit. And I think when people see ghosts, they see the spirit of that person. But I think it's people who are more haunted and not places or homes."

Jimmy shook out his arms and legs. "Maybe when some spirits don't feel like they are being listened to, they get really pissed. That shadowy guy, I think we've both seen, looks really upset. I just don't know why."

"So what are you saying?" Seth asked. "You think we're seeing ghosts?"

"I'm beginning to like that idea more than that we're suffering from hallucinations. Multiple people have the same hallucination, so it doesn't make sense to think that. Or maybe we're haunted and we're picking up some psychic traces from the past."

Seth sat down and stretched his legs. "Have you tried looking up the history of the university?"

"Dude, I've been in the library for days, and I've been on the internet. I've got no idea what makes this place any different. I thought it was chemicals, but no."

"Well, you're in the right place, man. This school is full of books."

Jimmy believed that was part of his problem. "Hell, I can see that. I go into the library and I just stand there and wonder where to begin. I'm overwhelmed. There are five floors and each floor has shelf upon shelf filled with books. I could spend years here reading and the information I want might not even be in those books."

Seth placed his leg on Jimmy's shoulder and stretched. "Ask for help."

"I have already. It didn't get me anywhere. If only I knew exactly what I was looking for. No matter how much I read, I'm still in the dark. I feel like I'm stranded out in the middle of the ocean and I can only see water. There's no land in sight."

"I know if you need a history book; as I recall, the history books are on the third floor."

He felt a wave of annoyance. "Yeah, I know that. But do you know how many books there are on one floor? I've found plenty of American history books and textbooks on Virginia's history. But I'm not sure if I need a history book on people or businesses or events."

"You know who I think you should talk to?" Seth asked. "Go see Dr. Johnson. He likes to read history, and he can tell you anything you want to know about Morganburg."

"Okay, I'll do that right after class." Before he left, he said, "Hey, Seth, we have to talk soon."

"About what?"

"Leaving Morganburg."

Seth smiled. "Jimmy, don't you know? We're here for life."

Seth walked off.

Jimmy shivered. That didn't even sound like his voice.

After class, Jimmy stopped by Dr. Johnson's office. Jimmy figured his article-writing days were over, but that didn't mean he still couldn't satisfy his own curiosity. Dr. Johnson sat at his desk when Jimmy told him he wanted to ask him a few questions.

Dr. Johnson set down his history book about Venice and smiled. "Have a seat. What do you want to know?"

Jimmy's chair hissed like an angry cat after he sat down. He thought about the cemeteries. If there were ghosts, maybe the cemeteries had something to do with it. "I always wanted to know why is that old cemetery between this art building and the poli sci department?"

Dr. Johnson's smile faded. "A lot of students are curious about that little graveyard. That's the original cemetery of this town. Morganburg was originally centered here on campus. As the university expanded, it built up around the graveyard."

Jimmy noticed a Playboy calendar hung on Dr. Johnson's wall. "Why didn't they just remove it?"

"They couldn't, and they can't. It's unlawful to knowingly dig up a graveyard. When this art building was being built, they dug up a bunch of old bones. So they stopped construction. State and county officials were called in to remove the bones."

That stunned Jimmy. That meant he was literally standing on top of a former graveyard. "What happened then?"

"They were buried in one of the cemeteries just outside of the campus. It was believed the bones were either bodies of slaves from the people buried right next door, you know, their bodies were just dumped in a mass grave, or those bones were from Yankee soldiers thrown in an unmarked mass grave during the Civil War."

"Jesus," Jimmy muttered. "So you're saying the Civil War was fought right through this town? Civil War soldiers died on this land?"

Dr. Johnson shuffled some papers and placed them in a box on his desk. "Jimmy, the Civil War was fought all over this state. It's a given the war marched through here. It started on what is now fraternity and sorority row. There was a bloody battle in this town that killed a couple of hundred men. I know someone at the history department who can tell you more."

Jimmy squirmed. He remembered the soldier he saw in that art building. Was there a man trapped there? A ghost didn't go where spirits are meant to when they die? "What became of Morganburg during the war?"

Dr. Johnson grunted. "It was burned to the ground."

"What else can you tell me about this town?"

"I can tell you several things. Are you looking for anything specific?"

"What do you know of Morganburg prior to the folks who moved here and built it?"

Dr. Johnson set some books on a shelf. "Prior to that? Next to nothing. It was all wooded land. Tribal America ruled here. Look, if you want to know about Virginia and this area, the state history books are on the third floor of the Main Library. There I'm sure you'll find whatever it is you're looking for."

Jimmy nodded. "Thanks." Before he left, he asked, "When are you planning to vote to get those woods cleared out of here?"

Dr. Johnson frowned and nodded. "Just as soon as this fall semester ends."

Jimmy felt an icy cold breeze cut through him. The wind blew through the hallway from the studio beside him. The balcony door was open. He saw the forest through the window. The trees whispered in the breeze. Their branches touched like they spread messages to each other.

CHAPTER TWENTY

That Saturday, Jimmy slept in late at Traci's. When he got home, he jumped on his computer, proofed his second short story, and emailed it off. Ever since he decided to give up his newspaper story, he suffered no hallucinations or weird visions. Nothing scary happened to him. He would feel great, except that Rafe and Pete have been reported missing. He was the last person to have seen them. The police had nothing useful to say.

When he was done, Seth was already up and drinking a soda in the kitchen.

Jimmy said, "Let's go. Pizza time, remember?"

He wished Seth would hurry up. Traci, Natalie, and her parents waited at the pizza joint.

Seth dragged his tail all morning. Jimmy drove to the post office just to waste some time. He thought Seth would be done showering and getting ready by now, but he was still drinking lots of water to rid himself of cottonmouth from last night's bingeing. Jimmy got into Seth's car and waited for him to finish drying all his long curls.

"I really don't want to do this," Seth moaned after he got into his car. "Not only do I not want to meet Natalie's parents, but she also picked a football Saturday to do it. Morganburg has a home game today. And you know the pizza places are going to be packed."

Oh, Jesus. Jimmy could smell alcohol on Seth. "Did you drink this morning?"

He smirked. "Just a little beer to steady my nerves. I really don't feel up for this today."

Jimmy grimaced. *That ought to make one hell of an impression on Natalie's parents. And you don't smell like beer. You reek like the hard stuff.* "Chill out, dude. Practically the whole town is at the game. Only a few people will be at Italy's Finest. It's not really a big deal. If you really are that nervous, just be quiet, and you can't go wrong. Only talk when they ask you something."

"Yeah, okay, I'll do that. Remember, you got to take off to meet your sister at the airport, and I have to take you there."

"Yeah, yeah," Jimmy said as they hit the main intersection in town. He had no sister. That was Seth's plan to get out of lunch early.

Seth pulled up to Italy's Finest. "All right, let's get this over with."

The football game had already started. Several people ate at the pizzerias. The radio carried the game and a loudspeaker pumped it to the people outside. Almost everyone sat inside to see other games on TV. The aroma of freshly baked bread and pizza wafted outside. It smelled fantastic.

Jimmy's stomach grumbled. He didn't love meeting anyone's parents, but he figured it would be no big deal, and he'd sit through worse than this for pizza.

Natalie, Traci, and Natalie's parents sat out on the deck. They smiled when Jimmy and Seth arrived.

Natalie stepped off the deck to greet Seth. She kissed him and gave him a curious look as she held his hand. "Mom, Dad, this is Seth."

Natalie's father was balding and a little overweight. He wore glasses. Natalie's mother looked younger, short blonde. Seth shook their hands. Natalie introduced them to Jimmy and Seth. Jimmy immediately forgot her parents' names.

Jimmy watched Seth. He could tell Seth was nervous, but he looked cool. They made small talk for a few minutes. Jimmy thought everything started out well. Natalie's parents were nice.

They weren't snobs, and they didn't give Seth a hard time.

"Let's order," Natalie said. "Do you guys know what you want on your pizza?"

They agreed on what they wanted, sausage, pepperoni, and black olives.

"We'll pay for this," Natalie's father gave Seth some cash.

"You stay here," Seth said. "I'll put in the order."

"Order us another pitcher, Seth," Natalie said.

Seth took the money from Mr. Dupree and stepped through the open front door. Before he ordered the pizzas, he noticed the liquor bottles behind the bar. Italy's Finest and Geribaldi's weren't just pizzerias but also full-service bars.

TVs hung over the bar and all over Italy's Finest. Games aired from across the country as the radio blared away. The Pirates led the game in the first quarter. Students inside ate pizza and drank beer. Seth ordered another pitcher but stared at the liquor bottles. Jimmy followed after him to make sure he didn't get any extra liquor, but he was too late.

The bartender, a thin guy with his long dark hair tied back, gave Seth his pitcher. "You, my friend, look as though you desire more than just beer."

"You got that right, Jack. I've got my future in-laws outside there. I'm meeting them for the first time."

The bartender grimaced. "Ouch. I can understand the need. Talk to me. Help me help you."

Seth ordered a couple of shots of whiskey. He slammed them.

Jimmy grabbed the pitcher. "Come on, Seth." He wanted to really chide Seth, but a fight right now was not a good idea, especially with all the booze Seth had already put down.

"Anything you say." Seth sat down and poured a beer. It was like a hole was in the bottom of his glass, the way he drained glass after glass.

"Seth, slow down," Natalie said. "You're not in a race."

"Oh, sorry," Seth muttered. "I thought I'd get a head start before all of the students get here after the game and drink it all up."

Jimmy made eye contact with Traci. She looked concerned as she cupped her hands around her beer and ran her thumbs around the rim of her glass. She had stopped drinking.

Jimmy couldn't tell what Seth was up to. He hoped Seth wasn't planning on getting flat-out drunk in front of Natalie's folks. Seth liked his pranks, but he was serious about Natalie. He didn't want to ruin that relationship before they'd even married, did he?

"Natalie has told us so much about you," Natalie's mother said to Jimmy and Traci. "Both of you are studying to be writers?"

Traci sipped her beer. "I'm a journalism major. I want to be a writer for a newspaper. Jimmy wants to be a novelist."

"Is that so?" Natalie's father asked. "What sort of novels do you want to write?"

Jimmy smiled slightly. "I'm rather partial to mysteries."

"Jimmy has been writing short stories," Natalie said.

"Pirates intercepted a pass!" the announcer exclaimed. The tiny crowd inside erupted.

"Do you have anything published yet, Jimmy?" Natalie's mother asked.

He shrugged. "When I was a freshman, I got a couple of poems published for a campus publication at the college Seth, and I went to before we transferred here. I'm working on a short story now. I've sent out a couple. I'm still waiting to hear back."

"Oh, my," Natalie's mother said. "You must be so excited."

Jimmy grimaced. "Actually, I'm only cautiously optimistic. I'll get excited if I get a story published."

"Jimmy and I have already got an article published in the campus paper," Traci said.

"You did?" Natalie's father asked. "What was it about?"

The hairs stood up on Jimmy's arms. He wasn't sure he should discuss this with Natalie's folks, especially right before lunch. "We interviewed the frats. We asked them questions about rape and violence. We were stunned to find how many of them had a desire to rape if they thought they could get away with it."

The crowd inside cheered again. Morganburg just blasted through their opponent's defensive to the goal line. The announcer sounded like he might have an aneurysm. "The Pirates just scored again!"

"What made you think of doing a story about that?" Mrs. Dupree asked.

"My girlfriend was murdered last summer," Jimmy said.

Natalie's parents looked shocked. They asked him what happened. Seth kept glancing back to the front door. Jimmy didn't know if he tried to get a glimpse of a game on one of the TVs if he wondered when the pizza would be ready or if he eyed the bottles behind the bar.

"I want to solve her murder," Jimmy said.

"Natalie told us you also went to Morganburg," Traci said. "Did you have a lot of violence, rape, and murder back then?"

"Absolutely not," Natalie's mother said. "I can't believe—"

"Wait a minute, dear," Mr. Dupree said. "We had no murders. I remember a couple of rapes happening when we attended school here."

"But we didn't have a rash of them."

"How would we know? Rape wasn't reported as much back when we were in college."

Natalie's mother started to say something, but she stopped. "Well, maybe you're right."

"What does the university have to say about this?" Mr. Dupree asked.

Jimmy set his beer aside. He was interested in asking Natalie's parents about Morganburg, as they might know about the university. "I haven't actually contacted any of the university officials for a response yet. So far, I get the feeling the university doesn't care. There is no actual class or subject, or program that addresses campus violence. So therefore, it's not a concern to the college. I'm sure they feel this is an issue for the high schools and parents to deal with."

"I'm sure they care," Mr. Dupree said.

Jimmy didn't bring up that he'd quit the paper. He didn't want Natalie's parents to think he was unreliable. "I'm not so certain about that," Jimmy said. "Have you heard about Laura Jenkins? She was my girlfriend."

Natalie's parents said they didn't. Jimmy noticed a concerned look on Natalie's face. Seth chugged his beer.

"Seth, slow down," Natalie said. "The beer won't evaporate if you drink slowly."

"She was murdered last August," Jimmy stated. "And so far, Traci and I couldn't get any official word from the university or any information from the police. They seem to care more about the image of this university more than what happened to Laura."

Natalie's parents were shocked to hear that happened.

"Do you know of anything strange happening on campus when you attended?" Traci asked.

"Strange?" Mrs. Dupree asked. "Like what?"

"Like disappearances," Jimmy said, thinking of Pete and Rafe, as well as Deanna.

Traci shot a concerned glance at Jimmy. She watched Seth downing another glass.

Mrs. Dupree said, "Actually, now that I think about it, there was an unwritten rule that we women never went out at night."

"Why?" Natalie asked.

Her mother looked down. "We didn't feel it was safe."

"That figures," Seth grumbled after he finished another beer. "The frats here are a bunch of Neanderthal hillbillies."

You're going to get down-in-the-dog-dish-drunk right here and now, aren't you, Seth?

Jimmy wanted to him and ask him if he really wanted to embarrass himself in front of Natalie's parents.

Mr. Dupree blanched. "Now that I think about it, I can remember when I first came here; the upperclassmen warned us to never go near the woods at night."

"Why?" Traci asked.

"Because they said if you did, you were never seen again," Mrs. Dupree said.

Jimmy felt an icy tingle lurch down his spine. He suddenly became more interested in his beer again. He joined Seth in gulping some down.

"Of course, we just thought the upperclassmen were trying to scare us," Mr. Dupree said.

"So one night, a few friends and I waited for it to get dark, and we walked into the woods."

Seth got up. "I'll get us some more beer."

Jimmy was stunned. Seth didn't want to hear Mr. Dupree's story. Jimmy wondered if Seth was even listening to the conversation. He'd thought Seth cared about Laura's death, his investigation, and the town mysteries, but Seth never cared at all.

"Seth, why don't you wait to get another pitcher when the pizza's ready," Natalie said.

"No, that's okay. I can get it now." Seth went inside.

Natalie wrung her hands.

"So what happened?" Jimmy asked, unable to meet Natalie's eye. She would want him to do something about

Seth, and he wasn't willing to get in Seth's way when he was this drunk.

Natalie's father shook his head. "We got caught in a frat prank, but it was the scariest thing I've ever seen."

"Gerald, you never told me about this," Mrs. Dupree said.

Mr. Dupree frowned. "I didn't want to scare you."

"What happened?" Jimmy demanded.

Natalie's father drank some beer and hesitated as if he mulled over whether to tell the story or not. "We saw, well, what we really saw were a bunch of frats dressed up as Civil War soldiers, all in blue. They scared us all right. We got the hell out of those woods and never went back. And we stayed off the campus at night."

"How was seeing a bunch of Civil War soldiers scary?" Traci asked.

"At first, we weren't scared. We thought it was a hoax. But—

"But what, Dad?"

"You should've seen them. Their faces were chalk-white. Some looked blue. Others looked like they had parts of their faces blown off. Some had no heads at all. But—" He looked away for a moment. "For a while, we held our ground. But the closer they got, the more real they looked, and we took off."

Jimmy was shocked, and he wasn't sure why. If Civil War ghosts are haunting this campus today, then they'd certainly would've back then.

Again Jimmy's heart leaped in his chest.

Natalie asked, "Are you sure that's what you saw, Dad?"

He said, "If those were frats, I don't know how they pulled it off, but they didn't look like they were walking. They floated. And they called all of our names and told them to join us."

Jimmy jumped when Seth set the pitcher of beer on the table. He never heard Seth come back outside. Seth didn't waste any time pouring himself another beer.

"Are you still talking about this miserable little redneck town?" Seth asked.

"I don't understand what makes you dislike it here, Seth," Mr. Dupree said. He frowned at his future son-in-law.

"Take a look around you, old man. This is a little backwater country fuck town with a university jammed into the middle of it. Nothing goes on here! If you want to see a show or go see an event or festival, you have to drive to Richmond or Virginia Beach."

Seth's language surprised the Duprees. Natalie's eyes were wide with rage.

"That's true," Mr. Dupree said. "It's secluded, but that way, you have fewer distractions, and it's supposed to inspire you to keep up with your studies."

Seth scoffed. "They have plenty of universities in big cities. I wish like hell Jimmy, and I didn't transfer from the community college in Virginia Beach to come here. I wish we stayed there in that city and went to a school there."

Jimmy felt compelled to start slamming his own drinks. "Seth, you know we didn't because this was a college our parents could afford and the dedication it had to the arts. Based on our success in high school, and everything that was going on when we were teens, we had few options. I thought the University of Morganburg was right for us."

Seth chuckled bitterly. "Yeah, well, I think we made a mistake, man."

"I think Natalie's right, Seth," Natalie's father said. "You need to slow down. You've probably had enough already. And I don't like the way you describe this town. It's a good town with good people. This is a fine university. You ought to be thankful you are able to attend this school."

Seth poured himself another beer. "I pity anyone who thinks this god-awful hell hole is a good place to be."

Natalie's father was going to respond to that, but a loudspeaker blared, "Party of Williams. Your pizzas are ready."

Seth stood up. "I'll get those."

"You're going to need help with those pizzas," Jimmy said. "I'll go with you."

"I think maybe we should switch from beer to soda," Traci said. "I'll go get us a pitcher of root beer."

"I need to go the bathroom," Natalie said.

Seth walked inside and got his pizzas. Jimmy followed him. He saw the bar. A mirror hung behind the rows of liquor bottles. But Jimmy didn't see Seth in the mirror. He saw a person with long straight hair, sunken, dark eyes, draped in black. He smiled so coldly Jimmy felt goosebumps crawl like black widows down his body. His knees quivered.

"What the hell?" he gasped.

Traci walked in behind Jimmy. "What is it?" she whispered.

"Look," Jimmy said. He pointed at the mirror. "Tell me what you see."

Natalie exploded into the restaurant. "Seth!"

Seth turned around.

Traci said, "I just see Seth's back. And some people."

People stared at them.

"What?" Traci asked.

Jimmy spun around. He saw Seth's curly black mane that ran down the middle of his back. Jimmy rubbed his eyes. "Nothing. Never mind."

"What did you see?" Traci whispered. "Something bad?"

"Yeah."

"Seth, what are you doing?" Natalie demanded.

"What now?" Seth said.

"You're embarrassing me and you're embarrassing yourself! You're acting like an ass! You're drunk again and acting rude. Why are you doing this?"

"Your old man is all pissy because I don't love this precious redneck college."

"You're being an obnoxious drunk! My parents want to get to know you. Instead, they're getting to know a drunken slob. You're not giving them a chance. You're being as prejudicial about them as you have accused older adults of being with you."

"So what? They were going to hate me anyways. What's the difference?"

Someone muttered, "Can you two assholes go home and war with each other? We're trying to watch the games here."

Jimmy knew a way out of this nightmare, at least for himself. He grabbed Seth's arm. "Hey, I just got a phone call. I have to pick up my sister at the airport. Her flight got in early, okay? Unfortunately, I have to go and I'm with you, so let's call it a day, all right?" He would miss the pizza, but it was for the best.

Seth's angry expression switched to one of relief. "Good. Let's get the hell out of here."

Morganburg scored again and the bar exploded. Jimmy glanced at the mirror and he saw that dark-eyed stranger grinning at him. This time Traci also saw him. She gasped. But he knew she'd seen it.

When Jimmy looked back in the mirror, the vision was gone.

Jimmy quickly looked at Natalie. "You two will have to try this again, but without the beer. I'll get him out of here. You smooth things over."

"And how am I to do that?" Natalie barked.

"Tell them Seth hadn't eaten yet today, and he's on some pain medication for his back from weightlifting and the mixture of that with the beer was the cause of this." He didn't much like lying, but Seth hadn't been okay lately. He deserved another chance.

Natalie rubbed her brow. "I suppose that could work."

Jimmy always thought writers make good liars. They know how to con their way out of jams. "Plus, he's under a lot of stress because he's having some trouble in his art classes. His paintings just aren't coming out the way he wants them to. That much was also true."

Natalie forced a smile. "Thanks, Jimmy. You always know how to get out of bad scrapes, don't you? I'll tell your folks about your, uh, sister." She talked through her clenched teeth when she looked at Seth and said, "I'll talk to you later."

Jimmy looked at Traci. "I'll call you, okay?"

Traci grabbed him. Her flesh was clammy and cold, and her face was white like chalk. "What was that in the mirror?" she whispered.

Jimmy put his hand on her shoulder. "We'll have to talk later. You're not going crazy. It's real." He led Seth outside. "Let's get out of here. And I'm driving."

"Sure thing," Seth tossed his keys to Jimmy and eased himself into the seat like he poured himself into the car. "I owe you a favor for getting me out of there." Jimmy drove while Seth sulked. At least Traci had seen the figure, not a hallucination, but some glimpse into some other reality. What did it want from him?

"So I suppose you want to lecture me too, don't you?" Seth asked.

"No," Jimmy said. "You're already pissed off. I'm not going to tug on a panther's tail."

Seth remained quiet until they got to their house. "I screwed up, didn't I?"

"Seth, you screwed up like a cork in a bottle of poisoned wine. Congratulations, Jack! You just made enemies of Natalie's parents, and you very well may have ruined everything between you and Natalie."

Jimmy and Seth got out of the car. Jimmy hand Seth's keys back, and he got in his car.

"Where are you going?" Seth asked.

"I don't know. I guess I'll know when I get there. I need a breath of fresh air."

Jimmy raced back to campus. The place was still devoid of people since the game was at halftime. Jimmy parked the car behind the art building. He walked to the yellow spot where Rudy was murdered. It looked like a murderer left a cowardly imprint. An icy cold wind blew through Jimmy. He made his way to the white brick wall that surrounded the graveyard. He stopped when he saw a tree growing outside the cemetery. He glanced up at the art building, then back at the tree.

No. It couldn't be. That looked like where he and Seth saw that guy planting the tree that one afternoon. The tree was now taller than Jimmy. But that couldn't be the same tree! Trees don't grow that fast.

Jimmy hopped the fence and walked up to the woods. The tips of the trees looked as if they reached to grab the sun and drag it under. No birds sang like they avoided those woods. The trees looked like obstacles to obscure a sinister crime inside.

Do something, Jimmy thought. He wanted to see something, anything. He wanted to understand what the hell was going on in this town. What's out here? Maybe it was time for him to face his fear of the woods. If Natalie's dad was brave enough to come in here, maybe he should as well. He could ask the dark figure why it kept following him around and abducting his friends.

Why are you making me see these things? I quit the newspaper. You can have whatever you want, so take it!

Jimmy saw nothing, no movement in the woods, no figures with haunting eyes that appeared out of nowhere. Jimmy looked behind him. No soldiers crept up behind him. Jimmy heard no screams. No strange-looking people stood in the cemetery. Jimmy slammed his hands on his hips.

Why are you doing this to Seth and Natalie? Is this part of a curse? You make all couples fight? Jimmy was sick of all of this. He muttered, "Do you just like to ruin relationships? Do you like to see us fight each other? Since you like fighting so much, why don't you come out here, whoever or whatever you are, and face me? Or do you want Seth for some reason? I wonder if you could fight an entire biker gang. Could you? I wonder if I got the Black Knights, could you stop me from taking Seth away from you?"

Nothing happened, and that enraged Jimmy even more.

"Come on, god damn it! Where are you? You're really fucking tough at night. Where are you during the day—!"

And then there it was. Darkness oozed out of the woods at his feet. It heard him. It listened. And it was creeping out. Jimmy backed away and it kept coming. The mysterious black fog crept out and expanded to envelop him. After what he had seen with Traci behind the art building, he was unwilling to let that get anywhere near him. He ran out of the cemetery and to his car. The dark fog spread over the fence. Jimmy hit the gas and sped out of the parking lot. The darkness continued out of the woods and spread into the street. Jimmy floored it away from the art building and off campus, regretting he'd said anything.

Jimmy returned home, and he wanted to talk to Seth, but Seth was in his room drinking while working on a painting. After his fight with Natalie, he figured it would be best if he just left Seth alone for a while. He sat down at his computer and tried to calm down. Whatever is out there in those woods is evil and powerful. It's determined to do whatever it wants to….But what does it want?

Jimmy was working on his computer when someone pounded on the door. Seth wouldn't answer it, so Jimmy got up to see who it was.

"Where is he?" Natalie hissed.

"He's in his room, and I'll warn you, he's in there drinking."

"I don't care." Natalie stormed into Seth's room. "What the god damn hell did you think you were doing?"

Seth didn't say anything immediately. "Listen, you're obviously pissed off, so why don't you go away for a while, and we'll talk later."

"Oh, you better believe we're going to talk right now, buster! What the hell is wrong with you?"

"What did you really expect from me, Natalie? I'm nothing but a fuck-up! The only thing I had going for me is my painting and I can't even do that anymore."

Jimmy couldn't believe he just said that. He never referred to himself that way before. He never got down on himself like that or his art…until we moved to this house.

"Is that what all that was about?" Natalie raged. "You're feeling sorry for yourself because a few paintings are bothering you? So you got drunk and acted like a buffoon to my parents?"

Jimmy recognized that look on Seth's face. That was clearly not the thing to say to him.

"Natalie, you need to leave right now."

"I'm going nowhere! Not until you tell me why you spoke to my folks that way? They were being nice to you and you acted like an obnoxious jerk."

Seth stepped closer to her. "Your father reminded me of my old man. He had that look in his eye like my father had. The look that said you're never going to amount to anything. He had that stuck-up, rich look that said I had no business even being in the same room with you. I could just see him sitting there wondering, how dare you fuck my daughter."

Jimmy didn't think that was what Natalie's dad had looked like at all. He feared this was about to get violent. He was stunned to hear Seth speak to her that way. Even when Seth was drunk and stoned on the streets of Virginia Beach, he never talked like that.

"Seth, why are you talking this way?"

Seth smashed a painting. "Because it's the way I talk, honey!"

Natalie froze for a few moments. "Seth, in two years I've known you, I've never heard you speak like this before. You hardly ever swear. And right now, you're offensive and absolutely disgusting. How dare you talk about my father like that?"

"Hey, if you don't like it, then fuck off! No one asked you here. In fact, I asked you to leave, but you just had to stay here to be an obnoxious bitch!"

"You asshole!" Natalie screeched. "You have no right to speak to me that way!"

"Hey, you're in my damn home; I'll speak to you any God damn way I please!"

"You most certainly will not, and you will not talk to me this way when we're married!"

"Fuck off, bitch!"

"I ought to slap your face!"

"You lay a hand on me, woman, and I'll make it so they'll need a spatula to scrape you off the floor to throw you in the ambulance!"

Natalie cried. "You know, I don't even know you anymore, Seth. I can't believe what I'm hearing from you. This is completely the opposite of who you are. The person I fell in love with was never like this. Now I'm wondering if I made a mistake. Maybe we need some space."

"I know right now I wish you would go to hell!" Seth threw his beer bottle at Natalie, and she ducked. It narrowly missed her head and clunked against the door. Beer pooled on the carpet.

Jimmy leaped from his chair and ran into Seth's room. "All right, enough from both of you! Natalie, get the hell out of here! Just go. I'm sorry. I really am. At the rate you two are going, someone is going to end up in the hospital. Go on, Natalie."

Natalie took off.

Jimmy stared at Seth. "She's right, you know. I don't know you either anymore, man. You're not just drunk. You've become just plain cruel. And I'm beginning to not want to know you anymore."

Jimmy grabbed his cell phone and called Traci. He left to spend the night on her couch again. He didn't know what was going on with Seth. He was beginning to hate him. No, he was beginning to fear him.

CHAPTER TWENTY-ONE

The next week after classes, Jimmy headed his way to the art building. He missed Seth and was no longer mad at his best friend, but he was concerned. He wanted to try to talk Seth into leaving Morganburg after the semester. He hoped Rafe's and Pete's disappearance would help his cause. As he made his way through the courtyard, Michelle, the business major from upstairs, stopped him.

Jimmy said, "I read in the paper your sorority is putting on some kind of brunch."

She forced a slight smile. "We are. We're celebrating the end of midterm. And Sunday, we're taking Cassie away from here."

"Why, what's wrong?"

"She's drinking so much lately. And she's not acting herself. A bunch of us from Tri Delta are getting Cassie away from campus, far away, and we're going to have Anne Marie's mom look at her. She's a doctor. We think something's really wrong with her."

That's what that note meant that I found on their floor when Seth and I were up in their home. "Maybe that's a good idea. I think I need to do the same with Seth. He's also drinking a lot and not acting like himself."

"What's up with him hanging out with Cassie so much? Isn't Seth supposed to be engaged?"

"I didn't know they were hanging out a lot. He is engaged, and I plan to go over and see him now. I'll try to find out what's up."

"Good luck."

"Yeah, you too. Let me know what happens."

"You bet. And likewise."

Jimmy had been avoiding him all week. He wanted to talk to Seth into getting the hell out of Morganburg, maybe even skipping their final semester there, going somewhere else, and transferring their credits over.

In all the years Jimmy knew Seth, they never had any bad words to say to each other, and he never spoke to Seth the way he had last Saturday. Jimmy walked slowly across the street. He stepped quietly into the studio to find Seth working on a painting and drinking a beer.

When Seth saw him, he smirked and shook his head. "I thought I probably saw you for the last time."

More miserable turpentine fumes again. It smelled like Seth had flung the stuff all around the studio. Jimmy wished the university would provide the building with a decent ventilation system. "You can't get rid of me that easily, asshole."

"It sounded like I nearly did. Haven't seen you all week."

Jimmy sat down on the mobile stage in the middle of the studio. "Look, I'm sorry about what I said the other day. I was just pissed."

Seth stepped away from his painting to look at it. "You know, I can't believe I acted that way. The next day after I got up, I wondered why did I say those things? What was wrong with me? I'm sorry I was such an ass. I'm sorry you had to get between me and Natalie. I should've called you to apologize. I thought you didn't want to hear from me. I don't know what got into me."

Jimmy wondered that himself. "You didn't eat all day. Then you started slamming drinks. You were nervous, and school had been bothering you. It all came to a head last weekend."

"I tried to call Natalie, but she's still really upset. She won't talk to me. I guess I can't blame her. I think we're finished."

Jimmy truly hoped not. She was good for him and a fun girl. "Oh, I doubt it. She'll probably be back. But you're going to be on a double probation with her. That was one hell of a fight you had."

"Yeah, that was the worst fight I've ever had with Natalie. I feel really bad about that. She can hate me forever. I just wish she'd let me apologize to her. I owe her at least that." Seth picked up his paintbrush, looked at his painting, frowned, and tossed his brush back down again.

"Are you still having the same problems with your paintings?"

"Yes! This one is driving me up the wall. I swear I want to take a butcher knife and shred this."

Jimmy gazed at it. The painting was a floating nude woman reaching down to a man sinking into the sea. He didn't understand what was wrong with it. "I'm no art major, but it looks fine to me, man."

Seth smiled. "Yeah, you're right. You're no art major. I hate this water. It's too muddy. I want it to look as though it has more depth. I don't know about this woman. There's just something about her that I don't like. I think I'm going to let the paint dry and rework it later."

"It probably has to do with that bottle you're nursing. You could lay off a little. That might help. Why are you drinking here anyways? You know it's illegal to drink on campus."

"Of course, I know that. You want one?"

Jimmy wanted to decline, but then he changed his mind. Hopefully, that would relax Seth and he'd talk to Jimmy if he accepted one.

"Yeah, what the hell."

Seth reached into a small cooler stashed in the corner of the studio and grabbed a couple of bottles. He handed one to Jimmy and opened another one for himself.

"Lately, it seems like I want more than one of these," Jimmy said.

Seth smiled. "What's the matter, Jimbo? Classes bothering you?"

"No, it's not my classes. School is okay. It's just everything else. " It's you and this town. Since Seth was already drinking, Jimmy thought if he could get him off campus and out to a bar, and they could talk. Reason with him. Get him to listen. Then maybe he could reach Seth to get him to realize they need to leave Morganburg for at least the Christmas break, maybe even convince him they need to leave Morganburg forever. "It's just that I'm exhausted. I'm cranky. It's Friday, and I'm ready to go out and pound down a few."

Seth set his paintbrush down. "I won't give you an argument there."

Jimmy sat back down on the stage. The walls looked grayer than before, like they needed a new coat of paint. "Then why don't we get out of here and take a break."

Seth sighed heavily. He cleaned his brush. "Well, I know how you feel. I've had it with this painting. I think maybe what I need to do is just blow off some steam. Do you know of a good party to go to tonight?"

"No, but how about we hit a bar tonight? We haven't done that together in a long time. You can get away from campus, your paintings, and everything for a while."

"Right now that sounds like the best idea I've heard all day. Let's blow this taco stand."

Jimmy and Seth drove to a big downtown sports bar. He liked to come in there, watch some games and write during the ads and half times. TVs lined a shelf for people sitting at the bar. TVs sat all around the rest of the place. UVA, VTU, and Pirate football memorabilia covered the walls and filled a display case. The strong smell of fish and fries saturated the air.

As soon as they stepped inside, the bartender saw them. "Jimbo!" Buddy, a tall, husky guy with a beard, shouted. "You ain't dragged your God damn sorry ass in here in ages. Where the God damn hell have you been?"

Jimmy was glad to see his old friend. "School, man."

"Where do you find these dives?" Seth asked.

"Girls before I met Laura," Jimmy said. "They brought me to places like this to get me drunk and get me into bed." He laughed at the memories.

Jimmy and Seth got a couple of corner seats at the bar. The place was full, and the music was a little loud.

Buddy didn't need to ask what Jimmy wanted. He already had a beer ready for Jimmy when he and Seth walked through the door. "And what can I get you?" he asked Seth.

"That's a damn good barkeep that already has your drink ready before you even get on the barstool," Jimmy said. The beer tasted better in a glass Buddy kept them chilled. Jimmy gulped his beer and said to Buddy, "So, what's new with you?"

After Buddy turned on all the TVs to one channel for a Friday night college football game about to come on, he leaned both hands up against the bar. "You know, I've had it with this town. Last night I had a bunch of kids egg at my home. You know how hard it is to wash dried egg off the side of your house? It's the third act of vandalism on my home I've had to deal with this year."

Jimmy sipped his beer. It sounded like this whole town had problems. "Bummer, dude."

"So you know what I'm going to do?" Buddy asked. "My wife and I are taking the kids and moving out. There's just something not right about this town. The last bunch that threw the eggs, I chased one of them down and grabbed him. Do you know he had these bizarre gray eyes? It was like he was sleepwalking. He acted drugged or hypnotized."

"What did he say when you caught him?" Seth asked.

Buddy held out his hands. "The kid just said, 'I've got no eggs on me. Call the cops. I don't care.'"

"Wow," Jimmy said. More fighting. This place seemed to thrive on conflict. "He threw all his evidence, huh? But did you still call the cops? You could still make a complaint at least; then the cops would have a record of him for being a suspected vandal."

Buddy poured another beer for a regular and put it on the guy's tab. "Nah. I just let the punk go. What the hell. I'm out of this town. What do I give a damn anymore?"

"You really hate it here that much?" Seth asked.

"I don't just hate it," Buddy said. "There's something unnerving about Morganburg. That kid I grabbed with the funny look in his eye, that's not the first time I've seen that look. And I keep seeing it more lately. I fear it's actually spreading. No, I don't just hate this town. I fear it."

Jimmy remembered Ed Frank and the detectives. "I've seen that look."

"It's scary, isn't it?" Buddy asked.

"Yeah," Jimmy said. "It's as you say, unnerving." He wondered if Buddy didn't know something about Morganburg. "Tell me, how long have you lived here?"

"It's been eight years." Buddy leaned against the bar. "My advice to you guys, transfer to UVA or V-Tech or anywhere. Just get out of this redneck town."

"Why?" Jimmy asked. He had his own ideas about why by now, but he wanted to hear what Buddy thought.

"When I first moved here, things were fine, but five years ago, things started getting really bad. I've had friends get that gray look in their eyes. I saw their personalities change. People who I considered good friends have changed so greatly; I can't even stand them anymore."

"What happened to them?" Seth asked.

Buddy wiped down the bar and refilled a dish with beer nuts. "I have no idea. I'm close to leaving. I'm tired of dealing with the vandalism. I'm moving to Charlottesville. I'm going to UVA to work on my Master's."

"Damn," Seth said. "We've got us a damn brainy barkeep."

Jimmy smiled slightly at the joke, but he felt uneasy after what Buddy told them. He wished he never came to Morganburg.

"Damn straight," Buddy said.

Jimmy savored his beer. "Seth, what do you think about us going back to Virginia Beach this winter break?"

"Virginia Beach?"

"Yeah."

Some guys cheered at the bar and shouted after a team scored.

"Want another beer, guys?" Buddy asked.

"No, we're good for now." Jimmy stood up. "Let's go to a table." He wanted to go where it was quiet, and he could really talk to Seth.

Buddy grabbed their empty glasses. "Okay, guys. I'll see you around."

"How do you even know these places exist?" Seth asked.

Jimmy chuckled. "Honestly, I can't even remember. Some girl brought me here about three years ago. Sometimes I like to come here just to reminisce about how much you and I used to drink when we first got into college and before college." The two of them sat down at a corner booth. The place reeked of cigarette smoke, but there were only a couple of people in there, and it was quiet. "I can't remember the girl's name, and I can't remember her face. I can only remember she was blonde and beautiful. She sat me down at this table."

"What happened to the girl?"

"I don't know." Jimmy smiled. "I can remember that some friends joined us. I think she helped me home. I never saw the girl again. I wish I could remember her name."

The guys ordered a pitcher of beer from a waitress, and Jimmy knew this was a good time to ask him about getting the idea of leaving into his head. "So what do you say? Let's get out of Morganburg for a winter break, at least."

"Yeah, I hate it here. I really want a break."

Jimmy was thrilled. He could finally get him to agree to leave. "Now, what do you say about—" Before he could say anymore, Cassie came into the bar. She wore a tight black dress that tied up the front.

Jimmy groaned. Not you, he thought. Not now. I was just starting to work on Seth.

Seth grinned. "What brings a sorority girl to a dive like this?"

Cassie laughed. "This place isn't that bad."

Seth scooted over in the booth. "Here, sit down. I'll buy you a drink."

The waitress brought them a pitcher of beer, and Jimmy said they'd need another glass. Seth threw down his first beer like the county was going to go dry in the morning.

Three of Cassie's friends walked into the place, and she said, "I want you to meet them, Seth." Two brunettes and one blonde sat down at the bar. They all wore short dresses and looked like they wanted more than just alcohol that night.

Jimmy regretted coming in here. He wished he picked a bigger dive way on the outskirts of town.

Cassie and Seth visited with the girls at their table while Jimmy settled up for their round of drinks. Jimmy heard Seth say, "Girls, my name is Fun. Want to have fun?"

Jimmy hung his head. Seth is really hammered again. If he didn't place a least a couple of days in between that sort of drinking, he won't be able to anymore.

Jimmy rushed to Seth and grabbed his arm. "Come on, Seth, dude. Remember, you already have a steady girl, Natalie."

"Who?" Seth asked.

"Natalie," Jimmy said angrily. "You know, the girl you're going to marry?"

"Oh, yeah," Seth said. "Natalie."

Jimmy dragged Seth out of the bar and away from Cassie, but she followed them. Damn it. Can't you take a hint for just one night? "Come on, big guy," Jimmy said. "I'm taking you away from here."

"Where are we going?" Seth asked.

"Somewhere else where we can talk," Jimmy said.

Seth playfully moaned. "But I was having so much fun."

They started back to Jimmy's car. A silver BMW sped up to them and onto the sidewalk. They slammed on the brakes before hitting Jimmy and Seth. Four guys swarmed out of the car. Cassie groaned. Jimmy recognized them. The frat boys making all of the noise at the pizzeria jumped out of the car. They wore dress shoes and slacks. One wore a tie. They looked dressed for a job interview rather than a night to go out to drink and watch the games or see a band.

Jimmy felt like getting a hammer and slamming it against his temple. *Now what? Every time I try to get Seth away, something stops me.*

Suddenly Jimmy realized they were on campus at night. Bad things happened here at night.

The art professor was right about that, even if he didn't understand why. Jimmy broke out into a sweat.

"Ernie, what are you doing here?" Cassie asked.

"Ernie?" Seth said before he laughed. "Where's Bert?"

"What the hell are you guys doing with my girl?" Ernie demanded. He had a smug face and a paperclip for a body.

"Ernie, fuck off!" Cassie shouted.

Ernie pointed at Seth. "What are you assholes doing with her?"

Jimmy looked into the eyes of Ernie and the rest of the frats. They had that creepy, fuzzy, gray color. Jimmy grabbed Seth's arm. "Seth—" he tried to say.

Seth jerked away and pushed Jimmy aside. "Stay out of this," Seth said. "So she's yours? What do I care?"

"Just get away from her!" Ernie screamed. "You two hippies shouldn't be anywhere near her! Haven't you done enough? First, you perverts go upstairs and mess around in the girls' dressers, and now you're after Cassie!"

"What are you talking about?" Cassie asked.

"It was those two who went up to your friends' place-!"

"Ernie, you liar!" Cassie shrieked. "It was you and your friends, you fucking prick! Don't bring them into this."

"It wasn't me!" Ernie screamed.

"I don't know anything about being up in anyone's home or their dressers," Seth lied. "And I don't care what you think about anything else. Cassie chose to hang out with us. Whether you rednecks like that or not isn't my problem. But if you bunch of square heads have a problem with that, then why don't you do something about it."

"Seth," Jimmy said as he tried to get space between him and the frats.

He grabbed Seth's wrist, but Seth twisted away. He feared what Seth was capable of then. He wished those bunch of hicks would just fuck off for one night. He didn't want anyone to go to jail or die that night. Damn it, he just wanted to talk to Seth for about an hour.

Ernie threw a punch, but Seth blocked it. He punched Ernie in the throat. Ernie crumpled to his knees. Seth kicked him in the head twice. The second kick smashed Ernie's head into the fender of the BMW. It was an ugly sound, like a fist crushed in the jaws of a panther. Ernie didn't get up. A blonde guy tried to help him up. The other frats huddled around him.

The one with the tie and baby face shouted, "You've just got thirty guys on your ass!"

"Ward, please calm down," Cassie pleaded.

"Listen, go get thirty of your out-house Jack friends together to beat us up. All of you be up at the old water tower at midnight, and I'll have my people there waiting for you."

A tall one with dark hair and a slight paunch laughed. "You got it, asshole! You get whatever friends you've got to fight. We'll be there. If you're not, Phi Beta Kappa will find you!"

The frats piled into the car, carrying the lurching, wounded dumbass, and they sped off.

"Who the hell were those fools?" Seth asked.

"The Phi Beta Kappas," Cassie said. "Ward was the one wearing the tie. He's their president. The tall guy with dark hair was Jerry. Seth, you shouldn't have done that. Phi Beta Kappa really does have thirty guys, and I'm sure Ward and Jerry will get most of them."

"I expect him to," Seth said as he looked around.

Jimmy was angry that he wanted to pick a fight with those gray-eyed, buzzy-brained frats. "What the hell are you doing, man? Are you nuts? Why didn't you tell them we'd call the cops? I've got my cell phone in the car. We can have all of them up on disorderly conduct and terrorist-threat charges at least."

"Yeah, I know," Seth said. "But did you get a look at their eyes?"

"Yes, I did," Jimmy grumbled. "They had that glazed-gray look that Buddy talked about."

"Exactly. And the way those guys talked, I figure the cops may cool them off for tonight, but those rednecks will be back. If we don't get rid of them, they'll be constantly harassing us." They returned to Jimmy's car. Seth picked up Jimmy's cell. "You know, Jimbo, I once was glad we got a chance to come here to this university, but I'm starting to get over it. I miss the city and city people."

Jimmy nearly wanted to hug him after hearing that. "I do, too."

Seth dialed a number, but the phone wouldn't put the call through. "I know another college in Virginia Beach wouldn't look as good on a resume, but I can't stand the mentality here."

Jimmy grinned. He almost jumped up and hugged Seth. Awesome! Then we can get the hell out of here in December.

They drove to a payphone in front of an abandoned gas station. Jimmy couldn't believe any still existed. And to his surprise, it still worked. "You're not calling any of our friends from here, are you?"

"No way," Seth said. "I'm calling Billy. It's going to take a couple of hours for Billy and the Black Knights to get down here. By midnight, we should have a nice little set-up waiting for those frat fucks. They will never mess with us again."

Jimmy knew those frats didn't know their past. They had no idea what they were in for. In fact, Jimmy wasn't even sure what the frats were in for. He feared what Seth planned for them.

Before midnight Billy shot off his headlights and slowly crept up the hill near the old water tower. Jimmy, Seth, and Billy got out of Billy's van and ducked behind a pair of trees.

They waited for the rest of the gang to get set. Thirty frats waited impatiently at the town's old gray steel water tower. It looked like a large bullet pointing at the sky. Among the BMWs and the Mercedes, the frats stood outside in their dress shirts, ties, and sweaters, ready to fight.

Jimmy knew these fools didn't know what the hell they just got themselves into. That bunch might be angry, up-tight, fuzzy-headed dumb clucks, but they knew nothing about fighting, especially fighting a biker gang.

One of them said, "Those two sons of bitches better not have chickened out on us! They can't hide. We'll just kick in their front door and get them!"

"Where do they live?" one frat asked.

"In that old white house on the hill just off campus," another one said. "They live in the basement beneath Michelle, Elizabeth, and Anne Marie."

"You're lucky we're not met with a bunch of cops," another frat warned. "We could get in a lot of trouble both with the law and the university."

"Hey, shut up, Jerry!" Ward shouted. "Ernie's in the hospital with a concussion. Fluid has built around his brain. There's a chance he could die. I want those two assholes!"

"Who do you think those two guys are going to get?" Jerry asked.

Another frat chuckled. "They'll probably get a bunch of tie-dye hippies who will attack us with peace signs and love beads."

They laughed.

"Yeah, and they'll probably come up to us and say, 'Hey, man, like chill. Peace, dewd. Like, why can't you just experience non-violence? Smoke some dope and be one!'"

They all laughed again.

"Those two longhairs aren't showing!" one of them yelled.

"We'll wait here another five minutes," Ward said. "And if they don't show—"

Jimmy let out a slow breath. Maybe they'd just leave if they waited. He'd rather not have a fight if it could be avoided, but he also didn't want the guys showing up later at their house when the Knights had gone.

Ward stopped. He saw a single beam of light crack a round hole in the night. Another beam of light did the same on the other side of them. The frats whirled around. Another beam of light came on, then another, and another until the frats were bathed in light. The roar of the engines erupted like a chorus of demons in the night. Suddenly a mob of bikers, many with beer guts, long hair, and beards, surrounded the frats and sped around them and their cars. Several of the bikers' "old ladies" rode with them. Some girls swung chains. They knocked a few of the frats to the ground. The bikers fired guns and knocked out car windows. Several frats ducked behind their cars while a few others climbed into their cars and locked the doors even though the windows were already shattered. Ward and Jerry watched the bikers speed around them. Exhaust and gunpowder filled the air.

Finally, a pair of headlights turned on in the distance. The bikers stopped racing around. Billy drove his van towards the frats and bikers. He had his girlfriend, Tabatha, with him. The bikers cleared a path for him, and Billy stopped his van. He got out. The back doors flew open. Jimmy and Seth jumped out. They wore their leather jackets with the colors of the Black Knights' on the back. Cassie got out of the van with Tabatha, a busty short woman with lots of blonde hair.

Jimmy found himself smiling. Okay, now you idiots are going to get a heavy dose of reality and find out all about our past.

Seth and Jimmy walked up to Jerry and Ward as he nursed a beer bottle. "We're here! I see you guys are dressed for a fight."

Jerry and Ward stood there with their jaws hanging around their toes. The smell of fired weapons and exhaust from the bikes saturated the air.

"I'm ready to fight, aren't you, Jimbo?"

"Yep," Jimmy said. He was actually ready for anything that would get these boobs to leave them alone. But maybe this isn't all bad. You guys actually have him thinking that he wants to leave here.

"Are the rest of you Knights ready for a fight?" Seth asked.

"Yeah!" they shouted.

"So let's go!" Seth said. "Let's fight!"

"Hey, w-we were just kidding," Jerry said.

"Yeah, kidding," Ward said.

"Kidding?" Seth said. "That's like humor, right? I don't have a sense of humor, do I, Jimmy?"

By the looks on the frats' pasty faces, they finally understood picking a fight with them wasn't such a hot idea. "Not in the past couple of weeks, you haven't."

"See? So now, when you guys say fight, the first thing Jimmy and I think of is our past. Dig our past?"

"Really, guys, we didn't mean it," Jerry said.

"Didn't mean it?" Seth asked. "But you guys are all out here—"

Snake, a skinny guy with thick, curly brown hair, held his hands over his stomach. "Hey, Seth."

"Don't interrupt me, Snake!" Seth shouted.

Snake got off his Harley Hog. "Oh, Seth, I just gotta—"

"Snake-man, I'm warning you! Don't interrupt me!"

"Seth, really! Twirlin' around on my bike has done made me ill."

Seth turned around. "Is that so?" Seth walked up to a convertible. "It looks to me like we got a toilet right here."

"Oh, good." Snake ran to the car, bent over, and threw up in the front seat. The smell of partially digested tequila wafted through the crowd.

"Hey!" Ward shouted. "Hey, that's my car!"

Seth slammed some more beer. "I don't give a shit-ass." He looked at Snake. "Feel better, dude?"

Jimmy couldn't help but chuckle. He wondered if the frats now realized just what they got themselves into.

"Yeah," Snake said before he spat into the car. "Except now I gotta go the other way."

Seth finished his beer and tossed the bottle into the car. "The other way?"

"Yeah, all of that rotgut I drank before we got here is making my bladder feel like it's going to burst." Snake climbed into the backseat, unzipped his pants, pulled out his male member, and urinated all over the front dash, the front seats, the stereo, and the speakers. "Oh, yeah," he muttered. "I feel much better now."

"Hey, that's my car!" Ward screamed. He started to run towards Snake, but Seth grabbed a shotgun from one of the Black Knights and shoved it into Ward's face.

"Stay right there, asshole," Seth shouted. "Or I'll blow your god damned useless head right off!"

Jimmy couldn't understand it, but he again saw Seth's eyes turn from brown to black. Seth leaned on his gun and stood confident like David by Donatello. Seth chuckled.

Seth raged as he wandered around the frats. "I want you bunch of clods to realize I'm not like you. I didn't go to some well-to-do high school and then come right here to our proud, beloved, prestigious University of Morganburg, isn't that right, Jimbo?"

Jimmy gulped some beer. "Yep."

"Jimmy and I spent a couple of years on the streets in between high school and college. We were in this gang, the Black Knights. So if you nerds threaten me or Jimmy again, we're going to make a little phone call again, and we're getting our old gang back down here, and we will burn your precious frat house to the ground, and then we're going to come after all of you."

A lot of the Black Knights laughed. Jimmy looked at all of the frats. Their clammy, white faces contrasted greatly against the dark of night behind them. Jimmy knew Seth got what he wanted. Those frats looked like they were caught gang-raping the homecoming queen. But Seth wasn't done with them yet.

Seth stepped up to Ward. "Now, what you need to ask yourself is, have we pissed off this big Freak People to the point where he's reverted to the maniac he used to be on the streets, or is he still more like college-boy, the kinder, gentler art major he has been after he became more educated and enlightened?"

Ward breathed like an asthmatic. "Please, man—"

Seth pointed the gun at Ward's head and cocked the hammer. "What do you say? Which person do you believe I am right now? Do you think I could kill you? Do you?"

Jimmy wasn't sure if Seth meant it. Would he really kill that guy? For the first time in his life, Jimmy feared Seth might murder him. He believed they taught the frats enough of a lesson. It was time for them to get out of there.

"Please, man," Ward said as his voice quivered. "We were just fooling around!"

"Fooling around?" Seth screamed. "It didn't sound like that to me! Did it to you, Jimbo? It sounded like if we wouldn't fight you, you bunch of two-faced mental midgets were going to come after us. You said you going to kick our ass."

"Please," Ward pleaded. "We didn't mean it!"

Jimmy said, "Seth, come on. Let's go—"

"Then why the fuck are all of you here?" Seth screamed. Ward didn't answer. Tears slipped down his face. Seth shoved him into a car. He fell to the ground. "Get up, you dumb son of a bitch!"

Ward covered his head and cried, "Please…please…please!" Snot ran down his face.

Seth pointed the shotgun in Jerry's face. Then he shoved it into his mouth and said, "How about you? Do you think I'm still the guy from the streets? Do you know what I did to people there? Do you know what I was capable of then? Huh? Speak up!" Seth looked around. None of them said anything. "A couple of hours ago, when it was four against two, I had no problem hearing from you. When you threatened to get thirty people, I heard you boast quite clearly. Now I don't hear anything out of you tough guys!"

Seth ripped the gun out of his mouth.

"Hey, calm down, man," one of the frats said.

"Yeah, fuck off, redneck!" Seth shouted.

Jerry sobbed, "Please don't shoot me."

"Oh, please don't shoot me," Seth mocked. "And you guys wanted to fight. Look at you, dressed in your ties and sweaters. What the hell would you rednecks know about fighting? You wouldn't know the difference between a headlock and a pair of headphones. You people wouldn't last ten minutes on the streets I used to walk." Seth smirked and stepped away, but he stopped and jammed the butt of his shotgun into the base of Jerry's sternum. Jerry collapsed. Seth turned around and glanced at Jimmy, Billy, Snake, Tabatha, and the rest of the Knights.

Jimmy grabbed Seth's arm. "Come on, Seth. Enough."

Seth pointed the gun back at Ward. "Now I want all of you to get the hell away from us and I don't want to even see you looking at Jimmy and me on campus!" Seth grabbed Ward by the tie and jerked him towards his convertible. "I want this dumb ass to get in his pissed-in, barfed-up seat and lead the way, now!"

Jimmy was relieved to see the situation end with no further violence.

Ward looked disgusted as he sat in his car. The Knights on their bikes, cleared a path for the frats. After they all left, Jimmy, Seth, and Cassie joined the gang to drink at the Hawk's Nest, the bar he wished he'd taken Seth to just as soon as the frats confronted them.

Billy, the Knights' leader, with shaggy golden brown hair and a thick beard, slammed whiskey shots and then drank his beer before he said, "Damn, Seth, I thought you were really going to shoot one of those guys."

Seth smirked. "So did all of those geeks."

Billy sloppily gulped his drink. "Seth, when I heard you call me, at first, I couldn't believe it. You needed our help?" Billy burst into laughter. "Hell, man, you were the toughest, dirtiest fighter among us. But then when you said it was, like, thirty guys that were after you and Jimmy, I called everyone, and we hauled ass down here."

Jimmy was grateful for his help. "Yeah, we appreciate that, Billy. I was afraid we wouldn't be able to get any of you on such short notice."

"Aw, hell, Jimbo," Billy said. "You guys ought to know we'd be here for you. After all of the things you did for us, we probably owe you two guys about twenty favors. Besides, we'd just like to see you two again. How long has it been since the whole gang seen you? Four years?"

"Damn near," Seth said. "Jimmy and I really miss Virginia Beach. We miss the city. I miss the beach, the boardwalk, Beach Street, Atlantic Avenue, and that awesome statue of King Neptune. I want to move back after I work on my Master's, maybe a Ph. D. at UVA."

Jimmy was again ecstatic to hear that again. If Seth really believed that, Jimmy believed he'd had no problem getting him out of there. "Yeah, I miss the nightlife and the bands. And you can bet once I graduate, I'm moving right back. I've had enough of this little backwater town."

Billy poured another bottle. Beer foamed over his wrist. "We'd definitely be glad to see both of you come back. We miss you two nuts. And if you get any more trouble from that bunch of punks, don't be afraid to call us, or if you run into any trouble at all, and we can help, call us."

Jimmy was glad to hear him say that. "You never know, man. We may have to take you up on that offer."

Billy smiled. "Cool!" He slammed his beer. "I like beating up stupid punks."

Seth introduced Cassie to several members of the gang. She met Snake, their friend from high school who got Seth and Jimmy into the gang, Hat Trick, Nick, Hammer Head, Spike, the Spider, Poseidon, and others. Jimmy was sure she had lost track of all the names. After a few hours of drinking and telling old tall tales, the Black Knights roared back to Virginia Beach. Jimmy wished he could have joined them. He drove Seth and Cassie back home. Seth walked Cassie to the door of her apartment building. After Seth said goodnight to her, Cassie planted a big kiss on him.

Uh-oh, Jimmy thought.

CHAPTER TWENTY-TWO

Monday morning felt awful. He and Seth drank all weekend. The stress of living in a town he feared and hated was getting to be too much. He went on campus and went to one class. Something on the front page of the campus paper caught his attention. He grabbed a copy and read the front article. The Tri Delts became sick from the fall festival brunch. Some of them had to be hospitalized.

Damn, that probably means those girls didn't get Cassie out of here.

Jimmy returned home and grabbed a Coke. He returned to his bedroom and tried to get his eyes to focus on a story he was working on for a class. Someone knocked at the door, and it felt like a ballpoint pen ramming into his ear.

"Oh, enough already," Jimmy moaned. He opened the door without even looking at who was there. He sat down on the couch. "Please enter quietly. There's a hangover in progress."

Traci folded her arms. "I guess I don't have to ask you what you've been up to, Jimmy. Yet another drunken debacle of a weekend?"

He rubbed his unshaven face. "You got it, honey."

"Why, Jimmy? Why do you keep doing this to yourself?"

Jimmy sighed heavily. "Hell, I don't know."

"Damn it, Jimmy!"

Jimmy cringed and held out his hands. "Easy, dear."

"Ever since the day after you were with Rafe and Pete, the night they disappeared, I've been trying to call you. I've been really worried about you. Where have you been?"

"I don't know. I got to drinking with Seth."

"Drinking with Seth? From what I've seen, I think that's the last thing he needs right now. Don't you realize you're only enabling him?"

"Yes, I do—"

"And if he doesn't stop, he's going to get addicted."

"Look, I love that guy like a brother. I was looking to get him alone to talk to him. I think maybe I succeeded. But he kept drinking and so did I."

"Why? Why did you keep drinking? Did you and Seth get drunk because you're worried about Rafe and Pete?"

"Yeah, we were, I mean, we are, I mean, I am." Jimmy breathed deeply. He gulped some of his Coke. He figured maybe Seth was right. He should tell Traci. "Look, I've been drinking like this because of Laura."

"Laura? Jimmy, this sort of drinking isn't going to bring Laura back. It's not making you feel any better."

"I know that," Jimmy grumbled.

"Do you think Laura would want you to deal with her death by this sort of drinking?"

"No, damn it," Jimmy said so loudly the pounding in his head increased. His stomach rolled with the pain.

"You're not to blame for her death."

"I know, I know."

"So why are you drinking this way?"

Jimmy rubbed his forehead. He finished his soda. His mouth still felt like a layer of carpeting covered his tongue. "The night she was murdered, she had an exam. She wanted to stay home to study. I was done for the semester. So I went out with Seth and some other friends, and we partied the night away. If I had stayed home with her, I know she'd still be alive."

Traci knelt down at Jimmy's feet and held his hands. "I never knew that."

"Few people do. Obviously, Seth knows about it. So do a few others, but actually, you're the only person I've ever talked to about that."

Traci squeezed Jimmy's hands. "You never talked about this to anyone?"

He never wanted to. He wished the night had never happened. "No."

"I'm sorry."

Jimmy shrugged. "Not as much as I am."

"Did you ever think you would've been killed, too?"

Jimmy's mouth was so dry; he could barely talk. He got another Coke. He chuckled bitterly. "There are days when I wished I died with her. Some days I think that would've been the best thing that could've happened to me. I'd rather die with her and still be with her than live like this."

"Now, don't talk like that, Jimmy. You know you have a chance to help find her killer. And you may have a chance to uncover whatever the devil is going on here."

Jimmy's hangover suddenly faded, and his stomach settled. He chugged some more Coke. He no longer felt so thirsty. He wanted to find out what happened to Laura, but the price was too high. And his relationships seemed doomed. "I don't seem to be good luck to girls."

"What do you mean?"

"In high school, I had a girlfriend who was in a really bad car accident. She was nearly killed. She was in a wheelchair for a while. After we graduated, we didn't stay in touch. I wonder about her sometimes. Laura helped me not be afraid to get close to a girl again." He scoffed.

"Then she was murdered."

She smiled sadly. "I always thought you've been doing all this drinking because of Laura. Now I realize it's more complicated than that."

Jimmy sat back down. "It hasn't exactly been a fun life. My parents were always fighting, fighting with each other, fighting with me. I think that's why I started writing as a teen. I can create my own worlds where the ending is a happy one."

"You and Seth use your art to cope. It sounds like that's how you got through your childhoods."

"Yeah, it's been a lot easier for me to deal with characters than real people. I love my characters in my created worlds. But people out there, as soon as I find someone to love, this world takes her away from me."

Traci sat down next to him. "I think I can help you get close to someone again, Jimmy."

Jimmy smiled weakly. "Really? Do you know magic?"

Traci squeezed Jimmy's hands again. Her hands felt cool. His heart raced. He had just told her he was bad luck to girls, but she smelled nice, and she seemed to like him.

"From now on, I'll stop bitching to you about your drinking."

Jimmy wiped his eyes. "No, you're right. I shouldn't be drinking this much. It isn't helping, and it really bothers you, doesn't it?"

"Why do you think I'm complaining about that?"

Jimmy set his can of soda down. "You must not like it."

She frowned. "Yeah, but why?"

"I don't know."

"Jimmy, tell me about the time when we first met."

"When we first met? We met when we were juniors. Natalie introduced you to me at the student center. Seth was with us. We all had lunch together."

"No, Jimmy, try again. We met before then."

Jimmy didn't understand what she meant. He didn't know why she asked about this. "What do you mean try again? That's how we met! Hello? What are you talking about?"

Traci shook her head. She sat down next to him. "We met when we were sophomores. You had just transferred from Reynolds College to here. We met at Rafe's and Pete's. Try again."

Jimmy didn't know what she was talking about. What did she want him to say?

"Sophomores? Rafe's and Pete's? Honey, I never forget a face, and I never forget how I met someone. You and I met on a Friday in October when we were juniors."

"No, Jimmy. We met when we were sophomores at Rafe's and Pete's party, and you talked me into bar hopping. We went to Allen's."

Jimmy felt the blood rush away from his face. "No, way," he breathed.

"Oh, yes way."

"You were that blonde that took me to Allen's?"

Traci frowned. "That's right. I was a blonde. And I went out with you that night."

"My God," Jimmy whispered. His eyes scanned Traci up and down. "That was you?"

"Yep. My hair is a little longer now, but that was me."

"I can't believe it. That was really you? What happened? Did you take me home?"

"No. A bunch of your friends came into the bar, and you left with another girl."

Jimmy couldn't believe what he was hearing. He didn't remember any of this, and apparently, Seth didn't either. He felt lost, not knowing what he did. "What girl?"

Traci's glare made him feel as though his skin had begun to melt. "It was Laura. You looked like you met her already."

Jimmy groaned. "Oh, man, I met her in a creative writing class. I think that was the first night we went out. Jesus, you mean to tell me I just left you? While we were on a date?"

Traci said disgustedly, "You got it, buddy."

"So that's why you've always been on my case about the drinking. I can't believe it. How could I leave you?"

Traci stood up and shrugged her shoulders. "Because I think even then you knew you really liked her, and you wanted to get serious with her."

"Did I say goodbye or anything?"

"No way. You just took off with your girl and left me stranded."

He had no idea he'd done any of that. Was that who he was when he was drunk? "Christ, Traci, I am sorry. Please believe that. I drank a lot heavier back then. I drank even heavier when Seth and I were with the Knights. Ever since I met Laura, I slowed down and even stopped. Then, well, you know."

"And since she was killed, you've been really pounding down the booze."

"I've been starting up again because of everything going on lately. I had been drinking to forget, but I wasn't forgetting. I need to get over it and move on. If I stop drinking so much,that'll make you happy, won't it?"

"Yes, it would. I'm glad I didn't know you back when you were with the Knights. I doubt if I would've liked you back then."

Jimmy forced a slight smile. "Aw, come on. You would've loved me back then. I was Captain Party. I'm the guy who made the party into a verb."

"That doesn't surprise me."

Jimmy finished his soda and stood up. He asked her if she wanted a Coke. She accepted.

"Why didn't you ever say anything, especially the day Natalie introduced me to you?"

"I wanted to hear what your excuse would be for ditching me like that. But then, when you didn't even recognize me when Natalie introduced us, I was even more furious with you. I was hoping at some point and time you'd remember, but you never did. I thought you were a real creep." She took the can of Coke from him.

Jimmy shook his head. "That wasn't my intent. I'm afraid I was. Now I know why you've been so hostile to me."

"Your drinking reminded me of my father's drinking. He used to drink like that. Finally, my mother threatened to leave him if he didn't stop. But he didn't. He picked the booze over her and left us."

"I see." Jimmy preferred to take life over liquor, so he believed stopping would make her ecstatic. He glanced out the window. He believed those woods actually spied on him. "I can't wait to get out of here."

She cracked open the can. "Neither can I. I hope to find a job back in Virginia Beach."

Jimmy smiled. "That's where I'm from. Maybe we can move back together."

Traci grinned. "I'd like that."

Jimmy stepped up to the window. The trees swayed back and forth. They moved in uniform. A chilly breeze blew through the window.

"I hope we can," he whispered.

The next day after Jimmy finished his classes, he found Natalie across the campus in the law library. Compared to most of the campus, which was either old antebellum houses converted and renovated into academic buildings with classrooms or unimaginative structures that were built four or five decades ago, the law library looked modern. It stood three stories high. The front doors opened to a huge lounge. Shelves filled with magazines lined the walls. The leather couches and chairs looked brand new.

Everyone saw where the university put its money. Even though this school was founded by the arts, the art and English departments looked like they were beginning to fall apart, but the law and business schools have the newest, best, and most modern facilities. Jimmy knew where he stood with the college.

Natalie sat at a large wooden table, taking notes from a textbook. Several people studied at tables around the library. He sat down next to Natalie. "Hey, good-looking."

Natalie smiled slightly. "Hi, Jimmy. What brings you over here?"

"You busy?"

She nodded. "Pretty much, yeah. I'm working on a really tough paper for class."

Jimmy's heart sank a little. "Okay. I was just wondering if you're still mad at Seth."

Natalie set her textbook aside. "Pretty much, yeah."

"I know that fight you had with Seth was really awful. And Seth acted like a jerk. In fact, he was downright scary. And he's acting that way more and more. I swear he's getting worse than when we were on the streets. I'm really getting worried about him. I'm sorry. You know I wouldn't let him hurt you."

"Jimmy, do you know what's going on with Seth?"

"I can't prove it yet, and I don't know how, but I think this town is having a negative effect on him. I know this sounds nuts, and you're the only one I'm willing to say this to because you know me so well, but if I didn't know any better, I think Seth is becoming another person. It's like he swallowed poison, and he's become Jekyll and Hyde." Jimmy couldn't help but wince. It's what Traci accused him of acting like. Jimmy thought that the way he fought with Traci sometimes, maybe she was right. Maybe everyone in town is becoming like that.

"I've noticed that. One moment Seth is his old self and the next, he's an out-of-control madman who is screaming and raging."

"Yeah, I have to admit, even I feel as though this town is twisting me inside out. I'm getting a real bad attitude about this school and this town. I can't really explain it, but some days I feel like getting a lighter and torching the whole campus. I just want to see this university burn."

"I think you're getting senioritis. You're ready to graduate and get on with your life. Maybe that's Seth's problem, too."

It's a lot more than that. If only you had seen that black fog like Traci and me. "Look, I know Seth said some pretty hateful things to you, but if I think it's possible, he's become an alcoholic. If I could arrange an intervention with you, me, and Traci, would you be willing to do it?"

"You think that's what's wrong with him?"

Jimmy looked around. People glared at him. He didn't realize he talked that loudly. He lowered his voice. "I think it's possible that could be happening to him. Actually, I think that could be a symptom of something much worse. Would you help me if I asked?"

"Yes, of course. You know I love Seth. I'd do anything for him."

"I want to get him away from campus. I have to get him to agree to go out for lunch or something. Then we'll take him out of here."

"Yeah, the way Seth is talking lately, I think once he graduates, he wants to get out of here and go to grad school somewhere else. He hates Morganburg."

"I think we just need to get him out of here. He's not happy in this town, and I think if we just get him back to Virginia Beach, we'd get our old Seth back."

Natalie sighed. "Yeah, you may be right. We'll see. First things first. We have to graduate."

He didn't care about that; he just wanted to get out first and then figure it out. Maybe there was no point in trying to get others to leave, even though he was scared of the campus and the spirits or curses or whatever that were there.

She leaned her head in her hand. "I can't take much more of this, Jimmy. I really can't. The one thing I didn't want a problem with was a boyfriend. I've got enough on my plate dealing with school and trying to get into law school."

He felt bad for her, but he felt bad for Seth and himself, too. Everything has gone to hell since he moved here.

"How did things go with your folks after we left?"

She wiped a tear from her eye. "They're understandably upset. They think I should stop seeing him, graduate here and move back to New York with them."

"Are you?"

"I really don't want to. I don't miss New York winters."

He hoped she wouldn't take his head off when he asked this. "Would you be willing to do an intervention on him?"

She nodded. "Yeah. I still love him. I'll do anything to help him."

"Good. I'll call you." People still stared at him. Jimmy couldn't understand it. He couldn't whisper any more softly. "Until then, stay away from that house. Fights keep breaking out both upstairs and downstairs. I think there's something wrong with that house. I swear, there are days when I think the only thing that house is missing is a moat. The basement makes me feel as if I'm in a dungeon."

CHAPTER TWENTY-THREE

Jimmy saw Laura come to him that evening as he sat on the couch. He saw her as she looked the last time they went out. She wore a black flowery dress. He stood up and held her hands. "It's okay, Jimmy, with you and Traci—"

"Laura, I still love you!"

"I know you do. But it's over, Jimmy. Face reality, hon. I'm gone. Traci is alive. It's okay about you and her. Take her and Natalie and get out now—"

"Wait! There's so much I need to ask you! Who murdered you?"

"I can't talk long, Jimmy. They're constantly after me. I can't keep running and hiding from them forever. They killed me. The force here. Sent a soldier after me. Didn't know when I answered the door…I have to go, Jimmy. Please listen to me. Get out while you still can. Forget Seth. You've lost him. Go *now!*"

Jimmy woke up and looked around. He was in Traci's apartment. He looked at her bedroom. The door was open.

That Friday, Jimmy called Traci, and she agreed to come along. She was just down the street in the news office. He wanted to try to set Seth up for an intervention. He wanted Natalie to join him, but since she was working on a poli sci paper, he hoped Traci's presence would help, and Seth would be less inclined to start an argument if she was there. They darted into the art building and found Seth standing back away from one of his mud paintings and staring at it. He tried to paint a still life of flowers in a vase, wine bottles, and a dish full of fake fruit over a draped blue table cloth that stood at the center of the back wall. Easels with paintings on them circled the room.

"Why?" he mumbled. Seth rolled the stage closer to the painting and he sat down. He gulped some beer as he gazed at the disaster before him. Seth never heard someone open the studio door behind him.

"Why don't you give it a rest, Seth?" Jimmy asked.

Seth turned around and glared at them. "I'm taking enough shit here. Why don't you go blow and do me a huge fucking favor?"

His words felt like a punch to the gut. *Damn it. He's back to being Mean Seth.*

"Seth, why are you so mad all the time?" Traci asked. "What's wrong?"

"What's wrong is you people keep harassing me and then I can't concentrate on what I'm doing."

Jimmy couldn't deal with Seth when he was like this. He's drinking and mad at his painting. He'd rather deal with him in the morning. "Fine. We're outa here."

They left the studio, and Jimmy said, "We have to get him off campus. And I think we're going to need Natalie's help. We need to do an intervention."

They started to leave, but he caught a glimpse of Cassie through the large back window in the stairwell. He ducked into a hallway, and Cassie headed to the studio where Seth painted.

They ducked into a hallway and watched Cassie go into the studio with Seth.

"What the hell is that bitch up to?" Traci whispered.

"Let's find out."

They went to the studio door and peeked inside.

She snuck up behind Seth and asked, "What are you thinking about?"

Seth nearly jumped into his painting. He leaped from the stage like one of the bodies from the graveyard next to the art building rose up from the ground and put its icy-cold withered hand on the back of Seth's neck. Seth exclaimed, "Jesus, Cassie, what the hell are you doing?"

Cassie giggled. "Don't tell me that little ol' me scared a great big man like you."

"Crud, Cassie, you scared the shit-ass out of me."

She pouted. "Mad with me?"

Seth smirked after he caught his breath. "No. I'll be fine, so long as I don't choke on my heart, which by the way, is in my throat after that."

Cassie giggled. "Are you making a painting or a mess?"

Seth shook his head wearily. "Oh, don't you start in on me too, okay? Jimmy and Traci were just in here and told me to take a break from it. I really bit their heads off about it. I wish I hadn't done that. Lately, every little thing seems to make me mad."

That's what Jimmy tried to tell him. Jimmy wished they got that warm and fuzzy Seth.

"It's probably that beer you're drinking. It's illegal to have alcohol on this campus, you know, Seth."

"I'm aware of that. Want one?"

"Yeah, sure."

Seth reached into his cooler and handed Cassie a bottle. Cassie popped the top. "So, what's up with this painting?"

Seth smirked as he sat down next to her on the stage. She held his hand and pressed his arm firmly against the side of her breast. "I don't know. I was trying to paint an ocean scene, but instead, I have ended up with a rat hole painting. I think I'm going to let that debacle dry and just paint over it."

"So Jimmy said you should take a break, and you read him the riot act?"

Seth sipped some beer and moaned. "Yeah. I guess maybe I should. Honestly, it's worse than awful, and I took it out on him."

Jimmy couldn't believe what he was hearing. Seth was like two different people lately.

"What's going on with you?" Cassie asked.

"I'm pissy because I've been fighting with Natalie and our relationship is hanging by its fingernails. The two best friends I've ever had, and I've literally told them to go to hell."

"Maybe you should take a break."

Seth set his paintbrush down.

Jimmy figured if a person is beautiful enough, Seth would listen to them.

"Jimmy, we should leave," Traci whispered.

"Hold on. I want to see what she says to him."

"Have you and Natalie split?"

Seth slammed some beer. "Aw, hell, we're still together. But now I am no longer sure if we're getting married."

"What happened?"

"I think some of our problems are due to the fact that we're both workaholics. She wants to graduate and go to law school. I want to work on a Master's in drawing and painting. Sometimes our busy schedules force us to be apart for long stretches. I believe that's what's really hurting us."

Cassie played with Seth's hair and touched his earring. "Ow!" Seth said.

"What is it?" Cassie asked. She looked at his ear. "My gosh, Seth. You should see your ear. It looks infected."

Seth felt his ear. "Damn. I didn't realize."

"Can't you feel it? It's really red and swollen."

"No. I'll take a look at it and clean it later tonight."

"You better do that then right away; otherwise, you could lose that ear. It really does look bad. You haven't noticed?" She held his hand. "Besides that, are you all right? You look really tired."

Jimmy opened the door a little wider. He wasn't surprised Seth was tired, he ought to be. He was drinking all the time.

"I am." He couldn't believe how those women upstairs acted with their boyfriends. They sounded like mating elephants. "Your friends keep me awake a lot. What's wrong with them? They get into huge fights with their boyfriends, especially late at night. I've had to call the cops on them a few times. It sounds as if I've stopped a couple of attempted rapes."

"I didn't realize it was that bad. I do know that those girls have complained that everything is fine with their boyfriends, but once they get back to that house, they start screaming at each other."

"Why can't they just split up if they hate each other? I already left my parents behind, and I figured once you did that, you could leave any relationship. It was freedom."

"I really don't know. Hell, you remember that night you, me, and Jimmy were out, and Ernie and his friends threatened you. He turned out to be a real prick. And so did all of his friends. Maybe Anne Marie, Michelle, and Elizabeth will split up with their boyfriends, too."

Seth stared at his painting for several moments. "You know, I've had the same problem with Natalie. We're fine with each other until we're at that house. Maybe there's something wrong with that place."

Jimmy believed there was definitely something wrong with that place. There was something wrong with the whole town. He wished he had never even heard of Morganburg.

"Like what?"

"Jimmy, we should really leave," Traci whispered. "This is none of our business."

"I can't believe what I'm seeing," he muttered. "It's like it's not even Seth."

Seth used his utility knife to scrape off old paint from his pallet. "I don't know."

Cassie touched it. "I've never seen a glass pallet before."

"Most of us art students use them. We get them at the art supply store. We can get a piece of corkboard cut exactly the size of the glass. Then we duct tape them together. The pallet is easy to clean. We can scrape off the hardened clumps of dry paint. And turpentine can wash off the rest."

"What's the corkboard for?"

"Easier to handle, harder to break. Taping the edges makes it so we can't get cut from the edges of the glass. And when the duct tape wears out, it's cheap and easy to re-tape it. A glass pallet will last forever."

"That's good." Cassie slammed the last of her beer. "Got more?"

"Oh, yeah." Seth got up and grabbed another bottle.

Cassie looked down. "What's this we're sitting on?"

Seth opened the bottle and handed it to her. "It's a stage for models. We can move it around to accommodate the size of a class."

"Nude models?"

Cassie looked around and Jimmy let the door nearly close. He feared where those two were going with that.

He grinned. "That's the only kind of models we have, you know. You think we can study figure anatomy looking at some guy in his boxers?"

"I see. I doubt if I can help you with Natalie or Jimmy, but I do know how to help you with your painting."

"And how's that?" Seth asked.

Jimmy breathed deeply and cracked the door open a little more again. He was relieved Cassie didn't see him.

"Jimmy, we need to go," Traci pleaded.

Cassie picked Seth's painting up from the easel as if she was touching a dirty, foul-smelling pair of underwear. "Do you have another canvas to work with?"

"Oh, yes. I put gesso on this one yesterday. I can use it." Seth placed the stretcher on the easel. "Why?"

"I know that if artists get stuck in a rut, they drop what they're doing and work on something else. I think that's what you need to do. It will free your mind and it will still keep you working. Then maybe when you come back to your ocean painting, it will work out for you."

He nodded. "So, what do you want me to paint?"

"Me," she whispered.

"You want me to paint you?"

"Yes. Will you do it?"

"Sure."

Cassie gulped some of her beer and set it down. "You ready?"

"Hang on, honey," Seth said. "I need to mix paint to get your skin tone and your hair color."

Cassie walked back to the stage. Her high heels smacking against the floor sounded like someone locking a graveyard late at night. Cassie stepped up onto the stage and walked around it.

Seth mixed his paint. "I'd be happy to paint such a beautiful woman. You know, Natalie and Jimmy are trying to talk me into leaving Morganburg and going to school somewhere else."

"They're what?"

"They're trying to talk me into leaving. I'm really beginning to consider it. I don't like it here."

Jimmy believed they needed to get Seth out of there. He wasn't sure if he should quit spying on his best friend and leave it or try to put a stop to that. *"Maybe we should—."* He looked over his should and Traci was no longer there. He looked further behind him. She was just standing at the hallway entrance of Dr. Johnson's office.

He wondered what she was looking at. He didn't want to call her for fear Seth and Cassie would hear him.

Cassie said, "Michelle, Mary Anne, and Elizabeth have been trying to do the same to me. I don't understand what's making these people think this. Are you really serious, Seth? Do you really want to leave?"

He was surprised she asked. Outside of the university, there was nothing there. "Yeah, I really do."

Cassie swayed back and forth on the stage. "So models just stand up here?"

"Yeah, or they sit or lie down."

"For how long?"

"Studio classes are two hours," Seth said as he finished mixing paint for Cassie's hair, black and a little red, and the paint for her skin, black, white, red, and a little blue and yellow. "It depends on the class and what the professor wants. For the upper-level figure anatomy courses, a model can sit for half an hour, an hour, two hours, or for several days."

Jimmy thought he smelled something bad, and it wasn't the turpentine. He wondered what was that? He looked behind him, but he couldn't see anything to cause that stench. He couldn't believe they couldn't smell it, too. He looked back at Traci, and she was still staring down the hall.

What is she doing? he thought.

"In the same position?" She asked.

Seth found the colors he needed and mixed a bigger batch to paint Cassie. "They get breaks. For very long poses, we get the models to get into a comfortable position so they can stay that way for a long time. If they get a limb that goes numb or if they need a break, they can ask to get up, walk around, go to the bathroom, or go have a smoke. We don't mind. Artists need breaks, too. Think you're up for it?" He grinned at her.

Cassie picked up her beer and sat back down on stage. "How do you want me to pose?"

"How long do you want to be in your position?"

Cassie shrugged. "Just tonight."

A few hours was going to be tough to finish if she didn't want to sit for him again. "Pick any position you want then. You will probably still want to be sitting." Seth started to mix paint for her clothes. "You know, your skin is sort of dark, but not very dark. Are both your parents European or do I detect a mix of something else inside you?"

"My mother was tribal American. What about you, Seth? Do you have roots from one of the American tribes?"

"Yes, I do, but I'm not sure which one. I was adopted. I know my father was tribal American, but I don't know anything else about my real parents."

The smell grew worse. He stepped into another painting studio, but he saw nothing. "Traci," he whispered. She still stared down the hallway.

"You're adopted, too?" Cassie asked.

"Yes, I was. I only know a little about my real parents. I never really cared. I figured if they didn't want me, it's probably best they gave me up." Seth finished mixing the paint. "Okay, I got your hair, skin, and your clothes. Did you decide how you wanted to pose?"

Jimmy tried to call Traci again without being heard by Seth and Cassie. Traci remained staring down the hall. He wondered if she could be in some kind of trance. The stench grew worse, first like burning sulfur, then more like diseased flesh with open wounds and decaying bodies. He couldn't believe neither one was mentioning it.

Cassie kicked off her high heels. "You don't need to worry about the color of my clothes, Seth." Cassie unbuttoned her white sweater and let it slip from her shoulders.

Oh, shit, he thought. *What the hell does she think she's doing? Seth is engaged. Or at least Jimmy thought he still was.* He glanced back at Traci. *What is going on with her?* He closed the door, stepped closer to her, and whispered, "Traci."

Seth nearly dropped his brush. "You want me to do a nude?"

"Yes, baby, I do. Haven't you always wanted to since you met me?" Cassie unfastened her jeans and unzipped them. She kicked them aside as if they were a burden. She stood on the stage in nothing but her lacy black bra and panties. "Let's see," she muttered as she sucked on her beer bottle as if she was performing fellatio. "How should I do this?" She put her bottle down and unfastened her bra. "Does Natalie have breasts like mine?"

Jimmy cracked the door back open.

Cassie's breasts were larger. Her dark nipples protruded outward farther than Natalie's. Seth smiled. "No, she doesn't."

"You like them more, don't you?" Seth's smile widened, but he said nothing. "Tell me, Seth."

"Okay, they're beautiful. And they're nicer than Natalie's, okay? You happy now?"

Jimmy had to put a stop to this. Seth had Natalie, and he still would if Jimmy could get him out of there. But the stench grew overpowering, and Jimmy nearly threw up. He ran to her and grabbed her hand. "Traci—!"

She stared into the interior design studio. Through the glass wall and door, they could see nothing but black. She lazily raised her hand and pointed. "It's the Darkness, Jimmy. It's *coming*." Then she laughed.

Oh, shit, Jimmy thought. *Don't tell me this crap has her, too.* He shook her. "Traci, snap out of it!"

She came to and said, "What?"

"Come on! We have to help Seth."

They ran back to the studio, and he cracked the door back open.

Cassie sat down on the stage. "Tell me. What's a good pose?"

"The best pose is the one you feel comfortable with holding for about an hour or so. I assume that's what you want me to do, paint you for about an hour."

Cassie smiled. "I guess so." She positioned herself a couple of ways until she found one that she liked. "Oops. I almost forgot one last thing." Cassie peeled off her panties.

"Classic Venus pose," Seth said.

"Is it? I've always wanted to be your Venus, Seth."

"*Jimmy,*" she whispered as she tugged at him.

"Come on. We have to stop them."

"Jimmy, look!"

The Darkness floated down the hallway.

What the fuck? Jimmy thought.

"My God, Jimmy. We have to get out of here!"

The black fog also penetrated the back-open studio door and into the room. Jimmy gasped, and they fled the building through a side studio door. He started to run to his car but stopped.

"No. I can't run. I have to get Seth out of there!" He gave her the keys. "Start the car and drive to the street. I'll get him."

"Jimmy—!"

"Do it!"

He ran back to the outside glass door, which led to the studio Seth was in, but no longer saw the black fog.

Jimmy wondered why it retreated. Was it just to chase him away?

As Seth painted, the two of them made small talk for several minutes. Seth rubbed some of the paint with his finger on the canvas to create a coarse appearance against Cassie's arms. He smeared some paint with a putty knife into the background. Then he rubbed his thumb against the canvas. Seth put the brush in his mouth and studied the painting. He finished one bottle of beer and started another. Cassie stole a couple of long gulps of her beer while Seth got another one for himself. She spread her thighs and smiled.

Seth nearly dropped his brush. "Now, that's definitely not part of a classic Venus pose."

"No?" Cassie asked as her smile widened.

This time Jimmy was putting an end to this.

Just as Jimmy opened the door, the Darkness oozed back into the studio. He froze.

"Come here, Seth," Cassie whispered. "Come here, baby. Come here and make love to me."

Seth shed his clothes like a reptile's skin and became entangled with Cassie like a couple of vipers coiling around each other for a deadly strike. They kissed and rolled their tongues around each other. Seth grabbed Cassie's breasts and sucked on them as if he was trying to drain them of blood. Cassie grabbed fistfuls of Seth's hair and sucked on his neck. Seth shoved Cassie onto the stage and rammed his erection deep inside her. Seth drove into her like he stabbed her with a butcher knife. Cassie screamed in ecstasy like she had never had sex ever before.

"Oh my God, Seth! Yes! Harder! Just like that! Yes, baby!"

Seth planted his seed in her and grinned like a decaying corpse. Darkness roared back into the studio like diseased vermin and slithered up to the stage and spun around it as Seth pumped Cassie full of his seed. Seth and Cassie kept drinking while they grabbed and groped after Cassie got on top of him.

Jimmy had to end this now.

He ran inside. The Darkness surrounded them, crept up on stage, and rose around them like a moat of protection. It entered Seth, and then he down up at Cassie. Seth looked ill, even ghastly white.

Jimmy couldn't understand what was happening to Seth.

Then blackness poured out of Seth's mouth as he looked up with those black eyes and grinned.

How do I fight evil that is this powerful? Jimmy thought. *How can I ever hope to free him of this and bring him back to me?*

The black fog rushed Jimmy, and he stumbled backward, tumbling over the vase behind him and smashing it. He got up and ran, colliding with the easels and knocking them over along with the paintings. The Darkness nearly enveloped him when he sprang to his feet, ran out of the studio and into the next one, and escaped through a side door that led outside.

Traci pulled up in front of the little cemetery. He ran to his car, and they sped off.

CHAPTER TWENTY-FOUR

As they flew to Jimmy's apartment, he asked, "What happened to you back there?"

"What do you mean?"

"When you were at the edge of the hallway staring into the interior design studio. It was like you were in a trance."

"I don't know," she muttered. She looked like she might start crying. "I can only remember peeking in on Seth. Then I remember you grabbed me, and we ran back to the studio."

They pulled into the driveway, and she parked his car.

She asked, "Do you want to come with me?"

"Yeah. I don't want to be in that house alone at night."

They went inside. "I'm never going to be on campus unless I absolutely have to. Just for classes. That's it."

Jimmy grabbed some clothes and everything he needed for school.

As he stuffed books into his bookbag, she asked, "What is that?"

Jimmy looked back at some paintings scattered on the floor. "This is what Seth calls his paintings now. Hideous, aren't they?"

"No, I don't mean the painting itself. I mean right there on the painting. What has he written in the corner?"

Jimmy had to stare at the name before he could attempt to pronounce it.

"Riapokemobataconno. Don't ask me what the hell that means. I think he's using a pseudonym now. A lot of Italian Renaissance artists he likes used pseudonyms."

"What's it mean?"

"I have no idea."

They ran out of the apartment and sped to her place.

Jimmy and Traci talked little as Jimmy drove them to his apartment. Once inside, Traci grabbed a couple of Cokes. Jimmy collapsed onto the couch in the living room.

"After everything we've been through, we deserve these," Traci said. She handed Jimmy a can.

He still breathed heavily. "I've got no argument with you there." He gulped nearly half of it. "Can you believe what we saw tonight?"

She sat down next to him and held his hand. "We're done, right? We're done trying to find out what's wrong with this town."

It felt nice to have her touch him. He didn't want to lead her on. He said, "Yeah, we're done. I didn't go there to find out anything; just talk to Seth. People who have tried to investigate have ended up dead. Dangerous, scary, and crazy stuff keeps happening to us. Rafe and Pete are missing. I think they're dead."

"I realize that. The more we get involved and the deeper we dig, the worse things become. I'm scared to death for both of us. I will not help you with this story anymore, and I want you to promise me you'll stop. Please, baby? Please, let's stop."

"Yeah, after all I've seen, I think I know who and what killed Laura. It's got to be the curse in this town. But I still don't know why, and I think I may never know. I feel like I failed her and in trying to find answers, and I've put other people's lives in danger trying to find out."

"That's not true, Jimmy."

"Yes, it is. I failed Laura. I failed Rafe and Pete. They're probably dead because they tried to help me. I think I've failed Seth, too. I fear I've also lost him. I quit before I do any more damage." Jimmy believed someone else could figure out what was up with this town. He was ready to let go and move on with his life.

"You haven't failed me. You've saved me. More than once."

He pulled back, but she pulled him closer. "It's okay, baby. I promise. I know you still love Laura, but it's going to be all right."

Traci smiled slightly and the two of them stared at each other for several moments. Traci kissed him. She placed his hand on her breast. Jimmy led her to his bedroom. Jimmy still felt attached to Laura, but after everything that had happened to him the past several months, finding some sort of happiness in this horror around him felt right.

Jimmy wanted to feel good again. He wanted to have a normal life.

Traci unzipped her top. She took off his pants and kissed him again. She unfastened her bra and lowered his head to her bosom. Traci's large, pink erect nipples looked awesome. He kissed and licked them. He sucked on them until she moaned. He gently bit one of her nipples, and she gasped. He shed the rest of his clothes. Traci lied down. He kissed her body all over. He pulled her panties off and buried his face between her legs. Traci moaned louder.

"Yes, Jimmy," she whispered.

Jimmy slipped his erection inside her and pumped her hard. Traci screamed. They made love all night long. Traci was a gentle lover. Jimmy loved the way she moaned his name after she got on top of him. She touched him all over. When they finished, Jimmy held her.

"Promise me you'll never cheat on me," Traci said. "Promise me nothing will ever come between us, especially alcohol. Promise me you won't leave me. Promise me we won't let all of this here split us up."

Jimmy smiled and kissed her forehead. "I'm not losing you, too. I promise." To think he'd found this girl annoying. Now he thought she was the hottest thing around and someone he could even love.

Tuesday after Jimmy's last class, he had to run to the Academic building so the university could confirm he had all of his credits to graduate at the end of the spring semester. It was a pain-in-the-ass formality, but he had to do it. When Jimmy walked into the office, for a moment, the guy behind the desk looked like a rotting corpse with hollow eyes and insects crawling all over. Jimmy rubbed his eyes, and the vision was gone, replaced by a balding, forty-ish man with a potbelly.

Christ, Jimmy thought. *This again?*

The advisor asked, "What can I help you with?"

"I got an email that said I need to come here to confirm all my classes for graduation."

"Oh, yes. You're Jimmy Durham?"

"That's right."

He reached for a folder on his desk, opened it, checked a piece of paper, and signed it. "You've got all your credits. Just one semester to go and you can graduate. Any questions?"

"Yeah, one. Of the classes I have left, could I take them at Reynolds College and have them transferred over like I did when I came here as a sophomore?"

The advisor checked Jimmy's final classes. "Yes, you can. Are you getting a job?"

The guy smiled slightly and that foggy gray look filled his eyes.

"Yeah, that's it. A job."

"Sure. You can do that. Leave here. Take Traci with you and have a good life."

Painful, icy shivers ran down the length of Jimmy. In a dream, he saw Laura warn him about 'it' being in government. The spiritual force has control of the campus, City Hall, and probably the police. *I really do need to leave.*

"Okay, thanks."

Jimmy wasn't about to reveal what he was planning. Nothing was going to stop him. Yes, he was leaving, but not without Seth.

Jimmy couldn't find Seth all week. He was never at the studio or home, and Seth wouldn't answer his phone. He didn't know where Cassie lived, and he stopped to ask the girls upstairs where she lived, but they also were never home.

He glanced at the woods before he drove away from the house. *You really think you're going to keep him, don't you?* he thought. *That's not going to happen.*

CHAPTER TWENTY-FIVE

That Sunday, Jimmy finally reached Seth over the phone to go out for lunch together that day. Quickly Jimmy called Natalie and Traci, and they agreed to come over to take Seth to Traci's apartment to do an intervention on Seth.

Jimmy came home, and Seth wasn't there yet. He decided to fix a snack before Seth arrived. Just as Jimmy placed a leftover piece of pizza in the oven for lunch when he heard Seth come home. He heard him talking to a woman and thought it was Natalie.

Finally, Jimmy believed, they were going to get to Seth to talk to him.

But when he went into Seth's room, he found Seth with Cassie.

"What are you doing here?" Jimmy barked at her. "Haven't you done enough damage?"

"What's your problem, biker boy?" Cassie sneered.

"My problem is—"

"That's enough, Jimmy," Seth said. "I've heard enough from you. You owe her an apology."

Before Jimmy could think, he felt rage boiled inside him and suddenly erupted. "An apology? To *her*? You owe an apology to Natalie!"

"It's over between Seth and Natalie." Cassie held Seth's hand. "I'm pregnant with Seth's child. We're going to be together forever. Isn't that wonderful?"

Wonderful? Jimmy wanted to shout. At first, he thought it couldn't get any worse. Now he was wondering just how bad could it get.

Jimmy said, "Seth, what the hell has gotten into you?"

"You know—!" Seth started to say.

Someone knocked on the door.

"This isn't like you," Jimmy said. "In all the years I've known you, my God, you—"

The knocking grew louder, and Jimmy answered it.

Natalie gripped her purse tightly. Her smile quickly faded. She recognized the look in his eyes. "Is something wrong?"

"Honey, this is really a bad time."

"You think I should leave?"

"Honey, I think you should head for the highest hills in town. Run to the protective mount of the gods. Dionysus is livid and his wrath is great."

Her chest heaved. "Damn it. I wanted to do that intervention on him. Now what's gotten into him?"

"He's just drunk and in a mean mood. I would just strongly suggest to you to get the hell out of here."

Natalie's shoulders sank. "We were supposed to talk today about where we wanted to get married and who we were going to invite."

He didn't understand why she couldn't take a hint. Now really wasn't the time. "I'll you. We'll plan to do this some other day—"

"Natalie," Seth called. "Is that you?" His cold small smile showed no teeth, like a vengeful God who finally found his hapless devotee. "Natalie, I wasn't expecting you today."

His eyes were black.

"My God, Seth, what's happened to your eyes?"

"What about them?" he snapped.

"They're *black.*"

"I don't know, Nat. Why are you here today? I wasn't expecting you."

"What? But we were supposed to go out for lunch today. We were all going out for lunch, you, me, Jimmy, and Traci. Don't you remember?"

"No."

"Seth, you're drinking again," Natalie said. "You promised me you were going to stop that."

Cassie came out of Seth's bedroom. Her eyes were also black.

Jimmy realized the evil has her, too.

"What's *she* doing here?" Natalie snapped.

"What's she doing here?" Seth grabbed Cassie and kissed her. "That's what. Meet my new fiance, Natalie."

Natalie gasped and ran out of the house. Seth chased after her, but Jimmy tackled him.

"What the hell do you think you're doing?" Seth roared.

"Christ, Seth!" Jimmy yelled. "What's wrong with you? You act as if you're *possessed*!"

"What's wrong with me? What the God damn hell is wrong with you? Let go of me!"

Jimmy released him, and as he was getting to his feet, Seth shoved Jimmy into the dresser. Jimmy nearly lost consciousness. His head hurt from where it bashed up against the dresser, and he fell. He was stunned. He had never been in a fight with his best friend. Jimmy again felt a surge of rage rise inside him like someone opened a cage door and a Minotaur roared through the pit of his gut and right to his brain.

Jimmy got to a knee. "Seth—" he started to say.

Seth's eyes turned black again, and he launched Jimmy back into the wall and clubbed Jimmy in the back of the head. Pain exploded through Jimmy's head and shot down his spine. His vision swam as he looked up at who used to be his best friend.

"You're nothing, Jimmy! You always were!" His voice turned deeper when he said, "You serve us no purpose! *We don't want you!*" His voice changed to gruff and inhuman when he said, *"You're weak! You're not like us!"*

Seth roared out of the house.

Jimmy tried to get up, but his vision was blurry. His legs wouldn't move beneath him to support him. He reached forward, but everything faded to black.

Jimmy heard pounding. Something kept banging over and over again. He also heard someone hammering at the front door. "Jimmy!" Traci screamed. She ran around to the back of the house and pounded on the living room window. "Jimmy, wake up!"

Jimmy shook the cobwebs, and he smelled smoke. He forgot he had left the pizza in the oven. It had burned in the kitchen, and the house reeked of gas. Seth's door slammed shut by itself. After Jimmy came to, the door slammed shut even faster. Jimmy got to his feet, and Traci ran back around to the front door. Jimmy felt something wet running down the side of his face. He touched it. Blood covered his hand. Jimmy had split his head wide open after Seth shoved him against the dresser. If the metal latch kept scraping together by the door slamming shut, it could create a spark, and the whole house could blow apart like a giant grenade. Jimmy darted into Seth's room, reached beneath the bed, and pulled out a dumbbell. He braced the door and kept it from slamming closed. Jimmy staggered to the kitchen. Thick smoke obscured his path to the oven. He found the burners on high and the pilot lights out. Jimmy turned off the gas and the oven and he took the charred piece of pizza and put it in the sink and drowned it. Jimmy opened a couple of windows, ran to the front door and he fell into Traci's arms.

"My God, Jimmy, what the hell happened? What was going on in there?"

"I don't know," Jimmy said as he gulped fresh air. "Seth came home with Cassie and that screwed the intervention. It all went downhill from there. Natalie got there and Seth kissed Cassie in front of her. Natalie ran out, and Seth and I got into a fight. I lost that battle. Whatever is wrong with this town has definitely got hold of Seth. Jimmy couldn't wait for the next semester to get Seth out of there.

After Jimmy caught his breath and the smoke cleared out of the house, Jimmy wanted to leave. He wasn't sure he could spend any more time here, not with Seth like this. They drove to her apartment.

"Lucky I got there when I did."

Jimmy smiled slightly, but it faded fast. "Yeah. I think our luck is running out. And so is time."

CHAPTER TWENTY-SIX

Jimmy couldn't find Seth again for several days and gave up. He would try to find him again after the holiday.

Early in the morning on Thanksgiving Day, Jimmy drove Traci to Virginia Beach. They went to Billy and Tabatha's to have turkey dinner. Billy and Tabatha lived in a big, dark blue house among the trees. Billy was a big Cavaliers football fan. He kept Virginia memorabilia everywhere. Above the fireplace hung a big orange and blue trimmed V and two crossed swords, just like the emblem on the Cavaliers' helmets. Jimmy assured Traci she would like them. He told her some of the other guys would be there, too.

As they walked up to the door, Jimmy said, "The Black Knights grew older, and a lot of them started families. They also grew mellow in their old age."

"Are they dangerous?"

"No way. They didn't bully people and they didn't break the law, except a few of them still take drugs every now and again. But mostly, they like to ride and hang out in bars and listen to bands and drink."

Jimmy had forgotten how much Billy's place was like a home away from home for him. "They're a good bunch of guys. I miss all of them. I now wish Seth and me never left Virginia Beach to go to school at Morganburg. I wish we stayed there for school."

Traci smiled. "I'm sure I'll like them."

After Jimmy introduced Tracy to Billy, Tabatha, and a couple of the guys, Snake and Hat Trick, a tall beefy guy with a thick beard who always wore a black undertaker's hat. They sat down at the kitchen table. Billy passed around beer to everyone. Tabatha returned to the kitchen to place the stuffing in the turkey and stir the vegetables on the stove. Traci noticed Billy kept a bottle of whiskey in the fridge.

"You're the only person who I know needs to have his whiskey chilled," she said.

Billy grinned. "I always like my drinks ice cold." He popped open a soda. "I always mix it with this so the next morning my stomach isn't hanging out my mouth."

Hat Trick opened the fridge and grabbed a beer for himself. "You guys want one?"

Jimmy no longer cared that much for alcohol anymore. "Yeah, okay," Jimmy said unenthusiastically. "I don't drink much anymore. But what the hell. It's the holiday."

"You haven't quit, have you?" Snake asked.

Jimmy opened a bottle of Sam Adams. "Not officially. But I've certainly cut way back."

Tabatha set the table. "Where's Seth? In the past, he and Natalie always came here for Thanksgiving."

Jimmy spun the beer bottle in his hands but drank nothing. He didn't really want to tell them he thought Seth was possessed. They'd think he left for college and lost his noodle. He wasn't so sure that wasn't actually happening. "I don't know, Tabby. I couldn't find him. Lately, he's making himself scarce. There's something wrong with him, and I'm not sure what it is. He's changed. He cheated on Natalie, and she found out about it. It was horrible. I think those two have split. I honestly don't know what is going on in his head."

Traci started to sip her beer, but she set it back down hard on the table. "Seth cheated on Natalie?"

"Afraid so," Jimmy said.

"With who?" Traci asked.

"Cassie. He met her at one of Rafe's parties. Do you know her?"

Traci shook her head. "No, but I know you went to that one sorority with her. You've talked about her. I think I may have seen her at Rafe and Pete's house."

Tabatha put the mashed potatoes and margarine on the table. "Seth cheated on Natalie? That doesn't sound like him. He was always a loyal person."

Not anymore, Jimmy thought. "Yeah, I know. Now he's something else. The place has changed him."

"I never liked that town," Billy muttered. "I've known people who have moved there to go to school and moved back. They all said they hated it there."

Jimmy wondered if he could still get Seth to move with him. "Listen, Billy, if I run into a jam again, can I call you and get the whole gang to come to Morganburg again? I think I really need you, and I need you to keep your calendars clear until the end of the semester."

"Of course. I told you I would. What's up?"

Jimmy glanced at Traci. "I'm planning on leaving Morganburg after this semester. I'm going to finish my last semester at Reynolds College here in Virginia Beach. I can't take it there anymore."

"That's a shame," Tabatha said. "But we'd love to see you again."

Jimmy grinned. "You don't know how much I want to come back. I really do miss the big city."

"You know we'd always help you, Jimmy," Tabatha said as she put the big brown bird on the table. It smelled wonderful. "You and Seth and Natalie."

Billy grabbed a knife. "Yeah, if you can stay here with us if you need a place."

Jimmy was relieved to hear that. At last, he could finally see a light at the end of that endless tunnel called Morganburg. "If Natalie agrees with me to give Seth another chance, I'd like to get him out of Morganburg and to a hospital or clinic where we can get him to dry out. I may need help getting him back here, help from you and the gang."

"Sure thing, Jimbo," Billy said. "You know I'd do anything for you two guys. I know the whole gang feels that way."

Snake said, "We'd be more than willing to help him."

"Just say the word," Hat Trick said. "We'll get everyone."

Jimmy smiled. "Thanks, guys. I sure do hope I won't need you."

Billy started to carve the turkey. "That's all right. We'll help you bring him back if that's what you need. Then maybe I'll have a word with that kid. Maybe I'll knock some sense into him."

Jimmy smiled a little, but he feared it could come to that. He would need the whole gang to subdue Seth.

The following Monday, late that afternoon, Jimmy stopped by the art building to see Dr. Johnson.

Jimmy sat down in his office. "I wanted to ask you about Seth."

Dr. Johnson squirmed in his chair. "You stole my line. I wanted to ask you about him."

"How is he doing in class?"

The doctor frowned and shook his head. "Not well. For whatever reason, he's painting a series of tar pits. He's missed a lot of class. He's moody. He keeps to himself. He seems to be struggling with something, although he won't say what. He's not talking much lately. Is he having problems with his fianceé?"

Jimmy thought that was the understatement of the year. "He's having problems, that's for sure."

Dr. Johnson straightened out his desk. "I'm sorry to hear that."

"Yeah," Jimmy said weakly. "Can you call me if you see him? He still owes rent, and I haven't seen him since before Thanksgiving."

"Sure."

Jimmy gave him his number. "The other reason why I came here was to ask you about that thing at City Hall you plan to vote on. Are you still on for that?"

"Oh, you're talking about the variance request to level those woods out there so we can expand the university. Yes, it's still on Monday, the last week of finals. I'm not going anywhere that whole day except here early in the morning to post grades. Why?"

"Because I believe it when you say there's something wrong here in Morganburg. And I think those woods should be leveled. I wish I could raze the entire town."

"I certainly will be there for the vote. Nothing could keep me from doing that."

Jimmy felt relieved. "I'm glad to hear it. There is something definitely out of whack and dangerous here in Morganburg. Something needs to be done."

As Jimmy left Johnson's office, a brutally cold wind blew through the open door of the interior design studio. Jimmy fled the campus.

The Friday before finals week, Jimmy drove to the apartment to look for Seth. He got a message from the property manager that Seth still hadn't paid the rent. Seth wasn't there, so Jimmy grabbed a soda before he took off, but he heard the girls upstairs talking in the kitchen. Voices rose, and then a woman started shouting at them. Her voice sounded hoarse, like a feral cat.

"That's just in your heads! Can't you see that?"

Jimmy thought he heard Cassie.

"What's wrong with you girls? Are you losing your minds?"

"Cassie, what's wrong with you?" Elizabeth pleaded.

Now Jimmy knew Cassie was up there. And then hopefully Seth was, too.

Jimmy ran outside and around the house.

"Leave me alone!" she shrieked.

Jimmy heard things getting thrown and smashed. Then heard a metallic "ding," and one of the girls screamed.

Cassie ripped the back door from its hinges, kicked the porch door open, and froze when she saw Jimmy.

"You!" Her voice wasn't female. It wasn't even human. "Stay away from us! Leave here and *leave us alone!*"

Jimmy was terrified. *Us.* That's what Seth said. But who's us?

She darted to her car and sped off.

Cassie was possessed, too. Jimmy couldn't believe what these spirits wanted with Seth and Cassie.

Jimmy ran into the kitchen and was horrified by what he saw. Anne Marie helped Michelle from the floor to a chair. Michelle was holding her head. Blood was running from her forehead. A broken pot and broken dishes were on the floor. Elizabeth bolted into the kitchen with some first aid supplies.

"What the hell went on in here?" Jimmy gasped.

"We tried to talk to her," Michelle cried. "And she did this to me."

Anne Marie said, "We showed her a picture, and she freaked out."

Elizabeth wiped the blood from Michelle's face and said, "We always knew this place was bad, those woods and this town. But this is more dangerous than we ever realized."

"She's possessed by something," Michelle muttered. "Look at what she did! She smashed the door, kicked the porch door to pieces, and broke that pot over my head."

Elizabeth taped Michelle's forehead. "Cassie isn't strong enough to do all that."

Jimmy couldn't believe it. "What picture did you show her?"

"*This.*" Anne Marie reached for a photo sitting on the counter.

It was a photo of the girls together, standing in the backyard with the woods behind them.

Michelle said, "That was taken two years ago when we first moved here. We were having a cookout with a bunch of friends. I had Cassie take that picture. Look at the tree line. And look outside now."

Jimmy thought he might pass out. *No way. And I mean no fucking way. No way could that happen.* The tree line had moved several feet closer to the rock wall outside. He couldn't believe it. He thought that was even worse than Seth's painting. "Trees can't grow that fast, that numerous, and that large in that kind of time."

Elizabeth set the first aid supplies on the counter. "That's right. It's unnatural and it's evil."

"We were meeting here with Cassie," Michelle said. "Because I had heard she's pregnant, and it's with Seth's baby."

Jimmy winced. That brought back a horrible memory. "There's also something very wrong with Seth."

"We're in agreement there," Elizabeth said. "I liked him at first; we all did. He's handsome and super talented. But things got weird fast, and he's definitely not the person we met at the beginning of the semester."

"Did you girls ever get Cassie out of town to have her checked out by a doctor like you had planned?" Jimmy asked.

Anne Marie crossed her arms. "No. We all got food poisoning that weekend. We didn't go anywhere."

"That was really suspicious," Elizabeth said. "Too much of a coincidence."

Michelle held her head. "That was no coincidence. We were stopped from taking Cassie away." She cried a little. "I wanted to go to college and get a degree so I could make a better life for myself. I never thought the most important thing about being here would be to save a friend's life."

Elizabeth placed the broken dishes in the trash beneath the sink. "She's right. I feel awful, ashamed, really. I thought the most important thing about being here was about getting a degree so we can make a lot of money. Now I realize the most important thing about our time here is our friendships and how we help each other when we need it."

Michelle shook her head. "We're not sitting by and letting this happen any longer! We still have plans to meet with Cassie for a celebration of the end of the semester. At least that's what she thinks."

Anne Marie rubbed Michelle's back. "Yeah, we have to act. We can't run from this anymore."

Jimmy always thought he could read people well after being on the streets. And Anne Marie always impressed him as someone who was pretty timid, unlike Michelle and Elizabeth, who were more assertive and unafraid to tackle adversity. When he heard Anne Marie say that, now he knew these girls meant business.

He figured he'd lay his cards on the table. If the girls didn't already know about the dark figures he thought were influencing Seth and Cassie, he would tell them about it. "I think this place is possessed by a demonic force. And it's possessing people, including Seth and Cassie."

Elizabeth grabbed a bottle of water from the fridge. "I agree. I've always believed there was some sort of strange force in this town, and now it's got Cassie. I think we should take her out of here and to her parents' home up in Norfolk. We need to get Cassie to a hospital and see if she's okay and her baby's okay. And I want to see if we can get out old Cassie back."

"When are you going to do this?" Jimmy asked.

"Let's do it the weekend before finals," Michelle said. "None of us has any exams until Wednesday. So why don't we plan to do it Sunday afternoon when everything's quiet, and most people are studying. If Cassie misses her exams, that's too bad. Her health is more important."

"That's right," Anne Marie said. "We're getting her out of here as soon as possible."

"What about Seth?" Elizabeth asked. "The baby's his. He'll want to know what happened to Cassie and where she's at."

"I'll deal with Seth," Jimmy said. "I think you're right. Seth needs to go to the hospital, too."

"So this is it then?" Anne Marie said. "We're all agreed? This Sunday, we get Cassie the hell out of here?" Michelle and Elizabeth agreed.

Jimmy asked the girls where Cassie lived. Once he wrote down their address, he knew he could now check her apartment to see if Seth was staying there.

Jimmy felt energized after he said goodbye. He and the girls now had a plan set to get Seth and Cassie out of Morganburg. Hopefully, then sanity would return to his life.

As the door closed behind him, he heard Michelle mutter, "Hang in there, Cassie. Help is on the way."

Jimmy returned to his car. Now if he could just find Seth.

Jimmy only had one final exam and it was Thursday for a literature class, and he was well prepared for it already. While

Traci studied for her finals, he wanted to calm his shattered nerves and get somewhere he felt relatively safe, so he drove out to the Hawk's Nest that night.

Jimmy bought a *Richmond Times-Dispatch* before he stepped inside the bar. He hadn't looked at a paper in days. He glanced at the front page before he tucked it under his arm and sat at the bar. A tough-looking guy with high cheekbones, a crew cut, and a level-headed skull that looked like it was flattened by a shovel poured the drinks. Two older women, heavy on makeup, jewelry, and drinking, sat at the bar and talked quietly. A couple of guys wearing dirty jeans and shirts played a game of pool while they drank bottles of beer.

Earlier in the week, he had put up flyers around campus to sublease his apartment. He checked his phone. He was happy to find a few inquiries on his phone messages.

Jimmy snagged a menu and ordered a Coke. He flipped open the paper. Something about a tragedy captured his attention. He set his phone down and flipped to the local section. Suddenly he felt cold. Two people sat down on either side of him. He nearly fell out of his chair. It was Rafe and Pete. They looked pale and thin.

"My God, where have you guys been?" Jimmy almost shouted. "Do you realize your parents reported you missing? The police have been looking for you? Do you know we all thought you were *dead*?"

"Relax, Jimbo," Rafe said. "We got picked up on possession. We're out now."

"Yeah, we're fine," Pete said. "Don't worry about ditching us that day. We got a ride."

Jimmy wanted to grab them, hold them, and shake their hands, but he stopped. Their cold black eyes told him his friends maybe didn't make it out that night after all, but he couldn't be sure. "I just came here for lunch. I'm leaving Morganburg this weekend. I'm trying to find someone willing to sublet my apartment for next semester. I might take my classes at another school and have them transfer my credits back to Morganburg."

"That's a good idea, Jimmy," Pete said. "You take Traci with you and go have a good life."

Jimmy felt Rafe place his cold hand on his shoulder. A cold wave of icy shards crawled down the length of his body. He thought he'd be relieved to see them because it meant they were alive, but they didn't seem okay. He spotted an article about Morganburg. "Hey, how did you guys know about me and Traci?"

Rafe smiled coldly. "It's all around town, Jimbo."

Jimmy's eyes darted back to the article. He read, "*The bodies of Pete Sanders and Rafe Katz were found on campus in the woods behind the Department of Art. Police will not say how they died, but they have said they suspect foul play. They were reported missing—*" The paper shook in his hands.

Jimmy wondered if Rafe and Pete are dead, then who was sitting next to him?

"What's the matter, Jimbo?" Pete said. "You look like you've seen a ghost."

The guys chuckled. Jimmy looked away from his paper. Rafe and Pete were gone. Their chairs were empty. It was as if they had never entered the bar.

Jimmy left his Coke and paper and drove to Traci's apartment.

He left the streets of Virginia Beach to go to college because he thought life just had to get better than what he had there. Instead, it got *much* worse. And he feared if he didn't get out soon, he may never get out of there alive.

Part Three

"Bloody Sabbat"

CHAPTER TWENTY-SEVEN

Jimmy saw Laura step out of the woods behind his home.

She said, "Jimmy, you have to listen to me. Their power is stretched to its limit. The force here is possessing so many people, and Seth and Cassie proved to be stronger than they imagined."

Jimmy reached out to her. "Laura, what—?

"Just listen, Jimmy. I don't have much time. They burned a lot of power taking control of them. That's why they can't possess you. The spirits don't have much power to stop you. And their power is weaker during the day, so go now, Jimmy!"

Jimmy tried to run to her, but his legs felt like lead. "Laura! I can't believe it's you. I just want to hold you again!"

"Listen to me, Jimmy! Your wills were just too strong. They can't possess you *and* Seth. Take Natalie and Traci and get out of here!"

Jimmy kept trying to run to her but couldn't get his legs to move.

She said, "The spirits here were always angry, troubled, and felt like they couldn't or shouldn't leave. But then Christine opened a portal, and it remains open. Demonic spirits have been coming through, and they've taken possession of the spirits already here, the Powhatans and the soldiers. The demons are in control now."

Jimmy still tried to run to her but only got a few feet closer. "Laura, I just want it to be the way it was with you, me, Seth, and Natalie. I can still get Seth!"

The Darkness bled out of the woods and started to envelop her.

"No, you can't, Jimmy. It's too late for me. And Seth is gone. Do you hear me, Jimmy? Get out now!"

The Darkness consumed her like a flood. It was up to her neck. He reached out to her and screamed her name.

"Jimmy, do you hear me? If you find a cross, ignore it. Just leave today and leave right now! I can't fight them off too much longer. Go! You have to go now, Jimmy!"

"Jimmy!" Traci shook him awake. "Christ, wake up. You were having a horrible nightmare. You kept calling for Laura."

He sat up and rubbed his face. He wanted to cry. That dream was so real like he really was talking to Laura. "Oh, my God, that was awful."

"You okay?"

Jimmy breathed deeply and looked around Traci's bedroom. "I will be as soon as we're the hell out of this town."

That morning Jimmy was nervous as hell. The nightmare looked so real, and he couldn't shake it from his mind. But he was also happy. He and Traci planned to get out of town the next day. He couldn't wait to start a new life, no more University of Morganburg, no more strange town, and no more strange visions. He was saying goodbye to the insanity forever.

Jimmy drove to his apartment and found Seth's car wasn't parked outside, so he stopped to pick up some things and check the mail. As Jimmy made his way up the front porch, he spotted something. The fall shed all the leaves from the bushes and allowed Jimmy to see something shiny and black on the ground. He went back down the steps and picked up the object. Jimmy looked up. It was from the middle of the metal design above the porch.

My God, it's a cross, Jimmy thought. *That's what's broken from that metal design.*

He heard wild crying and chanting from the woods behind the house. It sounded like a tribe preparing for battle.

His heart pounded, and his palms turned sweaty. *What the hell?*

It grew louder and louder until a car pulled up behind him. Then the chanting stopped.

Herbert Dunn from Remonds and Associates, the real estate agent who operated the house, opened his car door and leaned on it. Jimmy was glad to see him. He wanted to ask Dunn if he could help get new people into the apartment.

The gray, balding, pudgy man asked, "Is Seth around?"

"No, he isn't."

"Seth is late on the rent, and I've been trying to get in touch with him. Do you know where he is?"

Jimmy chuckled bitterly. He had been looking for Seth for weeks. "Try the bars. That's always where he is nowadays, drinking up his rent money. That's why he's late on the rent."

"If you see him around, tell him I need to see him. If he doesn't get a hold of me soon, I'm going to begin dispossessory proceedings."

Before Dunn drove off, he saw the black metal in Jimmy's hands. "Hey, I see you found the cross. Where was it?"

Jimmy was surprised he knew about it. "Right here in the bushes."

"I always wondered what happened to that. Lightning struck it. I guess the Great Spirit doesn't want it there. So be it. I'm not spending any money to try to fix it."

"Great Spirit?"

"Yeah. This land was originally owned by the Powhatan tribe. I was told the final battle between the Powhatans and Europeans was fought about where this house stands. Legend has it that the last leader of that decimated tribe was killed here. What was his name? Riakpe…something, I think."

It felt like the blood rushed from Jimmy's head to his feet. He thought he might faint. *Wasn't that the name on Seth's paintings?* "Powhatans?" he muttered. *That was the name Laura mentioned in my dream.*

"Yeah. Maybe the spirits here don't like any crosses here. The Powhatans had their own religion. That leader was supposed to have cursed this land before he died." Before Dunn got back in his car, he said, "If you see Seth, let him know he needs to get in touch with me right away."

"Okay." Jimmy watched him drive away. He realized he had forgotten all about asking if Dunn heard from any of the people interested in subleasing the place. Then he looked back at the faces on the chimney. They still grinned. Jimmy glanced back at the porch above him. A cold breeze blew from the woods. The frantic crying and chanting resumed. Jimmy dropped the cross and sped to the library.

While on his way into the library, he got a call from Dr. Johnson. Jimmy stayed outside to take the call.

Dr. Johnson "I saw him in the studio painting."

Jimmy felt relieved. "OK, good." *Now I know where you're at.*

"Oh, wait. He's just leaving."

Crap, he thought. *The bars are open now and he's probably off to one.* "All right. At least I know he's around."

Dr. Johnson said, "Listen, I just drove to school to post grades for those students who wanted to see them early." Jimmy heard him open a door. "I'm taping the posted grades to his office door right now. "I'm planning to avoid the campus until Monday. I don't even want to take a chance, not even during the day. I'm only going to town to vote that morning. I suggest you stay away from here, too. I—"

He coughed and choked like he was gagging.

"Dr. Johnson?"

"Oh, no," he gasped.

"Dr. Johnson? What's wrong?"

"Dr. Johnson," someone with a thick, Hispanic accent said angrily. "It's time to come now, Dr. Johnson."

"*Rudy,*" Dr. Johnson cried.

"Dr. Johnson?" Jimmy gasped. "You see Rudy? Get out of there!"

The phone went dead. And then he saw Seth's car drive past the library. He tried to call Dr. Johnson back, but he wouldn't pick up. *Good Lord,* he thought. Jimmy hoped he was okay. But he was not going back to that art building.

He called Seth. He was surprised to hear him pick up. "Seth, where are you?"

"I'm on my way to Allen's, Jimbo."

"Seth, go home. And stay there. And while you're there, write a check out for the rent, okay? The property manager needs that rent from you."

"I've got a little present waiting for those girls when they get home." Then he laughed.

Jimmy hung up. *That didn't even sound like Seth. He had to find out what's going on in this town.*

He tried to call Dr. Johnson again, but he didn't answer. *Jimmy hoped he was all right.*

Before he ran inside, he got a call. He thought it was Dr. Johnson, but it was Laura's mom.

"Jimmy, you haven't called me. Have you found out anything?"

"Brenda, give me a couple of hours. I think I might have something. I think I might know everything."

He hung up and ran into the library.

CHAPTER TWENTY-EIGHT

Seth drove back home that afternoon. He looked at several of the drunken abominations he painted the past few days. He grabbed a package of chicken from the refrigerator and threw it on the kitchen counter. He turned on some music and clutched a butcher knife from a drawer. As he cut the chicken, Elizabeth came home.

He heard her and her boyfriend talking at the side door. "Thanks for lunch," she said.

"Call when you get up to Norfolk, okay?"

"I will. I want to try to get a nap in before we drive up there."

Lights out. Seth cranked down his music. Seth grabbed a bottle of beer and cut apart the rest of the chicken while he waited for Elizabeth to fall asleep.

CHAPTER TWENTY-NINE

Jimmy grabbed his cell phone before he ran into the library. He remembered he was going to check at the library again to see if they had more books on the fourth floor, but something stopped him. It was Amanda. *I forgot all about that. Then Traci stopped by, and all hell broke loose.*

The security guard, a beefy overweight guy, glared at him as he rushed by the gate. The library looked empty. He said to the woman behind the front desk, "I need to know about the Powhatan tribe of Virginia," he said. "Do you have any books on them?"

She checked on her computer. "Oh, yes. We have history books about Morganburg and the Powhatan tribe, but those books are rare or out of print so we keep them on the fourth floor with all our rare books and historical papers. But you can't check those out. "

The fourth floor. That was it! That was why Laura had written the number four beneath Rudy's name.

"Oh, man," Jimmy groaned. He felt like a fool. The information he needed was under his nose the whole time. "That's okay. I won't need to."

Jimmy ran up to the fourth floor. The woman behind the counter there looked up the books Jimmy wanted. She handed him a clipboard. "Yes, but you have to sign them out here and return them to me when you're done."

She looked for the books Jimmy wanted before she stepped into the room behind her. Jimmy signed his name and felt the blood drain from his face. A few lines above his was Laura's. Below hers, he found Deanna Matthews. He noticed several pages of signatures below the top page where he had signed. He glanced at the librarian, still looking for books. He flipped through the pages and felt faint when he found Rudy's.

She handed four books to Jimmy. "This should get you started. I have more if you need them."

"Thank you," he muttered. He sat down at the nearest table at the front counter and opened the first book. I'm about to discover the same thing that got Laura, Deanna, and Rudy killed.

CHAPTER THIRTY

Seth sat in the living room, drank beer as he listened to music and waited. Once the sun went down and the Darkness bubbled and oozed from the woods, he stood and grabbed the butcher knife. He crept around the back of the house and the Darkness flowed around him as he walked to the concrete steps to the side door of the upstairs residence. After the Darkness surrounded his feet, he floated over the stairs. He stepped into the side porch. He saw Elizabeth's dark blue BMW parked in the driveway. He opened the screen door. He tried the side door and found it unlocked. He grinned as he let himself in. He stepped into the kitchen. The basement door that led down to his apartment was to his immediate left.

Seth popped into the living room. Several dirty dishes, glasses, and crumpled napkins sat on the coffee table. He stepped lightly over the hardwood floor. An end table stood next to the couch facing him. To his left, Seth saw a bedroom with no one in there. To his right, he saw the bathroom in between the other two bedrooms. Elizabeth slept on her bed in the bedroom to the left. He smiled as he tip-toed into her bedroom and raised his knife.

CHAPTER THIRTY-ONE

Jimmy pored through the old musty-smelling books. He read for hours. He didn't finish until the evening. Finally, he found what he wanted to know. It was worse than anything he could've imagined. "Dear God," he whispered. "I need to get Seth out of here tonight."

Before Traci woke me up this morning, was that nightmare just a dream or was that really Laura's spirit coming to me in my sleep to warn me?

The dreams Jimmy had with Laura in them now all made sense. He discovered the Powhatans and the Europeans warred right here on campus. Later it's believed the leader of the decimated Powhatans, Riapkemobotoconno placed a curse on the land, the land the Powhatans considered sacred where they worshiped. They also believed this land held spiritual power, the same land they believed the white man raped and desecrated.

Jimmy knew this was what Laura found. She was a crusader. She would've published her story, made the student body aware of the past here and pushed the university to investigate whether there were graves beneath the campus and out in the woods. She would've pushed to help Dr. Johnson to get those woods leveled.

He bet she saw the black fog or the spirits around campus. No wonder she had never told him what she was working on. He was sure she figured he'd never believe her. But with this sort of evidence and things she may have seen, he would never suggest to Seth that they move into that house.

Jimmy darted from the third floor down the stairs and started to head out when he got a call.

Traci said, "Jimmy, where are you? I'm here at your home."

Jimmy almost forgot they planned to leave Morganburg today. "Traci, you need to get down here to the Main Library right now. I've finally found out everything I've been looking for since I started work with the paper."

"Jimmy, you promised me you stopped that."

"This isn't about the story. This is about Seth. I've found out what's wrong with him. He needs our help."

"What are you talking about?"

"*Get down here,* and I'll show you. It all makes sense now. The couple I've seen floating around campus, the Civil War soldiers, the guy I saw with the black eyes, the rapes, violence, and everything else. I'm calling Natalie. I'm going to get her down here, too. Will you come?"

"Yes, of course. I'll be over there in a few minutes."

Jimmy called Natalie. At first, she wasn't interested in hearing about Seth.

"No, Jimmy. I don't want—"

"Natalie, you have to listen to me. This whole university is haunted. Seth is possessed and I found out who is in control of him."

"Possessed? Jimmy, I— wait. *Possessed!* My God, that's why Seth has been acting so strange. That's why I saw Seth with those black eyes!"

"That's right. You need to get down here right now."

Natalie said she'd be right over. Jimmy tried to call Billy, but suddenly his cell wouldn't work. He ran down to the first floor. He didn't dare ask to use a phone on campus. He didn't think he could use his phone at home.

Jimmy only had to wait a few minutes before Traci and Natalie found him. Natalie looked beautiful in her flowered sundress. Traci wore a shirt and shorts. The girls sat and Jimmy handed each of them a history book. "Read this right here," he said to each girl. Both of them moaned after what they read. He switched textbooks, so each of them got to read both books.

Traci cried and hung her head. "Good God," she mumbled.

Natalie shook her head. "My God, Jimmy, what does this mean?"

"I'll tell you what it means. These two books have the key parts of what I learned."

"So this campus used to be all Powhatan territory?" Traci asked.

"Yes," Jimmy replied. "There were small skirmishes at first, but then war broke out."

Traci flipped through a few more pages. "So the Europeans fought with the Powhatans and pushed them out of their homeland?"

Jimmy said, "Exterminated is more like it. Nearly a hundred were initially slaughtered here in 1625, all on land they considered sacred. There was peace for a while, but the Europeans kept pushing them aside. They wanted the Powhatans out of their way, so they were forcibly moved."

"Where did they go?" Natalie asked.

Jimmy believed they never really went anywhere. "Those that didn't die from starvation, dehydration, exposure, and disease during the trip moved to a camp near here, maybe at the house I live."

"When did this happen?" Natalie asked.

"This second bloody battle happened in the fall of 1676. Honestly, I couldn't find out if those Powhatans were buried or just left to rot out on the land."

Natalie pushed her book aside like a bad meal. "Why did you show us this other book, Jimmy?" Natalie asked.

"Because I've seen Civil War soldiers standing around campus."

Traci said, "I've seen that, too. I thought those were frats pulling a prank."

"That's what I thought, but I don't think that anymore. The soldier I saw was a Yankee. In that history book, I found a fierce battle was fought right through this town. It's believed about two hundred Yankee soldiers were slaughtered in the battle."

"And that was here in Morganburg?" Natalie asked.

"Yes. Rebel soldiers dumped the Yankees in a mass grave somewhere around here, probably underneath this campus. Remember I said Dr. Johnson told me about the bones that were dug up when they began to build the art building?"

"Yes," Traci whispered.

"I think the university uncovered some of the bodies of those Yankee soldiers." He flipped through a few pages and said, "The Powhatan that led that last bloody battle was a little-known leader named 'The One with the Devil-Black Eyes.' That name in Powhatan was Riapkemobotoconno."

Traci's eyes went wide, and Natalie gasped.

Jimmy explained to Natalie everything that happened when he and Traci visited Meyer Hall.

Then he said, "That leader is supposed to have cursed this land. Riapkemobotoconno is the pseudonym Seth has been using on several of his paintings lately. And those things looked like mush. Riapkemobotoconno was a leader, a warrior, and a hunter. He wasn't an artist. He couldn't paint his own ass if he smeared paint on his butt cheeks and sat on a canvas."

Natalie began to cry. "That old spirit has possessed Seth? That's what's wrong with my Seth!"

"Yes. And I think that Christine Walters, who hanged herself in Meyer Hall became, used black magic and opened a portal to a demonic presence so the Powhatan spirits could obtain more power, but I think the Powhatan spirits are now possessed by demonic forces and those spiritual forces not only have control of Seth but many people in Morganburg."

Traci asked, "Didn't Laura write something in her notebook about using Christine to wage war?"

Jimmy nodded. "She meant the demonic force is waging war against humanity."

"But why?" Natalie asked.

"Why?" Jimmy said. "Because we're standing on a powder keg of spiritual power. And I think the demons are using the anger of the Powhatans and manipulating them, possessing them and making the tribe take their land back."

Traci closed her textbook. "Why Seth?"

Jimmy wished he didn't know. "I think maybe they've found a way to make themselves born again, one body at a time. They've used Seth to impregnate Cassie."

"Oh, my God, Jimmy," Natalie gasped. "You're not serious, are you?"

"Yes," he said. "And why Seth and Cassie? Seth has tribal American blood in him. Maybe Cassie does, too."

"So that's why Seth has been not acting like himself," Natalie gasped. "Because it's not him."

Jimmy wished he never saw the ad to move into that house. "Yeah."

"What are we going to do?" Traci asked.

"We need to get Seth the hell out of here tonight," Jimmy said. "We can't wait until the end of the exams. Seth doesn't have any exams anyways. We've got to move now. I think once we get him away from here, we'll get our old Seth back."

Natalie wiped her eyes with a tissue from her purse. "What about Cassie?"

Jimmy glanced back at the clock. "I already talked to the girls that live above me. Those girls are also worried about her."

"What do they plan to do?" Traci asked.

"They're taking her back to her folks and to a hospital to get her checked out. I expect they're already on their way to Norfolk now."

Jimmy asked Traci to give him a piece of paper from her purse. He jotted down a phone number. "Now, I want you girls to listen to me very carefully. I want both of you to stay together and go to Traci's home and stay there. Off-campus is probably safe."

They said, "Okay."

"Traci, I want you to call Billy. I tried, but my cell isn't working here. Use your phone at home."

"All right," she said.

Jimmy said, "I'm going to need the gang's help to get control of Seth, at least physical control. Natalie, I may need your help so we can regain control of Seth's mind. Together I think all of us can subdue him and get our old Seth back. He needs us now."

"What are you going to do?" Natalie asked.

"I'm going to find Seth," Jimmy said. "But not to confront him. I just want to find him. I'll call you, Traci. You tell me when Billy and the Black Knights are on their way. Now have both of you got this straight? Get away from campus and stay away. Don't deviate from this plan, all right?"

"Okay," they said.

Jimmy collected the books. "You girls get going."

Natalie started to leave, but Traci remained. Natalie waited on her.

"I wish I could stay with you," Traci said. "I don't want to be alone—"

Jimmy grabbed her by the arms. "You can do this. Just drive home. You have to do this for me. And for Seth. For all of us. Now get going."

She nodded. Before she took off, she grabbed Jimmy by the arm and said softly, "You be careful, baby; you hear me?"

Jimmy had to be more careful now than when he was on the streets. "Yeah, you be careful, too."

"I care about you," Traci said.

He felt taken aback and slightly embarrassed but then warm all over. He smiled. "Do you?"

"Yes," Tracy said before she hugged him.

He was too flustered to know if he should tell her he had feelings for her.

"Okay. Now you get out of here."

"Hang on, Seth," Traci mumbled. "Help is on the way."

Traci and Natalie rushed down the stairs while Jimmy gave the books back to the librarian.

Jimmy sprinted down to the first floor, but he walked to the front door.

"Hey!" the security officer said. "Where do you think you're going?"

He was going to ask, "What's it to you?" until he saw his gray eyes. "I'm dealing with an extreme emergency. And I must go."

"I don't think so. You need to stay here while I call the campus police. There's a problem."

Jimmy clenched his fists so tightly that his fingernails cut into his flesh. *Don't go there with me, whoever or whatever you are.* "No, I'm leaving, and you're not going to stop me."

"The only place you're going is to jail," the guard said. "You can tell your story to a judge."

"I don't think so," Jimmy said. He kicked the guard in the gut and then the head. The guard flew backward into the podium and knocked it over. Then he whirled around and kicked him in the side of the face and knocked him out. Jimmy ran out of the library to his car. Before he unlocked the door, he heard a noise. It sounded like wet burlap ripping.

Then he heard what sounded like rocks cracking and breaking.

What the hell? He looked up and gasped, "Oh, dear God, no!"

CHAPTER THIRTY-TWO

Seth had nearly plunged his butcher knife into Elizabeth's head when a car pulled up to the house. He rushed to the entrance of the kitchen. Seth gazed out the kitchen window. Michelle had returned home. He recognized her car. Seth glanced back at Elizabeth. The sound of Michelle's driving up and slamming the car door didn't wake her up. Seth looked around. He glanced at the two unoccupied bedrooms for him to hide in.

He ducked into the empty bedroom on the other side of the bathroom and frantically looked for a place to hide. He couldn't hide underneath the bed. The bedspread didn't hang to the floor. Michelle stepped into the porch beside the house and opened the side door. Seth stepped into the closet. Michelle walked through the kitchen and into the living room. She glanced into Elizabeth's bedroom and saw her roommate asleep. She headed straight for the room Seth chose to hide in. Seth snagged his knife on one of Michelle's sweaters. He freed his knife from the sweater just before Michelle entered her room.

From between the clothes, Seth watched Michelle let her hair down and kick off her shoes.

She looked at herself in the mirror before unbuttoning her burgundy dress. Michelle slipped out of it. She sat down to peel off her stockings. She removed her bra and panties. Seth smiled. Michelle grabbed her white robe and went into the bathroom. She closed the door and got into the shower. Seth slithered out of the closet and crept by the bathroom.

He peered into Elizabeth's bedroom. The sound of the shower didn't wake her. The hardwood floor creaked beneath Seth's feet. He froze. Elizabeth looked like a corpse. He crept up to her bed and she up into a ball. He saw the sheet rise and fall with the rhythm of her breathing. Seth gazed at her face. She was a pretty woman while she still breathed.

Death calls, honey.

Seth stabbed her in the head. Elizabeth made a muffled whimper like a cat struck by a car, its skull crushed beneath the wheel. Michelle never heard her faint cry over the shower. Blood splattered Seth and the wall next to the bed. He stabbed her in the head again and again and again.

He shook his knife free from her skull like he merely slipped his knife out of a melon.

Blood, bits of brain, and stringy gray fluid stuck to his knife like the guts of a pumpkin. Her body slumped over to the bed. Elizabeth's head hit the floor like a bowling ball. Blood gushed from her wounds and spilled onto the wooden floor, staining the white sheets. He grabbed Elizabeth by the hair and glanced at her mutilated face before he dumped her crumpled body back onto the bed. He stuck his bloody knife in the belt loop of his jeans. He ripped away the bloody sheet from the mattress cover and threw it over the body. He wrapped up her body into the sheet, slinging the corpse over his shoulder like he took out the trash.

One of Elizabeth's bloody hands slipped out from a tear in the sheet, and it rubbed a bloody smear across the bathroom door as Seth walked by. He took her outside, and the Darkness came to him, and he floated past the stairs to the grass. He stepped onto the rock wall and crossed the threshold of the woods. He threw Elizabeth's body to the ground. He turned around and looked up. The bathroom window was open, and he heard the shower still running. He grinned like the eerie faces on the chimney.

CHAPTER THIRTY-THREE

Before Jimmy could get into his car, the ground broke open on the lawn beside the library, in the street, and in the library parking lot. The moaning of the starved, beaten, tortured, shot, stabbed, and those left to die in the cold filled the night. Civil War soldiers rose from the ground.

Jimmy dropped his keys. Soldiers clawed away at the dirt and stood up.

A small chorus of the long-dead voice rising to drift on the cold wind called, "Jimmy…"

Jimmy tried to find the key that opened the door. "Damn it!" he screamed.

The soldiers limped to him. Jimmy found the key and unlocked the door. He jumped into his car. Jimmy put the key into the ignition. He glanced out the windshield. Dead, disjointed Yankees walked awkwardly to Jimmy's car on all sides. The engine turned over but died. He pumped the gas and turned the key again. His eye caught something in the rearview. A soldier raised a rifle, aimed squarely at the back of his head through the windshield.

Shit!

Jimmy turned the key again. The motor rose from its own grave.

Yes!

He threw the car in reverse and turned out of the line of fire. The soldiers blew each other apart.

Decomposed soldiers with missing heads and limbs limped and stumbled their way to Jimmy. Two soldiers, one decapitated, staggered in front of his car and aimed their rifles at him.

Jimmy floored the gas and drove right through them, sending body parts and decayed history flipping over the hood. Another soldier stepped into the parking lot and took aim. Jimmy caught a glimpse of him in his rearview mirror just in time. He slammed the car back into reverse, smashed into the soldier, and broke him into several pieces. He rammed the car back into forward and the car stalled.

Good Lord! Fucking really? Not now, god damn it!

Jimmy cranked his key again; the other keys jangled against the dash like small warning bells. In a frenzy, he pumped the gas, his left hand pounding on the steering wheel. The engine groaned and clanked, mechanical parts reluctantly grinding together.

"Come onnnnnn! Come onnnnnnnn; god damn it!" Jimmy screamed as the soldiers slowly aimed their guns at him. *Start already.* Then came the victorious roar as the engine came to life.

More soldiers closed in. Jimmy pounded his foot on the gas as a soldier freed himself from his unmarked grave in the cemetery between the art and political science buildings. The dead soldier aimed his gun. Jimmy screamed as he ducked his head beneath the dash. The soldier pulled the trigger. The gun fired and backfired. The upper body of the soldier blew to pieces while the remainder of its body crumpled to the ground. Jimmy's door window shattered.

He steered the car to the right and sped by the poli sci building. Another soldier punched a hole through the middle of the street. Before it could aim its rifle, Jimmy drove through the corpse. The soldier flipped end over end over the car and broke apart after it hit the pavement. Bones snapped and his car shook as he ran over the soldier. He hung another right before the Darkness crept out of the woods, around the campus buildings, and reached out like a claw to grab his car. He raced away, hung another right, turned left, and escaped the campus. He drove to Allen's, but Seth wasn't there. Then he drove to the next two bars in his path, but Seth was in neither one. He jumped back into his car and drove out to the Hawk's Nest, the place where this nightmare all began, but he wasn't in there.

He called Seth, but he didn't pick up.

He got back in his car.

Seth, where are you?

CHAPTER THIRTY-FOUR

Seth crept back into the house. His eyes looked as black as two deep puncture wounds. He grinned like a hungry demon as he knocked on the bathroom door.

Micheeeelllleee," Seth growled. "It's time to plaaaaay!"

Michelle jumped. She shut off the shower. "Hello? Is someone there?" Michelle never bothered to towel off. She stepped out of the tub and threw on her robe. Water dripped at her feet. "Elizabeth? You up?" Michelle received no answer. She opened the door to a crack. "Elizabeth? Anne Marie?" She waited for a response. "If you guys are kidding around, this isn't funny!" She only heard silence. Michelle opened the door wider and saw the blood smeared across the bathroom door. "Oh, my God!" she gasped.

"Tag, you're it, sweetie!" Seth shouted after he flew out of Elizabeth's room.

Michelle screamed. Seth slammed the knife into Michelle's chest, right in the breastbone.

Michelle fell backward. She kicked and screamed. One of her feet connected with Seth's knee.

Seth fell to the floor and on top of Michelle. She squealed louder and fought to keep him from stabbing her again. Seth placed his hand on her bloody chest and held her down. Michelle used her one free hand to claw at Seth's eyes. Michelle broke free of him and tried to sprint away, but her feet could get no traction on the slippery tile. She crawled furiously to get away from him. Seth whirled around with a discus swing. His butcher knife sliced the back of Michelle's thigh all the way past the muscle and down to the bone. The slash sounded like a dull metal hoe scraped against a dusty chalkboard. He couldn't believe how hard it was to kill this woman.

Michelle wailed like a dog that took a hatchet in the back. She could no longer run. She couldn't even stand upright. Seth lunged at her but only snatched a fistful of her robe. Michelle tried to break free, but Seth pulled her towards him. Michelle shed her robe, letting him have it. Seth's momentum launched him backward, and his head hit the toilet. He dropped his knife, and Michelle crawled away. He groaned and held the back of his head. He nearly blacked out. He shook his head and saw a nude Michelle groping her way into the living room. He grabbed his knife and ran to her. She left a bloody, watery trail as she snaked through the living room to the phone. He slipped on the wet floor and fell onto Michelle's back. He tried to stab her but missed. Seth drove the knife into the floor, right in between Michelle's thumb and forefinger. She fought and bucked like a ram. She head-butted him in the face with the back of her head. He bounced back and was stunned for a moment. He punched her in the kidney, and she collapsed to her stomach. He plucked the knife from the floor and lifted it high above his head. But as the knife came down, Michelle got back to her knees. She threw off his aim, and he stabbed the floor again, this time in between her forefinger and middle finger.

"Damn, woman!" Seth screamed. "Will you sit still so I can kill you?"

Michelle screamed louder and fought harder. She knocked Seth into an end table. He bashed his head into the corner of the table and knocked the phone to the floor. The phone came off the hook. Michelle grabbed a glass from the coffee table and whacked Seth over the head. She clubbed him again on top of the forehead. Michelle dropped the glass and leaped over him. She clutched the phone and dialed nine-one-one. Seth punched her in the ribs. He grabbed her around the waist and pulled her away from the phone.

The operator answered, "Nine-one-one. What's your emergency?"

"Help!" Michelle screamed. "Help me! I'm at—"

Seth punched her in the throat. She choked and gasped. Seth grabbed her by the face and shoved her back.

"Hello?" the operator said.

Seth smashed the phone with his boot. *Not this time, lady.* He threw the shattered pieces across the living room. Michelle kicked the butcher knife beneath the couch as she scrambled away from Seth. She clawed her way to the kitchen. Seth tried to snag his knife beneath the couch, but he couldn't reach it. She lunged into the kitchen and grasped the oven to pull herself up. She fought through the pain to force herself to walk. Seth heard her reach the side door as she turned the doorknob and opened it. Seth tackled her and kicked the door shut. He dragged her back into the kitchen by the stove. He seized her by the hair and yanked her head back. He stuck his fingers in her eyes and gouged them out. Blood so thick his fingers looked black. She wailed as she reached out for the oven and found it. She pulled herself up again. Seth ran back into the living room. He picked up the sofa and tossed it across the room.

"Help me!" Michelle screamed. "Somebody help me!"

"Oh, shut up, bitch!" Seth growled before he slammed the butcher knife into her mouth and through the back of her throat. Michelle collapsed to the floor one final time. "Why don't you try screaming, fighting, and making noise at all hours now, you dumb, useless piece of shit!"

He chuckled as he picked up her lifeless body. He slung her corpse over his shoulder and walked outside into the Darkness. He dumped her body into the woods. Seth found Cassie in the forest, and they waited for Anne Marie to come home.

Seth held Cassie's hand. "*At last, my wife, we are reunited in life again.*"

She grinned. "*Yes.*"

"*And you know what you have to do.*"

She nodded and disappeared into the woods.

CHAPTER THIRTY-FIVE

Jimmy drove to two more bars looking for Seth but still couldn't find him. He then sped back off campus to the parking lot of the Hawk's Nest; his cell phone started working again. He tried calling Seth again. This time he picked up.

"Seth, where are you?"

Seth laughed. "You want to know where I am? I'm right here. Let me send you a little pic I have. This is what happens when you stick your fucking nose where it doesn't belong."

Jimmy received the picture on his phone and gasped. It was a mutilated picture of Elizabeth in the woods. Jimmy wanted to call Seth right back, but Traci's picture appeared on his phone. He got a call from her.

"Jimmy, I don't know what happened to Natalie. I was driving right behind her. We were on the phone together, and she was crying, and then all of a sudden, she got really mad when we were stopped at a light. She told me she wanted to see Seth to talk to him. She said she believed she could reach him and drove off on her own. She said no one would take Seth from her. I told her not to go near him. I reminded her of your plan, but she just hung up on me. I think she's headed in the direction of your apartment."

"God damn it!" Jimmy shouted. "Okay, you go home. I'll try to stop her." He hung up. *Dear God, no, Natalie. Not there. That's the last place you want to be right now.*

He tried to call Natalie, but then his cell phone cut out. His battery had plenty of juice, but it just shut off as soon as he neared the campus. He roared back to the Hawk's Nest and his cell started working again.

Jimmy got out of the car and started to double-check to see if Seth was there, but two drunk rednecks came out.

"Looks like the biker boy is all alone," the taller one said.

"Ain't that a shame?" the shorter one said. "He has no one to help him."

Jimmy glanced back behind the guys and the bar. He was far away from campus, but the woods were right behind the Hawk's Nest.

"Guys, you really don't want to fight me right now."

"No," the taller one said. "We want to *kill you.*"

Jimmy kicked one of them in the knee and heard a grisly crack. The guy screamed and collapsed to the blacktop. "Oh, my God! I think he broke my fucking knee!"

The other guy punched Jimmy in the head and knocked him over. He fell to the ground and his phone slipped beneath his car. Jimmy got up, and kicked the guy in the gut and then in the head, sending the guy reeling backward.

He wanted to really kick the shit out of them, but more soldiers marched out of the woods as more people came out of the bar.

Jimmy groped for his phone beneath the car, jumped back inside, and sped to a nearby liquor store. There were no woods behind it. He called Traci using a video on his phone.

I want to see her get home so I know she's safe. I don't want to lose her like I lost Laura.

"Damn it, Traci, I told you to stay together!"

Jimmy couldn't believe Natalie didn't do as he told her. He and Seth never had problems with the Black Knights' girls. Those girls always listened when they warned them danger was near.

This is insane. Seth is obviously either in the woods or at home. We can't do this tonight. Laura said their power is weaker during the day.

She glanced at him as she drove. "I couldn't do anything about it, Jimmy. We came in separate cars and we left in our cars. She was right behind me up until a minute ago." She nearly hit an oncoming vehicle and swerved back into her lane.

"Traci, watch the road! Just let me see you while you get all the way home."

Traci drove just off campus to the lot of the abandoned gas station. The university's welcome sign stood behind her across the road. The only pay phone in town sat at the edge of the lot.

"Traci, listen to me. We need to change our plans. I want you and Natalie to meet me at your place. We're going to drive to Virginia Beach tonight. We'll get Seth tomorrow morning."

"Hold on. I'm off campus now. I've tried to use my cell. You're right. I can't get a call through to Virginia Beach. I've found this abandoned gas station just off campus. It has a payphone out in front. I hope it still works. I can phone Billy twenty minutes earlier this way. Something tells me every minute is going to count."

That was the payphone Seth used to call Billy to get the Knights to come here. "Traci, don't do that! Go home like I told you. We can get Seth in the morning!"

"Don't worry, babe. I'm off university property and I think I'm safe here. I'll be careful." Traci hung up on Jimmy.

I wish Traci would've listened to me. It's safer if we get Seth tomorrow morning.

"Will neither one of these women listen to me?" He couldn't believe it. Jimmy called Natalie and shouted, "Natalie, what the hell do you think you're doing?"

"I'm just driving to your apartment, Jimmy," Natalie said. "I want to see if Seth is there."

Jimmy wanted to strangle these girls. "Natalie, don't go over there! Go to Traci's apartment and stay there. We had a plan; now stick to it!"

"Damn it, Jimmy! You said yourself you thought I would be the one who could talk to Seth and bring him back. I *know* I can! I love him. He loves me. Not you or anyone in your old gang can say that."

"Natalie, listen to me. Seth is dangerous right now. Traci is going to have the Black Knights here in about an hour. After the gang and I get control of him, we'll get you, and we'll all be on our way to Virginia Beach, and then you can talk to him. He'll need you then."

"Jimmy, he's *my* fiance. He's been my man, and I'll always love him. What has happened to him is a crime. It's unfair, and it's disgusting! I want him back now! He's mine, and I'm going to get him back. And no— Jimmy, I'm at hour house. I see someone. It's Seth! He's carrying something into the woods. I can't make out what it is. I'm going to talk to him."

Jimmy headed back to his home. "Natalie, don't! Do *not* go anywhere near him, and don't go into those woods! Natalie, do you hear me?"

Natalie hung up.

"Damn it!" Jimmy screamed as he bounced his cell phone off the front seat of his car. He couldn't believe this was happening.

Jimmy, still in the liquor store parking lot, started to call Natalie back, but Traci called him first, again using video.

"Okay, sorry I hung up on you," she said. "That was an accident. I'm here. Everything's fine. I'm calling Billy now."

"This time stay with me. Don't hang up. And watch what's going on around you! If you see the dark fog, get the hell out of there!"

Traci dug into her purse, looking for change. "Don't worry. I can take care of myself." She propped up her phone against the payphone as she looked for change. A street light stood right over the payphone. She dumped the change on the ledge in front of the phone.

Jimmy saw the abandoned white gas station illuminated by a street light behind her. Beyond that, it was too dark to make out anything behind the gas station. Only Darkness.

Wait a minute. Behind that gas station was the woods. "Traci, get out of there!"

"I'm off campus, Jimmy."

"But just barely. The woods are right behind you. Go home, Traci!"

She found more change. "I'll be fine. This will just take a minute. If this phone doesn't work, I'll go home." She unloaded some of the junk from her purse to make it easier for her to find money. She grabbed a few more dimes and set all of her change in front of the phone. Some of it rolled to the ground.

"Shit," she whispered.

Jimmy panted. "What? What happened?"

"It's nothing. Just spilled some change."

"Look behind you! Tell me what you see."

Traci glanced over her shoulder. "I see nothing. There's an abandoned gas station behind me. That's it."

Traci picked up the change. She put in the change and dialed the number. "Okay, I've got a dial tone….Come on, Billy," she muttered. "Answer the damn phone." She glanced back. "Just stay with me, Jimmy. Please don't leave me."

"I promise. I won't."

Jimmy realized he couldn't see the gas station anymore. Darkness coiled around it and crept forward like a hoard of large black tarantulas.

Jimmy screamed, "Traci, look out! Get out of there! Run to your car!"

"What—?"Traci turned around. Darkness billowed up behind Traci, and Cassie floated out from it.

Billy picked up the phone and said, "Hello."

Cassie put her hand over Traci's mouth and whispered into her ear, "You should have stuck to Jimmy's plan." Cassie slashed Traci's throat so badly that she nearly decapitated her. Cassie let Traci's body fall to the ground and giggled as she floated back into the black mist. The Darkness retreated back into the woods.

"Traci!" Jimmy shouted. "What is it? Who's there with you? What's happening?"

"Hello?" Billy said again.

Jimmy heard a strange, throaty, gurgling sound. "Billy! Is that you? Can you hear me?"

"Hello?" Billy said once more.

"Billy! It's Jimmy! Can you hear me?"

Billy hung up and then the line went dead.

"Traci!" Jimmy cried. *Oh, God no. We're finished. There's no way we can get Seth now without her.*

Then Jimmy got a message from Seth. This time it wasn't Seth's voice. "*Come home, Jimmy, and see what's waiting here for you.*" Then he laughed. It sent chills down his spine. Then he saw the pic sent to him.

"Oh, no," he gasped. "No, Seth, no, no, no!" Jimmy put the car back into drive, nearly rammed into a car, to avoid that car, nearly hit an oncoming car, and sped back to campus.

CHAPTER THIRTY-SIX

Anne Marie drove home and parked her car next to her roommates' cars. She was about to go into the house. Someone was walking downstairs and around the house to Jimmy and Seth's apartment. It looked like Cassie.

"Cassie!" Anne Marie yelled. Anne Marie ran down the concrete steps and again shouted, "Cassie!"

She walked around the house and peered into the hallway toward Jimmy and Seth's apartment. The door stood cracked open. "Cassie?" She pushed the door farther open and peered inside. Horrid paintings and empty beer bottles littered the living room.

"Cassie?" Anne Marie called. "Seth? Jimmy? Anyone home?" She stepped farther inside the apartment. "Hello?" She stepped inside, and the voices stopped. She found no one. Anne Marie turned around to leave. Just as she whirled around, the door slammed shut. Seth stood behind it. The door locked by itself.

Seth grinned. "How nice of you to drop in, Anne Marie."

Anne Marie looked stunned. The handsome Seth she met at the beginning of the semester was gone. Seth looked bony and emaciated from the heavy drinking and skipping meals. His eyes looked black, even the whites. What stood before her now was a *ghoul*. Seth held a butcher knife. He approached Anne Marie. She backed up.

"My God, Seth, what's happened to your eyes?"

Seth only answered with a grin.

"Seth, is Cassie here?"

"Nope. She's gone into the woods. Care to join her?"

Anne Marie glanced out the window. Darkness oozed out of the woods. "Seth, I need to go."

"Yes, you do!"

Anne Marie squealed as she ran around the dinner table in the living room. "Seth, what's happened to you?"

Seth didn't answer. *This land is now ours.* "Come on, Anne Marie. This playing hard to get garbage is getting old. You came down here wearing that cute little blue sweater and skirt. You look just like a little cheerleader. It's obvious what you've got in mind. It's been obvious what you've wanted from me all along. So let's not fool around anymore. Let's get down to business!"

Anne Marie shrieked. Seth chased her around the table but couldn't catch her. He stopped.

"Seth, I'm dressed like this for my boyfriend, not for you! And I only came down here because I thought I saw Cassie. Obviously, she's gone, so I have to leave. Now let me go!"

"You want to see Cassie? You're about to see her. In fact, you're about to join Elizabeth and Michelle!"

Anne Marie saw Seth's knife was stained with blood. "Seth, did you hurt Michelle and Elizabeth? Did you kill them? Did you?"

Seth's breathing grew more rapid.

Anne Marie eyed the front door. She cried, "Please tell me you didn't kill them, Seth. You couldn't have! Please tell me you didn't do that."

Seth hyperventilated.

"Why, Seth? What did they ever do to you? You're not a killer! You're a college student and an artist. Why would you hurt anyone?"

Seth's hand shook, so the butcher knife rattled against the table like hatchets hitting bone during the war. Seth dropped the knife and bowed his head. When he looked up again, his eyes faded from black to brown. *You can't have me. What you're doing is wrong. I don't care what injustice you suffered.* "Run, Anne Marie!"

"Seth!" It's *you!*"

But I can't hold on. He's too strong. "Run!" Seth screamed. "I can't fight Riapokemobataconno and the demons who control him too much longer. He's too powerful!"

Anne Marie glanced at the door. "Riapke who? What? Demons? What are you talking about?"

"Run, damn it!"

"Seth, is that really you? Jimmy said you're being possessed." Anne Marie crept to the door. She hesitated. Seth still stood between her and the door. "Yes, Seth! Fight it!" She inched her way closer to the door. Seth screamed and lowered his head again. Anne Marie stopped and stepped back. When his head rose, his eyes turned devil-black again.

Seth smiled and grabbed the knife. "No, Seth! Keep fighting it!"

"You should've run when you had the chance. These games stop now, bitch!" Seth lifted the table and tossed it across the living room. Anne Marie screamed and ran into the dining room.

Right outside one of the second dining room window, stood the concrete stairs that led up to where she parked her car. She opened the window and kicked out the screen. Seth kicked in the door as she climbed out the window. Seth threw his knife onto the dining room table. He caught Anne Marie by her foot. Only a few more inches, and she would've been out of the house.

She reached for the railing that led upstairs. Seth tried to pull her back inside the apartment, but he lost his grip on her slick nylons. His hands slipped down her leg to the shoe. Her shoe flipped off and she slipped free. She was out of the house. Seth lunged at her and grabbed her foot again. Half of him dangled out of the window. She desperately clung to the railing. Seth gouged his fingernails into her leg. Anne Marie screamed and kicked. Seth tore away her nylon to get a hold of her. Seth sat on the window ledge as she tugged with both hands on the railing. She was nearly free of his grasp when Seth grabbed her skirt.

You can't escape me, little woman.

"No!" she screamed.

Seth began to pull her skirt off. Anne Marie reached down with one hand to keep Seth from ripping it off. Seth was able to yank her one hand free of the railing. He tugged on her skirt harder and it tore. Seth stepped back into the dining room. He grabbed her sweater and jerked her back into the house. Anne Marie's other shoe flipped off. She hit her head against the window frame when Seth dragged her back inside. She tried to get up and run but Seth clubbed in the back of the head twice. He picked her up and threw her against the table.

"I want these clothes off and I want them off now!" Seth raged.

Seth grabbed her skirt and tore it more. This time Anne Marie let him have it. Seth tossed it aside. He grabbed her other foot and tore away her other stocking. She crawled to the living room. Seth grabbed his knife and seized her by the sweater and dragged her into his bedroom.

"No!" she shouted.

Seth tore at her sweater. She fought him. She punched him in the head. Seth tossed her around towards the bed. Anne Marie kneed him in the groin. He screamed and toppled over her.

They fell onto the bed together. She pushed him off her and snatched an empty beer bottle from the nightstand and clobbered Seth over the head. She broke free of Seth's grasp and started to run. Seth reached out and snagged the front of her sweater. He tore the front of it open, sending the buttons flying like missiles to all ends of the bedroom. She slipped out of her sweater and ran out of the bedroom to the front door. Dressed in only her bra and panties, she unlocked the door. Seth dropped his knife on the nightstand and bolted into the living room and smashed his body into hers. He jerked her back to the floor and buried his fist into the back of her head and neck until he nearly knocked her unconscious. He dragged her by the hair back to his bedroom.

"No," she begged.

"Oh, yes."

Seth threw her up onto the bed and unfastened her bra. He ripped it off and threw it to the floor. Her nipples were small and pink. He fondled her breasts until her nipples turned erect. He sucked on both of them. She became fully conscious again when he jammed his tongue into her mouth. She punched him, and clawed at his face and neck. He reached for the butcher knife from the nightstand and placed it against her throat.

"Stop fighting, or I will cut off your head and do it to *your corpse*! Do you hear me?"

Anne Marie shook her head as she sobbed. Seth used his knife to cut off her panties. "Let me do this, and I'll let you go." Before Seth entered her, he said, "You're going to love this."

After Seth had gotten bored of Anne Marie, he got off her and pulled his pants up.

Anne Marie sprang from the bed, but Seth grabbed her by the arm and threw her back on the bed.

"Seth! You promised me you'd let me go!"

Riapokemobataconno chuckled and said in a deep, inhuman voice, "You really think I'd let you go after what you planned for Cassie?" Seth thrust his knife into her heart.

Anne Marie screamed loud enough to be heard on the other side of the woods where the art building stood.

CHAPTER THIRTY-SEVEN

Natalie grabbed a can of mace from her purse, got out of the car, and ran up to the woods. "Seth!" she shouted. "Seth!"

The Darkness bubbled and oozed out of the woods. It slithered around her feet and wrapped around her hips. Natalie squealed and ran into the woods. Darkness rose until she saw nothing but black. Darkness lowered and spun away from her waist. She saw the trees in front of her. She turned around. She couldn't see the house, only trees that stretched for several yards. Beyond that, she only saw Darkness.

"Seth!" Natalie shouted.

Yes, my dear sweet, I'm right here watching you the whole way.

She heard moaning and groaning. Natalie ran a few steps and tripped over rough and uneven ground. A small twig shot up beneath her middle fingernail all the way to the quick. The can of mace slipped out of her hand and sunk into thick, black, bubbling goop. She shrieked and jerked her hand away.

Natalie yanked the stick free. If only she could talk to Seth, maybe this would all make sense. She did love him a lot. And he wasn't well. He needed her. She recovered and tried to search for her mace. She stuck her hand in oily, soupy slop. A bloody, pasty hand grabbed her and pulled her toward the ground. She wailed and wrenched free of it. Something screamed in the distance like men on horseback crying and shouting as they battled. Horses' hooves were pounding like thunder and Natalie sprinted away.

"Seth!" she screamed.

"Naaataaalie," a voice called.

"Seth?"

"Yes, Natalie."

"Seth, where are you?"

"Here, Natalie."

Natalie looked around. "Where's *here*, Seth?"

Something huge meandered among the trees. The dark mass with red eyes stood twenty feet, its head hovering near the treetops. The thing stunk worse than two hundred corpses rotting in the sun. It heard Natalie call out to Seth and looked down at her, grinning and growling.

Not much farther, Natalie. You and I are almost reunited. "Run, Natalie!" Seth said. "Run!"

Natalie flew through the woods. She nearly fell several times over the broken branches, partially exposed tree roots, and rotting leaves. Two soldiers rose from the ground and tried to grab her. She screamed and sprinted by them as gunshots echoed in the woods. Tree branches above her cracked and fell on her. A decaying stench followed her every step. Hands reached from the ground and touched her legs and her dress. She darted around decayed soldiers buried in the ground. Some looked like bony, emaciated monsters, while others were mere skeletons. A few sat up and begged.

"Help us, Natalie."

"Thirsty, Natalie. We need water."

"Go back, Natalie," a couple of them warned. "Save yourself!"

Jimmy called her back. "Natalie, thank God you answered! Where are you?"

She cried, "Jimmy! I'm in the woods. I'm lost!"

"Natalie, go back! Get out of there!"

"I don't know where 'back' is!" She sobbed now. "I don't know how to get out of here!"

Dark hands reached up to grab her. They wrenched her phone free, and it sunk into the earth.

"Nat—!"

You're too late, Jimmy. Much too late.

Natalie shrieked, broke free and she sprinted through the forest. Faces emerged from the Darkness. Men with long hair tied tight to the sides of their scalps. She shielded her eyes and kept running. She tripped and burst out of the woods. The large, imposing art building stood before her.

"Seth!" Natalie shouted.

"Yes, Natalie," Seth said.

"Where are you?"

"I'm here, Natalie, in the art building."

Natalie got up and ran through the back doors and yelled, "Where are you, Seth?"

"I'm upstairs, Natalie."

Natalie ran up the two flights of stairs. She stepped through the glass doors. "Seth, where are you?"

"Right here, Natalie."

Natalie looked to her left and down the end of the hallway towards the drawing and painting studios. "Seth!" Natalie shouted.

Seth outstretched his arm. "Natalie, take my hand."

Natalie ran to him. She hugged Seth. He grinned as he put his arms around her.

"Seth, we have to get away from here!"

"There, there, my dear."

Natalie felt something plop against her shoulder. Maggots fell from Seth's swollen, infected ear. Underneath his hair, part of his ear and face rotted away. Darkness bled out of his eye sockets and down his cheeks. Natalie screamed. Seth laughed hysterically. Natalie turned to run, but Cassie, Elizabeth, Michelle, Anne Marie, Laura, Deanna, and Traci walked into the other end of the hall. Blood covered three sorority girls from head to foot. One had been stabbed in the head so badly she didn't even look human. The other two were completely nude. A butcher knife stuck out of the chest of the blonde. Traci's slashed throat spewed blood. Her head hung back and to the side.

Natalie looked the other way. Several people walked up behind Seth. Blood poured from Dr. Johnson's mouth and from a large hole in his chest. Another man walked backward, but Natalie could see his face. A girl walked beside him; blood dripped from her mutilated wrists. Civil War soldiers marched behind them. Rafe, Pete, Deanna, and Valerie followed.

"Join us, Natalie," Seth said.

Darkness spread across the floor, flowing down the hallway like blood. Icy cold, icy hands reached up her dress from the black fog and touched her legs. They pushed her panties aside and slipped inside her. She swatted them away, but they continued to grab her and penetrate her.

"Good God!" she cried. "No! No!"

"Join us, Natalie!" Seth said. "Join us or die!"

Natalie couldn't escape. The doors to the classrooms were locked. She continued to hit and push away the icy hands below.

"Die, Natalie, die!" Seth screamed.

"No! No! Leave me alone! No!" Natalie shrieked as her knees buckled and her back hit the wall. She crumpled to the floor and clutched her hair with both fists. She tried to kick away the dead, purple, black, and green hands that reached up from the Darkness.

"Die, Natalie, die!" everyone shouted. "*Die*, Natalie, *die!*"

Natalie couldn't fight through the evil that surrounded her. So she escaped the only way she could. She walked into a mental cellar, closed the door behind her, and locked it.

Jimmy found Natalie's car back at the house. He jumped out of the car and shouted, "Natalie! Natalie!"

He stood at the edge of the woods. He couldn't see her. *Do I dare go inside there?* He wanted to, but not in *those woods.* He tried calling her again, but she wouldn't pick up. He stepped just inside the tree line. He thought of running in there, but then he heard the war chant again. Then he saw many dark figures moving toward him.

I don't want to go, but I have to. I have to save Natalie.

Darkness poured out of the woods. Jimmy ran back to his car. The Darkness kept coming, and he sped off.

The only thing I can hope for is Natalie came out the other end.

Jimmy sped to the art building and slammed on his brakes after he rolled over the sidewalk.

He hoped he'd find Seth and Natalie on the other side. He flew into the building. He only saw Darkness out the back window. No trees, grass, or anything else. He immediately found Natalie to his right. The stench of death filled the building. The Darkness retreated away from the hallway and into one of the studios. He bent down and held Natalie's arms.

"Natalie! What is it? What's wrong? What happened?" He couldn't get Natalie to let go of her hair. Her face was a frozen mask of terror. "Oh, dear God, no," he mumbled. This was bad. This was *very* bad. He reached for his cell phone and called nine-one-one. He ran to the studio, where he saw the Darkness disappear.

Jimmy ran through it and to the balcony outside. Darkness flowed back into the forest.

"You sons of bitches!" Jimmy screamed. "What have you done to her?"

Jimmy heard Seth laugh hysterically somewhere deep inside the woods. Jimmy closed the back door and locked it. He found Dr. Johnson's body lying outside his office. Hideous black and purple bruises covered his throat. Half of his tongue lay on his stomach. His partially consumed heart was carved out of his chest and left on the floor. He ran back to Natalie and knelt beside her.

He cried as he said, "*Please* be okay, Natalie. Just say something to me. Something, *anything*!"

Natalie didn't speak, although she was breathing. A brutally cold shiver washed down Jimmy's body. He tried to call Traci again but got no answer. He tried to call her at home. She also didn't pick up there. Suddenly the phone rang. It was Laura's mom. He threw his phone against the floor and smashed it.

Please, God, make it so Traci is okay. But he knew why Traci wasn't answering.

Jimmy sat down next to Natalie, touched her knee, and sobbed. "Jesus, Natalie, I'm so sorry.

I should have got you and Traci out of town first and driven to Virginia Beach with you. Then I could've driven back with the Knights to get Seth. I totally screwed up."

Jimmy felt like he had his guts ripped out. He thought maybe Natalie was better off than everyone else. She no longer had to deal with any of this. Her mind must've shut down to protect her. He wanted to join her. He grabbed his hair just like her and cried. He didn't care if dead soldiers came into the building and shot him. He didn't care if he saw what Natalie did. He didn't care about anything anymore. But he didn't fade away like Natalie.

I thought I was dealing with the real danger by trying to locate Seth. I thought by sending Natalie and Traci away, I was keeping them safe. I wanted to take this…Darkness on myself. Instead, I put Traci and Natalie in greater danger. I failed everyone, Natalie, Traci, Seth, even Deanna, Rafe, and Pete.

Red and blue flashing lights illuminated the art building. Jimmy stood and tried to think of what to tell the police. One thing he knew for sure. The power of the Darkness in that town could never be broken.

CHAPTER THIRTY-EIGHT

Jimmy told the police he found Natalie there like that. He said nothing else, letting the cops ask the questions. He answered as rationally as he could. The police found Traci's body later that evening.

Police discovered the house above his apartment was covered in blood. Seth, Cassie, Michelle, Elizabeth, and Anne Marie were missing. Because of the blood up there, the police expected foul play. They searched the woods but found only a blood trail that led to the woods, but then just disappeared like the land swallowed its victim. Seth and the girls' boyfriends were considered suspects for the disappearances of the three sorority girls, plus the death of Dr. Johnson and Cassie's disappearance.

The police would've liked Jimmy as a suspect as well, but his story checked out. The librarian on the fourth floor vouched for him for most of the afternoon. Bartenders and security footage confirmed Jimmy came in at night asking for Seth. Cell phone records at least proved Jimmy spoke on the phone with Natalie and Traci. Police found it hard to connect him to any disappearance or murder.

Jimmy left town. Billy and Tabatha took him in. For a week, Jimmy hardly ever got out of bed or ate. He wanted God to let him die, but Jimmy woke up every morning. Each night of the week, Jimmy suffered terrifying nightmares.

He saw Seth, his face a grotesque demon with horns, fangs, and a garish grin, slip into Elizabeth's room and stab her repeatedly in the head. Then Seth wrapped her up in a bloody sheet and carried her out to the woods.

He then saw Michelle come home, and Seth waited for her in her room. When she opened the bathroom door, Seth buried his knife in her. He attacked her and slashed her, beat her, and stabbed her to death.

He saw Seth trap Ann Marie in the house, savagely beat her, heard the fabric tearing away from her body, and rape her.

And finally, he saw Rudy walking backward with his head turned around, killing Dr. Johnson. Then he saw a terrifying vision inside the art building where several murdered people, along with Seth, confronting Natalie and driving her mad.

Then he saw the dreams change to Jimmy doing the murders and rape, felt his hand hurt as it repeatedly stabbed into the girls, felt him penetrate Ann Marie and assault her and carry their bloody bodies to the woods. He heard Seth's thoughts screaming inside his mind, "No, no, no!" as he stabbed Elizabeth. And then, "You can't have me! What you're doing is wrong!" when Seth attacked Michelle.

He woke up screaming several times, and sweat poured down his head like blood. Billy and Tabatha admitted they feared they were going to have him committed. After a week and a half, Tabatha and Billy finally convinced Jimmy to eat. After a few weeks, Jimmy became concerned for Natalie. He got in touch with her folks. Natalie's condition hadn't changed. She had a nervous breakdown, and her parents couldn't reach her. No one could. Jimmy asked their permission if he could see Natalie to try to bring her out, and they allowed him to.

Jimmy wouldn't return to that town without all of the Black Knights with him. He visited Natalie alone, though with the gang waiting outside. Several vases full of flowers were set in her room. Natalie was in bed. She didn't react to him. The look of terror was gone from her face, but that girl had aged. She was only twenty-two, but now Natalie looked over thirty. Lines cut into her face. She had a few gray hairs. She lost weight. He held her hand and talked to her for a while. He told her he loved her and missed her. She was his best friend's girl. He should've been able to protect her.

Natalie didn't respond to his touch or his words. He pressed her hand up against his head and cried.

"Jesus, Natalie, I wish I could right this wrong. I can't help but feel I'm to blame for the way you are now. This is all my fault."

Natalie still didn't change. Before he left her, he wondered if some shred of Seth didn't try to spare Natalie because he still loved her. He didn't kill her. Seth gave her a chance to escape, and she could later recover and make something of her life.

I should've never taken Traci's call. I should've just driven back to my place, got her, got you, and drove us all to Virginia Beach. Hell, even if I left on my own, the girls would've still been safe.

As long as Jimmy was in town, he decided to have the gang drive him over to the house to retrieve his clothes and other possessions. The house was still roped off, but the police gave Jimmy permission to enter his basement apartment. Jimmy was surprised to see the police kept the house as a crime scene. He couldn't understand why they hadn't finished their investigation. Being in a small town, maybe the cops still waited on lab results. Perhaps the cops didn't want to disturb anything since the case still remained open. Or maybe the force in that town maintained control of the city police, too. The grisly aftermath was left as a statement and a reminder. Maybe that's why Natalie wasn't murdered like the rest. The Darkness left a warning.

Don't get too curious about our affairs, or we can do this to you, too.

Jimmy ducked beneath the yellow tape to see if he had any mail left. After he checked the mailbox, he peered inside the upstairs residence. Blood covered the floors and the walls. The coffee and end tables were tipped over. The couch was in the corner and upside down. Jimmy knew there was no way those girls were alive after seeing the state of the house. He supposed he'd never get his rental deposit back either.

Jimmy had received no mail. He asked Billy and Snake to join him in his old apartment. There was a blood trail that came out of the side door of the upstairs residence down the back steps to the driveway and into the woods. Jimmy saw some sort of fight happened in his apartment, too. The dining room table was overturned. In Seth's room, he found one of the window screens smashed open. It all looked exactly like what Jimmy saw in his nightmares.

Jimmy went into his room, and Billy said, "Everything looks clear here. Do you want us to stay?"

"No," Jimmy said. "You and Snake can go back outside or hang here if you want. This won't take long."

Billy and Snake went back outside. Jimmy opened up his closet door and began dumping his clothes into a couple of boxes. He only was in his room for a few moments before he heard the upstairs neighbors come home. Jimmy smiled.

He remembered the herd of water buffalo that lived above him. He missed those simpler times. His smile faded. *Those girls were presumed dead.* And with all of the blood all over the place, no chance existed that any of those girls were still alive. The upstairs residence was still considered a crime scene. No one was allowed up there, let alone lived there. Yet Jimmy heard several girls in high heels walking around. He looked up. He heard them talking and laughing. Then they ran to the side of the house. They opened the basement door and ran down the stairs. The door in the kitchen rattled.

Three women sang, "Jimmy, are you there? Please open up! Please? We want to see you!"

Jimmy packed faster. He grabbed a couple of notebooks and then emptied his closet.

He finished grabbing everything when he heard a fourth woman walk into the house upstairs.

She rushed down the stairs and rattled and pounded on the basement door. He recognized the voice. It was Traci.

"Please let me in, baby. I want to talk to you. I miss you! Please let me in!"

Jimmy felt compelled to walk to the door and let his lover in. He so desperately wanted to see Traci again. *But she was dead!*

"Jimmy! Please let me in!" Her voice became angry. "Jimmy!" he heard a deeper, angry voice demand. The lock on the door started to bend and give as Jimmy sprinted outside. He ran straight into Billy.

"Whoa, man!" Billy said. "What's wrong?"

"Let's just get the hell out of here!" Jimmy said.

"What is it?" Billy asked.

Jimmy hurried to Billy's van. "I heard people come into the house upstairs. They were walking all around, just like the upstairs neighbors used to do in their heels."

"Upstairs?" Billy asked, grinning and folding his arms over his chest. "No way, man." Billy walked around the house and called to a bunch of guys standing upstairs at the side entrance of the house. Gang members surrounded the property. "No one just walked into the house, did they?"

"No way," they said.

"There's someone up there, Billy," Jimmy said.

"Do you want us to check it out?" Billy asked.

"*No.* We're getting the hell out of here *permanently.*"

"Okay," Billy said. The guys saddled up their metal steeds. Jimmy climbed into the van with Billy and Tabatha. As Billy drove away, Jimmy wouldn't look back at the house. He knew if he looked back and saw Traci staring out from the front window, he might turn into a vegetable like Natalie.

Jimmy only had one semester left, but he never returned to the University of Morganburg or that town. A year later, Jimmy felt like he could go back to school. He finished his final semester and had his credits transferred over. He heard the message that the town had sent him. Don't meddle. Mind your own business. And don't attempt to butt heads with power. He never considered returning to a land filled with nightmares of destroyed youth, blinded sight, and stolen dreams. If he should ever waver in that consideration, he knows the Darkness is out there to remind him that it possesses the power to crush him at any time. Every late autumn, when it's still warm but cool at night after Jimmy has gone to bed, he is awakened by Traci calling him.

"Jimmy? Won't you come with me? I miss you, baby. I love you. Won't you join me?"

Jimmy always shuts the window, rolls back over, and goes back to sleep.

Jimmy believed college changed him, but not for the better. Jimmy left the streets to go to school to have fun, study creative writing, and earn a degree. He did all of that, but he also learned that when humankind isn't carefully watched and allowed to go unchecked, an evil power can mushroom and take control, a power that hides out there in the Darkness.

The Bloody End